Mystery Authors Love
Blondes Have More Felons!

"Not only does the old cliché say that blondes have more fun, but Alesia Holliday proves blondes have brains as well! And when it comes to a new law practice, fair-haired heroine, attorney December Vaughn, takes us on a wild— yet hilarious—ride through the justice system. And for an added bonus, we get treated to hunky Jake Brody. Yum! Holliday does an excellent job in this fast-paced read."
—Lori Avocato, award-winning author
of the Pauline Sokol mystery series

"I'd judge this book a bar above the rest! An intriguing premise and endearing characters will draw you into the wacky legal world of hotshot lawyer December Vaughn. Lawyer jokes mixed with blondie cracks—what an irresistible combo!" —Nancy J. Cohen, author of the
Bad Hair Day mystery series

"The verdict is in for Alesia Holliday's debut into the world of chick-lit mysteries: delightful, delicious, and just plain fun! Readers will root for spunky attorney December Vaughn as she wrestles with bad guys, tainted drugs, and an alligator with an attitude in *Blondes Have More Felons*. So move over, Miss Marple, 'cuz this girl detective rocks!"
—Susan McBride, award-winning author of
the Debutante Dropout mystery series

Praise for Alesia Holliday and her novels

"Nice Girls Finish First is a hoot! This book is funny, entertaining, and heartwarming—a well-written, fast-paced story all wrapped inside one little book cover . . . a top-notch story for a summer beach read, and one not to be missed." —*Romance Reviews Today*

"I'll warn you right now, this is a definite two-boxes-of-tissue book; you'll laugh yourself to tears. Charming characters come to life immediately. This is without a doubt in the top ten books of the year." —*Huntress Reviews*

"With the quirky characters and sometimes laugh-out-loud madcap moments that Holliday is known for, *Nice Girls Finish First* is a completely enjoyable read." —*Chicklitbooks.com*

"[H]ard not to feel a sense of kinship as [Jules] marvels at the confidence of inept contestants or shares her insights on the reality TV phenomenon . . . a zany debut." —*Publishers Weekly*

"[W]ell worth the crazy ride." —*Booklist*

"Featuring an appealing heroine with a sense of humor and a sexy hero who is there when she needs him, this smart and sassy first novel makes marvelous fun of the 'reality' TV craze and offers a bit more substance than the average chick-lit romp." —*Library Journal*

Blondes
Have More Felons

Alesia Holliday

BERKLEY PRIME CRIME, NEW YORK

THE BERKLEY PUBLISHING GROUP
Published by the Penguin Group
Penguin Group (USA) Inc.
375 Hudson Street, New York, New York 10014, USA
Penguin Group (Canada), 90 Eglinton Avenue East, Suite 700, Toronto, Ontario M4P 2Y3, Canada
(a division of Pearson Penguin Canada Inc.)
Penguin Books Ltd., 80 Strand, London WC2R 0RL, England
Penguin Group Ireland, 25 St. Stephen's Green, Dublin 2, Ireland (a division of Penguin Books Ltd.)
Penguin Group (Australia), 250 Camberwell Road, Camberwell, Victoria 3124, Australia
(a division of Pearson Australia Group Pty. Ltd.)
Penguin Books India Pvt. Ltd., 11 Community Centre, Panchsheel Park, New Delhi—110 017, India
Penguin Group (NZ), Cnr. Airborne and Rosedale Roads, Albany, Auckland 1310, New Zealand
(a division of Pearson New Zealand Ltd.)
Penguin Books (South Africa) (Pty.) Ltd., 24 Sturdee Avenue, Rosebank, Johannesburg 2196,
South Africa

Penguin Books Ltd., Registered Offices: 80 Strand, London WC2R 0RL, England

This is a work of fiction. Names, characters, places, and incidents either are the product of the author's imagination or are used fictitiously, and any resemblance to actual persons, living or dead, business establishments, events, or locales is entirely coincidental. The publisher does not have any control over and does not assume any responsibility for author or third-party websites or their content.

BLONDES HAVE MORE FELONS

A Berkley Prome Crime Book / published by arrangement with the author

PRINTING HISTORY
Berkley Prime Crime mass-market edition / March 2006

Copyright © 2006 by Alesia Holliday.
Cover illustration by Cheryl Hoffman.
Cover design by Rita Frangie.
Interior text design by Stacy Irwin.

ISBN: 0-425-20892-3

BERKLEY® PRIME CRIME
Berkley Prime Crime Books are published by The Berkley Publishing Group,
a division of Penguin Group (USA) Inc.,
375 Hudson Street, New York, New York 10014.
The name BERKLEY PRIME CRIME and the BERKLEY PRIME CRIME design are trademarks belonging to Penguin Group (USA) Inc.)

PRINTED IN THE UNITED STATES OF AMERICA

10 9 8 7 6 5 4 3 2 1

Dedication

This one is for Steve Axelrod, my brilliant and low-key agent, who says "I like it. It's fine," when he's getting ready to make the magic happen. Thank you for believing in me.

As always, for Judd, who knew I was a lawyer but fell in love with me anyway. Thanks for ten years of the craziest and best marriage in the world.

And for Karyn Lyndon, for the title.

Dear Reader

Thank you for joining December on the first of her new adventures! For news, contests, and a members-only lawyer joke forum, please visit me online at www.alesiaholliday.com.

Happy reading!

Alesia

Acknowledgments

It takes the support of so many wonderful people to make a book happen. I'd like to thank some of them here.

First, I'll admit that the characters tell me their stories, and I can be stubborn about them. So, most of all, to my editor, Cindy Hwang, who is not only brilliant and kind, but who understands that lawyers can *tell* jokes and not just be the butt of them. Plus, she never, ever says, "Alesia, this book doesn't look much like your synopsis . . ."

Leslie Gelbman, who keeps her eye on everything; Susan McCarty, who works so hard for me and on my behalf; Cheryl Hoffman for the beautiful cover; and the entire marketing and sales team who get my stories out to the world.

December would be committing malpractice in print if not for the counsel and insights of amazing trial attorneys Kim Evers and Jim Thies. Any mistakes I've made are strictly in spite of their very best efforts.

Suzanne Brockmann and Ed Gaffney (and Eric Ruben!), who trapped me in a minivan for a week and kept saying, "You *must* call Steve." I even forgive you for the bluegrass. And the wonderful readers on Suz's message board, who help me with research and ask me naughty questions.

Christine Feehan, who understands and talks me down when I'm crossing the mountains with my cardboard boxes. Chris, Cheryl Lyn Wilson, Kathie Firzlaff, and Val Phillips for one of the funniest weeks in recorded history. Crouching writer, hidden crumble.

Lani Diane Rich, Michelle Cunnah, Barbara Ferrer, and Marianne Mancusi—for way more than I can say without sounding girly.

Lori Avocato, Nancy Cohen, and Susan McBride, who were kind enough to take time from writing their own fabulous mysteries to do an advance read for me.

My new friends at www.themysterychicks.com—thank you for inviting me to the party. I'll try to live up to your example!

The Cherries, who are funny and wise and always quick to answer research questions, even when they begin, "I just murdered somebody, and I need to know . . ." And to Jenny Crusie, for so graciously allowing us all to play.

Catherine Chant, who was kind enough to bid on having a character named after her. Here's wishing that your own characters find their way into print very soon.

As always, to Judd for patience, cheerleading, and support. To Connor, who is my research assistant and biggest fan. And to Lauren, who is a writer like Mommy. I love you all more than the universe.

Finally, to all the lawyers with whom I've ever worked. Some of you were brilliant examples, and some were terrible warnings. With both kinds, laughter helped.

Chapter 1

Nobody ever tried to stab me when I did corporate work.

"Hey! All I did was suggest that your neighbor have his property surveyed." I shoved my desk chair between me and a hundred and ten pounds of angry senior citizen. "I never told him to bulldoze your lawn shed if it crossed over the property line. You need to calm down, Mr. Ellison, or I'm going to have my assistant call the police."

I eyed the distance between my desk and the door. Surely I could outrun this guy, even in my heels. He had to be ninety years old.

"Don't even think about it, girlie. I've got pepper spray, and I ain't afraid to use it. Those self-defense classes down at the Seniors' Center were good for something." The little white-haired troll brandished a menacing-looking can in the air with one hand, while still pointing the knife at me with the other. If I hadn't been in imminent danger of being filleted, I would have laughed.

My name is December Vaughn, and I'm a lawyer. That means that I'm usually the most annoying person in any room, even when I don't have PMS. Not *this* morning, though.

I tried reason. "Look, you have a claim against him for the shed. He has to pay to replace it, okay? The shed and any tools he may have destroyed. Now, put that knife down before somebody gets hurt."

Ellison lowered the knife, but it was still pointing at me.

This was not how I generally liked to start my Mondays, being chased by somebody's rabid, weapon-toting great-grandfather. Especially not before coffee.

"He ain't been the same since that testicle problem. Man's got half his left nut missing, and it drove him insane." He squinted his eyes at me behind his bifocals. "Can I garnish the rat turd's Social Security?"

"I can't really advise you on your actions, since you are an adverse party to the rat turd, er, my client, sir. However, I'd be glad to recommend somebody—"

"*Ha!* I knew you'd say that. You lawyers are all the same. Cause problems and then weasel out of trying to fix 'em. I don't want another lawyer. You started this; you can figure it out." He shuffled around the edge of the desk and sat down, looking a lot like a prune, or somebody who needed to eat one.

Maybe *lots* of prunes.

I could hear my teeth grinding together, and forced myself to relax. "Okay, Mr. Ellison, what exactly is it that you want? I really, really need some coffee before my life is threatened any more this morning. Would you like some coffee?"

"Wouldn't mind some coffee. None of that fancy flavored crap, though. Just straight up normal coffee with some cream. Make it fresh cream, too, not that powder." He watched me closely as I walked out of my office door to the tiny adjacent kitchen. Weasel lawyers couldn't be trusted to make good coffee, I guess.

My new assistant and best friend since high school rushed in behind me. Max "never, *ever* call me Maxine" Emmanuel Hutton was five feet, four inches of beauty pageant alumna, from the tips of her silky brown hair to the toes of her rounded-in-all-the-right-places body. Luckily for the state of my office management, she was also unbelievably efficient, when she wasn't dating one of the series of losers who always managed to find her.

"What's going on with the geezer?" she asked, voice low. "I just got here and heard the end of it. Do you want me to call the police?"

I turned to face her, holding two mugs, which I promptly almost dropped. "*What* are you wearing?"

"Oh, this old thing?" She did a slow turn, treating me to a 360-degree view of the most bizarre outfit I'd seen outside of a bullfighting ring. She had tight black silk pants tucked into knee-high black leather boots and a flowing, ruffled white shirt, with a red, embroidered vest topping it all. All she needed was a cape and a sword, and I'd start yelling *Toro, toro*. Since she normally wore your standard office-worker clothes, this new look was a teensy bit unexpected.

"Where's the bull? Or is this Be Kind to Matadors Week? I forgot to check my calendar."

"Very funny, especially coming from the queen of bargain-basement shopping. I'll have you know, this is the very latest knockoff of a Mistraldi original last seen on the Milan runway not three months ago. It's not like *you* have any fashion sense anymore, December." She sniffed as she took in my sensible navy suit, white blouse, and (okay, let's admit it, boring) navy heels. "You moved to Ohio and morphed into Midwestern-lawyer drone somehow. I'll bet you don't even own any tube tops anymore. At least you didn't cut your hair off."

I cringed, remembering Orange Grove High fashion. "Hey, one of us has to look like somebody who works in a lawyer's office, don't you think? I figure it may as well be me, since you've lost your mind." I touched the clip holding my shoulder-length blond hair off my face, wondering again if I should cut it.

"Oh, ho, Miss Big Stuff. Three whole weeks of owning your own practice, and already you're acting like the big boss. What's next? Unpaid overtime?"

It's tough to get respect from someone who knows you stuffed your bra in tenth grade. Even worse when she'd helped you stuff. (Hey, it was prom—I was nervous!) I was considering booting her in the silk-covered butt with one of my ugly pumps, when the voice of doom broke in. "Where the heck's that coffee? Did you have to go to Colombia and pick the beans? I'm getting bored in here." Quavery and demanding at the same time. Neat trick.

"I'm on the way, Mr. Ellison," I called, then turned back to Max.

"Don't bother with the police. I'll get him calmed down and out of here. If he ruins my new furniture with his knife or pepper spray, the police will be the least of his worries."

I brushed past the office toreador and marched back into my office. "Here's your coffee. Freshly made, unflavored, and with cream. Now let's talk."

He sipped his coffee, peering at me over the mug. I noticed he'd taken the time to pat down his wisps of silvery white hair and straighten his tie while I was making the coffee. The knife and pepper spray were nowhere in sight. Maybe he was ready to be reasonable.

"I think you and Mr. Bessup will be able to work this out in an amicable manner, Mr. Ellison. If you'll just—"

"Does somebody who would bulldoze my shed without even discussing it with me first sound amicable to you, girlie? The old fart hasn't been right in the head since he lost his wife." His hand darted behind the desk, and he pulled the pepper spray back out.

I sighed. So much for reasonable.

"My name is December Vaughn. You can call me December, or you can call me Ms. Vaughn, but *girlie* is definitely out. Please treat me with the same respect I'm giving you, sir." Eight years of litigation in a corporate firm had given me a bellyful of condescension. I wasn't about to take it when my name was finally the one on the door.

Well, it *would* be on the door as soon as I got a sign. "Also, don't you think you should give the man a break if he's recently widowed?"

"Okay, December—and just for the record, what the hell kind of name is that? Parents some kind of hippies? And widowed, hell. His wife ran off with the UPS driver. They live down in St. Augustine now," he said, shaking his head. "Hated to see her go. She had the nicest set of bazumbas in the neighborhood."

My lip did an involuntary kind of curling thing at the idea of Mr. Ellison scoping out his neighbor's wife's *bazumbas*.

He smacked a hand on my desk for emphasis. "Anyway, here's the deal. I'm out twenty-five hundred dollars, and I know that rat bastard is never going to pay it. For one thing, he don't have no money, and for another he's about the most contrary individual I've ever come across. So, the way I see it, *you* owe me the money." He sat back in the chair with a flourish, clearly pleased with his solution.

I gaped at him over my mug. "How do you come up with that? I gave my client legal advice about his property line. He went way, way beyond anything I discussed with him and bulldozed your shed. You're *nuts* if you think—I mean, it is clearly an incorrect conclusion for you to assume that I am liable to you for the damages."

Sometimes I lose my grasp of lawyer-speak when I get

ticked off, which—to my mind—calls into question the value of a sixty-thousand-dollar legal education. If you can't *res ipsa* and *tortfeasance* at the drop of a hat, you're not worth the paper your bar license is printed on.

"Damage is right. Twenty-five hundred dollars' worth of damage. I don't expect you to just give me the money. I don't want your charity. The way I figure, you owe me a job. I'll work for you, until I earn back the money. I'm only seventy-two years old and can do just about anything." He smiled in triumph and smacked the spray can down on my desk.

"There is no way . . ."

Sadly, my do-gooder gene picked that moment to kick in. *He's just a lonely old man.*

He beamed.

"You can definitely *not* work for me . . ."

Probably no friends or family.

He folded his arms over his chest.

"I don't even need more . . ."

He smiled all over his prune-cheeked face.

He'll give up and lose interest in a couple of days anyway.

"Fine. So, what can you do anyway?" I slouched back in the visitor chair, and then changed my mind and stood up. "Hey, if you're going to be working for me, get out of my chair. Get over here on this side of the desk and hand over the weapons." I held out my hand.

He pushed himself out of my chair, grinning, and walked around the desk. "Here's the knife, girl—er, December."

"This is a butter knife! You chased me around my own office with a butter knife?"

He grinned, unapologetic. "You run pretty good in a

skirt, too. Nice legs. Not much in the way of bazumbas, though."

I closed my eyes and prayed for patience, then snapped them back open and glared at him. "First rule of employment: No comments on your *boss's* personal baz—*person*. Hand over the spray, too."

"Now, you wouldn't want to leave an old man helpless against the muggers, would you?" He gave me a puppy-dog-eyes look, which might have worked if he hadn't threatened my life a few minutes earlier.

"I think it's the muggers who would be helpless against you," I muttered, still holding out my hand.

He grumbled, but pulled the pepper spray out of his pocket and handed it over. I tried not to think about what other instruments of death might have been concealed in his pants, the old pervert.

"Max, get in here," I yelled.

Max, who'd been lurking right outside the door—if a woman dressed up like a matador can ever lurk—popped her head in the doorway.

"You bellowed?"

"Mr. Ellison is going to be working for us for a while. I have to get ready for my ten o'clock, so please get his information for the employment forms and figure out something for him to do."

Max stared at me in disbelief. "You're kidding, right? What's *he* going to do?"

"Hey, I'm right here, chickie. What the heck are you wearing anyway?" My new employee drew himself up to his full nearly five-and-a-half-foot height and squinted down at Max. Visually speaking, it was an interesting contrast. Matador meets shuffleboard chic.

I sighed. Hugely. "Mr. Ellison, what did you do before you retired? I assume you *are* retired?"

He puffed up his tiny chest. "You bet. Forty-five years as a school bus driver. Best safety record in the Claymore County School District."

I dropped my head in my hands as Max led my new employee out to the reception area. School bus driver. Well, *that's* surely an underused talent in a law firm. I tried not to think about what adding another person to the payroll was going to do to my rapidly vanishing bank account. I'd shoveled everything in my 401K plus the small inheritance from Dad into the new practice. I'd traded in my sweet Mercedes convertible for an ugly but practical Honda and some cash. I was even living in my aunt and uncle's rental house for no rent, like some kind of deadbeat college kid.

One of my ex's pet phrases for me flashed through my mind. *You jump without bothering to figure out where you're going to land, December. You're suicidally optimistic.*

I refused to admit he might have had a tiny point.

I would have pulled out the file on my ten o'clock, but I didn't have one. He was a potential new client, referred by my Aunt Celia. So I shuffled papers around, grabbed a clean legal pad, and practiced looking like a seasoned personal injury attorney, trying to ignore the crashing noises coming from my file room.

"I'd go with the pose where you lean forward with your hands clasped on the desk, honey. You look all Lawyer Barbie that way."

I jerked in surprise, then glared at Max. "Do you need something, or are you just here to mock me?" I'd been hearing "Barbie" since I turned about fourteen. The long legs, long blond hair, and blue eyes made me an easy target. Sometimes I thought about dying my hair brown, just for a change, but I never did.

Maybe red?

"Well, Mr. Deaver is here for your appointment, but mocking is good, too." She grinned at me when I gave her my Reserved for Opposing Counsel Death Glare.

"Save your death glares, girlfriend. You forget I've known you since high school, when you were the annoying dweeb who sat in front and raised her hand all the time." She had a little dimple when she smiled. It'd been her pageant circle secret weapon.

Then the smile faded. "Plus, you owe me for putting up with your new hire. That . . . mean man called me chickie. He does it again, and I'm going to help out our nation's Social Security deficit by one paycheck." Max being scary wasn't actually scary. It was mostly just cute. But I could never tell her *that*. It would hurt her feelings.

"Quit with the scowl. You'll scare the clients. Plus, I stopped doing the hand-raising thing in tenth grade. You better . . . Oh, forget it. Please show Mr. Deaver in." I shook my head. So far, if my first two employees were an indicator of the future success of my firm, I was in big trouble.

My dad's words rang in my ears. *Great at book learning, but no common sense.* Even two years after he'd died of the heart attack he'd spent forty years chasing, Dad liked to pop in occasionally and poke at my self-esteem.

Putting aside for the moment the fact that I was arguing with a dead guy, I poked back. *Ha! Takes more than book learning to run your own law firm, doesn't it?*

As he always had in life, Dad had the last word. *Three weeks isn't exactly a track record.*

I shook off my burgeoning brain meltdown and stood up

to greet my new client, as Max showed him into my office. "Mr. Deaver, I'm December Vaughn. How are you? Can we get you some coffee or water?"

"BDC Pharmaceuticals killed my wife, and I want them to pay."

Chapter 2

Okaaaay, no coffee, then.

I stepped forward to shake Charlie's hand, then dropped into one of the guest chairs and gestured for him to take the other. Charlie Deaver was a young guy, good-looking, probably no more than twenty-four or -five, with dark hair and eyes. He was dressed neatly, in khaki pants and a white shirt, and he was twisting a Florida Gators ball cap in his hands.

He grimaced. "I'm sorry, I'm just, well, so angry, and this is taking so long. My other attorney quit, and I need help now." He thrust a hand through his short brown hair and clenched his eyes shut for a moment. Then he blew out a breath and leaned forward, gazing intently into my eyes.

"They killed her, and I want them to pay. I want to hurt them so bad that they can never, ever do this to anybody again. They're a big drug company, and they never should have sent that insulin out without checking it or testing it or something. I had to watch her slip away in the coma, day after day."

He leaned forward and grasped both of my hands in his own. *"I want to make them pay."*

"Charlie, I'm so sorry for your loss. Let me help you."

I gently pulled my hands out of his and reached for my legal pad, trying to swallow past the lump in my throat. "Tell me what happened."

He slumped back in his chair. "I don't even know where

12   Alesia Holliday

to start. You've seen the commercials, I'm sure? If you're injured, call 1-800-BAD-INSULIN, that sort of crap?"

I nodded. Since moving back to northeast Florida a couple of months earlier, the barrage of TV ads for law firms had amazed me. I'd been staying with my aunt and uncle, and Aunt Celia liked to leave the TV on all the time. There's nothing you want to see while you're having breakfast like a commercial about bedsores and nursing home abuse. I almost tossed my Cheerios over that one just last week.

Not that I didn't think the public had a right to information about lawyers who could help them, but some of the ads crossed over the line into seriously tacky. The recent wave of solicitation ads for anybody injured by an allegedly defective batch of insulin were among the worst. They featured a close-up of a child in a hospital bed, surrounded by grieving relatives. I was sure that kind of thing had to be against the Florida Bar rules, but the firm airing the ads probably made enough money to scoff at any fines that might be imposed.

"Well, I called after my wife died. I'm not some kind of vulture, I mean, I don't want any money off of her death. But somebody needs to teach that company a lesson. So these lawyers told me all about how BDC was wantonly and brazenly negligent in putting that insulin on the market."

"Willfully and wantonly negligent?" I was taking notes, but I really needed to review his files. Florida's Wrongful Death Statute should be cited in the complaint. The old common-law standard was willful and wanton negligence, which translated into reckless indifference to human life. But Florida, like most states, had codified its torts law, so we weren't still using the same system the colonists had carried over from England.

"That's right. They were wantonly negligent, and Faith died. So I agreed to sue them, and my lawyer has been working on the case for about six months. Now he's retiring, and I need another lawyer. He referred me to a guy in downtown Jacksonville, but my mother plays golf with your Aunt Celia, and she said you were somebody who really cares about your clients. So here I am."

He stopped and looked around, seeming to take in his surroundings for the first time since he'd walked in the door. My office looked pretty good. Max had insisted we spend most of the decorating budget on the seating area in front of the reception desk and on my office, because that's the part of the firm that clients would see. The doors to the file room and the kitchen were kept closed at all times, so nobody would wonder why a successful law practice housed rooms that were only slightly more elegant than your average county jail holding cells. We'd get to them when we had more money in the budget.

A mahogany desk with matching credenza and bookcase over tasteful-but-boring beige carpet—I'd won the battle with Aunt Celia over mauve—dominated the room. My diplomas were out in the lobby on the requisite ego wall, so two subdued prints hung over my office bookcases, and a framed cover of my Uncle Nathan's first mystery novel held a place of honor on the wall behind my desk.

Charlie finished his visual tour of my office and looked at me. "Is it only you?" he asked, head tilted to one side. "I mean, no offense, but this is going to be a big case fighting against a huge drug company. Do you think you can handle it on your own?"

I figured *I'll give it my best shot* wasn't really what he wanted to hear. "Yes, I can handle it. Let me tell you about my background, Mr. Deaver."

"Call me Charlie."

"Charlie, then. I graduated *summa cum laude* from law school and then took a job with the top corporate firm in Columbus, Ohio. I spent eight years specializing in the defense of products liability cases, with a concentration on pharmaceuticals. When they offered me a partnership, I realized I didn't want to spend the rest of my career managing huge corporate clients by committee. So, yes, definitely I can handle it. In fact, of all the cases that have come across my doorstep since I opened the firm last month, yours is the one that most perfectly fits my talents and experience. Not only can I handle it, but I can't wait to dive into it."

(I was trying for assured self-confidence and hoped it didn't come off as wishful thinking.)

"Also, in mass torts like this—where many, many people are harmed by the same product—the plaintiffs' lawyers on all the cases generally team up and share their resources in order to best serve their clients. I imagine this litigation is on the way to being MDL'd, if it hasn't been already."

He looked a little more convinced. They taught us that in law school: Use legal acronyms whenever possible to confuse the issue and impress the layman. It's generally pretty effective. The ABCs of billing two-fifty or more an hour.

"What's MDL?"

"Multidistrict litigation. It means that a lot of similar cases—same product, same type of injury—are brought together to be handled by one judge for judicial economy and for consistency of results. In other words, to save the court's resources, and because it wouldn't be fair if two cases with exactly the same injury and damages were decided two different ways. Anyway, I've been following the insulin cases a bit. Evidently the bad batch was only distributed in Florida, and the defendant company is head-quartered here, so the cases can stay in state court. That's good for us. I'll have to review your files before we get started, though."

"You're not sure you want to help me?"

"I just want to be sure that I *can* help you. Let me read through your files and review where you are so far, to confirm your lawsuit is what I think it is. If I think you'd be better off with a different attorney, I'll tell you that up front. And there will be no charge for my initial review."

Charlie looked at me somberly for a long minute. Then he seemed to reach a decision and drew a deep breath. "Okay, you're in. I think Faith would have liked you, and you seem to know what you're talking about, which is more than I can say for my other guy. He just made a fortune on some big case anyway, so he plans to spend the rest of his life fishing. He says he'll send his files. I hope you decide to work with me."

"Thank you, Charlie. I hope so, too. I promise you, if we do work together, I'll do the best job I can for you and for Faith."

We stood up, and I walked him out to the reception area. "Max, will you please take Mr. Deaver's preliminary information and the contact information for his current attorney? I'll call this afternoon and arrange for him to transfer the files to us. We'll need to file a notice of appearance, too, if suit has been filed."

"You bet, December." My office manager, in spite of her sudden flair for dramatic fashion, was the best person I'd ever known for putting people at ease. She could elicit information that people would *never* think to tell me.

"I have to leave for my, er, appointment now. I should be back midafternoon."

Max grinned at me. She knew that what was left of my furniture was arriving that morning from Ohio.

"Wait up, girlie. If you're leaving, you can give me a ride home." Mr. Ellison burst out of the file room door.

Great. I'd almost forgotten about him.

"I took the bus to get here, and there's all sorts of weirdos on the bus. Not so's you people would notice," he added, aiming his chin at Max. "Let me just grab my sweater."

"I don't really have time to . . . Oh, fine. Let's go. But do you really need a sweater? It's June in Florida. You're going to melt." I studied him as he pulled on the thick cardigan. His belt had surrendered to migration and rested snugly under his armpits. I'm *so* not even going to discuss the black socks/white shoes combination. I leaned over and whispered to Max, "Try to get Bessup on the phone. If we can solve this problem, maybe we'll get rid of Ellison."

She grinned at me. "Way ahead of you, boss. Already left three messages for him."

Ellison stared at us suspiciously as he creaked his way across the room, but didn't ask any questions. "Old bones get chilled easy, girl—*December*," he said, brushing past me and out the door.

Amazing. In the space of a single morning, I went from assault victim to chauffeur for the old blackmailer who was somehow my new employee. *Really, could my Monday get any better?*

Chapter 3

"It's a U-Haul." I stood on the sidewalk in front of my brand-new house and looked down at the driver. He was about five-eight and built like an aging professional wrestler whose muscles had melted into Jell-O. I'm five feet ten, even in the flat sandals I'd changed into to go with my shorts and Sun Records T-shirt, so I tend to look down on most of the rest of the world.

Strictly from a height perspective, not like an arrogance thing.

He peered up at me. "Are you Deborah Vaygan?"

"It's December Vaughn, and *that* is a U-Haul. A very small U-Haul. It's not a moving van at all. Where's the rest of it?" I looked down the street. This must just be the overflow.

"What rest? This is a delivery for Deborah Vaygan. Household furniture and personal belongings. Shipped from one Gareth in Columbus, Ohio."

One Gareth. One Michael E. Gareth, or Doctor Mike, as he liked to introduce himself to his patients. I'd told him once that it was a little too fake-buddy-buddy for people who were expecting a shrink to look and sound like Freud, but he'd just smiled a calm smile and quizzed me about my tendency toward passive-aggressiveness.

Which kind of summed up our marriage. He was too passive. I was too aggressive. We're great friends but sucked at being husband and wife.

The sweaty driver interrupted my thoughts. "You need to sign here, lady. I don't want to stand around all day. I'm burning up. I don't unload either, so you better have help." He swiped at the sweat dripping off his face with one beefy arm and rubbed it on his shirt.

I snatched the clipboard out of his other hand, wishing I had sanitary wipes or rubber gloves, and stabbed the pen at the paper. One lousy U-Haul. Where the hell was my furniture? Mike probably forgot to put it in his daily planner, which meant it would never happen. This was a man who literally wrote "Brush teeth" in his daily planner. Every single day.

Twice.

After I had unloaded the U-Haul—with no help from the driver, as promised—I collapsed inside my front door on the floor, saying a prayer of thanks for whoever'd invented air-conditioning. Then I pulled out my cell phone.

"Dr. Gareth's office, Brenda speaking."

"Brenda? *My* Brenda? Is that you?" I was sure I recognized my secretary's voice. Or at least, she had been my secretary, back at my law firm in Columbus.

She giggled. Yep, that was her. Nobody else had that sultry giggle. "Oh, hi, December. Yes, it's me. I work for Dr. Mike now. I thought he told you? I started last week."

Brenda was a bizarre combination of pinup-girl body and brilliant organizational mind. I'd usually spent a good part of my day wading through all the male lawyers sniffing around her desk. I'd tried to convince her to go to law school, but she only wanted to get married and have enough babies for her own soccer team.

"No, he didn't mention it. Is he in? I'm having problems with the moving company."

"Sure, let me put you through. His last patient just left. And let me know if you need any help with the movers."

"Thanks, Brenda. Talk to you soon. And congrats on the new job."

She giggled again. I had to grin; I hadn't heard anybody giggle for a few months. It didn't surprise me that Mike had hired her. He'd often said he wished he could find an assistant who was as efficient as my Brenda. She wasn't crazy about lawyers either; she'd planned to leave the firm when I did.

Mike's soothing voice came on the line. I'd always told him that his voice should be bottled and sold to help insomniacs everywhere. Unfortunately for our marriage, its soporific tones meant almost all I ever did in our bed was sleep.

Well, that and other reasons, like the fact that his equipment apparently only worked on national holidays.

"December. So good to hear from you. How are you? What's the problem with the moving company?"

"I'm not so great at the moment, Mike. All that showed up was one small U-Haul with my most beloved—but least useful—possessions. So now I have a new house with nothing in it but my carnival chalk horse collection, my antique side table, my stuffed tigers, and Grandma's Depression glass. None of this is very helpful for daily life, you understand." I blew out a breath. "By the way, when did you hire Brenda? What happened to Mrs. Prosser?"

"She retired to Florida to be with her grandchildren. Seems like all the women in my life are moving to Florida."

I could hear the sadness in his voice. Mike had believed that another year or two of marriage counseling would fix us. I knew it wouldn't—all the talking in the world can't create chemistry where there isn't any. Best friends should never get married just because it's comfortable.

I tried for humor. "Well, the women may be moving to Florida, but the furniture isn't. Are you sure you shipped everything?"

"Absolutely. Let me check my daily planner. Hey, I got one of those PDAs—my daily planner is electric now. You should get one. Okay, here it is. Yes, exactly one week ago today at four thirty-five, we finished loading your things into one large moving truck and one small U-Haul. ETA your house is listed here as today. So, you're saying the big truck didn't show up?"

"That's right. I called the moving company, but the dispatcher is gone for the day, and nobody else knows what's going on. I thought I'd confirm with you before I start yelling at them tomorrow." I sighed and studied the ruins of my manicure. This is why I went to law school in the first place. So I didn't *have* to hump boxes. I sighed again.

"Let me know what they say, and whether there's anything we can do on this end. Brenda said she'd be glad to follow up with them for you."

I could hear Brenda's muffled voice in the background and was tempted. But no, this was *my* new life. I could handle my own problems. "Thanks, but I've got it under control. I'll let you know what happens. Take care, Mike, and hugs to Brenda for me."

I stood up and stretched and thought about how much I didn't want to unpack right now. Especially collections of fragile items when I had no shelves. Or tables.

Or a bed, come to think of it. I sighed again. Better see if I can borrow a sleeping bag from Aunt Celia at dinner tonight. *The deadbeat college student theme continues.*

•   •   •

When I pulled up in the driveway of Aunt Celia and Uncle Nathan's two-story Georgian, I saw that Max's Mini Cooper was already there. I parked my despised ("It's practical, and you need a practical car, now that you're spending all your money on this new venture," Mike'd said, which is one of the many reasons I'd divorced him. Who wants to be married to a man who thinks practical cars are the way to go?) ten-year-old Civic behind it and slammed the door.

"Oh, for Pete's sake, December. Move it in here and tell us all about poor Charlie." Max was standing at the door, wiping her hands on a dish towel. The matador look was gone, replaced by a pink-flowered summer dress. She looked like an ad for some Florida tourist resort aimed right at the male market; all "come drink your fruity umbrella drink with me." I looked like a sweaty, dirty escapee from a home for frizzy-haired women, just from the drive over. By the time the AC in the Honda cranked up, I'd usually already gotten where I was going.

Freaking practical cars.

"I hate this freaking car. Have I told you about my precious baby? My darling convertible? My lipstick-red, sunshine-convertible, rolling example of brilliance in German engineering that shouted, 'I am a wanton sex goddess'?"

She rolled her eyes. "Your car was a wanton sex goddess?"

"Not the car, you idiot. Me! And you know, now that you work for me, you might try treating me with a little respect," I said, grinning as I walked up to the door. Max was kind of the tiara-wearing sister I'd never had.

She snorted out a laugh. "Yeah, keep dreaming, O Wanton One. The chicken is almost ready, and the kids are out on the back deck, bickering."

We walked through the house, comfortably decorated with overstuffed sofas and bright colors. As the president of the Orange Grove Senior Citizens' Center, or the Center, as she called it, Aunt Celia entertained quite a bit, and the profusion of red pillows and miniature parrot figurines from her collection made her home as warm and quirky as she was.

Max headed for the kitchen, and I followed, hoping for a quick bite of something and maybe a glass or six of wine.

"Are you all settled in?" She put a glass on the breakfast bar and pushed an open bottle of Chardonnay toward me, then started chopping salad vegetables. The spicy aroma of whatever was simmering on the stove almost made me drool.

"Don't get me started. Not only am I *not* settled, but my furniture truck is somehow missing in action. My house is currently decorated with cardboard boxes filled with carnival chalk horses and Depression glass."

"Chalk horses?"

"It seemed like a good idea at the time. Don't ask."

I poured a healthy dose of wine and then looked out the sliding glass doors at Celia and Nathan. She was standing over him and shaking her finger as he sat, arms folded over his chest, in a wooden deck chair.

"What's up with them?"

Max laughed. "Nathan came down from his office in the middle of Celia's board meeting luncheon and begged a sandwich, then stood there and went off on a riff about how easy it would be to poison chicken salad, and what if there were a serial killer who murdered random social club committee members from town to town and—this was in total gorefest mode, mind you—how *ooky* death by arsenic would be."

I was laughing helplessly by the end of the story. I could visualize it perfectly. Nathan always got this blank, glazed look in his eyes when he was plotting a book, and he loved the gory details. "Oh, no."

"Oh, *yes*. Cleared the room in no time, according to Celia, who is especially miffed that they never got to try the mini–pecan cheesecakes she'd made. So, be prepared to eat a lot and pile on the compliments over the cheesecakes, or we're all in for a long night."

Max had finished cutting veggies and was mixing oils and vinegars in a mysterious blend, with some fresh herbs. She and Celia each had the gourmet cooking gene that I totally lacked. I'm a champion eater, though.

I heard the sound of the glass door sliding open and turned on my stool.

"Deedee! Why didn't you come outside and tell us you were here? I want to hear all about your meeting with poor Charlie."

My Aunt Celia was gorgeous, and the only person in the universe I'd ever allow to call me Deedee. Her peaches-and-cream complexion—"Never, ever sit in the sun, December, unless you want to look like a rhinoceros when you're fifty"—and strawberry-blond hair still drew male attention. From the stories Uncle Nathan liked to tell, she and my mom were the prettiest sisters in northern Florida "back in the day."

All of his stories ended the same way: "Could have had any man she wanted, December. But she picked me." After which Celia would blush and smack Nathan on the arm, muttering something about old reprobates. Their marriage was the kind of wonderful I'd always secretly hoped for, but never really expected. I wasn't making much progress either, going from a mediocre marriage to *no* marriage in one easy step.

Which reminded me that I didn't have any furniture either. I moaned and rested my head on the countertop.

"Oh, no. Is it that bad? Did that other lawyer mess up poor Charlie's case?" Celia stuck her face really close to mine and peered into my eyes.

"No, no. I was moaning about my missing furniture, not poor Charlie, er, I mean Mr. Deaver. And you know I can't talk about my clients, Aunt Celia. Client confidentiality and all that."

Celia *tsk*ed. She thinks client confidentiality shouldn't apply to the relatives who practically raised you. She wandered off to the other side of the counter, peering in the pot simmering on the stove.

"What is that, Max? Did you add the rosemary? What about the fresh peas?"

Max put her hands on Celia's shoulder and drew her away from the stove. "Yes, I did. Don't you think you should wear those nice glasses of yours, so you can see what's cooking without having to stick your face right in the pot?"

"Hmmph. I don't need glasses. Anyway, they make my face look fat."

I rolled my eyes. "Right, fat is a big problem for all one hundred pounds of you. Do you want me to get Uncle Nathan?"

"I don't care if you get him or not. That *man*. Honestly. Margaret Pelman clipped half of my azalea bush with her Continental, because she was trying to get out of here so fast. If he'd just *think* before he goes all plotty in the middle of a luncheon. A board meeting luncheon, no less."

Nathan had walked inside during the last part of her

recitation. "Me going all plotty is what paid for our cruise to Alaska last summer, dear. And the tour of the Pacific Northwest. You seemed to like Vancouver well enough at the time." His voice was mild, and I could see the amusement in his eyes. Sometimes I thought he pulled the absentminded mystery writer act to get a rise out of Celia.

It always worked.

As we dished up and dug into the delicious chicken-something-with-a-French-name that had been this month's cooking magazine's featured selection, Celia turned her attention to me. "I've referred all my friends down at the Center to you, dear. I hope you're up on your wills and trusts law. These people aren't getting any younger. We've had three different quadruple bypasses in the past six weeks."

Before I could respond, she moved on to Max. "Speaking of not getting any younger, I've found the perfect man for you. He works on the construction crew that's renovating the kitchen at the Center, and he's a total hottie."

She beamed a smile at Max. She'd been trying to fix both of us up with "a nice boy so you can settle down" for about ten years now. Well, except during my marriage.

Max paused, fork halfway to her mouth. "Total hottie? Have you been watching MTV again? You didn't order any more DVDs, did you? That teen queen pop festival you put us through last month nearly melted my ears."

Celia narrowed her eyes. "I have to say, Maxine, you were much nicer during your pageant years. Whatever happened to *world peace*?"

"*You* try being peaceful when you have to superglue swimsuits to your butt."

I stepped in to help. "What does he do on the construction crew? Is he the foreman or just a lowly carpenter? Nothing but the best for our Max, after all."

Celia stopped buttering her roll. "Hmm. I'm not sure, but he has a drill kind of thing. And a really big hammer."

Chapter 4

After we'd finally quit laughing and cleaned up the dishes, while Celia issued a good-natured lecture on childish behavior, I borrowed a sleeping bag and headed out to my house. Celia and Nathan had invited me to stay with them until my furniture arrived, but I wanted to spend the first night in my new rental house actually *in* my new house. (Not that they were letting me pay any rent yet, but still. I was keeping track and was going to pay it all retroactively once I got the business going.)

Thirty minutes later, I sat on the floor in my borrowed sleeping bag, surrounded by boxes, and toasted myself with a paper cup of wine and a Krispy Kreme donut.

To a new life and a new December.

In fewer than seventy-two hours, I'd find out that my old life wasn't quite done with me yet.

Polished hardwood floors are much better to look at than sleep on, so I gave up and headed for the office early. Getting in at seven would be all productive and business-owner-like. I'd have at least an hour and a half of quiet time to catch up on the paperwork I hadn't had time for the day before. Law is usually about five percent excitement to ninety-five percent paperwork, despite what you see on TV.

As I pulled in to my private parking space—Max had

painted my name on it in big blue letters—I smiled to my-self. *I can do this. Running a law firm isn't that hard.*

"Are you running a law firm here or what? Where the hell have you been?"

I jumped at the first screechy word and almost spilled coffee all over my skirt. I looked up at the culprit and tried not to growl. "Hello, Mr. Ellison. Is there a problem, or do you usually lurk in parking lots trying to scare people?" I swung my car door open and stepped out, which made me about half a foot taller than him.

Always take the position of power for the psychological advantage. Lawyer 101.

"I've been waiting for you since six o'clock this morn-ing. Don't think that you don't have to pay me for the past hour and seven minutes just because *you* don't have any work ethics, young lady."

I gritted my teeth, peaceful feeling evaporated. "I think you mean work *ethic,* Mr. Ellison. And please call me De-cember. Or even *Boss.* Boss would be great, actually."

Subtle didn't really work on Mr. Ellison. "Well, I guess if you only have the *one* ethic, that's how you say it. I've got lots of ethics. And you'd better give me my own key, so I can get to work while you lollygag around in the morning. Where's the chickie?"

I juggled my briefcase and coffee as I unlocked the of-fice door. "Max. Her name is Max. No girlie, no chickie. Try to keep up with what century you're in, Mr. Ellison. She usually comes in at nine, like me. How about you just come in at nine, when we do?" *That way you can't break anything.*

He stomped off toward the file room. "Fine, but you're paying me for this morning. And make a different kind of coffee today. That stuff yesterday gave me the runs."

I made a face at his retreating back. "TMI, Mr. Ellison. TMI."

He stopped at the doorway and turned around. "By the way, your butt looks huge in that skirt, *Boss*."

This whole boss thing isn't all it's cracked up to be.

After a fairly calm morning spent reviewing Charlie's file and refereeing arguments between Mr. Ellison and Max — who was back to normal clothes, thank goodness — my phone rang as I was pondering the vital decision between Wendy's and Taco Bell for lunch. Praying that Mr. Bessup was finally returning our calls and would magically appear and take Ellison off my hands, I snatched up the receiver. "December Vaughn."

"Ms. Vaughn, this is P. Addison Langley the Third. You can call me Addison." The dulcet tones of Southern charm flowed out of the phone.

"Okay, Addison. How can I help you?" Probably selling long-distance services. Perfect telemarketer voice.

"No, it is I who wish to help *you*, Ms. Vaughn. I understand you filed a notice of appearance in the Deaver case this morning."

I glanced at my watch, surprised. "You've got pretty good information, Addison, because I just filed that about an hour ago, after I talked with my client. Who are you, exactly?"

He laughed. "It's been a very long time since a lawyer in this town — or anywhere in northeast Florida, for that matter — asked me who I am, young lady. Where have you been? I am the managing partner of Langley, Cowan, and Allens."

Ah, Langley, Cowan. Now *that* I'd heard of. Langley,

Cowan was a hundred-year-old white shoe defense firm that represented all of the biggest companies in the area, and several from out of state. They'd been colead counsel for the defendant manufacturers in the latest round of diet drug litigation, and I'd heard some interesting tales of them butting heads with the New York firm that served as the other colead. Not to mention that they were BDC's defense counsel on the Deaver case, although Langley hadn't personally signed the pleadings I'd seen so far.

If this Langley was *that* Langley, I was seriously outgunned.

"Ms. Vaughn? Are you still there?" Suddenly his voice didn't sound all that charming to me. More . . . *smarm* than charm.

"I'm here, Mr. Langley. What can I do for you?"

"Call me Addison. May I call you December? It *is* December, isn't it? Curious name."

This from a man named *Addison*?

"Well, then, December, as you surely know by now, we are chief outside counsel for BDC Pharmaceuticals and are defending BDC in the insulin cases. Since you're apparently taking over Charles Deaver's case, I thought I'd give you a call. All in the spirit of cooperation, you understand."

I understood, all right. I'd made similar calls myself, under orders when I was a baby lawyer. First you get the solo practitioner or generalist attorney to think you're her friend. Then you quickly offer to settle, before one of the huge plaintiff's firms that operate on the industrial model swoops the plaintiff up in the giant Hoover suction of client solicitation.

Let me back up a minute. The mass tort model was pretty simple, really. The FDA would recall a drug for what they called Adverse Events, and what the rest of us called reports of seriously bad side effects. Like cancer, or heart disease, or death.

The kind of side effect that could ruin your day.

Then, when the pixels had barely settled from the FDA's Internet press release, an elite group of plaintiffs' attorneys from law firms based throughout the country would hop on their private jets and head for a central meeting place. Someplace simple, like the Four Seasons in New York or the Bellagio in Vegas.

These particular plaintiffs' attorneys are really into under-statement, you understand.

They'd put an action plan into effect, based on the many, many cases they'd worked together in the past. Quickly draw up teams and designate which did what. Discovery, expert witnesses, medical knowledge, Daubert and other evidentiary challenges to the science. Then they'd drink a few dozen thousand-dollar bottles of wine and head back to their respective states to start the real work: pulling in cases.

There's a fine line between solicitation, which is illegal in most states, and advertising for cases. The line has to do with the directness of the approach. For example, an attorney can't approach a *specific* person known to have a *specific* problem and say, "Hey, I'm a lawyer. Hire me for your case."

But we can advertise and say, to the general public, "Hey, I'm a lawyer. *If* you have a case, hire me."

(If the distinction confuses you, you're not alone, trust me.)

Then, when somebody's wife or child suffers an injury that may be related to a bad drug, they call their family lawyer. Or their friend's lawyer. Or the lawyer who did their taxes or their divorce or their will.

None of these lawyers will have a clue about how to run a drug case, so they refer the case—for a fee, of course—to one of the big firms in the private jet-set group. So basically, a handful of law firms who never, ever meet their clients run all the cases against the manufacturer or manufacturers of the drug in question.

It's efficient. It's expedient.

I'm not sure it's exactly *justice*.

The defense side of the cases operates with similar war-room strategies and battle-honed precision. If a few plaintiffs (or a few hundred) get crushed under the wheels of the machine, well, that's how it goes.

It's also efficient. And expedient.

I'm not sure that it's always justice on *that* side of the playing field either.

Not really the time for philosophizing, though. Sometimes you're the windshield.

"Sometimes you're the bug." But I didn't intend to let Charlie Deaver be crushed.

"Excuse me?"

"Nothing, Addison. Thank you for the call and for the spirit of cooperation. I'd like to talk about some of your discovery responses, which appear to be seriously past due. If you—"

"Oh, no need to get into all that, now, is there?" He chuckled warmly, all jovial-let's-you-and-me-be-buds now.

"Excuse me?"

"Well, you and I both know, no offense, that you don't have the expertise to handle this case. Your client deserves experienced counsel. You don't want his case to suffer while you try to learn your way around a mass tort case, do you?"

I leaned back in my chair, intrigued. Now *that* was a new

tactic. Trying to get the inexperienced lawyer to give the case to somebody better equipped to handle it? It wasn't an arrow in any defense counsel quiver I'd ever used. The cynic in me wasn't buying altruism as a motive, however.

"So, you're suggesting I refer the case out?" I tried to keep the surprise out of my voice. I couldn't wait to hear how this played out.

"Definitely. And I know just the lawyer. Sarah Greenberg at Greenberg and Smithies. I'll give you her direct dial number. She's handling all of the cases that have been filed against BDC to date. She's been doing this almost as long as I have, the old battle-ax."

I'm sure Greenberg would get all warm and fuzzy over being called a battle-ax. I might have to mention it when I met her around the bar someday. (That's bar association, not the beer-and-nuts kind usually. But whatever works.)

"Okay, just to get this straight, you want me to refer my client's case to a more experienced lawyer, so Mr. Deaver will achieve a better result. Against BDC Pharmaceuticals. Who happens to be *your* client. Is that about right?"

"You got it. After all, we're working for justice here, aren't we, December?"

"You know, Addison, I can't seem to remember *where* in the Rules of Professional Responsibility—you know, the part where it talks about a lawyer's duty to zealously represent one's client—I can't remember where the part about getting your client's *opponent* a better lawyer was written. It sure wasn't on the Florida Bar Exam I took last summer."

Addison's warmth turned cold fast. "Yes, last summer. So you've been licensed to practice law for what, six minutes? Do you really think that makes you qualified to go up against *me*? Lady, I've beaten the top plaintiffs' lawyers in the country. You might want to ask around before you decide to take me on."

I decided I'd heard enough. "Okay, then, Addy. Thanks for your advice and the spirit of cooperation and all that, but I think I'll keep this case. Mr. Deaver and I will do just fine on our own. Thanks for calling, though."

I slowly replaced the phone in its cradle, feeling my forehead scrunch up in confusion. I was going to look like a Shar Pei by the time I was thirty-five. Did the employee health plan cover Botox? Did we even have an employee health plan yet?

And more important: *What the hell was* that *all about?*

The phone rang under my hand, and I flinched back a little, blinking.

"It's for YOU, girlie," bellowed my new employee from somewhere down the hallway.

I picked up the phone and punched the button for Max's extension.

"Um, Max? Any chance you could teach Mr. Ellison how to use the intercom system or at least the interoffice extension?"

"I. Can't. Teach. That. Old. Buzzard. Anything." I'd never heard someone swallow her own tongue before, but this sounded close. Max was normally so calm she made Prozac seem hyperactive. Ellison must have been seriously pushing her buttons.

She took a deep breath. "Sorry, December. I'll see what I can do. It's Sarah Greenberg on line one for you, by the way. Snotty voice, good diction."

"Really? I was just talking about her. Well, being talked *at,* to be precise. The plot thickens, and all that mysterious crap. Thanks. And don't let Ellison get to you. Remember, you're better, you're stronger, and . . . um, you have more hair."

I disconnected the line quickly. That was *so* not covered in the "How to Be a Good Employer" manual. Taking my own deep breath, I pressed the blinking button with the big number one on it. *See, even I can learn this system. It ought to be a breeze for a retired bus driver.* "December Vaughn."

". . . tell her I'm not putting up with her shit. Two point five million, and not a penny less, or my next phone call is to the press. Yes, December? Sorry about that. You kept me waiting for so long, I had to discuss something with my secretary. So, welcome to the Florida Bar, yada yada. You need to transfer the Deaver case to me."

Chapter 5

I held the phone out and stared at it in disbelief. *Wow. That was blunt.*

"Hi, Sarah. You need to work on this problem you have with speaking your mind. Don't beat around the bush; just come right out and say what you think." I may have sounded just a teensy bit sarcastic.

She laughed, but it sounded brittle. *Snotty with good diction* had nailed her perfectly.

"Right. Sorry. I'm just so used to dealing with the big boys, and we don't play around making nice-nice. I heard you'd filed in the Deaver case, and I'm offering to help."

I jotted some important notes on a yellow legal pad.

1. Buy white legal pads. I hate yellow.

2. Sara(h?) Greenberg—check her Martindale Hubbell.

3. *Nice-nice?* Are we back in the third grade here?

"What is this town, Hotline Central? I filed that appearance just over an hour ago, and you're the second person to call me about it. Do you keep espionage agents on alert down at the courthouse?" I used my light, friendly, we're-all-in-the-same-treehouse voice as I doodled an angry face with ugly googly eyes next to item two.

Nice-nice. Puh-*leeze*.

"Cute. I assume, being fresh out of law school, that you

realize you're not anywhere near qualified to run a major drug case?"

Interesting. Almost the exact same words Langley used. Maybe they DO have a treehouse.

4. 411 on Langley-Greenberg connection?

5. Need toilet tissue for house and office. The good kind— no generic!

"Fresh out of law school? Where do you get that assumption? My previous caller seemed to have the same idea."

"We researched you, December. You took the Florida Bar last summer and were sworn in a few months ago. Am I wrong?"

6. I don't like this woman.

"Nope. You're right."

"It's not exactly rocket science." She laughed again. Still brittle; enunciation getting a little clipped.

7. She doesn't like me either.

I leaned back in my chair. "Except your information is a little off about the law school thing. I graduated eight years ago. *Summa cum laude,* actually, from Capital Law School in Columbus, Ohio, in case you want to check. Practiced in Ohio with True, Evers, and Johnson for eight years in the products liability department. Pharmaceuticals, to be precise."

There was a silence.

8. Her silence spoke volumes.

9. *What does that mean? How can a silence speak? Is it* Book *volumes, or volumes like in fluid? What would* that *mean?*

10. Am useless note taker.

I put my pen down, but still didn't say a word. I knew all about the "whoever speaks first, loses" trick of long silences. My old boss didn't have *Eat Breakfast with Machiavelli* in his bookcase for nothing.

She finally spoke. *Ha! I win.* "Well, then. I see. So you have eight years of defense experience. The plaintiff's side is very different. Plus, you don't have the huge law firm machine to back you up on this one. We represent more than one hundred clients in this matter, December. Twenty with wrongful death claims, the rest with substantial injury. We've retained experts and started the ball rolling. We'd love the chance to share our work with you. Why don't you just refer Mr. Deaver's case to us?"

Before I could respond, she hurried on. "Look, we'll keep you involved. You can attend his deposition, and we'll copy you on pleadings and such. I think forty-five would be fair, don't you?"

"Forty-five?"

"A referral fee. We'll give you forty-five percent of any recovery in the case, and all you have to do is read a few pleadings and hold Mr. Deaver's hand occasionally. Doesn't that sound like a more efficient way for you to start a new law firm? Rather than get sucked up in fighting Langley, Cowan on this case all by yourself?"

Snotty had turned patronizing, fast.

"You know, that's an interesting offer, Sarah. I guess, since you took the bar exam so very, very, *very* many years ago, you don't realize that a forty-five percent referral fee would violate the Florida Bar rules? Especially when I'm to have no input on the case beyond reading and hand-holding?"

"Fine. I won't waste any more of your time. If you change your mind, Ms. Vaughn, you know how to find me."

Click.

Hanging up on me probably gave her some small satisfaction after my low blow about her age. That third *very* was, maybe, over the top. Plus, it was totally unlike me. I'd practiced law for eight years and earned a reputation as one of the most civil of civil litigators, and now I was turning into a rabid pit bull after one day on this case.

I *so* needed chocolate. I tried to analyze why I was so averse to referring the Deaver case out anyway, with the amount of work and expense it was bound to cost me. Unfortunately, a "gut feeling" doesn't lend itself to analysis all that well. Something in Charlie Deaver had really touched my heart (not that tough trial lawyers have hearts, but still). I wasn't ready to give his case away so readily.

Mr. Ellison popped his head in my office just then. "Lunch?"

"Are you buying?"

He snorted. "Not on what you're paying me. Let's go, we're starving."

What am *I paying him?*

As we walked up to the front desk, the phone rang again. Max raised a hand to shush us and picked up. "Law offices of December Vaughn."

I grinned. Maybe I'd just sit out here in the reception area all afternoon and listen to her say that. *Law offices of December Vaughn. MY law offices. I really did it.*

"December? Earth to December? It's about your furniture."

"Oh, man, I've been so busy I forgot all about it. Hand me the phone, please."

Max stretched the cord across the desk.

"December Vaughn speaking. Is my truck on the way?"

"Well, that's the question, isn't it." The strident tones of the dispatcher slammed into my eardrum. I held the phone out a few inches from my ear. "What do you mean, that's the question? What's the answer? Where's my furniture?"

"Calm down, Ms. Vaygan. Here's the thing. We don't exactly know where your furniture is."

"What? How could you lose my furniture? And it's *Vaughn*." I clutched the phone so hard my knuckles turned white.

Max was making questioning faces; I waved her off.

"It's just that . . . er . . . this driver has kind of a history of the occasional bender."

"Bender? What do you mean *bender*?" It occurred to me that I was parroting everything she said, but my brain didn't seem to be functioning very well. "You hired a driver who goes on benders? As in drunks? So he's a drunken driver and a . . . a furniture thief?" My voice steadily rose until the word "thief" was fairly screechy.

"Now, just hold on a minute. He's not a drunk driver. He pulls off the road and gets out of the truck for a few days when he does this. He'd never endanger people by driving one of our big rigs drunk." She sounded offended.

She's offended?

"Look, all I want to know is where my furniture is, and when I can expect it to arrive. As much fun as I'm having sleeping on the floor, it doesn't really work for me."

"Um, that's a small problem."

"Another problem? What is it this time?"

"Your driver is the owner's brother-in-law. So he kind of

does what he wants. The last time he pulled this, we didn't hear from him for three weeks."

"Three weeks! Are you kidding?" Now I was full-out yelling. Max and Ellison both stared me with identical "Great, our boss is a nutjob" expressions.

These furniture people didn't know who they were dealing with. "You people don't know who, er, *with whom* you are dealing. I am a trial lawyer. We have a *contract*. As a lawyer, I understand contracts. I understand *breach* of contract, which is what you are now in danger of entering. I will pursue my full remedies under the law, if you don't find my furniture immediately and call me back by the end of business today with an ETA."

She laughed.

She *laughed*?

"Honey, the last person your driver pulled this on was an IRS auditor. If he didn't scare me, you got nothin'. I'll try to track him down, but the damn fool is good at hiding. I'll call you when I hear something."

"You'd better—"

Click.

I was so tired of people hanging up on me.

I unpacked two hundred dollars' worth of basics on my kitchen counters, still fuming about bully lawyers and incompetent moving companies. As I pulled various cleaning supplies out of the bags, I figured that it was lucky I at least had an island in the center of the kitchen for extra counter space, since it's not like anybody knew where my kitchen table was. Or my chairs. Or my couches.

Or my TV. How was a girl supposed to survive without her daily reality TV fix?

I sighed for about the fortieth time since I'd gotten home and held up one of my new buys. "Hey, at least I've got a toilet brush. Happiness is a clean toilet, right?"

"That's what I always say."

I whirled around toward the screened back door that I hoped I'd locked. You never know what kind of crazies may be roaming the neighborhood. "Um, hi?"

The woman who stood there had a cake. No crazy person would bring cake. Plus, it was chocolate. I was *so* letting her in.

She smiled. "Hi! I'm Emily Kingsley, your neighbor. I wanted to say welcome to the block in a warm and fudgy kind of way."

I opened the door and motioned her inside. "December Vaughn. If the cake under that frosting is chocolate, too, you may have saved a life today."

Emily laughed and put the cake down on the counter, then held out her hand to shake. "I'd settle for making a new friend, but rescue hero would be fine, too."

We shook hands, then I dug through my bags for the paper plates and plastic utensils I'd just bought, while trying not to drool too obviously. The whole missing furniture thing had ruined my appetite at lunchtime, so now I was starved. "Oh, sorry about the lack of proper plates and stuff, but my furniture is currently on vacation without me. With a drunken truck driver who profits greatly from nepotism." I scowled, but it was halfhearted. The delicious aroma of fudge was curing my bad temper pretty quickly.

Emily slid a plastic knife out of its box and started cutting the cake. "Wanna run that by me one more time? Family business, alcohol issues, your household goods are MIA; that about sum it up?"

I sighed. Again.

I had to quit doing that.

"Right. It's a long story, but the company reassured me that the longest he's been AWOL is three weeks. So I may have real plates by the end of June."

Emily handed me a plate loaded down with an enormous piece of cake. I raised my eyebrows.

She grinned. "Hey, if you're going to eat cake, eat cake, I always say."

I forked a huge bite into my mouth, and after briefly closing my eyes and offering a prayer of thanks for whoever created chocolate, I studied Emily. She was maybe my age or a few years younger. Slender, dressed in khaki shorts and sleeveless yellow top, no makeup. She had her shiny dark hair pulled back in a ponytail, and she probably looked about eighteen from a distance.

But I couldn't hate her. She'd brought me chocolate.

She swallowed and licked frosting off one of her fingers. "So, are you with the Navy? You said AWOL."

I shook my head. "No, I'm an attorney. I just opened up a small practice in town. But I grew up as a Navy brat. Dad was a chief petty officer when he retired and went corporate. Away Without Official Leave was a pretty common term when he and his buddies were complaining about the latest crop of squids. What about you? You said household goods."

She grinned. "My husband works for a firm that does a lot of business with the Navy. It's hard to escape all the jargon."

I took another bite of cake and almost moaned in ecstasy. It was a sad truth that chocolate was more important to my life than sex these days.

For the past couple of years, to be honest.

"This cake is unbelievable. Did you bake this yourself? My Aunt Celia is going to adore you." I finished the slice and looked longingly at the rest of the cake, but resisted. No need to be a total pig in front of the neighbors and make a bad first impression.

"I adore her. She and Nathan are darlings," she said. "I'm going to have another piece, December. To heck with the diet. Want more?"

I *loved* this woman. "What do you do, Emily?"

"I do a little bit of everything, but mostly I'm a stay-at-home mom. Elisabeth is four and Ricky is six, so they keep me really busy. T-ball practice and games, ballet lessons, swimming lessons, camp, Scouts. Pretty much go, go, go, as you might imagine. They're out at McDonald's with Daddy right now, so Mommy could have a little quiet before her head exploded." She laughed again, but seemed way too calm and together for any head exploding. Especially if she could bake chocolate cake this scrumptious for stress relief.

The doorbell rang. That made two more unexpected guests in one day than I'd had in the past five years. Florida was certainly a friendly place.

Chapter 6

"Will you excuse me a second?" I said to Emily, and then I walked down the hall to the front door. But my new guest started pounding on the door.

I yanked it open. "What do—Max? What are you doing here? Come on in and have cake. It's chocolate."

"You always say *chocolate* the way a person dying of thirst would say Evian, December." She thrust a bouquet of wildflowers at me. "Little housewarming present, even though you couldn't be bothered to invite me over."

"That is so sweet. Maybe they'll fit in a paper cup? And you know I was planning to invite you over when my furniture arrived. I'm totally going to hit you up for help unpacking, old buddy, old pal." I smiled hugely.

"Oh, no. Not that shark grin. I'm always in trouble when it's the shark grin."

"Shut up, already. I have someone I want you to meet. This is—"

"Emily! It's so good to see you again. What have you been up to?"

"Max! I haven't seen you since the fundraiser. How have you been?" She gave Max a big hug.

"I'm great. Working with December at her new firm now. What about you? How was Atlantic City?"

"Oh, same old, same old. Not to be trite, but you win some, you lose some." She grinned and put her plate and fork in an empty plastic bag. "Now, I have to get going and check my e-mail before the kidlets get home. It was so nice to meet you, December. If your stuff ever gets here, and you need any help unpacking, let me know. Oh, and we're going to have a block-wide garage sale and then a barbecue the week of July Fourth sometime. We'd love for you to join us at either or both. Bring this sweet Southern girl with you, please."

Max fanned herself with one hand. "Oh, it's an honor just to be here, darlin'."

I offered the plate with the rest of the cake to Emily. "Thank you so much. You should take the rest of this home to your family."

"Oh, no. You keep it and eat it for breakfast or something. I don't want to lose points on the Welcome Wagon scale. See you later." I watched through my window as she crossed to the house right next to mine.

I turned back to Max. "Wonder if she'd be willing to swap houses? Did you see that beautiful garden? What are those little purple flowers all over the front?"

"Impatiens."

"No, I'm not impatient. I've just got a yard full of weeds, and I want a garden like that. Now." I laughed. "Okay, maybe I am impatient."

"No, not impatient, impatiens. The name of the flower, December. Say it with me: im—pa—tiens."

I rolled my eyes. "Like I've had time to be Nature Girl during the past fifteen years, between college, law school, and working. I know a rose from a carnation, but the rest are mostly just *Look at the Pretty Flowers*."

Max leaned against the counter and folded her arms. "There's never a better time to start learning. Except not right this minute, because I'm taking you out to dinner at

Mama Yang's. Put some shoes on, girlfriend, and let's go. Giant cactus margaritas are on me."

I grabbed my sandals. "Are shorts okay? And, um, cactus margaritas? Sounds . . . prickly. Not to mention odd for a place called Mama Yang's . . ."

She picked up my purse and handed it to me. "This is Florida, darling. Shorts are always okay. Especially for someone who has an ass like that. How does a lawyer who sits all day long have an ass like that? It's so unfair."

I started laughing. "Like your ass isn't one of the Seven World Wonders. And why exactly are we comparing asses?"

As I locked my door, I glanced at Emily's house, where a minivan had pulled up in the driveway, and a couple of cute kids were chattering at full speed and top volume as they swarmed out of the car. I sighed again. For the forty-second time.

Stop that!

"Max, remind me again why I ever thought I'd fit in here in Leave It to Beaver–ville? Not to look a gift house in the mouth, or whatever, but I'm not exactly PTA material, like my sweet neighbor. They're all gonna hate me, aren't they? And how do you know Emily anyway? Have you been trolling bake sales for chocolate chip cookies?"

"I'm driving, December, because you need to get a good drunk on. I met Emily at an AIDS fundraiser for the Northeast Florida Beauty Queens for Literacy Alliance. We had a Vegas theme and raised over fifty thousand dollars. It was a great time, for a great cause, plus I got to wear sequins."

I looked at her as she slid in the driver's seat. "What more can a girl ask for? Emily's a beauty queen, too?"

Max started the car and laughed. "Not exactly. Emily was our celebrity guest. She's a professional tournament-poker player. One of the top players on the circuit. I guess she came close to winning the World Series of Poker last year."

I twisted around in my seat to stare back at the minivan. "Emily? A *poker* player?"

"They call her The Psychic on the circuit because she's uncanny about spotting tells. Claims to be able to spot a bluff from a mile away."

"What's a *tell*?" It sounded familiar, but I wasn't much of a card player.

"A tell is a twitch or a quirk that gives you away. Like if somebody always scratches his ear when he's bluffing, or taps his cards twice if he has a great hand."

"Come on, they don't really do that. Do they? The top players?" I was skeptical. I mean, it made for fun plot twists in movies, but would professionals be so unaware of their own tics?

Also: *How cool would it be to have Emily along in depositions and at trial?*

I didn't realize I was smiling, until Max did an exaggerated shudder. "Uh-oh. You're doing the shark thing again. Who's in trouble this time?"

"Addison Langley and Sarah Greenberg, if they try to push me around again. And I'm not making a shark look. That was a smile."

Max shuddered again.

"Fine, so it was a sharky smile. They teach us those in law school. Can we get to the margarita portion of the evening's entertainment already?"

"You're still pissed off about the calls from those attorneys on the Deaver case, aren't you?"

I'd filled her in during the afternoon, while we researched insulin and diabetes. Max had been furious when she heard about the intimidation tactics. I'd found myself back in my familiar role as the voice of reason; much more comfortable for me than the inner gorilla I'd channeled during my two phone calls.

My motto was, *Put the civil back in civil litigation.* Of course, my other motto was, *Take no shit, make no excuses.*

Okay, so I do see the contradiction.

Max pulled to a stop in the parking lot, and I stared at the flickering neon sign that read, MAMA YANG'S FINE ORIENTAL CUISINE.

Then I sighed. Again.

"Aaaarghhh! Forty-freaking-three! That's it! If you hear me sigh again tonight, hit me! No, make me do a shot of tequila. I'm sick of feeling defeated before I've even begun to fight. A shot of tequila is plenty of incentive to stop this sighing crap."

I blame the tequila for my ending up in jail.

Chapter 7

Mama Yang turned out to be Maria Garcia, a beauty in her mid-forties or so who was rounded in a forties movie star kind of way. I glanced down at my unrounded self and almost sighed again but tried for a teensy bit of self–pep talk. I'd been told once that I looked kind of like "Nicole Kidman on a bad day," and she does okay, right? Plus, some time in all this Florida sun, and I'd be tanned and gorgeous in no time.

Or with my Irish skin, more like sunburnt, leathery, and wrinkled, but let's try to stay positive.

"Mama, this is December Vaughn, one of my oldest friends. December, Maria Garcia." Introductions over, Max wandered off to the bar, hopefully to find giant margaritas.

Maria smiled at me. "You don't look very old to me. So how is the law business going? Sued anybody interesting lately?"

I grinned. "No, but the week is young. How did you know I was a lawyer?"

She took my arm and led me over to the bar. "Oh, everybody knows everything in this town. It's a hotbed of gossip and rumor—most of it totally untrue. And please call me Maria. Mama is Max's idea of a joke."

She introduced me to Catherine Chant, the bartender, who was in her mid-twenties or so and one of those bubbly people who make you want to smile a lot, once you got over the tattoos that covered both of her arms from wrist to shoulder. She didn't seem like a snakes-and-dragons person, but that just goes to show you that you never can tell about a bartender.

"Here you go, love. One of my Stress Relief Specials. A triple-shot cactus margarita. You'd better get some food with that. I've had men twice your size end up on their butts from my SRS margaritas. A skinny little thing like you will be flat out on the floor, unless you eat a burrito to soak up some tequila."

I hefted my giant drink and smiled at the idea of a five-foot-tall bartender calling me a "little thing." "Thanks. I promise. I think I'll go find Max."

I nodded to Maria and Catherine and wandered off to look for Max. The restaurant was still in conversion mode; the strings of chili peppers shared space with the Chinese dragon kites. A beautiful Asian doll in a glass case on the bar near the cash register cast a flirty glance at the miniature bullfighter propped against it.

"It's a melding of cultures," said a voice very near my ear. I sucked in a breath, both because I hadn't heard anybody walk up next to me, and because the voice itself was just a suck-in-your-breath kind of voice. A husky low tone that made me think of silk sheets and body lotion.

Of course, considering my celibate lifestyle lately, most things made me think of silk sheets and body lotion. Maybe I just needed to get laid.

I turned to face Mr. Sexy Voice and barely managed not to suck in another breath. The man was so hot he needed a warning label. From the black, tousled hair that was just a little too long, to the dark-chocolate eyes, to the long, lean body that had muscles in all the right places, everything about him shouted "Bad Boy Alert." My thigh muscles started twitching.

He smiled down at me—one of those slow, dangerous smiles that every mother warns her daughter about. Panties by the dozen fall off female bodies from smiles like that. I was a tough trial lawyer, though, and not easily charmed. "So, do you practice that smile?" I asked, tilting my head and giving him my best "you don't fool me" appraising stare.

He laughed, and something down low in my body clenched. My own traitorous panties were trying to disappear. *Damn, he has a great laugh, too.*

"Does it look practiced? Maybe I *should* practice, if that's the reaction I get. Wanna help?"

Luckily for my pathetic self-control, Max showed up just then. She gave the guy a cool look and stepped between us. "Hey, Jake. I see you've met December. Big surprise. Still on your quest to get naked with every beautiful woman in town? I saw Gina, by the way."

Jake smiled again, but his eyes narrowed. "You shouldn't believe everything you hear, Max. And no, we hadn't met. Jake Brody," he said, extending his hand to me.

I glanced at Max, curious about her flat-eyed stare, but took Brody's hand. It was a warm, firm handshake, from a man who actually knew how to shake a woman's hand. *I wonder what else he knows how to do with his hands?*

Stop it.

"December Vaughn. Pleasure. I'm—"

"Fine, you've met. Now let's go," Max said, grabbing my arm and practically dragging me off. I looked back at Jake, and he was staring after me, lips still quirked up in a smile.

I yanked my arm out of Max's grip, but kept walking with her. "What the hell was that all about?" I hissed. "In case you hadn't noticed, I'm not fifteen anymore and don't need you to be my big sister."

Max threaded her way through a few tables to one with a drink and a bowl of nachos on it and dropped into a chair. "You may not be fifteen, but you still need me if the first man you hit on is the infamous Jake Brody," she said grimly.

I slid into the chair and took a gulp of my margarita. "What's so bad about him? I mean, other than the obvious 'I'm big, bad, and dangerous' thing."

"More dangerous than you know. The man was a Navy SEAL, and now he runs the top private investigation firm in town. He has a rep for getting the job done, no matter the little details like legality."

I couldn't help it; my gaze cut to the bar, but Jake was gone. "What does that mean? Nobody can use him in court if his methods aren't aboveboard."

Max laughed. "They always are, if he's going to testify. But not all of his clients are law firms, if you get my drift."

I scooped up some more of the truly kick-ass salsa on what had to be a homemade chip and stuffed it in my mouth. "That is great salsa. Can we order some food now, before this margarita knocks me out? I'm not interested in Jake Brody, or any other man, for that matter, if it makes you feel any better. Recently divorced, remember? Not dating for at least five years."

My various body parts started shouting in protest at this, but I ignored them. Abstinence sharpens the mind, right?

Max wasn't buying it either. "Don't bullshit a bullshitter, D. I saw that look on your face. That was the Bobby Denaris look."

"Hey, Bobby Denaris was hot! Just because he only dated cheerleaders didn't mean I couldn't look. And can we quit rehashing high school, for God's sake? That was fifteen years ago!"

Max snapped her menu shut as the server approached, order pad out. "Patterns, D. We set our patterns at a young age. I'm just saying, as a friend, stay away from Jake Brody. The ones who make you rethink your policy on public sex are trouble."

"Why do I get the feeling that we're not talking about me and Brody anymore? When are you going to tell me what happened with Ryan? And hello—public sex? *Euww.*"

She wouldn't meet my eye. "He was trouble, too. Another Brody. And I was a damn fool."

"Want me to beat him up for you?"

She smiled, but it didn't reach her eyes. "Like you said, it's not high school anymore."

We sat there, both depressed all to hell. I grabbed my margarita, took a deep breath, and drained it, then held up my empty glass. "Next!"

Max grinned at me and drained her glass, too. "Screw all this depressing stuff. Let's get eat-the-worm drunk on tequila and see if we can show these rednecks something on the dance floor."

My dancing is even worse than my singing, and my singing caused my music teacher in fifth grade to take early retirement. But what the hell. Another Stress Relief Special, and I'd be doing my MTV-wannabe on the dance floor.

We heard it before we saw it, which wasn't saying much, because I was seeing everything blurry by that point.

"You keep away from my man, you low-rent ho!" The shriek drilled through my fuzzy brain.

The crowd dancing around Max and me parted, and people rushed out of the way, giving me a pretty clear view of four women facing off. Wait, two. *Two* blurry women facing off. Stupid cactus margaritas had me seeing double.

One was nearly as round as she was tall, with bleached blond hair teased up in a hairdo that was trapped in the eighties. The other looked like a mean version of Angelina Jolie, all hair and huge dark eyes. They were both seriously pissed off, and the Angie one had a knife.

Shit.

The blonde started screaming. "I didn't go near your man, you psycho bitch. I don't even know who the hell your man is!"

The brunette dropped into a crouch and did a "come and get me" gesture with the knife. She'd watched way too many movies, or else she knew what she was doing and Blondie was in trouble. Either way, I felt like I should do something. I started forward, and Max grabbed my by the sleeve. "What the hell are you doing? You're not a cop. You're going to get yourself stabbed."

I looked down at her with all the dignity I could muster. "I'm an ossifer of the court. I mean, an *officer* of the court. It's my sworn duty to uphold the lawn. Er, the *law.*" Okay, it wasn't a *lot* of dignity, but it's all I had at the moment.

I feinted sideways and then twisted out from her grasp and slipped in between two guys who were placing bets on the fight. By the time I got to them, the brunette was questioning the species of the blonde's parents in a very creative way.

I held my hands up and tried to be the voice of reason. "Now, ladies, I'm sure you can work this out—"

The blonde responded to reason by launching herself at the brunette, right through me. I tried to jump out of the way. Too late. She slammed right into my chest and knocked me on my ass. As I lay there on the ground, trying to catch my breath, I wondered if this reaction to my attempt to be the voice of reason meant I'd suck as a judge.

Then Blondie jumped up, stepping on my arm, and screamed at Knife Girl. "You bitch. I am so sick of your psycho crap. Are you the one who slashed my tires and wrote 'slut' on my car? I'll kill you!"

I yelled and yanked my arm out from under her foot, which toppled her and she went down again, this time taking Knife Girl with her. They both landed on me, slamming me back down to the floor. I couldn't see the knife, but Blondie started shrieking loud enough to wake a federal judge, so I figured she got stuck.

This wasn't going how I'd planned.

Chapter 8

I shoved at random body parts, trying to get them off me. It didn't help. Years (or *looong* minutes) later, arms yanked at both of them and pulled them up. Finally able to breathe, I stayed there on the floor, hacking and coughing to try to reinflate my lungs. It was way more comfortable without a couple of hundred pounds of screaming women on top of me.

Max looked down at me from where she stood next to the big guy who was holding Blondie by the scruff of the neck. "Are you all right, *ossifer*?" she drawled.

I hate it when she drawls.

I stuck my tongue out at her and mouthed the word "wimp."

She laughed and shook her head. The big guy handed the screaming blonde off to a bouncer. *Oh, sure. Now there's a bouncer. Fat lot of good he was. I hope Mama Maria fires him.*

"She cut me. The bitch stabbed me," the blonde shrieked, clutching her arm.

The brunette, meanwhile, twisted out of the hands of the man holding on to her shirt and dropped to the floor. I tried to roll out of her way fast, not wanting to be the next victim, but she curled up in a fetal position next to me and started sobbing.

Boy, do I know how to party or what?

Sobering up fast, I reached a tentative hand over and

patted her shoulder. "Hey. Hey, are you okay? Did you get hurt?"

She shook her head, but otherwise ignored me completely, other than a slight increase in volume. Two more big, burly, no-neck kind of guys shouldered their way through the crowd just then. One had a black shirt with the name of the bar on it, and the other guy wore a cop face.

Cop face introduced himself. "Deputy Marlin, ma'am. You're going to have to get up off the floor and hand over the knife."

Knife? Oh, yeah. I forgot about the fact that she had a deadly weapon. I backed away from her, fast. Two deadly weapons in two days were way over my limit.

She sat up all in one unbending motion, like a robot or something. It was kind of scary, to be honest. The silver blade in her hand didn't help.

The cop put his hand on his gun, but didn't pull it out of his holster. "Okay, just hand it over, nice and slow, lady."

She laughed bitterly. "It's Gina. Gina Schiantelli. And you're more than welcome to my nail file, you idiot." She flipped it up in the air so it twirled over and she caught it by the file edge, then extended it, pink plastic handle forward, to the cop.

He looked a little embarrassed, but I'd thought it was a knife, too. Sheesh. Butter knives and nail files. I was done being afraid of pretend knives, that's for sure.

"You're going to have to come down to the station with me, Ms. Schiantelli, and answer some questions, at the very least. We have witnesses who say you started this altercation, and it looks like your buddy wants to file charges."

The blonde looked at her arm. "Well, I'm not actually *bleeding,* but you're still a psycho."

Gina started sobbing again. "Great. Now I'm going back

to jail, right? You fall in love, and your life goes to hell. My life is a freaking country-western song. All I need is a damn porch with a dog on it."

I felt that little twinge under my left rib cage. I hate that twinge. It always means I'm getting ready to do something stupid for purely emotional reasons. I sighed and did it anyway. "Gina, I'm a lawyer. Do you need help?"

I ignored Max, who was violently shaking her head no, no, no. It was the twinge. Not my fault.

Gina sniffled and looked at me through the curtain of her dark, tangled hair. (Just for the record, I hate having clients who are so much better looking than me.) She looked me up and down for a beat.

It ticked me off. "Look, it's not like you can be all that picky right now. I don't see anybody else offering," I said.

She smiled a little. "You're right. Yeah, I could use some help. Can you meet me there?"

I returned her smile, but was already wondering what the heck I'd gotten myself into this time. I stood up and held my hand out to help her up. After she stood, I turned to the cop. "Officer, my name is December Vaughn, and I'm Gina's attorney. I'll meet you at booking."

He gave me his cynical face and then nodded, and snapped handcuffs on Gina, who was looking subdued but defiant. I watched them walk off, then turned to Max. "So. We need to call a taxi. Where do we go for booking?"

I'd been waiting for an hour and still no news on Gina. The waiting room was not exactly pleasant and peaceful. It smelled of old urine and fresh despair. Max had left about ten minutes ago to find us some drinkable coffee. The outside door opened, and the last person I expected to see walked into the room, looking like sex on a stick in his faded jeans.

"Jake Brody. Why am I surprised, after what Max said? Are you here for Gina?"

He sauntered over to me, and stopped when he was a fraction of an inch too close. "I was her one phone call."

My instincts pushed me to back up, but I didn't want to give him the satisfaction of knowing he made my warning bells clang. So I put my hands on my hips and gave him my best lawyer face. (I could play poker with that face, trust me.) "I bet you're a *lot* of people's one phone call. Friends in low places, much?"

He grinned. "Look who's talking. You don't even know her, but you're here. Business slow, Counselor? Going to run down some ambulances next?"

I sucked in a breath and told myself how bad it would be to punch somebody right in the sheriff's office. "Nice. Is this a sample of your much-vaunted charm?"

He reached over and tucked a strand of my hair behind my ear. The touch of his finger against the curve of my ear started other bells jangling. *Crap.*

"Nice to know you think I'm charming, Counselor. So, with all that gorgeous hair, do you get blonde jokes or lawyer jokes more often?"

I gaped a little. The man had balls of steel. "I think— you—oh! In your *dreams* do I think you're charming. And most people are too intimidated by me to make any jokes at all." I bared my teeth in my best scary-person grimace.

He laughed. "You might want to try harder. And you can go now. I called Gina's lawyer, and he's on the way down here."

"Fine. I'm going, I just—I just wanted to be sure she was okay." That darn twinge again. I didn't want to show any weakness to the wolf in black leather here, but I was worried about the missing marbles of somebody who'd start a nail file fight in a bar and then fall sobbing to the floor. I abruptly whirled away from Jake and headed for the door, but he stopped me with a hand on my arm.

I glared back at him, ready to bite his head off, but the look on his face stopped me. The cynical baiting expression was gone, replaced by something that looked . . . sincere. "Hey. Thanks. That was a nice thing to do," he said.

Sincere Jake was even more dangerous than Bad Boy Jake, I discovered. At least to my vow of celibacy. I didn't know what to say, so went with my default flippant tone. "Fine. Just don't spread it around. You'll ruin my tough trial lawyer image."

Before he could say anything else, I yanked my arm out of his hand and headed for the door, reaching it just as Max arrived with two coffees in hand. "What—" she said.

"We're out of here," I said. "Robin Hood arrived." Max nodded at Jake over my shoulder, eyes narrowing, then turned and went back out the door. I stopped for a moment and turned around. "In all seriousness, Jake, she needs to get help. If your girlfriend can't afford therapy, have her call my office, and we'll help her find a low- or no-cost program. No charge."

Jake's eyes widened a little, but all he said was, "Thanks. But she's not my girlfriend."

I didn't ask. I didn't want to know.

Liar.

After Max dropped me off at my empty house, I remembered that I'd wanted to pick up a few essentials, like a pillow. I stuffed some of my clothes inside of an old, stretchy t-shirt and figured it would work. Surely my stuff would arrive soon, right? Just as I started to climb in my sleeping bag, thinking dark thoughts about moving companies and wistful thoughts about air mattresses, I remembered to check the voice mail on my cell phone.

One new message: "Miss Vaygan? We have no news on your truck, but you'll be glad to know that the eighteen car pile-up on I-95 was not caused by your driver, as we'd thought. So your furniture is not in a smoldering heap of twisted metal on the side of the road, after all. Have a great day!"

Chapter 9

I splurged on donuts on the way to the office, figuring my all-fiber-bran-woodchip cereal would have to wait until I had a bowl to put it in. It was only eight-thirty in the morning, but the heat was killing me, so I ordered Diet Coke instead of coffee at the drive-through. At seven, it'd already been hot and muggy enough to steam up my sunglasses when I walked outside for the newspaper. Maybe I should have waited and moved to Florida in the winter, so I could ease myself into the heat and humidity.

"Woulda shoulda coulda," I muttered as I pulled into my parking place at the office. "Hindsight and blah, blah, blah."

Resolving to think cool thoughts, I balanced the box of donuts on top of my briefcase and walked into the office. Three pairs of eyes stared at me; *two* pairs of eyes immediately dropped their gazes to the donuts.

"Ah, we must have a new client," I said, smiling, as I walked to the reception desk. Max rescued the box of donuts from me, and then held them up high as Mr. Ellison immediately dove for them.

"Mr. Ellison, would you like to offer Mrs. Zivkovich a donut?" Max asked him through her clenched teeth.

Mr. Ellison's scowl turned into a beaming smile as he turned to look at the elegant woman sitting in our small reception area on the couch Max had re-covered in what she called "celery." "Mrs. Z? Would you like a donut to go with that coffee?" he asked in a weird, syrupy voice that sent a squicky feeling down my neck.

It was the same squick as the "bazumbas" conversation.

Mrs. Zivkovich looked to be in her early sixties. Her pale-blue pantsuit matched her pale-blue-tinted gray hair. She either wore makeup all the time—even in this heat—or had carefully applied it for our meeting. She shuddered delicately and shook her head. "No, I'm watching my carbs. Ever since Marge Diedenshour had that bleeding ulcer—and, you know, she was a donut eater—I stay far away from those things."

Mr. Ellison leaned against the counter, nodding. "Yeah, I know what you mean. Sandy down t'the Eagles got one of them, too. He had rectal bleeding, doncha know. Blood shot right out of him in the john during the Memorial Day barbecue. We had the E squad and everything."

I looked at the jelly donut I'd just grabbed and felt my lips curl back away from my teeth. I'd always had a teensy problem with the sight (or even mention) of blood. Max held up her hand. "Trash?"

"Trash," I agreed, handing it over. "Did I have an appointment?" I whispered.

Max shook her head. "No, she's a walk-in. Says she's a friend of Celia's, and she has a pest problem," she said in a low tone.

I turned back to Mrs. Zivkovich, shooting a glare at Mr. Ellison as I did, and smiled again. "Oh, you know my Aunt Celia? That's wonderful. Please come on back and let's talk."

As Mr. Ellison pushed off the counter, I whipped my head around to give him my "don't even think about it" glare. "Don't even think about it, buster," I hissed, in case he couldn't read glare language. "And keep the rectal bleeding stories for your . . . personal discussions. It's disgusting and not really appropriate for a law firm, don't you think?"

He blinked a few times, then looked at Max. "Oh, yummy! Jelly donuts!"

Max stared at me in disbelief as Mr. Ellison snagged two of the donuts and then sidled off down the hallway, blocking Mrs. Zivkovich's view of his death-dealing carbs. Max closed her eyes and took a deep breath, probably calling on her old pageant days for patience in the face of annoyance.

I led my new client toward my office.

After Mrs. Zivkovich had settled herself in a chair, declined coffee, and smoothed her hair away from her face, she finally started to talk. "I have this pest problem."

I waited patiently, pretty sure she didn't mean fire ants.

Her fingers worked at the clasp on her handbag. "It's . . . it's my son-in-law. He wants me to sign everything over to him. Some kind of power of eternity. He says I'm too old to make my own decisions, if you can believe that. And me only seventy-two!" She glared at me, indignation all over her too-young-looking-to-be-seventy-two face.

"Wow!" I said, staring at her.

"Wow? What do you mean, wow?" she snapped, leaning forward in her chair.

I laughed and shook my head. "I'm sorry, I just meant, Wow, I hope I look as great as you do at seventy-two. I was thinking sixty or so, tops."

She relaxed back into her chair, smiling, her cheeks tinting a pale rose. "Why, that's very sweet of you, young lady. Celia said you had a sharp legal mind, but she didn't mention that you were a sweetheart and a flatterer."

"No flattery, I assure you. But back to your pest problem. Does your son-in-law—and what's his name?" I asked, pulling out a pad of paper.

"Nervil. He likes for people to call him Croc, though, if you can believe someone would want to be named after a giant reptile," she said, sniffing.

"Well, at least it's better than Nervil, I guess. Let's figure out what you can do about him, and you certainly don't need to sign any power of attorney over to him. What does your daughter say about all this?"

Her face darkened. "I think he might be threatening her. She was my miracle baby—I had her when I was forty-four years old—and so she's very young. They have a baby, too. So she's trying to stay out of it for now."

My eyes narrowed. I hated wife abusers with an enormous purple passion. If Croc was threatening his wife, things were going to get ugly.

Really ugly.

"Okay, let's figure out some options for you. Don't worry about a thing. You did the right thing to come to me. Be sure and call me if you have any problems with him, all right? And call the police if he threatens you or your daughter or grandbaby in any way. Some bullies will back down at the first sign of police involvement."

She nodded and smiled a little, fluttering fingers finally calming from her compulsive fidgeting and resting in her lap.

"Thank you for coming in, Mrs. Zivkovich. I'm so pleased to be able to help you."

As I walked Mrs. Zivkovich out to reception to fill out our new-client form with Max, it hit me just how much I really *was* pleased to be able to help her. Not only that, but it was a relatively simple fix. Not like the corporate cases I'd spent my entire waking life for the past several years working on. Those cases usually took years and years to resolve.

This one might be over with a phone call.

Not so great for the billable hours, but pretty fantastic for the sense of accomplishment.

Life is good.

"Life is good, girlie."

I jumped. "Don't sneak up on me, Mr. Ellison! And why are you reading my mind—er, I mean, what do you mean, life is good?"

He nodded at Mrs. Zivkovich where she stood chatting with Max. "If we keep picking up hot numbers like that for clients, I might have to make this job permanent."

I rolled my eyes. "No hitting on the clients, Mr. Ellison. It's on page seven of the employee manual." I turned and strode down the hall back to my office.

"I didn't get no employee manual, girl—December," he called out after me.

"I didn't write one yet," I muttered. "But that rule is definitely going to be in it."

A few hours later, as I waded my way through scientific studies of the mechanism of insulin and wondered how much money expert witnesses were going to run me in Charlie Deaver's case, the phone rang. Inside line.

"Hey, Max. What's up?"

"I forgot to mention this earlier, but when you were meeting with Mrs. Zivkovich, I got the weirdest call about you." She sounded worried, which was totally unlike Max.

"What do you mean, weird?"

"Well, the guy said he was from the Ohio Bar Association, and wanted to confirm your Ohio bar number and your new address. But since when do they make phone calls for stuff like that?"

I shrugged, already back to scanning the data on the FDA's role in regulating insulin. "I don't know. Maybe some new intern is all eager-beaver or something. Did you eat lunch yet?"

She laughed. "Let me guess, that translates into 'Will you go get us some food,' right?"

"You know me too well. How about a big salad? Grilled chicken, if you can find one?"

"Back in a flash," she said, and hung up.

I heard footsteps and looked up to see Mr. Ellison shuffling his feet in my doorway. "Yes? Are you going to lunch? Done for the day, maybe?"

A girl could hope.

"Yeah, no, uh, I'm leaving soon. About that employee manual and the no-dating-clients rule. Does that apply to everybody or just me? 'Cause that sounds like discrimination against senior citizens, if you just made it up about me," he said, jamming his hands in his pockets and puffing out his scrawny chest. He looked like a sparrow on steroids.

If sparrows ever wore sandals with black kneesocks and baggy shorts.

I clenched my teeth to try to hold in the laugh, then slowly released a breath. Calm restored, I answered him. "Yes, it applies to everyone. Clients need to feel completely comfortable here, not worried that we're going to maybe take advantage of them in any way. Does that make sense?"

His balding head turned bright red, and I wondered if we should put a defibrillator machine on the office supply shopping list. "Look here. I would never think of taking advantage of an elegant lady like that. Sounds like this rodent son-in-law of hers is the one trying to take advantage. He better never run afoul of me, or I'll show him what for."

"How did you—were you eavesdropping on my client conference? Mr. Ellison, you really shouldn't—"

"I can't help it if you talk really loud, and I just happened to be standing in the exact part of the file room where the insulation is bad, and I could hear everything you said through the wall," he said, not quite meeting my gaze.

I stared at his red, pink, and green shirt, wondering for the third time that day where he'd found a store that carried plaid shirts with giant embroidered flamingos on them. "Look, I appreciate your concern for Mrs. Zivkovich. I really do. But—"

He interrupted me. Again. "What do you call fifty lawyers at the bottom of the ocean?"

"And definitely no lawyer jokes! Page *one* of the employee manual!" I shouted.

He snickered. "*A good start.* Catch ya later, girlie."

As he sauntered off down the hall, I dropped my head in my hands. I *have* to fire that man.

Tomorrow. I'm definitely firing him tomorrow.

My phone rang again. Outside line. "December Vaughn."

An unpleasantly familiar voice rang through the line. "Addison Langley here. I don't like dealing with amateurs, and I've had enough of you already."

Okay, so *certain* lawyers at the bottom of the ocean *would* be a good start.

Chapter 10

"Now what? And really, you don't need to keep impressing me with your charm and Southern hospitality, Addie." I pulled my legal pad toward me. I had a feeling I was going to need a very clear memory of this particular phone call.

"Look, Miss Vaughn, these cases are moving along at a very fast pace. Does your client really have time for you to piss around learning how to be a player in the big leagues? Sarah Greenberg is already up to speed. Wouldn't you be doing Mr. Deaver a favor by referring the case to her?" If a man's voice can sneer, his was doing it.

Creep.

"Hey, Addie, how about you let me worry about who does favors for my client? Speaking of moving things along at a fast pace, how about that past-due discovery that Mr. Deaver's previous lawyer served on you? Where are those responses, Mr. Speedy?"

He made some choking sound, but I barreled forward. "Right. I thought so. And you with two past-due letters already. Please consider this to be your single verbal follow-up. If I don't get those responses within forty-eight hours, I'm filing a motion to compel. I'll be sure and jot that down on paper for you, too. Are there two D's in Addison?"

He slammed the phone down with enough force that I flinched, and he probably cracked the plastic on his handset. Or maybe at Langley, Cowan they only had platinum-plated phones. As I replaced the receiver in the phone cradle, it rang again.

"He's probably calling back to apologize," I muttered, then picked up the phone again.

"May I help you?" I asked in my most sickeningly sweet voice.

"December?" Max asked. "Is that you? What happened to your voice? You sound sick."

I sighed. "Sorry. Long story. What's up? Where's our lunch? And please don't put Langley through again without letting me know first. I hate that guy, and I've never even met him yet."

It was her turn to sigh. "It wasn't me, D. It was Mr. Bus Driver. I had to pee, and he—"

"Okay, okay. What's up?"

"Jake Lady-Killer Brody is here to see you. Can I tell him to get stuffed?"

Heat shot up from the vicinity of my panties. Brody should bottle that; just the sound of his name was a guaranteed panty-warmer.

I'm in trouble, here, said the part of my brain that knew better.

Trouble would be a fun change, said the part of my brain that didn't care.

"Crap."

"What?" Max sounded like she was getting tired of my mumbling.

"Nothing. Send him in."

"But—"

"Please, Max. Big girl, remember? This is probably about Gina anyway," I warned myself, er, *Max.* I warned *Max.*

"Right," she muttered darkly, then slammed the phone down in my ear.

My eardrums were going to perforate at this rate.

I stood up, instinctively wanting to be on equal footing with the man. Then he walked into the room, and I sank back down in my chair. He was half a foot taller than me anyway, so it's not like it mattered. "Mr. Brody, how nice to see you. I assume you're here about Gina?" I picked up a pen and tapped it on the desk, trying for a "serious lawyer who is very busy" appearance.

He grinned at me and walked toward my desk, as I tried not to scoot my chair back. It would show weakness. The black pants and white shirt combination that put him in the *GQ* model league wasn't helping. "Nice to see you, too, Ms. Vaughn. But I thought we'd progressed to Jake and December, at least, the other night?"

I raised one eyebrow (this takes practice) and put ice in my voice. "Really? Would that have been before or after you called me an ambulance-chaser?"

Jake laughed and plopped his butt down in a chair. "Nice. Perfect degree of chill factor in your voice. I bet you've scared a lot of opposing counsel in your time. Sort of beach bunny meets ice princess, right?"

"What? You—I—*beach bunny*? Get out of my office, you offensive . . . buffoon," I said, no longer having to *pretend* to be immune to his so-called charm.

He leaned forward and propped his elbows on my desk. "Buffoon? Wow. Now you've wounded me. I guess I'll just have to take you to dinner to apologize."

The expression "balls of steel" popped into my mind.

"Look, Brody, maybe this tall, dark, and brainless thing you've got going on works with the Ginas of the world. But you might have noticed the degrees hanging on my wall? *So* not interested. Definitely not going to dinner with you. Now if you don't mind?" I pointed to the door.

He didn't move.

I stood up.

He still didn't move.

We started talking at the same time. "Look, Brody—"

"It's only dinner, Vaughn. I wanted to thank you for what you tried to do for Gina. The kid has had a rough time."

I folded my arms, ignoring the little twinge under my left rib cage that wanted to give him points for being nice to Gina. "Right. Except the 'kid' is a full-grown woman, and I've seen what happens to women who go out with you. I can live without being threatened with manicure implements, thanks anyway."

I walked around my desk and toward the door. "I really am very busy, and—"

"I didn't go out with that woman," he said in a very quiet voice.

"What?" I turned to look at him, and he was staring at me with that same look of serious intensity in his eyes that he'd had at the jail. The temperature in the room shot up a few hundred degrees.

"Not that it's any of your business, but I didn't go out with that woman in the bar. Or even with Gina, beyond two dinners more than a year and a half ago. She develops obsessions and has a hard time letting go, according to her shrink. You might quit jumping to conclusions long enough to listen to me, Counselor."

"I—"

"Right. Whatever." He stood up in a smooth motion that reminded me of a leopard I'd seen pacing at the zoo. I wasn't sure which of the two would be more dangerous.

Enough with the woo-woo stuff, December. He's just an ordinary, if good-looking, guy. Get over it, already.

He reached in his pocket, and I felt my body tense up.

He noticed it, too, and raised his eyebrows. "Do I make you nervous, December?"

I lifted my chin. "Not hardly, Brody. It would take more than one little PI to make me nervous. What are you, former Jacksonville Sheriff's Office?" A lot of the investigators I'd known started out in the sheriff's department.

He smiled that dangerous smile again. "No, I used to work for Uncle Sam. The Navy."

"Oh, my dad was in the Navy. He was a flight engineer on P-3s. What did you do?"

"I didn't get to wear the pretty uniform all that much," he said, taking a step toward me.

I took a step back, warning bells jangling.

He smiled again. "I do a lot of work for the law firms in town. If you ever need my services, just give me a call. I owe you one." He tossed a business card on my desk, then brushed past me on his way to my door. "Later, Vaughn."

I closed my eyes and let out the breath I'd been holding in for what felt like the past ten minutes, then my eyes shot back open as I felt his breath on the side of my neck. "Hmmm," he purred in my ear. "You have that effect on me, too. This is going to be an interesting friendship."

By the time I thought up a good comeback and whirled around, he was gone.

I'm in all kinds of trouble.

Almost time to go home, and the phone had been blessedly silent for the rest of the afternoon as I worked on Charlie's case and spent almost fifteen whole minutes wrestling with what Max liked to call our office budget.

We had no money and no real paying clients.

That's our budget.

My savings would run out in less than three months if I didn't start making some money. So of course I was planning out my *pro bono* work, right?

Suicidal optimism.

The phone rang, and I picked up. "Hey, Max. Why don't you head home? I'm almost done for now."

"Yeah, I'm on my way out. But you have Gina Schiantelli on line two for you. Good night."

"Maybe she wants help finding a therapist. Thanks for making that list of social services for me. Good night."

I picked up line two, smiling at the thought of playing Helpful Lawyer again. "Hello, Gina—"

Hideous shrieking cut me off. "You stay away from him! I saw him go to your office! You stay away from Jake, or I'll cut all that blond hair off and stuff it up your—"

"Whoa! What are you talking about? Jake stopped by to talk about *you*, Gina. You need to calm down, and we can—"

"No, you need to calm down, or you're going to be in big trouble. Got it? *Big* trouble!"

At least I held the receiver away from my ear as she slammed the phone down. I was getting plenty of practice.

Really, isn't this solo practitioner thing just the most fun I've had since that time I got food poisoning?

I opened my desk drawer and pulled out the business card, then dialed the number and waited for voice mail to kick in. "Jake Brody? This is December Vaughn. Keep your psycho girlfriend away from me!"

Then, for the first time all day, *I* slammed down *my* phone.

Oddly, it didn't make me feel a darn bit better.

Chapter 11

If you eat Wendy's chili with your french fries, you've got veggies covered, right? Think *beans*.

Tossing my take-out garbage in the trash bag hanging from a kitchen drawer, I weighed the benefits of a trip to the dollar store for important stuff like trash cans versus the productive qualities of a nap. Max had donated pillows and an air mattress, so I didn't have to face another night on the hardwood floor.

"Yoo hoo!" Emily's cheerful voice called in from the back door.

I walked over to let her in, smiling. "Who says 'yoo hoo' anymore? You are too cute for words!" I said, reaching for the screen door.

She had a folding table, folded, and two folding chairs, also folded, propped up against the side of the house. "Hey! I thought you might be able to use these. One thing we've got lots of is card tables," she said, laughing.

I lifted the end of the table and we carried it inside. "Thank you so much. Oh, and Max told me about your secret identity as a poker champ. I'd love to hear about that sometime."

We stood the table up in my empty dining room and went back out for the chairs. "Sure! It's tons of fun, really, and not as bizarre as it sounds. Lots of people play poker these days," she said.

"Right, but lots of people don't nearly win the big tournaments. I don't even know how to play. Ouch!" I looked down at my shin, wincing. "I just banged the heck out of my leg on that chair. I have the grace and coordination of a water buffalo."

Emily grinned. "It's all that height, stretch. Takes a while for your coordination to catch up. Like thirty years or so."

I grinned back at her. "Hey! Do we know each other well enough for you to mock me yet?" I put the chair down by the table and limped back into the kitchen. "Want some leftover cake?"

She shook her head. "No to the cake and sorry about the mocking. I tend to take to some people quick. I can tell you're going to fit in just fine around here. You can help me in my rebellion against the homeowners' association and their petty tyrannies."

"Well, I just rent from my Aunt Celia, but I'll do what I can. I always love a good battle with dictatorial homeowners' associations."

She started toward the door. "I just stopped by to give you the table. I really need to get back. Oh, and how would you like to go to a poker club with me Saturday, if you're serious about wanting to learn? I'll teach you how to play Texas Hold'em and you can tell me about the legal biz."

"It's a date! And thanks again for the table and chairs, and for the cake, too. When—or if—my stuff ever gets here, I'll have you all over for dinner or something," I said, wondering, even as I said it, when I thought I'd have time to learn to cook.

Hey, I'm in the South now. I need to do the Southern hospitality thing, right?

"Sounds great. Catch you later," she said as the door

closed behind her. I waved but the doorway was already empty.

At least I had a table. I grabbed a legal pad out of my briefcase and started a list of TO DO (including call the stupid trucking company) and TO BUY (two versions: "truck arriving" and "truck not arriving"). Fifteen minutes of list-making depressed me so much I decided to work.

Burying myself in work got me through all the tough times in my life so far. Why should "start a new business with no money and live in a house decorated in 'early yard sale'" be any different?

I read through Faith's medical records for an hour or so. I also spent some time on the personal things I'd asked for—photo albums, letters that weren't too intimate, year-books, and the like. I tried to get a sense of my client's life this way, and everything I saw and read told me that Faith had been one of the wonderfully happy people in the world, in spite of her illness. She'd taught preschool and Sunday school and volunteered for a dozen different causes. I gazed at a wedding picture, and the sheer joy on her face as she stared at Charlie brought tears to my eyes.

Pushing the papers to the side, I rested my head on my arms and closed my eyes to contemplate the next step I should take. Then I woke up to the sound of my cell phone ringing in my ear. "Wha?"

Blinking and wondering why my house was so dark, I fumbled for the phone. The little phone window said it was eleven forty-five. No wonder it was dark. I rubbed my aching neck muscles and flipped open my phone to talk to UNKNOWN NUMBER.

"Hello?"

"This town isn't big enough for both of us."

"What?" I was either still asleep, or I was trapped in an old John Wayne movie.

"Go back to Ohio, before somebody gets hurt." The voice sounded muffled, but I was pretty sure it was a man. A man with a horrible sinus problem.

"Do you have a cold?"

"What? No, I don't have a cold. What are you talking about?"

I shook my head, trying to come fully awake. "You sound muffled. Look, if it's just allergies, you should get a prescription. The pollen down here stuffs me up really badly."

"I don't have allergies," the muffled voice continued, getting louder. There was a pause. "Well, actually, my nose does run a lot in the summer. Do allergies get worse in the summer?"

"Mine do. All those flowers in bloom, plus grass seed and pollen. It's awful," I said, shuddering. "Have you tried Claritin?"

"No, I only—um, hang on."

I heard some mumbling and something that sounded like shouting in the background, then the guy came back on the phone. "Look, I don't have time to talk about allergies. You need to mind your own business, or else."

Silence.

Still more amused than concerned, I waited for a beat, but he didn't add anything. So I asked. "Or else what?"

"What?"

"Or else, what? I always wondered about that in books or movies. The bad guys always say 'or else.' Even with my dad, it was 'clean your room, or else,' but nobody ever specifies the 'or else.' So, or else *what*?" I was speaking in a very reasonable voice, I thought.

There was more mumbling, but I caught some of it. ". . . else what? . . . says . . . else . . . Ow! Right. Can't believe you freaking hit me!"

"Or else you'll get hurt," he said into the phone.

"Hurt how?" I asked, writing OR ELSE HURT on my legal pad after I'd peeled the top page from my cheek where drool had pasted it to my face.

That was some nap.

"Now don't start *that* up again! Or else . . . or else you'll get hurt really, really bad! And we don't want to hurt a nice little thing like you, even if you are stupid enough to fall asleep in full view of your window. Where the hell are your curtains anyway?"

A chill ran through me at the realization that somebody had been watching me sleep. Somebody was close enough to my house, in this peaceful family neighborhood, to spy on me through my window.

Suddenly, I wasn't amused anymore. "So you're spying on me and threatening me? That's got to be some kind of criminal offense! Probably a felony, even," I said, voice icy.

"What do you mean, *probably* a felony? Don't you know if it's a felony or not?" The voice was clear for a moment, as if he'd forgotten to muffle the phone.

"Well, not exactly," I said, suddenly embarrassed. "I don't know anything about criminal law."

"What kind of lawyer are you?" he shouted.

"Don't worry about what kind of lawyer I am, you idiot . . . *criminal!* You can't go around threatening people! Get off my phone right now, so I can have the FBI trace you, and you can go to jail for the rest of your pathetic life! I hope your allergies get worse!"

There was silence for a long moment. Then he came back on the phone. "How do you spell that Claretan stuff?"

"*Aaaarghhh!*" I clicked my phone shut, then immediately pressed REDIAL, only to hear the "This number is not available" message. I clicked my way over to RECENT CALLS RECEIVED but then remembered it had been an UNKNOWN NUMBER.

Crap. I finally have something exciting happen to me like those lawyers in the movies, and I get a loser criminal with allergies and a stuffy nose.

Where's the justice in that?

The air mattress would have been way, way better than the floor, except for the part where Max forgot to give me the air pump to inflate it. I stood in a hot shower for twenty minutes, trying to work the creaks out and figure out how much longer I could go before I had to take my dirty laundry to Aunt Celia's to wash it.

And I thought the *bad guy* was a loser.

I drove to work in my usual scenic way, down Argyle, down Blanding, by way of the donut shop, and wondered how much longer my skirts were going to fit with me eating donuts for breakfast every day. The waistband was already getting a little snug on the red one I'd squeezed into after my shower.

When I got to the office, it was only eight-fifteen, and nobody was there yet, which was nice in a peaceful kind of way. Except there were no appointments on my calendar, which meant no clients, which meant no money. I'd work on Charlie's case, but I still didn't have the discovery responses, and I'd given Addison forty-eight hours before I could file a motion to compel.

First, coffee. Then, decisions about the day's workload. As I poured water in the coffeemaker, I heard the front door open and Max's familiar voice calling my name. "I'm in here, Max."

She came rushing down the hall and stopped in the kitchen doorway, out of breath. "Did you see it? Did you see the *Post-Union* today?"

I glanced at her, wary of more bullfighter attire, but she wore a lovely green dress that made her look like Miss America at a tea party. All she needed was a tiara. Which she had, at home. Maybe five or six.

I so need to hire an ugly person, so I don't look like chopped liver next to her.

The door opened again. "I'm here, chickie."

Perfect. I'll go stand next to Mr. Ellison.

"Hello? Earth to December?" Max said, shaking the paper at me. "Did you see this? I'm guessing no, or you wouldn't be standing there in your precoffee fugue state."

"You know me too well," I said, putting the coffee holder in and then pushing the machine's on-button. "Did I see what?"

Mr. Ellison came stomping down the hall. "I ain't working for no druggie. You better go to rehab, or I'm quitting."

Max shoved the paper at me and then glared at Mr. Ellison. "You shut up. December has never touched drugs in her life. She's too much of a goody-goody. She wouldn't even drink beer in high school, for God's sake."

"Hey! I am not a goody-goody. I didn't like the taste!" I fumbled with the paper. "What am I looking at, and what the heck are you talking about, 'druggie'?"

I opened the paper, but Max snatched it out of my hands. "No, it's on the front page. *Above* the fold. Look here." She folded the paper and shoved it back at me, finger stabbing at the page.

I glanced down, then almost dropped the paper when I saw the headline.

JUNKIE LAWYERS MIGRATE SOUTH

Florida, long known as a haven for retiring northern attorneys, has a new label: Refuge for junkie lawyers. The *Post-Union* has discovered that six newly licensed Florida lawyers, all recently transplanted from northern states, have drug issues in their past.

December Vaughn, who was unavailable for comment when we went to press, admitted on her Ohio Bar Association application to "experimenting with marijuana on one instance" in high school. . . .

I clutched the paper so hard it crumpled, then looked up at Max, my mouth hanging open down to about my knees. "What? How? That bar app is confidential! How the hell did the newspaper get it? And how does trying pot one time—that was *your* fault, Max, if you remember—equate to being a 'junkie lawyer'? I'll sue their freaking pants off!"

I felt the blood drain out of my face as I contemplated all the clients I didn't even *have* yet bailing on me and running for more respectable attorneys.

"It gets worse," Max said. "Look below the fold."

I whipped the paper open and looked.

Addison Langley, top local trial lawyer, stated that the influx of the "lowest common denominator" attorneys could only have a negative effect on the level of practice.

There was a picture of the slimy turd. Top local trial lawyer, my butt. He looked like a pompous ass to me.

"I knew December was some kind of hippie name. I ain't hanging around if you're planning any drug parties or orgies," Mr. Ellison said, hopping up and down.

"I don't—"

"I heard about them orgies you druggies get going on. I ain't having no part of that. Although I've never been to an orgy. What all do you do at an orgy? Is it like on them movies down at the nudie bar? Them women have gigantic bazumbas, though. You ain't got much in the way of bazumbas. Do you lawyer types all have small bazumbas? 'Cause I don't see much point in orgying with a bunch of skinny women, really." He finally stopped to draw a breath, and I grabbed Max's arm before she punched him.

She tried to yank her arm out of my grasp and started yelling. "Let me go! Let me smack that little weasel! How *dare* you . . . you little ferret! December was kind enough to let you work here when you whined about your stupid shed, and how dare you accuse her of being a druggie or having orgies? And her tiny . . . *bazumbas* . . . are none of your business!"

I stepped between them, feeling my breakfast donut trying to come back up with about a quart of stomach acid. "Okay. Nobody is a druggie or an . . . orgier or . . . or anything else. No hitting, Max. Thanks for the 'tiny' part, too. And you," I said, turning to the little troll, er, Mr. Ellison. "We've already talked about the 'no commenting on your boss's body parts.' You won't have to worry about quitting if you do it one more time, got it?"

He had the grace to look embarrassed and shuffled his feet a little. "Ah, I didn't mean it, girlie, er, boss. You can't help what nature didn't give you. And I gotta agree that you seem like too much of a tightass, um, I mean, too . . . *serious* to be a druggie or do any of them orgies."

I closed my eyes and moaned. A goody-goody, tightass, orgying druggie. Well, there's a reputation that will certainly make the clients flock into my office.

Chapter 12

"So, I hear you've got a drug problem," said a familiar voice. I didn't even have to look up to know it was Jake; my thighs clenching was enough of a clue.

I switched the clenching from thighs to jaw and looked up at him. "I do *not* have a drug problem. And how did you get in here? I asked Max to lock the door when she and Mr. Ellison went to lunch."

He just smiled. "Sorry. The door was unlocked. I thought you might want to go get some lunch and repent your wicked ways. I can set you up with a good rehab program here locally, if you like."

No matter how good he looked in faded jeans and a black T-shirt, I was not going to lunch with this man.

No way.

"Are you buying?" somehow came out of my mouth. Damn traitorous body parts.

He grinned. "Yep. Is now good?"

I sighed and shoved my hair back out of my face. "It's not like the clients are banging down my door to get to me. Even if they'd been planning a visit to December Vaughn, Attorney at Law, that newspaper article would have scared them away."

"I wouldn't worry about it. This sort of thing blows over. Anyway, how many people who need a lawyer really read the paper every day?"

I groaned again. "Enough, trust me. The phone has been

ringing off the hook today with people wanting to ask questions about the 'junkie lawyer.' At least three different callers whom I seriously suspect of being drug dealers have called to feel me out about representing them 'on the barter system.'" I stood up and walked around my desk, taking care to avoid stepping too near to him. No need to get trapped in a pheromone cyclone on an empty stomach, I always say.

He laughed again and fell into place behind me on the way out of my office, so close I imagined I could feel his breath. Just thinking about it gave me the shivers.

"Are you all right?"

"Air-conditioning. Too high. Need to get that fixed," I squeaked out. *Seriously, I need to get a life.*

I reached the front door without spontaneously combusting and tried to open the door. The *locked* door. I turned to look at Jake. "I thought you said the door was unlocked."

He gave me his innocent face. "Maybe I locked it accidentally when I came in?"

"Hmmm." It sounded suspicious, but what was I going to do? Accuse him of breaking into my office? Picking the lock to invite me to lunch? It sounded crazy, even to me. But after the phone call the night before . . .

"Hey!" I opened the door and then held it for him. "Your friend Gina doesn't have a partner in crime, does she? A guy with bad sinus problems?"

He stopped and looked at me, eyebrow raised. "What are you talking about? Did somebody sneeze on you?"

"Very funny." I locked the door behind us and stepped out into the temperate climate that is Florida in June at lunchtime. It feels exactly like stepping into a wet blanket in the middle of a blast furnace. My hair instantly shot into frizz mode, which is not exactly a good look for me. But I did resist the urge to start panting like a dog. Barely.

Jake walked over to a very new-looking black Mustang convertible and opened the passenger door. Great. Good manners *and* good taste in cars.

Clearly, the man is scum.

"Nice car," I grudgingly said as I climbed into the car and sank onto the (leather, what else?) seat.

His gaze flicked over to the front of the building and back at me, and his lips quirked. "Well, it's no ancient Honda, but it'll do."

He shut the door just as I was working up a really good comeback, so I settled for steaming in my seat—literally and mentally. By the time he'd climbed into the driver's seat, I was ready. "Oh, yeah? Well, some of us have re-sponsibilities and drive grown-up cars."

He shot a glance at me as he put his seatbelt on. "You hate the Honda."

"I hate it."

"But it's . . . practical."

"Right. Practical sucks."

He grinned but didn't say anything else on the way to the restaurant. Too steeped in gloom and car envy to attempt small talk, I moped and stared out the window. By the time we arrived at Pete's Steakhouse, I'd nearly forgotten about my stupid criminal phone buddy.

Jake hadn't.

"Now, what about this guy with sinus problems?"

I rolled my eyes. "Some guy called me at home last night. Well, on my cell phone, but it was clear that he knew I was at home. He made some lame threats and mentioned my curtains. But after the allergies stuff, it was hard to take him seriously."

Jake stopped dead. "What the hell are you talking about? Curtains? Allergies?"

I walked past him on the sidewalk, intent on getting inside the restaurant, where there had to be air-conditioning. "Oh, he said, if you can believe it, 'This town isn't big enough for both of us.' Then I asked him if he had allergies, but he said 'or else' and I asked 'or else what?' and that made him mad, and . . ." I paused to push open the door and, *yes!* Cool air washed over my overheated face.

I walked inside and said "Two" to the questioning expression on the hostess's face, then turned back to Jake, who looked really confused, for some reason. "Where was I? Oh, right. There was no 'or else,' or at least it was just 'or else you'll get hurt really bad,' which is totally lame, but then he knew I didn't have curtains up and accused me of being a bad lawyer. Which, you know, creeped me out and honked me off all at the same time."

"This way, please," said the hostess. We followed her through the small, dim restaurant, which had about a dozen tables covered with traditional red-and-white-checked tablecloths. The air smelled incredible, though, like grilled steak with all the trimmings. I took a deep breath and realized I was starving. And the place was quiet enough, I could be incognito. Nobody even glanced up at me.

The hostess handed me my menu, and I sat down and opened it, then suddenly realized Jake hadn't said a word. He was staring at me with his mouth hanging open a little.

I watched the hostess amble away then snapped my menu shut. "What?"

He shook his head slowly, but at least he shut his mouth. Then he started laughing.

And he kept laughing.

Frankly, it was annoying.

Finally he calmed down and sucked in a big breath. "You—you—are you even sane? Why do I feel like you're speaking in a foreign language?" He looked around and lowered his voice. "Is it the drugs? Are you in withdrawal or something?"

"It is NOT the drugs! I. Do. Not. Do. Drugs!" I shouted.

All noise in the restaurant stopped, and I realized twenty-some people were all staring at me. "Way to be incognito, Vaughn," I muttered.

Brody clutched at his head. "Okay, okay, I was just kidding. Will you please explain what the hell you were talking about?"

I sighed. "Fine. As soon as we order. All this drama is making me hungry." I discreetly unbuttoned the button on the waistband of my skirt while he studied the menu. I was planning on eating a big steak. With dessert, even.

After the server took our order and spent a good five minutes flirting with Jake (not that it annoyed me), I told him the whole story. He didn't laugh it off as I'd hoped, and his mouth settled into a grim line.

"This bothers me a lot. Not so much the cheesy threats, but the fact that somebody was surveilling your house. This may be a stupid question, given your general pushy nature, but have you pissed anybody off lately?"

"Hey! Who are you calling pushy? I'm a trial lawyer, not a . . . a . . . florist. I do what I do to help my clients," I huffed out, tired beyond belief of hearing the same old song out of a brand-new singer.

"Right. I'm sure you're a terrific advocate, Counselor. I was talking about your prickly attitude around innocent by-standers. Like me, for instance," he said.

"I don't . . ." I started out snapping at him, but then had

to flash a sheepish grin. "I don't know. Something about you rubs me the wrong way, Brody."

He leaned forward. "I'll have to work on the right way, Vaughn."

My face flamed as red as the checks in the tablecloth, but I was saved from answering by the server returning with our drinks and salads. I dug in, famished. Being horny always makes me hungry.

If I spend much time with Jake, I'm going to need to buy pants with elastic waistbands.

"What is *that*?" I asked as Mr. Ellison dumped a giant metal monstrosity on my desk.

He looked wounded. "It's a toaster, of course. For you to borrow until your stuff gets here. I went home at lunch and picked it up for you."

I looked down at the most enormous toaster that I'd ever seen. It covered half of my desk. "What do you eat, dinosaur bread? Why is it so huge?"

"That's good old American engineering, girlie. Had it since nineteen forty-seven, and it's still going strong." He stuck his hands in his pockets and rocked back on his heels, smug in the knowledge of American superiority over sliced bread.

I gingerly picked it up, and watched a shower of toast crumbs rain down on my desk. "Er, not that I'm ungrateful, but have you ever cleaned it out in the past sixty years?"

He flashed a big grin. "I knew you'd ask that. I clean it out once in every year that ends with a three, whether it needs it or not."

Trial lawyer or no, I had no response for that, so I left it alone.

"Well, thank you. It was very thoughtful of you to, er, think of me. I'm sure I'll think of you whenever I toast something," I said, pasting a polite "I'm the boss, and I need to set the standard for courtesy" smile on my face.

"You're welcome. Now about Mrs. Zivkovich's problem. Me and Eddie from down at the chess games at the park can take care of that good-for-nothing son-in-law of hers for you. I still got my baseball bat from the old days."

I could feel the migraine itching to explode under my right eye. Threatening phone calls, junkie lawyer, Jake for lunch, toasters, and baseball bats. Somebody stick a fork in me. "Baseball bat? Did you play ball?"

He chortled. "No, I busted heads. Back in my union-busting days. Boy, I could sure tell you some stories. The lawyers like to got killed back then." He sighed. "Yep. Them was the good old days."

And lawyer-icide. Great. Shakespeare and Mr. Ellison.

"Breaking heads is *not*—"

"I could do kneecaps," he offered.

I closed my eyes and prayed for patience, or at least some migraine meds, then opened my eyes again. "Breaking heads, kneecaps, or any other human body part is *not* acceptable for any employee in this law firm. As much fun as you had in the good old days of assaulting people, we're going to handle this one my way, okay? A little more civilized?"

He frowned, and his scrawny shoulders slumped inside his winter-weight cardigan. "Fine. I figured you'd say that. But if you can't handle it your way, you let me know. I'll be glad to round up Eddie and the gang and help that scumbag see the light, if you know what I mean."

Probably satisfied that he'd left me speechless once again, Mr. Ellison turned and shuffled off down the hall, whistling tunelessly. I stared helplessly after him for at least a full minute, then moved the toaster to the floor in the corner and spent another five cleaning the crumbs off my desk.

The phone rang, and I glared at it. Probably the IRS, the way my day was going. "Max?"

"D, it's Charlie Deaver. He saw the paper and is upset. I think you should talk to him," she said. "Line two."

I punched the button. "Charlie? It's December."

"Hi, Ms. Vaughn. I, well, I saw the paper, and—"

"Please, call me December. And that libelous tripe you saw in the paper was ridiculous. I'm going to take strong action against them. Please be sure that I am certainly not, nor have I ever been, a druggie of any kind." I started jotting notes, trying not to bang my head against the desk.

Head banging is so unprofessional.

"Well, I know your Aunt Celia pretty well, and I can't imagine she would recommend a druggie—a person with drug issues—to me. So, if you're sure there's no problem . . ."

"Charlie, I promise you that there is no problem. I have never had a substance abuse issue of any kind in my entire life. I don't even smoke cigarettes! I hope this doesn't affect your good opinion of me, but of course I'll understand if you feel you need to seek different representation," I said, not holding out much hope. The poor man just lost his wife, and then he had to read in his morning paper that his attorney was a pothead.

Great start to our working relationship.

"No, it's okay. I'm a pretty good judge of people, and you looked like a good person to me. I'm sticking with you."

I silently breathed out about a lungful of air. "Thank

you, Charlie. You won't regret it. Now let me update you on where we stand with BDC's past-due discovery."

We chatted for about ten minutes about my pending motion to compel and the case, generally, and set an appointment for him to come in for an in-depth interview. By the time we hung up, he sounded a lot more confident in his decision to stick with me. I decided I'd had enough for the day and packed up my briefcase, then headed out to Max's desk. "I've had it. I'm walking out with you. Any progress on my furniture?"

She grimaced and shook her head. "No, and I think they're screening my calls now, because I got voice mail the last five times I called. But Legal Aid called to say they don't care if you're an ax murderer, they're still sending you the overflow cases for your *pro bono* day tomorrow. And your ex-husband called and asked . . ." She looked down at her notes. "Let me be sure I get this straight. Okay, three things: Do you want him to fly down here and help you with your furniture problem? Do you need money?"

I rolled my eyes. "Mike will never see me as a grown-up if I keep letting him bail me out. Plus, I think he's still trying to find a way for us to get back together. So, no, I—"

Max held up her hand. "I said *three* things. The third was, do you mind if he dates your former secretary?"

Chapter 13

As I contemplated pizza versus drive-through, in my quest to repress thoughts of my ex and my secretary doing the nasty, my phone rang. The caller ID said KINGSLEY, so I picked up. "Hey, neighbor! Come next door and have some dinner, if you're not doing important lawyer-type stuff. The kids are dying to meet you," she said.

"Hi, Emily. Thanks. I'd love to," I said, smiling for what felt like the first time in days. "I could use a break from my problems."

She started laughing. "Problems? What problems? Oh, those druggie friends of yours giving you a hard time, are they?"

Oh, not her, too. "Look, I promise I'm not a druggie. I—"

"Stop, already. This is the same paper that accused me of being a threat to the morality of all of northeast Florida, and the 'precursor of the gambling menace.' I don't care what they say about you. In fact, I might like you a little better now that the *Post-Union* has trashed you."

I could hear the laughter in her voice, and the tension in my neck and shoulders melted away. "I'll be right over. Oh, can I bring something?"

"Nope. Just your sweet self. But get over here quick, before the kids get any hungrier. They're cranky when they're hungry, and I don't want to scare you out of the neighborhood in your first week here."

I heard lots of singing and yelling in the background, so

I took her at her word. Grabbing one of the two bottles of wine that were the sole contents of my fridge, I headed across the lawn to her house.

A good-looking, bookish-type guy opened the door before I knocked. "Hey, December. Good to meet you. Emily said you're suffering from the local version of tarring and feathering. Welcome to our sinners' nest. I'm Rick."

Rick was tall and slim, with sandy brown hair, and the brown eyes behind his wire-rimmed glasses were warm and friendly. I shook his hand and returned his smile, but mine felt a little strained. "Yes, it's been an interesting day, to say the least. I've been offered a few cases of what you might call the lowlife variety since the paper came out this morning."

"Daddy, Daddy! Who's that? Can we play with her?" Two small and sticky-looking people shoved Ricky out of the way to get to me. I involuntarily backed up a step when the chocolate-covered one tried to jump me. I haven't had much experience with children, but I tried not to flinch.

"Hi, Miss December. We're so happy to see you!" The older one looked solemn. He held out his hand in imitation of his dad. "I'm Ricky Junior. That's Joker. She's only three, but I'm six. We had a dog, but he's in dog heaven now, where he gets all the biscuits he wants, but not chocolate. Chocolate is poisonous to dogs. Do you have a dog?"

I shook Ricky Junior's hand carefully, wondering which part to respond to first. Rick Senior stepped in to help out, catching his son's hand in his own. "How about we let Miss December sit down and relax before we bombard her with questions, buddy? Fifteen minutes of computer time, okay?"

" 'Putt Putt Saves the Zoo'?" Ricky asked, squirming out of his dad's embrace and jumping up and down.

"Yes, that's fine. Let Elisabeth watch," Rick called after

the kids as they made a beeline for the computer table in the corner.

He turned to me. "Come on into the kitchen. I think Emily is out back picking some peppers or something."

As I followed him into the kitchen, I tried not to moan. "She not only bakes cakes and cooks homemade food, she gardens? I either have to hate this woman or marry her myself," I said, laughing. The smell of something tomatoey and delicious wafted through the air, and I took a deep breath.

He nodded. "Yes, it's a little scary at times, isn't it? The Queen of Poker goes domestic. Oh, there she is."

Emily stepped in from the backyard with a basket of something green and leafy in her arms. "Hey, December. Glad you could make it. Oh, you brought wine! I love wine, and we seem never to have anything stronger than chocolate milk in the house these days."

"I always forget—is chocolate milk for fish or red meat?" I grinned and handed the bottle to Rick. "What can I do to help?"

"Not a thing," Emily said, then handed Rick the basket and went to wash her hands as he placed it on the cheerful yellow-and-white-tiled table. The walls were painted a warm, buttery yellow, and copper pots hung over a center island. Crayon art decorated every inch of the refrigerator. It looked like a kitchen where people actually cooked, like Aunt Celia's. I sighed, trying not to feel inadequate, and slid onto a stool near the counter.

"Seriously, I'm no Rachel Ray, but I can do something. I'm a terrific potato peeler, for example."

Rick grinned at his wife. "Er, you may not want to mention Rachel Ray here, December. Emily thinks any meal that only takes thirty minutes to prepare might as well be eaten from a take-out bag."

I looked at them both. "It can take thirty whole minutes to cook a meal?"

Emily did a mock shudder, then checked something in the oven. "Rick, will you pour the wine?"

"Gladly." He rummaged around in a drawer for a wine opener. "So, tell us about your druggie past, December."

I flinched a little, then dropped my head into my hands. "Aaargh. I haven't even called Aunt Celia yet. I bet she's hearing about this in a big way from her friends down at the Seniors' Center. Those women know everything about everybody."

I thought of the kids in the other room, and what I'd be wondering if I were a mom, and I sat up straighter on my stool. "Look, I know you don't know me, but I want to assure you that there is not the slightest hint of drug use in my past. Well, I did try one drag of that joint in high school, which is what they were talking about from my bar app, but that was it. It was disgusting. I don't even like to take aspirin. Seriously—"

Emily held up a hand. "Stop. We know Celia and Nathan. They never would have put some criminal in a house next door to our kids. Plus, we consider ourselves good judges of character, and we can tell that you're a good person."

Rick started putting plates on the table and laughed. "Well, The Psychic over there cooking lasagna is a good judge of character. I have a habit of giving fifty bucks to 'homeless, will work for food' people who turn out to drive convertibles."

Emily blew him a kiss. "You just have a big heart, sweetie. And I should have warned you about Glad Hand Luke. The intersection of Blanding and Argyle is his territory, and he talks about his weekly take when he's playing cards down at the Wild Card Room."

I took the silverware from Rick and started setting the places. "You have a panhandler who's a regular in weekly poker games? Now that takes balls . . . er, *basketballs*. I love to play basketball, don't you?" I grinned a huge, fake smile at a puzzled-looking Emily and jerked my head toward the kitchen doorway, where Elisabeth peeked out at us.

"Hey, punkin tater. Where's Mommy's princess?" Emily said, holding her arms out. The sturdy little girl, the exact image of her mother with her dark, glossy curls and pink cheeks (except Emily's weren't chocolate covered), ran to Emily to be swept up in a big hug.

"Did you meet Miss December?" Emily settled her daughter on her hip and turned toward me. "She's our new friend, and she lives next door."

"In Grumpy Gus's house?" Elisabeth looked scared for a minute.

"Yes, honey. Grumpy Gus is gone forever," Emily said, smoothing her daughter's hair back from her forehead. "Now go wash your hands and face for dinner and tell Ricky to wash his hands, too, 'kay?" She put her daughter back down on the floor, and Elisabeth ran off yelling *"Ricky!"* at the top of her lungs.

I raised an eyebrow. "Grumpy Gus?"

She shook her head. "He was newly retired from some big oil corporation, and his biggest enjoyment in life was yelling at the neighborhood kids to stay out of his yard and off of his grass. When I mentioned it to Celia, she and Nathan decided not to renew his lease. I don't know why he didn't just buy a house anyway. He had to be loaded, considering that car he drove. Jerk."

"Now, honey. Let's not scare December off on her first

dinner over here," Rick said. I got the feeling he was the pacifist in the family, and Emily was the mama wolf.

Emily carried the lasagna to the table, and I tried not to drool openly. I was *so* going to love living next door to people like this.

"Hey, speaking of The Psychic, tell me more about this. So you read 'tells,' Max said?"

Emily shrugged. "It's not that big of a deal. Trust me, after you've been a mother and your child stared you right in the eyes and swore up and down that he did not—and *never* would have—put the goldfish in the microwave because they were probably cold in their bowl, you can read grown-up poker players with no problem."

I laughed and made a face. "Did the fish survive?"

"Barely. They were never the same afterward."

Rick said, "She's being overly modest, as usual. It's a very valuable talent on the circuit. Some of these guys have been perfecting their technique for years, and nobody could *ever* read them until they came up against Emily." He rested a hand on her shoulder and smiled at her. One of those private smiles that some couples can share in the middle of a crowd, and you know they're only seeing each other.

I've never gotten a smile like that.

Emily smiled back at her husband then yelled for the kids. "Richard Kingsley Junior! I know you're still on that computer! Wash those hands and get in here."

Rick rolled his eyes. "He probably didn't even hear you. He goes into the zone when he reads or plays computer games. I'll go get him."

As he strode off in search of the kids, I looked at Emily. "So, have you ever considered consulting on any legal cases?"

• • •

"If I had even a millimeter of space in my stomach, I'd go for a third piece of lasagna," I said.

Elisabeth, or Joker, as her family called her, made an *"euuwww"* sound. "That's yucky, to eat more basketti after your dessert. Don't you know anything?"

"Elisabeth!" her mother said, looking stern. "Please apologize to Miss December. It's rude to ask someone if she doesn't know anything."

I laughed. "No problem. She's right. What kind of person eats more food after caramel pecan cheesecake? The kind who weighs four hundred pounds." I stood up, trying not to groan at the weight of my very full stomach.

"Now, you have to let me clean up the kitchen, since you cooked everything," I said, picking up a plate.

"No way," Rick said. "Tonight is my turn. Trust me, we'll let you do all the dishes you want, just not on your first dinner here. You and Emily go talk about girl stuff, and I'll take care of this. Ricky, will you be a big boy and help Daddy?"

Ricky nodded seriously, ready to take on his big-boy responsibilities. Joker pushed out her lip. "I wanna help. I'm a big girl, too, Daddy." She grabbed her Minnie Mouse cup as Ricky reached for it, then she yanked it away from him.

If I hadn't been the one covered in chocolate milk, I would have admired the perfect arc of the milk as it flew through the air.

I looked at my drenched clothes, hair dripping down my face, and thought about my day. Then I started laughing.

It might have sounded just a teensy bit hysterical.

Chapter 14

I woke up to the sound of classical music playing on the clock radio Emily had loaned me the night before, in the middle of a dozen or so apologies about the chocolate milk. Looking around the room at my motley collection of furniture, I realized I had to call the moving company again as soon as I got into the office. This sleeping on the floor on an air mattress was ridiculous when I had a perfectly good bed. Somewhere.

Plus living in a house furnished in "early yard sale" wasn't exactly good for the morale.

I jumped in and out of the shower, did a rushed hair and makeup thing, and put on my lightest-weight celery-green summer suit, since it was supposed to be a kajillion or so degrees by noon. Then I headed for the office, thrilled all over again to be running my own law firm. I'd tried for years to convince the partners at my old firm to have a *pro bono* day once a week. Even once a month. But nobody was all that interested in putting in unbillable hours in that corporate culture. Some lawyers had actually bragged about how long it had been since they'd seen their children when the kids were awake.

It was my show to run now, though. I could work all the unpaid hours I wanted. I winced a little as I opened my car door, remembering that *all* of my hours these days were unpaid, and then firmly shoved that thought to the back of my mind.

Nonexistent budget: Deal with later.

Twenty minutes of NPR and one difficult conversation with Aunt Celia later, I pulled up to my office, to find a long line of people snaking through the parking lot. The head of the line was at my office door. I parked and climbed out of the car, catching sight of Mr. Ellison rushing over to me. "Hey, girl—Ms. Vaughn."

I almost fell over. *Ms. Vaughn?*

"Are you sick?" I asked when he skidded to a stop in front of me.

"No, what? I'm fine," he said, panting, then snatched my briefcase out of my hands. "Give me that, and get going. You've got thirty-two people waiting to see you already."

I scanned the line, feeling last night's lasagna or something like panic roiling around in my stomach. "Thirty-two? I've never even met with thirty-two different clients in a week, let alone one day. How are we going to handle this?"

He looked up at me, chin thrust in the air. "You listen to me. If I can handle a whole busload of rowdy teenagers, you can handle this. You've got more backbone than you realize, I reckon."

With that, he wheeled around and marched to the door, leaving me gaping after him in surprise. "Finally, a comment on my anatomy that I can live with," I muttered. Then I took a deep breath and pasted a huge "I can do it, I can do it; I've got backbone" smile on my face and nodded to the people in line as I strode over to unlock the door.

NOTE TO SELF: *Give Mr. Ellison a key. After this, he deserves it.*

He stood at the door, rocking from side to side. "By the way, I gave everybody cups of coffee from the diner down the street. You can't expect clients to wait out in the cold. You owe me thirty-seven dollars and sixty-two cents."

"In the cold? It's nearly ninety degrees out here, Mr. Ellison," I said.

"Still, it's the principle of the thing. Don't want to get a rep as a cheapskate after you-know-what," he mumbled out of the corner of his mouth.

In a weird way, it was touching. He was trying to protect my reputation. He'd even called me Ms. Vaughn, instead of girlie, in front of my prospective clients. Plus, he'd said I had backbone.

Oh, oh. I was starting to like him.

"Tell Max to give you the cash out of the petty cash box. Just give her the receipt for the taxes, okay?" I said, unlocking the door. "And Mr. Ellison?"

He turned to look at me, eyes narrowed, probably ready to argue about coffee.

"Thank you," I said.

He flashed a huge smile at me, and it was my turn to narrow my eyes. *Damn. I bet Mr. Ellison was quite the hottie in his day.*

Okay, now that I've officially gone over the bend, it's time for me to talk to my new clients.

"I'm here, I'm here," Max called, hurrying up behind us. "Sorry I'm late. I . . . I didn't get much sleep last night."

Uh-oh. That was the "Ryan screwed me over again" voice.

I pulled Max to the side, and Mr. Ellison escorted the clients inside and started unfolding folding chairs at the edge of our reception room. "Folding chairs? Where did . . . never mind. Please tell me that wasn't your 'I gave Ryan one more chance, like a big fat idiot' voice."

She wouldn't look at me, but moved so the reception

desk was between us, stuffed her purse in a drawer, then locked it. "Full house today. We'd better get started."

"Look, Max," I said, then glanced behind me. Thirty-plus faces looked at me expectantly. "Fine, but we'll talk about this later, okay? You know I worry about you."

"I don't need a big sister anymore either, D," she said.

"Maybe I still need to be one," I mumbled, then straightened my shoulders. "Okay, triage. Let's take the eldest and anybody who looks frail first. Also," I said, glancing around again, "that woman who's breastfeeding in the corner. I don't want to make a woman and her baby wait around for hours."

I swung around to face the room, then stopped and looked back at Max. "We need to file the motion to compel in Charlie Deaver's case first thing this morning. I e-mailed it to you last night after I showered the chocolate milk out of my hair."

"What?"

"Never mind. Long story, and I shouldn't eat my 'basketti' after my dessert. Tell you later." I grinned and faced my new clients. "Welcome, everybody. I'm so glad you're here, and I hope we can help every one of you. My name is December Vaughn, and I'm a lawyer."

Why, again, did I ever want to be a lawyer?

"No, Mrs. Stilkich, I am not a loser druggie. As I said, the reporting was grossly inaccurate. But we've been going around and around on this topic for nearly"—I glanced at my watch and did a mental eyeroll—"nearly twenty minutes. I'd completely understand if you choose to seek different counsel." I stood up, smiling and holding out my hand, figuring I'd be way better off if she'd just go away.

Mrs. Stilkich was a big woman with a slight trace of an accent and a bright yellow scrunchie holding her hair up in a big knot on the top of her head. She was somewhere between fifty and seventy, and suspicious as hell. Whether about me personally, or lawyers in general, I didn't know yet.

Naturally, after ten minutes of grilling me about my background and "addiction issues," she suddenly changed her mind. "Oh, no, no. Lordy, anybody can see that you're not a drug user. I mean, if you want to take that jacket off and show me that you don't have any trackmarks . . ."

"Mrs. Stilkich!" I said and crossed my arms. "I'm running out of time and patience, to be honest. There are still more than a dozen people in the waiting room, and it's almost two. I haven't had any lunch, and I'm getting cranky. So either tell me your legal problem, or go get another lawyer, but do it now, please."

Maybe not the preferred method of winning over your new client, but sometimes a lawyer's gotta do what a lawyer's gotta do.

"Speaking of which, excuse me for a moment," I said, picking up the phone and pressing a button.

"Hey, D, what's up? Ready for the next person?"

I sighed. "I wish. No, I'm ready for lunch. I'm starving, here. Let's order pizza, okay? And get enough for any clients who are still waiting, too. Take the money out of petty cash."

"D? We have twelve cents in petty cash, after I paid Mr. Ellison for the coffee. Any other ideas?"

"Oh. Right. I'll bring you out my credit card." I hung up the phone and looked at my recalcitrant potential client. "Are you coming, or would you like to wait for me, ma'am?"

She opened her mouth, then shut it again. Settling back

in her chair, she said, "I'll wait here, young lady. I think you can help me after all. Anybody who'd feed that crowd in the waiting room can't have much of a need for drug money, right?"

Saved by the pizza. Who knew?

I walked down the hall to give my credit card to Max, who had the pizza place on the phone. She gave me a thumbs-up signal, then continued ordering extra cheese and pepperoni.

Mr. Ellison barreled his way over to me when I walked back to my office. "Hey! Did you know none of these people plan to pay you?"

"Yes, that's why they call it *pro bono*. It means 'for the public good.' We're doing something to give back to the community here." I smiled, feeling benevolent again.

He scowled at me. "Sounds like *pro stupido* to me. And now you're buying them pizza, too? Bunch of deadbeats with no jobs? How do you expect to pay my salary if you don't have any clients that got actual cash?"

The headache that had been lurking behind my skull started pounding again. "Don't worry about it, Mr. Ellison. Everything will be fine."

He snorted and stomped off down the hall, muttering something about "damn fool women." I stood there and watched him go, wondering suddenly what his salary *was*. Come to think of it, I wasn't exactly sure what Max's salary was either. We'd sort of discussed working the details out when money started coming in the door.

My forehead was doing the scrunchy thing again. Max couldn't afford to go without a paycheck for very long, in spite of her pageant-winnings savings. I needed to make money. I needed to—

"Are you coming or what?" Mrs. Stilkich yelled down

the hall. "Don't make me change my mind about you, young lady."

I needed to get Mrs. Stilkich out of my office.

"Okay, we did it. Somehow, we saw twenty-seven clients," I said, sprawled out on the couch in reception.

"I thought there was thirty-two," said Mr. Ellison, who was slumped in a chair.

"Five were friends or relatives who came for moral support," Max said from her position draped across the other chair.

Mr. Ellison squinted at us. "You two look like you been rode hard and put away wet."

I was too tired to argue with him about being PC. Max lifted her head briefly, then sank back down on the chair. "Whatever. You're not exactly fresh as a daisy, you old geezer," she said.

He puffed out his chest. "Hey! I've got twenty years on you two!"

I lifted an eyebrow. "Twenty? Which would make us what? Fifty-two or so? Nice. Very nice."

He snickered.

Max raised her head again. "Oh, by the way, D, that annoying Addison Langley called. He wanted you to hold off on filing your motion to compel. I told him you were busy, but that we'd already filed it. He got pretty nasty about it and told me the boxes are on the way. Said he hoped we could *handle* them when we got them, whatever that means."

I waved a hand in dismissal of Addison Langley and his condescending ways. "Who cares? We'll withdraw the motion if he actually serves the discovery. We did intake on twenty-four new cases today. At least a half-dozen were about collecting disability or unemployment benefits, which I know squat about and should probably start researching right now."

I closed my eyes and started neck rolls to ease the tension. "But all I want to do right now is go take a *loooong* bath and go to bed. Or go to air mattress. Oh, crap!" I smacked myself in the head. "I totally forgot about calling the moving company. I'm never going to get my stinking furniture."

"I called them," Max said. "No news. They're hoping he'll call his mom for her birthday this weekend, so she can figure out where the heck he is."

"Aaarghhh!" I pounded my head against the back of the couch a few times. "What did I do to deserve this? I need my furniture!"

Out of the corner of my eye, I saw the front door swing open. "I thought we locked that?"

An enormous, bushy head peered around the edge of the door about a foot higher than you'd expect a head to be. I stared in surprise as the biggest man I'd ever seen outside of the movies walked in. "Hello? Is this where December Vaughn works? I'm Bear Anderson, and the folks over at Legal Aid sent me over. Is it too late?"

Mr. Ellison whistled. "What'd you do, son? Sit on somebody and squash the life outta them?"

Even as I shushed Mr. Ellison, I could understand why he'd asked. Bear was nearly seven feet tall and probably three feet wide across the chest. He wore a T-shirt with a giant panda bear on it and a pair of denim shorts, plus running shoes. He had bushy red hair and a bushy red beard, and thoughts of the books I'd read as a kid about Daniel

Boone, Davy Crockett, and the mountain men flashed into my mind.

That and Paul Bunyan.

Bear's eyes widened, and he shook his head. "No, I took a really pretty lamp home for Grandma, but I guess I didn't pay for it." He looked down at the cap he was twisting in his hands. "I kinda get forgetful and do that sometimes. I guess they're planning to prosecute me this time. But I always give it back!"

I dragged myself up out of my chair and tried to look perky.

Or awake, even.

"Sure, Mr. Anderson. Why don't you come on back, and let's see what we can figure out."

Max sat up straight in her chair, eyes narrowing suspiciously as she gave Bear the once-over. "I'll just wait out here for you, December. Waiting for my large police officer boyfriend, who will be here in a few minutes to pick me up."

I turned my head so Bear couldn't see me and hissed at her. "Nice. Subtle, even."

She hissed back. "So you want me to leave you alone here with *him*?"

"Don't even think about it."

Chapter 15

"Please tell me exactly what happened, Mr. Anderson," I said, trying to find a clean legal pad amid the stacks of new files on my desk. It had been a really, *really* long day.

"Call me Bear, please, ma'am," he said. For such an enormous guy, he had a soft and gentle voice. Soft and gentle blue eyes, too. Bear didn't look like somebody I needed to be worried about, in spite of the fact that each of his biceps was as big around as my waist.

Plus, there was the panda bear on the shirt. Not a lot of crazed serial killers wear those, I was betting.

"Okay, Bear. Call me December."

"Like the month? That's really neat," he said, beaming. The expression "gentle giant" came to mind.

"Thanks, I like it. Or at least I do now. School was tough. Now, let's talk about your case. What exactly happened?"

"Well, it's kind of hard to explain," he said, apparently suddenly fascinated with his shoes.

I leaned forward and caught his gaze. "It's okay. I'm a good listener."

"Um, okay. I saw a real pretty lamp at the Lighting Shack store, but I waited and waited, and nobody would talk to me. There was a girl talking on the phone." He stopped talking and his eyes widened. "I think she was talking to her boyfriend. She kept yelling about 'that slut, that slut,' and the s-word is bad, isn't it?"

I nodded slowly, thinking that poor Bear's brain hadn't grown at quite the pace his body had. Did he even have capacity to form intent? I grabbed a pen off the desk and starting taking notes.

1. Intent? Capacity? [What am I doing with a criminal case when I know nothing about criminal law?]

"Mr. Anderson, maybe we should back up a minute. I'm a civil lawyer. Do you know what that is?"

He blinked. "Um, no. You're friendly?"

"Mostly. But no, 'civil' means that I don't work on criminal cases. I don't know much about criminal law, and you'd be much better served with a criminal attorney. In fact, if you don't have the resources to hire one, I'm sure the public defender's office . . ."

He shook his head violently. "No, no, no. Grandma says that those public defenders are no good. She says you get what you pay for, and you can't trust a Republican farther than you can throw one."

This time, I blinked. "Ah. Well. I'm not exactly sure what Republicans have to do with—how about this? How about you tell me about what happened, and then I'll make some calls and see what I can find out? If I can help you with any degree of competence, I will, but otherwise I'll help you find somebody you can afford. Does that sound fair?"

He stared at me solemnly, then smiled a sun-breaking-through-the-clouds smile. "Only if she's named after a month, too."

"I'll see what I can do," I said, smiling back at him. He was just as irresistible as Joker had been last night. A three-hundred-pound teddy bear.

He took a deep breath. "Anyway, when the girl wouldn't get off the phone and help me, I figured I'd come back later and pay for the lamp. But when I came back that afternoon, she started screaming and yelling and jumping up and down and then she called the police before I could explain."

"Explain? Oh, wait. You took the lamp earlier, without paying for it, and then you came back to pay for it later that same day?"

"Right! You get it!"

"But I'm guessing the police probably didn't understand?" I asked, scribbling notes on my legal pad.

"No. They wouldn't even listen to me. She wouldn't listen to me either. She called me a big oaf. It was very mean of her, wasn't it? You shouldn't call names, because sticks and stones, right?"

I nodded, amazed that anybody would pursue a criminal charge against this harmless man. "Okay, Bear. I think I've got enough. Let me make some calls Monday and see what I can find out for you, okay? Will you please give me your address and phone number so I can reach you?"

As he recited his address and phone number, I wondered how I was going to figure out what to do first. Then I realized I could call somebody at Legal Aid for advice. I'd said "ten or so cases" and ended up with twenty-seven. They owed me.

Big time.

After Bear had gone, charming Max on his way out, she and I looked at each other and both started to speak at the same time.

"Maybe we'll—"

"It looks like—"

We cracked up. "You go ahead," I said.

She switched off her desk lamp and grinned at me. "Looks like you might be some kind of lawyer after all, D."

"Yeah, and you're a hell of a legal office manager. How did I ever get so lucky in my choice of employees?"

"Oh, it's gonna cost you, trust me. As soon as we start making money around here. Speaking of employees, Mr. Ellison went home. And get this—*Mrs. Zivkovich* picked him up."

My mouth fell open. "No way. I told him we don't date the clients."

Max rolled her eyes. "Give him a break. It's not like he has all that many good years left."

"What? Since when are you on *his* side? What happened to 'troll, weasel, ferret'?"

We headed for the door and she shrugged. "I know, I know. But he was really great with everybody today. He even held that baby when the mother went in to talk to you. I don't know; he just kind of grows on a person."

"Yeah. Like fungus," I said, laughing, but I knew what she meant. I pushed open the door. "I only hope when I'm his age I'm a . . . STINKING BITCH?"

Max stared at me. "Why are you yelling? And why do you want to be a . . . oh. Oh, holy fudgesicles."

As the door swung shut behind us, we stared at my ugly Honda, which was now decorated with giant, hot-pink painted words and phrases.

STINKING BITCH was the nicest one.

We walked slowly around the car, then leaned sideways until we were looking at my back bumper from a nearly upside-down position to read one . . . *suggestion*. Max looked at me, her mouth hanging open. "Is this even anatomically possible?"

I said eight really, really bad words very, very loudly.

Then I ran to unlock my office door and dial 911. I wasn't some too-stupid-to-live coed in a horror film going down into the dark basement. I was totally calling for help.

Max looked at me. "Why wouldn't Bear have noticed this?"

"I get the feeling Bear doesn't notice much," I replied.

Max waited with me in the office until the police arrived, and we walked outside together. The younger of the two cops stopped dead to stare at Max. He couldn't help it; it was some kind of chemical response that men had to her.

Luckily for my self-esteem—and my chances of ever getting out of the parking lot—the other cop was quite a bit older and spared only a single appreciative glance for Max when I walked up to him, holding out my hand. "I'm December Vaughn. I called you. This is . . . was . . . my car."

"Deputy Reardon, ma'am. Do you know anybody who might have a reason to do this?" He pulled a notepad out of his pocket and scratched his scalp through his thinning hair. "Some of these comments are pretty personal. Sounds like somebody with a grudge."

Gina popped into my mind. But I hesitated to say anything that might cause serious problems for her without any proof. "Well, not exactly. But I did get this phone call . . ."

His ears perked up, and even Junior took a break from gazing worshipfully at Max (who was oblivious to all of it) and stepped over to us. He had gelled his hair into spikes which, however unfairly, made me wonder about the quality of his policework. I mean, gel spikes? In a sheriff's deputy? It just seemed wrong somehow.

"Ma'am?"

I blinked. Deputy Reardon peered at me, then jotted down another note. It probably said: VICTIM IS A FRAZZ BRAIN.

Shrugging, I told them about the phone call.

"That sounds pretty concerning. Did you report it?" Gel Boy asked, staring at me. Not in a "wow, you're hot" way, but in a "how do I know your name" way.

Or maybe I was just paranoid.

"No, it seemed kind of silly at the time, like some teenager playing a prank. Should I have?"

Reardon gave me his blank cop face. "If it happened, you should have reported it."

It took me a beat to catch the "if." "*If* it happened? What are you implying, Officer?" I could hear my voice ratchet up a notch.

Max, who'd stayed quiet up till then, put a restraining hand on my arm. "December," she murmured. "Calm down. The nice deputy is just doing his job, aren't you?" She flashed one of her stock pageant smiles at Reardon. He seemed unimpressed, but Gel Boy nearly fell over, hyperventilating.

Reardon shrugged. "I'm just saying, a smart woman like you might be able to figure out a way to take some attention off herself when she found herself in the news, for example."

Darn. Why does everybody have to read the newspaper?

I took a deep breath. "No, but a smart woman like me would know enough not to give false information to the police. They teach us that in law school. 'No lying to police' is a first-year course, in fact."

Reardon shoved his notebook in his pocket. "All right. We'll follow up and see what we can find out." He jerked his head at Gel Boy, and the younger deputy asked me for some contact information, then they headed out of the parking lot.

"Do you want to take pictures of the damage?" Max asked as we watched them drive off.

"What? Like I want a souvenir of this?" I kicked a stone off the sidewalk in disgust.

She sighed. "No, D. For the insurance claim."

"Right. I wasn't even thinking of that. Duh. Yeah, I'd better get some pics. Why don't you go home? You must be beat. It's not like the perps will be hanging around in the bushes, after all this time."

"Perps? Have you been watching *Cops* again? And no way am I leaving you here alone. I'll go inside and get my digital camera. Be right back."

As she walked back inside the office, only thirteen or so hours after we'd gotten there that morning, I thought about Reardon's reaction to the phone call.

And Jake's, come to think of it.

Maybe the savage sinus stalker was more of a menace than I'd thought?

Funny how I go all alliterative under stress.

I yanked my head up, heart pounding, as a car raced into the parking lot and swerved to a stop in front of me. I recognized Jake's Mustang about a heartbeat before I started screaming.

He stepped out of the car, and the look on his face didn't bode well for the person who had made him mad. I tried not to notice how well his T-shirt clung to his chest and biceps, which made me wonder about the kind of woman who notices things like that in the middle of a crisis.

A desperate woman, maybe.

Another man climbed out of the passenger side and stretched. He was tall, with a blond crewcut and a long, lanky body. His navy blue shirt said BRODY INVESTIGATIONS over the pocket. He nodded at me, and I started to say hello when Jake ambled over to stand next to me and stare at my car. He blew out a huge sigh. "Hello, Counselor. What happened this time? Are you okay?"

I blinked. "Do you have some kind of video surveillance set up in my parking lot? How did you even hear about this? And aren't you going to introduce me to your associate?"

"Police scanner, Vaughn. You were all over it tonight. We heard about the junkie lawyer with the great legs, and I didn't even need to hear your name to know you'd gotten tangled up in some new and improved kind of trouble."

"First off . . . great legs? Um, thanks." I felt my cheeks heat up and wondered why I always felt off balance around this guy. "Er, anyway, how is this my fault? Somebody paints nasty phrases—some of which are anatomically impossible, by the way—all over my car, and I'm the one getting tangled up?" I brushed past him to introduce myself to his colleague. I'd spent too many years at law firms being ignored to be rude to anybody else.

"Hi. I'm December Vaughn, as your rude friend may have told you."

"Wrench Carter. Pleased to meet you. By the way, that expression on the back of your car *is* technically possible. You just need to use a lotta lubrication and four pillows. Ya see, first—"

"Stop!" I said, staring at him with my lips curled clear back off my teeth. "It's nice to meet you, too, Mr. Carter, but I am not exactly in the mood for descriptions of techniques for an act that's probably illegal in all fifty states."

"Maybe not California," Jake said.

I whipped around and glared at him. He was leaning against the wall, lips clamped together and shoulders shaking. "Right. You're a lot of help. If you don't mind, I have pictures to take. Then I have to figure out what to do with my car."

Just then, the door opened and Max walked out, fumbling with the camera. "Sorry it took me so long, D, but I couldn't find the—"

She looked up, saw Jake, and stopped dead. "Brody. What are you doing here?"

He stood up away from the wall. "Wrench and I thought we'd lend a hand."

If I hadn't seen it with my own eyes, I never would have believed that old expression "The blood drained out of her face." But Max turned as white as the pages of my new legal pads as she slowly turned and saw Wrench.

Puzzled, I glanced at Wrench. His face had done a similar blood-drain trick. "Max? Is it really you? I thought you'd left town after . . ." he said.

I looked at Jake, but he seemed as mystified as I was.

Max stood there, staring at Wrench. "I . . . no. Well, I . . . kind of. Even . . . later. We can talk about it later." She almost visibly pulled herself together. "Right now, we need to deal with December's car. Can you two help?"

Jake stepped forward and gently took the camera out of her hands and held it out to Wrench. "All taken care of, Max. December is going to ride with me, and we're going to follow you home, if you think you're not too shaken to drive. Once you're safely inside, I'll take her home." He looked at me. "Unless you'd rather go to your aunt and uncle's house tonight?"

I hadn't thought any further than getting the car fixed. "Um, no. I should go home. As it is, I'm going to have to call her in case somebody else was listening to the scanner and called her with the good news that her least-favorite niece is in trouble again."

Max rolled her eyes. "You're her only niece."

"Well, whatever. But first I have to deal with the car."

"No, you don't," Jake said. "Wrench is going to document the damage, then take care of getting the car to the shop for you. Tomorrow's Saturday, but I'll drive you to work in the morning if you want to come in to the office. Your car should be good as new by tomorrow afternoon."

I looked at him, trying not to look a gift detective in the mouth, but my basic cynical nature popped up at the worst times. "Um, thank you, but I don't want to be a bother. I can call a cab. And anyway, why would you do all this for me?"

He grinned. "It's your charming nature, Counselor. I can't resist all that sweetness and light."

"Is that okay with you, Max?" I asked, too tired to resist the help. I worked the car key off my ring and handed it to Jake.

"Fine," she said, casting another glance at Wrench, who'd started taking pictures of my new paint job. "I'd be glad of an escort home, to be honest. This whole evening has me pretty freaked."

As I climbed into Jake's car, clutching my briefcase like a shield, he stopped to talk to Wrench and give him my key, then he slid into the car. I snuck a glance at him and tried for humor. "You don't have any ulterior motive for going all knight-in-shining-armor on me, do you?" Flirtation was way beyond me right then, but I tried to smile.

A little.

He put the key in the ignition and started the car, then turned to look at me. "Yeah. It's possible whoever did this to your car is waiting for you at your house."

Wow. I'm so glad I asked.

Chapter 16

By the time we got to my house, after escorting Max home, I was leaning against the window, dozing. The adrenaline spike had puddled somewhere around my feet, and the rest of me was just limp.

Jake touched my arm, and I realized the car had stopped moving and he'd shut off the engine. "Whaaa? I'm up. I'm up." I blinked and tried to open my eyes really wide, so he wouldn't know I'd been sleeping. I looked around and saw that we were parked a few houses down from mine.

He grinned at me. "It's okay, Sleeping Beauty. Your secret is safe with me. I promise not to tell anybody that the tough trial lawyer snores."

"I do not snore! And I wasn't even asleep! Just . . . just resting my eyes," I said, hearing how lame I sounded even as the excuse came out of my mouth.

He laughed. "That's what I meant. Give me your keys."

I automatically started to rummage around in my purse for them, then stopped. "My keys? Why? And this isn't my house. I live—"

"I know where you live. But I'm not pulling up in front of your house just yet. And I'm going to check things out before you go inside, that's why," he said, not smiling anymore. "If your stalker found out where you live, he might be here."

"Stalker? What do you mean, stalker? I was hoping this

was a teenager playing a prank," I said, my voice getting a little squeaky.

"I understand denial, but that's what you thought about the phone call the other day, right? Do you really believe in coincidences like that? And the stuff painted on your car was pretty damn hostile for a prank," he said flatly.

I grabbed my keys and clenched my fingers around them. "You're right. Denial is officially over. This painting episode is *really* personal. A lot like the conversation I had with your psycho girlfriend, actually. Does Gina have as much expertise with a paint can as she does with a nail file?" I folded my arms and glared at him, daring him to defend her.

He didn't.

"Hell, I don't know. Don't you think I've tried to call her about it? But she's not answering her phone, and I'll be stuck on a case for Langley, Cowan tomorrow."

"Well, I think—" I stopped in mid-sentence when his words penetrated the tiredness swamping my brain cells. "Langley, Cowan? You work for Langley, Cowan? As in Addison Langley the freaking Third, Langley, Cowan?"

"Yes, and why are you yelling at me?"

"I'M NOT YELLING AT YOU!" I yelled, then I clamped my mouth shut.

After I counted to ten, I tried again. "Okay, I was yelling at you just a teensy bit. Why didn't you bother to mention that you worked for Langley, Cowan? Are you spying on me for Addy?"

He faced me, and this time it was his turn to look surprised. "What are you talking about? Why would I be spying on you? Why would Addison possibly want to spy on you?"

"Oh, I don't know. Maybe because he keeps harassing

me about sending my new client, Charlie Deaver, to my competition. Maybe you've heard of her? Sarah Greenberg? *She's* very friendly, too, in a velociraptor kind of way."

"I don't know what the hell you're talking about, but how about we wait and discuss it some more once we're safely inside of your house? May I please have your keys now, or do you want to sit out here in the car all night?"

I bit my lip, considering.

"I haven't necked in a car since high school, but if you have romantic designs on me, that's fine, too, Vaughn," he said, smiling that wicked smile of his.

I handed my keys over, fast.

"Too bad. Well, maybe another time," he said, then he climbed out of the car. "Stay here," he said.

When I started to protest, he shook his head. "Please, December? Just give me five minutes."

The "please" got me. I nodded, then I locked the car doors after he'd shut his. No sense being foolhardy when I might have a stalker with a keen sense of the anatomically impossible. Somehow, that made my brain remember the lubricating lotion and the four pillows. Officially grossed out, I twisted around in my seat to watch Jake walk down the street toward my house. It was 9 P.M., and nobody was outside walking or watering lawns. I cracked the window a sliver to get some air, and the sharp smell of newly mown grass wafted in. My new neighbors were lawn fanatics in a big way. (Because it's so *normal* to work all week long, then get up early Saturday to mow a bunch of grass that will just grow again. Bluck.)

Jake stepped off the sidewalk to cut through the yard. The *wrong* yard.

Emily's yard.

Then he disappeared behind Emily's house.

Crap. He's got the wrong house. I should have made sure he knew which one was mine.

So I'll just have to go help him out.

Just go walk down the street, possibly into the clutches of an ax murderer with a kinky sex fetish, and help out the big, bad Navy SEAL turned PI.

Getting out of the car now.

Damn.

Okay. Getting out of the car NOW.

I stared at my hand, which didn't seem to remember how to unlock the car door, let alone pull the handle to open it. Then I shook myself all over like a wet dog, to shake off my fears.

NOW I'll get out of the car.

Nothing.

It's a new pair of Ralph Lauren boots if you'll just suck it up and get out of the stinking car, I growled at my stubborn self.

Magically, the car door opened, with my fingers attached to the handle.

Another nonbeliever touched by the power of quality footwear.

I climbed out of the car and headed in the direction of my house, my feet hardly dragging at all. As I reached the sidewalk bordering Emily's yard, the shadows deepened. The sounds of the neighborhood at dusk intensified.

The butterflies in my stomach turned into vultures.

Somebody grabbed my arm, and I shrieked at the top of my honed-from-the-treadmill lungs.

"Will you hush?" Jake said. "What is wrong with you?"

I quit shrieking and punched him in the stomach. "What is wrong with me? What is wrong with *you,* you . . . you *moron*? You scared the crap out of me!"

He shoved his hands into his pockets and made a *tsk, tsk* sound. "Which is why I wanted you to stay in the car, remember? Bad guys? The kind of thing I do for a living, not you?"

"Right, but you were going to the wrong house, genius," I said, smirking.

"No, I was circling behind Rick's house to approach yours undetected," he said, which ruined my whole smirking mood.

Then another thought occurred to me. "How do you know Rick? And how do you know where I live anyway? You *are* spying on me for Langley, Cowan, aren't you? And, um, what about my house?"

"What about your house?"

"Well, er, is there anybody there? Any intruder?"

He tilted his head and looked at me, narrowing his eyes. "Any reason I should tell you, after you questioned my intelligence and accused me of being a spy? Oh, there's also the part where you didn't want to make out with me in the car."

No *way* was I going any further with *that* conversation. I snatched my keys out of his hand and stomped up the sidewalk to my house. Damn alpha males anyway. I'd been a fool to leave a nice, gentle man like Mike.

Who would have hid behind me while I searched the house.

Okay, so bravery wasn't his strong suit, especially after that incident with the mouse and the hip waders, but he wouldn't make every nerve in my body jump, jangle, and jitter.

"*Aarghh!* Again with the alliteration," I muttered.

"What are you doing?" Jake asked, somehow right at my elbow, which caused me to nearly jump out of my Nine Wests.

"Stop sneaking up on me! It's very clear what I'm doing," I said, not looking at him. "I'm very calmly talking to myself like a total nutjob. Then I'm going to unlock my door and go inside, as soon as my hand stops shaking enough that I can get the key in the lock. What does it *look* like I'm doing?"

He didn't say a word, just reached around me and fitted his hand over mine to guide the key into the lock. Opening a door had never seemed like foreplay before. My mouth dried out, but I pretended it was because of the savage sinus stalker.

Jake leaned forward and pushed the door open, bringing his chest in contact with my back. (Did I mention he has serious muscles?) I stood there for a moment, dazed by the heat of his body and hoping I didn't swallow my tongue.

He chuckled. "Vaughn? Are you planning to step inside anytime soon? The house is secured, but I can go first if you want."

I stumbled forward. "No, I'm good. I mean, I'll do it. Well, not that I'll be *doing* it. I mean, not that I'll do it in a 'do me' kind of way. I mean, I'll do it in a 'walk in the door' kind of way."

When he stopped at the door and didn't follow me inside, I turned around, afraid of what might pop out of my mouth next. *Not in a "do me" kind of way??? I am a babbling idiot.*

"Are you okay, Vaughn?" he asked, amusement and something warmer in his tone.

"I'm good. Really. It's just been a seriously long day. Thank you for everything. Really. It was great of you. I should probably invite you in, but as you can see, I don't have any furniture, so it's either the card table or the air mattress," I said, then I nearly dropped my briefcase.

"Not that I was inviting you to the air mattress or any-thing. It's just that those are my only two pieces of furni-ture, so I was sort of listing them, you know, and then I didn't want you to think I was being a bad host, not that I needed to invite you on the air mattress to be a *good* host, but . . ." I had to stop to suck in a huge breath.

"Vaughn?"

"Yes?"

"Call me in the morning if you need to go anywhere, and Wrench will call you about your car, okay?"

"Okay. Um, thanks, Brody," I mumbled, not quite able to look at his face.

"Good night, Vaughn," he said, and then he turned and ambled back down the sidewalk, whistling. I thought I heard him say something like *"summa cum laude"* as he left.

But that was probably just my imagination.

Chapter 17

For some reason, my skull wouldn't quit ringing. As I fought my way up from the depths of drugged sleep (hey, cold medicine helps you sleep when your life is threatened, not just when you're fighting off the sniffles; they should put *that* on the commercials), I realized my skull was really the phone by my bedside.

Air mattress side.

I grabbed the phone. "What? And this had really better be very, very good. It's seven in the freaking morning."

"Nice. Do you always answer your phone like that, young woman? First, you block my parking lot with a line of bums, and then you're rude before you even know who's on the line?" The man did not sound happy. In fact, the word "crotchety" came to mind. I sat up when the words "my parking lot" sank in.

"What? And I'm sorry. I just had a very late night," I said, trying not to sound like somebody who just woke up.

"Your party-girl lifestyle is not my concern. The hundreds of cardboard boxes being unloaded in the parking lot outside of your—and *my*—offices, however, are. I'd suggest you get down here and resolve this issue immediately," he said.

"What? What boxes? Who is this anyway? And how did you get my number?"

"This is your office neighbor, Dentist Brill. Your answering machine listed this number as an emergency contact. Now get down here and get these boxes out of my parking space!" He slammed the phone down in my ear.

I was so tired of that.

I pulled on shorts and one of my faded Capital Law T-shirts, and tied my hair back in a ponytail. Grabbing a Buckeyes ball cap and my sunglasses, I ran out the door to my car.

My car that wasn't in the driveway.

The whole nightmare of Friday evening crashed back into my mind.

Crap.

I had to call Jake. Except everything in me rebelled against the idea, after what a buffoon I'd been around him. So I did the next best thing.

I called the cavalry.

"My baby! How have you been? How can you possibly justify not calling us last night? Your uncle has been a nervous *wreck* worrying about you!" Aunt Celia jumped out of Uncle Nathan's Caddy before he'd even come to a complete stop. Then she ran over and hugged me so hard she nearly broke my ribs. "Isn't that right, Nathan?"

Nathan climbed out of the car at a more sedate pace. "Wreck," he agreed, grinning at me.

"Why, after we saw that the paper printed such outrageous lies about you, I marched right down to Selma Macarbee and told her that her husband was a doddering old fool, and that nobody had ever liked her peach cobbler in the first place. It is entirely too dry, isn't it, Nathan?"

"Dry," he said, walking toward us.

"Um, Aunt Celia," I said, peeling her arms off me.

"Thank you for defending me, but what does peach cobbler have to do with the article?"

"Why, Toby Macarbee is the managing editor of the *Post-Union* and has been for the past eighteen years, since the prostate trouble took that dear Mr. Ollo, hasn't he, Nathan?"

"Prostate," he said, giving me a big hug.

"And his wife always brags about her important husband, but she makes the driest cobbler in Claymore County, of course," she huffed.

"Of course," I muttered, looking to Uncle Nathan to bail me out.

He looked everywhere but at me, conveying "you're on your own, kid" pretty clearly.

Traitor.

"Well, don't just stand there and babble at the child, Nathan. Let's get her to work to find out what that old toad Brill is complaining about. I never did like him. He did that work on Margaret, and her gums have never been the same since, have they, Nathan?"

He shook his head, then went to hold the door open for her. "Never the same since, dear."

Celia chattered all the way to my office, but I listened with only half an ear as I thought about my stalker. I really needed to call Jake and find out if he'd talked to Gina. It seemed a little weird that she would enlist a man's help to make that threatening phone call, but the way she looked, I had the feeling that she could get men to do almost anything she wanted.

Must be nice.

As we rounded the corner and pulled into my office parking lot, Uncle Nathan finally spoke in a complete sentence. "That's a big truck."

My jaw dropped open as I stared at the enormous gray-and-white truck blocking most of the parking lot. No wonder Brill had been upset. His patients had to park clear over by the eye doctor's office and squeeze past the big, burly men unloading . . .

"What the heck? That looks like hundreds of document boxes! I was hoping it was finally my *furniture* that had somehow shown up in the wrong place, but that is definitely not my furniture," I said.

As soon as the car stopped, I jumped out and ran over to talk to the men. "Excuse me. I'm December Vaughn. What is all of this?"

One of them swiped sweat off his red face with his beefy arm. "Lady, it's about time you got here. Although, signature or no signature, there's no way we're putting these boxes back in the truck. It's gotta be seven hundred frigging degrees this morning."

I folded my arms. "Yes, it's hot. Now, as I asked, what *is* all of this?"

He scowled at me. "Delivery from Langley, Cowan is all I know. What do I care what you lawyers send each other? Bunch of tree killers, every one of you."

Nathan and Celia walked up next to me and stared at the piles and piles of boxes. Nathan looked the surly delivery guy in the eye. "That's my niece you're addressing, sir. I'll thank you to keep a civil tongue in your head."

The man narrowed his eyes and opened his mouth, then seemed to change his mind and offered up a sheepish grin. "Sorry, man. The heat is just getting to us," he said.

Uncle Nathan nodded. "I don't doubt it. Celia, why don't you go inside and sit in the air-conditioning and make some phone calls. I'm going to run to the store and buy some cold drinks for these men."

All three of the moving men perked up a little at that. "We'd sure appreciate that. We're almost done here. We've already unloaded sixty-seven boxes and only have twenty-nine to go," the red-faced guy, who was apparently in charge, said.

"What? That's . . . seven and nine . . . ninety-six boxes! Is he insane?" I said. Then I remembered Addison's strange phone call to Max about "if we could handle it," and I started to get really ticked off.

"Thank you for your hard work," I said. "I'm going to make a few phone calls myself. Uncle Nathan, let me give you some money for those drinks, please."

He waved me off as he turned and walked toward his car. "Don't worry about it, December. Just keep Celia out of this heat. Knowing her, she'll try to lug some of those boxes."

Celia looked offended. "Really! Although the smaller ones look like something I could lift, dear. Do you want—"

"No! I mean, no, thank you. Please come inside." There was no way I'd let my aunt hump boxes in the June heat.

Of course, I didn't much want to do it myself either.

My cell phone rang as I unlocked the office door, and I waved Aunt Celia in and stopped at the doorway. Caller ID said Max. "Hey, Max. What are you doing up this early?"

"I didn't sleep much last night. Kept seeing wild, paint-brandishing thugs in the shadows. I finally turned on all the lights and slept on the couch. How about you?"

"I took cold medicine. Slept fine, but I had a tough time waking up when 'Dentist Brill' called to tell me that our parking lot was being overrun by boxes."

"What? What's that about? And I don't like that man. My brother's wife's cousin's Aunt Margaret had some work done by him, and her gums have never been the same since."

I rolled my eyes. "Small world, isn't it?"

"Huh?"

"Never mind. I know it's Saturday, and this is a terrible imposition, but any chance you can come down and help me figure out how I'm going to fit ninety-six boxes in our office, much less organize them?"

"What?" For an ex-beauty queen, Max has got some lungs on her.

"Hey! That was my eardrum. Yeah, Langley, Cowan dumped ninety-six boxes of what is probably our overdue discovery in our parking lot at seven o'clock on a Saturday morning. Sound sporting to you?"

I heard sputtering noises from her end. "Max? What's going on?"

"Oh, sorry. I said some bad words, and I didn't want you to hear."

"Ah. The Southern upbringing. I keep forgetting. You're going to say 'Bless his heart' any minute, aren't you?"

"No! And yes, I'll be right down. I'll bring donuts," she said.

"Bless *your* heart," I said fervently. "It's going to be a long day."

She sighed. "Long hours and low pay. This is my dream job." Before I could apologize, or offer her a raise, or start sniffling and throw myself on her mercy, she hung up.

At least she didn't slam the phone in my ear. I'd count that as a win.

December: One.
Life: Four hundred and eighty-two.

I flipped my phone shut and walked inside, to find Aunt Celia ensconced at the reception desk, with the office phone at her left ear and her cell phone at her right.

Naturally, I eavesdropped on the one-sided—well, two-sided—conversations.

"No, no, no. Stella already said tuna fish casserole. How about sweet potato pie?" she said into her cell phone.

She nodded and made a note on a sheet of paper, then held the cell phone a couple of inches away from her ear and spoke into the office phone. "Right. How about you for rolls? Nathan will do cold cuts."

Since it sounded like she was busy organizing some potluck dinner for the Seniors' Center, and that could take hours, I headed back to my office to call Langley. Five minutes and three "Will you hold while I transfer you"'s later, I finally heard his smarmy voice.

"Addison Langley."

"Interesting choice for document production, Mr. Langley. Not very sporting of you, though, was it?" I said, using my most syrupy voice.

There was a pause, probably while he decided whether or not to pretend he didn't know it was me.

He didn't bother to pretend. "Ah. Ms. Vaughn. To what do I owe the honor of this phone call?"

"Right. Like you don't know why I'm calling you. The number 'ninety-six' ring any bells?"

"Hmmm. A riddle. Let me guess. The number of days you've been licensed in Florida?"

I could grow to despise this guy.

"Cute. No, I'm talking about the ninety-six boxes that your flunkies starting unloading in my office parking lot

at, oh, probably six-thirty this morning. *That* ninety-six,"
I said, drawing a sketch of Langley as the devil, complete
with horns and a fat belly.

He sighed. "Ah, Ms. Vaughn. Most of us who work in
litigation spend all day Saturday at the office. How was I
to know that you and your associates are more . . . shall
we say, *lax* in your habits?"

Before I could singe his ears, he went on. "Oh, I'm
sorry. You don't actually *have* any associates, do you? If
this case is too much work for you, I'm sure Sarah Greenberg would be glad to take it. Just say the word, and I'll
send somebody over to deliver that discovery to her. Oh,
and by the way, Mr. Brody was quite amused at your predica-
ment last night."

The floor dropped out of my stomach. Jake had been
laughing it up with this pit viper about me? After how
scary everything was?

After he'd asked me to make out in his car?

Scumbag.

I stabbed my pen at the paper and started drawing Jake-
with-horns in slashing strokes next to Addy-with-horns.
"What is the deal with you and Sarah Greenberg? Are you
long-lost twins? Or secret lovers? I've already told you
once that I'm keeping this case."

I finished my sketch and started added flames burning
them both to cinders, then continued, "Addy, you keep
forgetting that I trained with the *masters* of gamesman-
ship. You'd better hope you didn't play the 'give the plaintiff tons of paper, but too bad if it's not legible' trick. I
have a motion for sanctions already in my forms file for
that one."

He started to speak, but I cut him off. "And I *win* with
that motion. Every. Single. Time. Good-bye, Addy."

He tried to say something again, but I'd had enough. I very, very gently placed the receiver in the cradle, not slamming it down in spite of how badly I wanted to do it. My hands might be shaking, but I'd faced down the big, bad wolf.

December: Two.

Chapter 18

When I left my office, Uncle Nathan was leading the burly mover guys, who each had a dolly loaded with boxes, toward the filing room. I squeezed past them and quirked an eyebrow at Nathan. He grinned and made a rubbing motion with his fingers and thumb, the universal symbol for "I bribed them with cash."

As much as I appreciated not having to carry ninety-six boxes in the stifling swamp of heat and humidity that was Florida in June, the idea of owing yet more money to Uncle Nathan made me twitch a little. Shaking my head, I walked out to reception and found Aunt Celia still on the phone and Max just walking in the door.

Max looked around, gaping in disbelief. "What the heck is going on? What kind of case has ninety-six boxes of discovery before experts are even called in?"

"It's the 'bury them in paper' trick. He hopes he can force me to go bankrupt or drop the case, either because I have to hire more staff to do document review, or because the case drains all of my time and resources. Either way, I won't have any hours left to devote to cases that might bring in some current cash."

She raised an eyebrow. "Do we even *have* any of those?"

"Very funny. Maybe you can take that act on the road. But in the meantime, how about you help me catalog these boxes and figure out some kind of organization?" I didn't even know where to start. If Addy were playing true to form, the docs would be organized in such a loose way that it could take months to figure out what I'd received.

The idea of transferring the case to a new—*non*-Sarah Greenberg—lawyer who had more resources than I did suddenly sounded awfully tempting. But I didn't want to give up on Charlie so soon. It might not be as bad as I thought.

"This is worse than I thought," I said a few hours later, tossing a file folder on top of the box I'd just pulled it out of. "There is no discernible organization whatsoever. He really messed with these files. The good news is, that's against the rules of discovery production. The bad news is, I waste more time and energy filing a motion against him. By the time I get a new, organized production, or at least some kind of key to this nightmare, we've lost another few months, minimum."

Max sighed and leaned against the mountain of boxes that partially blocked the doorway to the hall. She looked around at the cardboard looming over us on all sides of the file room and shook her head. "I'm usually pretty good with this, after five years working as a paralegal, but I can't figure it out either. The documents should be organized by matching them with the discovery requests—and they're not—or in the manner in which they were filed in the defendant's company, with an indication of which request they're answering—and they're not. It's a clusterfudge."

I had to laugh. Even in the face of my impending doom as a lawyer/business owner/somebody who could help Charlie Deaver, "clusterfudge" was funny.

Kind of.

"No worries, girlie. Sometimes you just need a man to bail you out of these things. Hey, did you hear about the three lawyers who walked into the bar?"

"MR. ELLISON!!" Max and I both yelled. "No lawyer jokes!"

He quit chuckling long enough to glare at us. "Hey! I don't have a hearing problem. No need to yell. So as I was saying, I solved your problem," he said, looking unbearably smug.

I looked at Max. "What is he doing here? Isn't this Saturday?"

She shrugged. "I didn't call him."

We both looked at him. He stuck his hands in his orange-and-white-plaid pants. As if the smirk on his face weren't bad enough, the pants were giving me a migraine. "You could just ask me why I'm here," he said.

I sighed. "I know I'm going to regret this, but why are you here?"

"Because Stella always calls me when she fixes tuna fish casserole. She makes the good kind, with green pea soup, not that nasty cream of mushroom that looks like phlegm."

I blinked. "Um, what does tuna fish casserole have to do with anything?"

He rolled his eyes and looked at Max. "For a big-city lawyer, she's not all that bright, is she?"

Max started sputtering, but he'd turned his attention back to me. "She's in the casserole brigade on its way down here to bring lunch and help out. When she said your name, I figured you were in some kind of big trouble for the casserole brigade to mobilize. So here I am to bail you out."

I stood up, brushing paper dust off my shorts and wondering when my poor teeth would crumble into tiny bits from all the grinding I'd been doing to them lately. "Mr.

Ellison, why—how—oh, hell. Just tell me how you're bailing me out, please. Let's start there."

He preened for a minute longer, then waved for me to follow him. I looked at Max and shrugged. "Let's go. It's not like we're getting anywhere on our own."

I followed the glow of Mr. Ellison's pants into the kitchen, where another dozen boxes were piled. He'd opened them all and written on the sides in dark green chicken scratch. There were neat stacks of paper lined up across the counter and all over the small card table and one of the two folding chairs.

Mr. Ellison stopped and swept an arm out. "Vowala!"

"Vowala?" Max asked.

"I think he means *voilà*. But anyway, what? Tell us already," I said.

"Don't you mean, 'Tell us, already, *please*'?" he asked.

"Tell us, already, or you're fired."

"Hah! Not very grateful, are ya? But out of the goodness of my heart, I'll tell you anyway. The code is on the boxes."

Determined not to say another word that might draw this out any longer, I folded my arms across my chest and waited.

He walked over to the table and picked up a sheaf of papers, stapled together. "These are the original requests for production. And by the way, talk about a lot of useless gobbledygook."

He started reading from the page. "'A copy of each and every document, correspondence, writing, communication, memorandum, handwritten note, typed note, worksheet, investigative material, report (including drafts), record, summary, test, study, chart, diagram, drawing, design, photograph, film, blah blah blah for three more lines, which convey any information relating to any and all tests per-

formed by you, or on your behalf, for the purpose of deter-
mining the effectiveness of the warnings issued and the
placement of the warnings.'"

He stopped to suck in a huge breath. "This is what is
wrong with you lawyers. Why couldn't you just say 'Give
us everything that has to do with any warnings on that no-
good insulin that killed Faith Deaver?' I'm guessing some
poor sap charged a thousand bucks to write up this crap."

"More like several thousand," I muttered, thinking of
my years of discovery management at True, Evers.

"What?"

"Never mind. And not that I need to defend the entire
legal profession to you, but there are reasons to be so careful. We lawyers, as you like to say, are careful not to leave
loopholes that can harm our clients. Not that I drafted those
anyway. That was Charlie's previous attorney."

I realized I was defending the entire legal profession to
him.

"*Aarghh!* Enough, already. Either tell me your miracu-
lous discovery, or I'm going to find us some lunch," I said
as my stomach growled again.

"It's simple. Sheesh, hold on to your panties. See the
one-one on this box?" He pointed to one of the open boxes,
labeled "11."

"Yes, that was box eleven out of ninety-six, right?"

"Wrong," he said, grinning.

"Wrong?" I looked at the numbering on the other boxes,
since I hadn't paid that much attention to the outsides before. "I'm not wrong. See, here is box twelve, box thirteen,
box . . . twelve hundred and twelve?"

"It's not box twelve hundred and twelve," Mr. Ellison
said triumphantly, almost jumping up and down with excitement. "It's the box that responds to request for produc-

tion twelve and interrogatory twelve. See? Twelve and twelve!"

I grabbed the document requests out of his hand and flipped the pages until I got to twelve. "Blah, blah, blah . . . communication with the FDA," I muttered, then put the papers down and started pulling file folders out of the box. "Regulatory division . . . *Dear Mr.* . . . holy crap, you're right! Do they all match up like this?"

"Every one in this room does," he said, grinning.

I grabbed him and hugged him. "Mr. Ellison, you are a genius! I—oh, sorry," I said, dropping my arms and backing away.

Not really a hugger. Plus, "don't hug your employees" is probably pretty standard in the employee manual I have yet to write.

He looked at the floor and shuffled his feet, the tips of his ears bright red. "Aw, that's all right. I can see how you might get carried away. I always did have that effect on the ladies."

Max, who had been standing there gaping, burst out laughing. "And you still do, Mr. Ellison. Because I just might have to kiss you."

He flinched and looked up at her, managing to appear alarmed and hopeful all at the same time. "Now, now. I don't want you two to ruin a perfectly good friendship fighting over me. I'm sure there are plenty of men out there your own age," he said, sidling toward the door.

Before either Max or I could say a word, we heard an unfamiliar female voice call out in a musical tone. "Oh, Mr. Ellison! Will you be a dear and come help me set up?"

He winked at us. "Too many women, not enough time." Then he rushed out of the room, leaving Max and me staring after him.

"Did he—" I asked.

"Does he—" she asked.

Then we cracked up. By the time I could catch my breath, I had tears rolling down my face. "This is . . . this is great, though. Saved by the bus driver."

"Yeah, it's a good thing his neighbor bulldozed his shed, or we'd never be able to get a thing done," she said, which set us off again.

Finally, the sounds of clattering and clinking broke through our laughter, and I looked up. "Wait a minute. Did she say, 'Help me set up'? And who *was* that? What is she setting up?"

Max grabbed my arm. "Even worse. Is that smell . . . *tuna fish casserole?*"

We hit the door running.

I slowed down at the end of the hall, to try to look more sedate and . . . lawyerly. Max didn't bother, so she shoved past me. When I reached her and looked over at her shoulder, Aunt Celia was standing in the middle of the room, directing a stream of blue-haired ladies—who each held a casserole dish—toward the table behind the reception desk. The unmistakable scent of tuna casserole perfumed the air.

And chicken casserole.

And—was that—Spam? *Euwww.* I plastered a smile on my face and threaded my way through what Mr. Ellison had called the casserole brigade to Aunt Celia. "Um, what's going on?"

She beamed at me. "Isn't it wonderful? All of my friends are here to help out. They brought lunch, and they're going to help you with all of those files. Stella and Margaret and Helen and so many others brought casseroles and lovely pies. Isn't that sweet?"

"It's very sweet," I said, then leaned over to whisper in her ear. "You have to tell me everyone's name, so I can say thank you. I really do appreciate the offer, but this is kind of complicated work. I'm not sure they would be able to help much."

She grabbed my arm and pulled me to the door, away from everybody. Then she put her hands on her hips and whispered back at me. "Now, December Vaughn. You were not raised to think that just because a person is a bit mature, she or he is not extremely capable. Mr. McChesney used to run our local branch of Bank of America. Stella was a paralegal for forty-three years. They've all offered to help you, and I'd think you'd be more grateful."

"Trust me, I'm very grateful for every bit of help I can get," I assured her, trying to put lots of enthusiasm in my voice, in spite of the fact that my bright and shiny new law practice was being bailed out by octogenarians armed with tuna fish casserole. It made me feel about twelve years old.

As I tried to find something else to say that would make Aunt Celia quit giving me the "I'm disappointed in you, dear" look, the door swung open and smacked me in the butt. Hard.

"Ouch!" I jumped and started to rub the place that was certain to have an enormous bruise by tomorrow, and my surprise guest walked in and looked down at me, grinning.

I should have known.

"Hello, Brody," I said, resigned to never looking like anything but a complete and total idiot around the man.

"I'm sorry, Vaughn. Didn't mean to hit you with the door. Are you okay? Anything broken?"

"You—" I started, but Aunt Celia put her hand on my arm and interrupted.

"Well, hello there! Are you a friend of Deedee's? Or Max's?" she said, suddenly all smiles again.

Oh, no. She smells fresh prey in the "let's get Max and December married off" sweepstakes.

Jake turned on the full-wattage smile, and one of the blue-haired ladies nearest to him nearly swooned. Not that I've ever seen anybody swoon, or even ever used the word "swoon" before, but trust me, that was a swoon.

Not that I blamed her.

"Deedee?" he asked.

"No, he's not. Well, yes, he is, in the 'I just met him, but he helped me out in a crisis' sense, but not in a 'Put your periscope up' kind of sense, Aunt Celia," I said, exasperated. "Jake likes to share private jokes about me with my opposing counsel, in fact."

Jake gave me a funny look. "I have never discussed you with Addison Langley, other than to tell him I couldn't go out of town today for him, since I had to do a job for you."

Then he held out his hand. "Jake Brody, at your service, Mrs. . . . ?"

I sighed. "Celia Judson, meet Jake Brody. Jake is a private investigator in town. Jake, this is my Aunt Celia. My Uncle Nathan is around here somewhere."

He shook her hand gently. "Mrs. Judson, I'm so pleased to meet you."

She nearly giggled. Boy, he was really turning on the charm. "Oh, please, Mr. Brody, call me Celia."

"Thank you, Celia. And call me Jake, please."

They stood there smiling at each other until I couldn't take any more, so I decided to go help set up casseroles. As I stalked off, I heard Jake's voice, pitched low. "Celia? Go ahead and put your periscope up."

Chapter 19

"You know I love you, but it's almost eight o'clock, and if I don't get out of here, I'm going to lose it," Max said, rubbing her eyes and yawning.

I looked up from the rough outline of the timeline I'd been sketching out, and immediately my jaw cracked open in a matching yawn. "You know, some of these entries are just not adding up for me. I mean, the—wow. How did it get so late?"

She stood up on the other side of my desk and stretched. "Gee, I don't know. Time flies when you're hiding from Jake and eating tuna fish casserole, I guess," she said drily.

"Hey! I wasn't hiding in the bathroom, I was having intestinal . . . issues. Each one of those women made me try some of her casserole. How could I be rude after they were kind enough to drop everything and rush down here on a Saturday?" I groaned and rubbed my still-distended stomach. "I never should have gone back for that second plate of dessert."

She laughed and shook her head. "Lessons learned. And yes, it was very nice of them, but I doubt they had a lot on their agendas to 'drop.' "

"Well, anyway. What time did Jake finally leave?"

"Around fifteen minutes after you disappeared with your intestines. He said he had stuff to do, but he'd be back with your car this afternoon," she said. Then she scrunched up her forehead. "Hey, where is he? It's way past afternoon already."

I stood up and stretched, too, not really happy with the creaky noises in my back. I was only thirty-two, not eighty-two for Pete's sake. "Hey, speaking of eighty-two, what happened to Mr. Ellison?"

Max rolled her eyes. "He left around four with Stella. That man is a player, if you ask me. I wonder if Mrs. Z knows about Stella?"

"Or any of the other ones. Did you see the way they fluttered around him?" I laughed. " 'Do you want some more casserole, Henry?' 'Can I get you something to drink, Henry?' It was disgusting."

"Yep. He was eating it up, and I'm not talking about the casserole either," she said.

"On the bright side, though, we finally know what his first name is," I said, perking up.

"We knew his name," she said.

"We did?"

Max tilted her head and stared at me. "You know, D, for a genius, you sure can be a little slow. We have his full name on his employment forms."

"Oh. Right. Of course, I knew that. I was just testing you."

"Riiight."

As she walked down the hall, I started after her. "Bet you don't know his middle name!"

"Percival."

I stopped dead. *"Percival?* Oh, I'm so gonna torture him the next time he tells me a lawyer joke."

Max crossed our small lobby, which seemed strangely empty without a couple dozen senior citizens eating casserole, and looked out the window. "Holy fudge. I think your car just pulled up."

"Why is my car pulling up holy fudgeworthy?"

I looked out the window next to her. "Holy fudge."

We both stared at the beautiful red BMW convertible as it parked in my spot in front of the building. "Nah. Somebody's just lost," I said, shaking off my momentary "they peeled off the ugly Honda's paint, and it turned into a beautiful convertible" fantasy.

Max sucked in a breath. "No, that's Wrench. He doesn't get lost, trust me."

We watched in silence as Wrench climbed out of the car. Then I realized I was missing a prime opportunity. "Just who is Wrench and who is he to you?"

"Long story, tell you later," she said, ducking away and running for the bathroom. "Don't tell him I'm here."

"Chicken!" I yelled after her, but without much conviction after I'd hidden from Jake earlier. One of those "the chicken calling the fowl feathery" moments.

"That was just sad, Vaughn," I muttered, then unlocked the door and opened it before Wrench had a chance to knock. "Hey, Wrench. What's up? And whose car is that? And where is my car?"

He blinked. He was wearing another Brody Investigations shirt and jeans, and he was actually kind of cute in an "I just got out of the Navy and still have a crewcut" way.

"Whoa. Slow down. Okay, this is your car. Your other car is kind of history."

"What? How can my car be history? All it needed was a paint job!" I walked outside and joined him on the sidewalk, and we both stared at the Beemer. I took a deep breath. "Will you please explain why my car is 'kind of history'?"

He didn't look at me. "Well, turns out that whoever did the job on your car used some kind of acid on it first. Some of the words were, ah, etched in the metal. Pretty permanent, if you know what I mean. So the paint place is loaning you this one until they can figure out what to do. Or until your insurance kicks in, whatever. Jake figured you didn't want to drive around with those words on your car."

"Jake likes to take charge, doesn't he?" I asked.

"Hmmmm," he said, not committing to anything.

I heaved a sigh. "Fine. I called my insurance agent this morning, and they said I have rental insurance. So what do I owe?"

"Oh, no. This is on the house. Part of the paint service." He still wouldn't look at me.

"Now, wait a minute . . ." I began, but my cell phone started ringing. I pulled it off the clip on my shorts and answered, "Vaughn here."

Wrench stepped back toward the wall, as if to give me privacy.

"This is Emily. Are you busy? I didn't want to bother you, but are you still coming to poker night with me? I'm getting ready to go, but you could meet me there."

"Oh, I forgot all about it, to be honest. It's been a crazy couple of days," I said.

"That's okay, if you can't make it—"

"No, I'd love to do poker night with you. Sounds like just the thing to take my mind off my troubles. Let me just finish one conversation; can you hold on a sec?"

I turned back toward the wall, but Wrench was gone. I grabbed the office door handle, but the door was locked, and anyway I would have noticed the door opening. He was just gone. I looked up and down the sidewalk in front of my office neighbors' doors.

Nothing. Shrugging, I put the phone back to my ear. "Emily?"

"I'm here."

"I'd love to. How do I get there?"

You could cut the tension with one of the cheese spreaders littering the dingy green felt table. The big man in the black cowboy hat slowly raised his head and speared Emily with his gaze. I realized I was holding my breath, and forced some out of my lungs.

Emily was a tall, cool drink of water. Not a bead of sweat on her forehead. Not a frown line in sight. She was Slow Hand Joe.

Cool Hand Luke.

Doc Holliday with a minivan.

She was ice, and the cowboy was going down.

Two hours of Texas Hold'em, and I'm talking like a B Western.

I covered my mouth with my hand and turned my laugh into a cough, but neither Emily nor Cowboy—known as Vernon the used-car salesman during the day—even glanced at me. Finally he spoke. "You're bluffing, Psychic," he drawled. "I call your two and raise you three."

By now, I knew that the two and three he referred to were two and three hundred dollars, which seemed to me like an awful lot to rest on a bunch of playing cards. To Emily, though, it was a friendly nickel-and-dime game, since she was used to thousands and tens of thousands resting on the turn of a card. The Turn was an actual term of art, by the way. It's the fourth card that goes in the middle. And the Button. It's the disk that indicates who would be dealing if there were no dealer.

And the lake. Er, I mean, the River. It's the final card that goes in the middle (community card) in Texas Hold'em. It's the one that lets you know who wins, pretty much.

Emily distracted me from my thoughts by sliding the rest of her chips to the center of the table. The two men who'd already folded whistled. Emily just smiled that demure, PTA-mom smile. "I'm all in, Cowboy."

"Damn!" he muttered. He glared at his cards, then considered Emily, then glared at his cards some more. He stood up and walked around the table, then sat down and shuffled his cards around in his hand, then glared at them a little longer. Emily just sat there, patiently waiting, not a hair out of place.

I, on the other hand, had to sit on my hands to hold still. There had to be nearly two thousand dollars in the pot, if I were calculating the chips right.

Two grand would buy a lot of paint for my car. Maybe I need to figure out how to play poker. Although the drive over here in that lovely sports car didn't exactly make me anxious to get the Honda back.

Finally, Cowboy curled his lip and threw his cards, facedown, on the table in disgust. "It's all yours. I'm done for the night," he said.

As Emily reached out to collect her winnings, I leaned over to peek at the cards she'd placed on the table. She caught my hand before I could turn them over, and smiled at me. "You have to pay to look at somebody's cards, December."

"But the hand is over. You won, right?" I was just curious.

Cowboy laughed, all signs of annoyance gone. "You never, ever look at another player's cards, rookie. If we let our opponents see our cards when they didn't pay to look, they could figure out our strategies."

One of the more cautious men at the table spoke up, patting his few strands of wispy white hair down over his mostly bald head. "That's right. How you bluff, how you bet, all the stuff that makes each poker player unique."

I nodded. It made total sense. "I get it. It would be like allowing opposing counsel to see my trial notes. They get all the facts, by reason of civil procedure. But if they know my strategy, I'm screwed. Same here. We all know what cards are in the deck. But you each play them very differently."

I looked at Emily and grinned. "Is the rookie catching on?"

She looked like a proud mama. "Definitely. Ready to try a hand of your own?"

A huge yawn escaped before I could catch it. "Oh, wow. I think I'd better give high-stakes poker a try when I'm not dead on my feet. Especially with you cardsharps," I said, grinning at the man on my left, who didn't look a day over ninety.

He flashed a huge, toothless grin at me. "Good thinking, cutie. If I was only twenty years younger—"

"If you were twenty years younger, you'd still be old enough to be her grandpa," Cowboy boomed. Then everybody started laughing. I shook my head and stood up, still laughing, and Emily stood up, too.

"I'd better go. PTA bake sale in the morning, and my brownies still need frosting," she said, which stuck me as surreal considering she was matter-of-factly sliding a mound of chips in her purse. "I'll cash this in next time. Thanks, boys."

They all stood up. "Thanks, Psychic. We'll get you next time," said Grandpa.

She smiled at him and gently patted his cheek as we walked past. "You always do, Mr. Spicey. You always do."

As we walked away, I heard them talking about her. "I love that girl. She puts the 'sweet' back in poker," Cowboy said, not bothering to lower his voice.

Emily's lips twitched, so I knew she'd heard it, too. After we finally weaved our way through the room, waving and chatting a bit with everyone, we walked out into an only moderately stifling night. It had to be down to at least ninety degrees.

Practically a cold front.

"How do you do that?" I asked.

"Do what?"

"Take all of their money, but leave them still happy and liking you. Trust me, lawyers would pay huge money for that secret," I said, only partly kidding.

She laughed. "It's a matter of dignity."

"Dignity?"

"Yes. I try never to lose mine, and I always leave them theirs. Have you ever watched poker tournaments on TV?"

We stopped at her minivan, since I didn't really want to have to explain the BMW. Especially since I didn't quite understand it myself, and I'd wimped out on calling Jake for an explanation.

"Well, no offense, but watching poker on TV sounds about as exciting as watching bowling. Or golf."

She laughed. "Yeah, I understand. Although Tiger Woods is a serious hottie. But anyway, there are always the hot dogs, just like in football or baseball or any other sport. Trash talkers, people who overcelebrate their wins, the guys I call the balloons."

"I know exactly what you're talking about. But *balloons*?"

"Balloon-headed. It's all 'me, me, me' with them, and they make other players feel badly about themselves. I never, ever do that, and so most people like to play with me." She looked around, then whispered, "Even when I beat their pants off."

"What about the Psychic part? I watched Cowboy non-stop and didn't notice anything. He liked to touch the brim of his hat, but he did that whether he had a good hand or a bad hand."

She hesitated. "Okay, but I tell you this under attorney-client privilege, right?"

I put my hand over my heart. "Cross my heart."

"He touches the left side of the brim more when he's bluffing."

My mouth fell open. "That's really subtle. You're *goooood*. Will you *please* come to court with me? Just for jury trials, seriously."

She laughed, and we said good-bye. I pretended to fumble for my keys and waved to her to go ahead, then I walked over to the gorgeous little convertible that was so sweet to drive.

Twirling the remote door unlocker thingy around like a magic wand, I said, "Abracadabra! Open Sesame!" and grinned at the lovely beeping sound that signified a car classy enough to have a remote door unlocker thingy. "I *love* that sound."

Then something really hard smashed into the back of my head, and I didn't hear anything else for a while.

Chapter 20

I opened my eyes slowly, wondering why my air mattress was full of rocks. A giant cowboy hat with blurry outlines did a wobbly dance in front of me, and I let out a little shrieky noise.

"Ah, I told you to get back out of her face, Cowboy. We need to call again and find out when that durn ambulance is going to get here." Mr. Spicey's worried face leaned into my line of sight.

I blinked a couple of times, and then I remembered. "I'm fine, guys. I'm sure I don't need an ambulance," I said, and sat up. Or rather, I started to sit up, and then the world went a little foggy, and I felt like I was going to vomit up about a gallon of assorted casseroles.

It wasn't a pretty thought.

Cowboy moved in to catch me, and I gratefully leaned back against him.

"What happened? We came out here just a couple of minutes after you and Psychic left, and she was gone and you were here on the ground," he said.

"Did you try to steal her winnings?" Mr. Spicey asked, looking hopeful.

"No!" I said loudly, sending a tidal wave of pain smashing through my skull.

"No," I whispered. "Emily is my friend. After she pulled out of the parking lot, something smashed into the back of my head. That's all I remember."

"And it's probably this," said a grim-faced woman I'd seen at another table earlier in the evening. She pointed at a rock the size of an orange lying on the ground next to me. It was dark and sticky on one sharp corner, and also had a few strands of what looked like my hair stuck to it.

The hair sent me over the edge.

"I'm going to throw up now," I said, as politely as I could, to Cowboy.

He sat me up a bit more and turned my head in the opposite direction from the rock. "Don't want to taint the evidence. Saw that on *CSI Miami*," he said, while I threw up tuna casserole and stomach acid.

"This may be the most humiliating moment of my life," I muttered, wiping my mouth on my sleeve.

Mr. Spicey and the others clustered around us had backed off a few paces, but Cowboy just chuckled. "Don't you worry about it, none. The wife and I raised five boys, and a little puke ain't nothing. Why, I could tell you times when—"

I held up a hand. "Thank you, but please don't tell me. I'm not sure I could take it right now," I whispered.

The shrill of the sirens cut across my words, and an ambulance and an Orange Grove PD car pulled in the parking lot, one right behind the other. "I really don't need an ambulance. It's just a bump on the head," I protested.

"Not with all that blood all over the place," Mr. Spicey said.

I looked down at where he was pointing and saw an enormous dark splotch on the ground. Then I touched the back of my head, and my hand came away sticky.

That's when everything went fuzzy again.

•   •   •

"It's a mild concussion. They did their tests and scans, and I'm fine. Nothing to get worked up over," I reassured Aunt Celia over the phone that a kind nurse had plugged in for me. "I'm only calling because I was afraid you'd learn about it over the scanner and freak out."

I looked around my curtained-off room in the ER, scrunching my nose. All hospitals smell like Lysol and sound like constant beeping.

"I think there is something you're leaving out of this, December. How could you accidentally fall down in a parking lot and hit your head? You are not the accident-prone type, by any means. Is there something you're not telling me?"

Now that she'd calmed down from utter hysteria to mild weepiness, she was starting to ask questions that I didn't want to answer. She and Uncle Nathan already worried about me enough.

"No, absolutely not. And no, I don't need a ride home. I have a friend right here to drive me," I lied. A taxi would be fine. Then somehow I'd figure out a way to pick up my car tomorrow.

"I don't believe you. You never call for help when you need it. Let me talk to this so-called friend," she demanded.

"Um, my friend just walked down to the coffee machine. But I'll have her call you later," I said, trying to be clever with a monster headache jackhammering my skull.

"No. You let me talk to her right now, or I'm coming to get you myself," she said.

"Aunt Celia! You're being unreasonable. Anyway, I didn't mean—"

The curtain to the ER bed swung open, and Jake and Max walked in together, leaving me sitting there gaping at them. Max grabbed me in a hug and burst into tears, and Jake took the phone out of my hand.

"Hello, Celia? This is Jake Brody."

He listened for a moment, then grinned. "Yes, it was delightful meeting you, too. Listen, Max and I are here, and we're going to take your niece home right now and put her to bed."

In spite of the headache, a little shiver rippled through me at the idea of Jake putting me to bed. I'm *so* not into the "damsel in distress" role, but if this is what it gets me, I can pretend to be helpless once in a while . . .

Snap out of it. I have more important stuff to worry about right now. Like the savage sinus stalker, who is now apparently trying to kill me.

Jake put the phone down, and the faint smile disappeared from his face. "What happened, Vaughn?"

I sighed. "Police scanner?"

"What happened?" He reached out and lifted a few strands of hair at the back of my head, and I noticed the bloodstains out of the corner of my eye. The room whirled a little, and I grabbed Max, who'd quit hugging me but was clutching my arms.

"Are you okay? How many fingers am I holding up?" she asked.

"You're not holding up any fingers. You're clutching my arms," I pointed out.

Jake moved behind me and looked at the back of my head. "How many stitches?"

There was ice in his voice, and I shivered again, but this time for an entirely different reason.

"Only two. It's really no big deal, except for the part where they tried to STAPLE MY HEAD. Anyway, it looks like somebody threw a rock and it hit me in the back of the head," I mumbled.

Max started crying again, and Jake moved around to stand in front of me, arms folded. "What did OGPD say?"

"They figured it was juvenile delinquents. And before you ask, yes, I told them about the painting incident, but they thought a connection was pretty far-fetched."

Max let go of me long enough to wipe tears off her cheeks. "Did you tell them about the threatening phone call?" she asked.

I winced. "No, I didn't even think about it, to be honest. My head was hurting, and after I practically threw up in Cowboy's lap, I was so embarrassed—"

Jake cut in, smiling and raising an eyebrow. "Who is Cowboy, and what were you doing in his lap?"

I started to shake my head, and then stopped, hissing at the pain. "No, no, he was playing cards, but he touches the brim of his left side, well, both sides, but left side for bluffing, and Emily said . . . but then she left, and I was walking to the car, which, by the way, is gorgeous, but we have to talk about how much I loan you for the owner, I mean owe you for the loaner, and . . ." I stopped dead and looked up at him. "What was the question again?"

The nurse walked in just then and saved me from whatever he'd been about to say. *Tracey Eller* was embroidered in flowing script over the pocket of her Winnie the Pooh scrubs. "Okay, dear. You're good to go home, but you need to follow the directions on this sheet. You can take regular-strength Tylenol for any discomfort."

"I'll take her home and take care of her," Max said. She was wearing denim shorts and a ratty old T-shirt, with not a stitch of makeup. She *must* have been worried about me.

Tracey smiled at her. "Okay, sweetie, but you might want to loosen the death grip on her arms."

I signed a few papers and took my copies as Tracey bustled off. Then I gingerly started to climb down off the table. Jake put his hands under my elbows and helped me down, and the temptation to lean against him and close my eyes was nearly overwhelming.

Nobody ever gave me a concussion when I did corporate work.

I stiffened my shoulders and stepped back from Jake, but smiled my thanks at him. I think the smile came out more like a grimace, but all I wanted to do was go home and take a shower and get the dirt and blood out of my hair.

Clean clothes would be nice, too.

I peered blearily up at Jake. "Why does that song about 'you've got to know when to fold 'em' keep running through my mind?"

He put an arm around me and helped me walk out to the car, in spite of the five times I told him I was fine. Max trailed behind us, carrying my purse and muttering very bad, un-beauty-queen-like words under her breath. When we reached the parking lot, Jake led the way to a late-model silver Mercedes sedan and opened the door. I looked at him and then at Max. "I'm sure Max can drive me home," I said, not wanting to go through the knight-in-shining-armor routine again, even if Max didn't really look all that stable, what with the hysterical crying and all.

He shook his head. "I called her when I heard the report and picked her up. I figured you'd rather have her spend the night with you than me."

Then he flashed that evil grin at me.

I rolled my eyes, too tired and sick to rise to the bait.

"Thanks, Brody. I'm still not really sure why you're playing fairy godmother, but I have to admit I appreciate it."

"You're interesting. Been bored for a while," he said cryptically, opening the door. "But don't call me a godmother."

Chapter 21

By the time I finally convinced Max to take me home on Sunday, after a rough night of trying to sleep in her guest room (she woke me up every hour, peering at me with a flashlight), Aunt Celia and Uncle Nathan were walking up the sidewalk.

"I tried to call you at Max's every hour to be sure you didn't fall into a coma and die like my third cousin twice removed Ingrid did after that frozen herring incident, but it kept ringing straight into voice mail, so Nathan said she'd probably turned the phone off. Max, not Ingrid," she said, practically yanking me out of the car in her haste to hug me and examine me for broken bones.

"Oooh, careful. My head is still aching, and I haven't taken anything for pain yet today," I said, trying not to whimper. Aunt Celia's fussing always put me back in little girl mode.

Next door, Emily came running out of her door. "Oh my goodness! December, are you okay? Celia told me all about it! I've been so worried about you! I baked you a giant chocolate cake, and Rick is bringing our guest room bed over for you right now so you don't have to sleep on the floor anymore."

Celia patted my arm. "I've made you your favorite pot roast and a pumpkin pie, dear," she soothed.

"With whipped cream?" I whimpered.

"I would never forget the whipped cream!"

Of course, with chocolate cake and beds and pot roast and pie and whipped cream, I could get into this whole pampering thing. I smiled as angelically as I could and tried to look fragile (not easy when you're nearly six feet tall).

"Okay," I said, making my voice as weak as I could. "I think I could eat something."

Uncle Nathan shot me a suspicious look, but I just blinked at him, sheer innocence written all over my soon-to-be-stuffed-with-pie face. He rolled his eyes.

Guess I don't do innocent face all that well . . .

Sunday rushed by in a blur, with food, family, and friends, plus naps and wincing around trying not to jar my head. But by eight that evening, I was tired of feeling sorry for myself and decided to get some work done. I had two boxes of Faith Deaver's medical records in my living room that weren't going to read themselves.

Naturally my cell phone rang the minute I'd arranged all the files around me on my new loaner bed (a full-size, even, not just a twin) exactly to my anal-retentive satisfaction.

The phone was still in the kitchen.

I contemplated ignoring it, and then I contemplated the problem of when I would remember to call to have a land line hooked up so I could have a real phone. My phone kept ringing, in spite of my attempts to dither around so long the person calling would hang up. I sighed and heaved myself up to go get it, and stubbed my toe on the file box sitting right next to the bed.

"Ouch!" I said, and did a hopping step over to the kitchen and grabbed the phone.

UNKNOWN NUMBER.

I flipped the phone open anyway. "What? This better not

be a sales call on Sunday night, because you'd better believe I know all about the Fair Debt Collection Practices
Act," I threatened in my scariest voice.

Jake laughed.

"It freaks me out that I recognize your laughter, Brody,"
I muttered. "Makes me think you've been laughing at me a
little too much."

"I just called to tell you that your car should be in your
driveway by now," he said in that low, silky voice that even
staticky cell phone reception couldn't disguise. "And I only
ever laugh *near* you, not at you."

"Right." I walked over to the window, and sure enough,
the red convertible was in my driveway. "Oh, great. Magic
tricks with cars, but where are the keys, answer me that,
Houdini?" I said, freaked all over again because I hadn't
heard anybody drive up with the car.

"Celia figured you'd be napping, so I asked Wrench to
be quiet and leave the keys with Emily," he said.

"Celia figured? What are you doing talking to my Aunt
Celia? I mean, I appreciate all of your help and everything,
but aren't you . . . getting a little too cozy with my family?"
I moved away from the window, not sure how I felt about
Jake being all buddy-buddy with Aunt Celia.

"I've got a lead on Gina," he said, trying to distract me.

It worked. "Where is she? Is she okay?"

There was a silence. "You know, I can't figure you out,
Vaughn. Most people would ask about whether or not Gina
had been behind the car vandalism first."

"I'm not sure how to respond to that. Are you accusing
me of not being practical?"

"No," he said softly. "I'm accusing you of having a big
heart."

"Oh. Well. Er, don't let it get around." I could feel my ears turning red.

"I'm sure it won't last. You *are* a lawyer, after all," he said.

"Nice. Very nice. Sneak in a compliment, then decimate them with an attack," I said. "Are you sure *you* aren't a lawyer?"

"Later, Vaughn. Try to stay out of trouble."

"I—"

Click.

I sighed. The man of mystery strikes again. What was it I'd ever thought was wrong with my dear ex-husband? I paused for a moment of wistful thinking. *Old, reliable Mike.*

Who wants to date your secretary.

The mere thought of Mike and Brenda sent me back to the refrigerator for my third slice of cake of the day. Chocolate is great for concussions, right? I carried my slab of cake and a glass of milk back to the bed with me and settled in for the night.

Those glamorous lawyers on TV got nothin' on me.

I woke up Monday morning and realized I was almost afraid to drive to work. The person (or persons, plural; I still had a hard time believing Gina Schiantelli was behind all of it, psycho nail file incident or no) who was stalking me had had the entire day Sunday to plot new tortures.

When I realized I was cowering in my bed, it ticked me off. There was no way I was going to let some low-rent thug get the better of me. Especially when I was freshly fueled with pot roast and chocolate cake.

After doing the shower/makeup/hair thing, I dressed in

my second favorite red power suit—the one with the extra couple of inches in the waist for those special, post-cake binge days—and black pumps with the three-inch heels. I figured if I had to go down, I was at least going to look good on the way. Then I headed out the door to get my keys from Emily and get on with my life.

I stopped on the sidewalk outside of my house and looked around for nefarious types, not quite sure what a nefarious type would look like, but sure it would involve hairiness and missing teeth. Tattoos, probably.

Mr. Feldman from down the street was walking Gigi, his Pomeranian, but he didn't really qualify, since he was bald and had enormous dentures. I waved to him and waited till he shuffled on by, then I made as hideous a scowling face as I could, kind of "constipated pirate," and swept the street with my fearsome gaze.

"Watch out, stalker. I'm in the mood to take names and kick ass," I growled.

Then I felt stupid, because I'm *so* not a growler, but at least it made me laugh. It's hard for your teeth to chatter when you're laughing.

Not that I was scared or anything.

Much.

I was the first one at the office, and I walked from room to room, making sure nothing had been vandalized. Everything looked fine, so I brewed a pot of coffee and dove into the Deaver production. Now that we had the key, the documents were starting to make sense. I wanted to establish at least a rough timeline by the end of the day of *who* first had notice *when* of the potential problem with the insulin. I also needed to start calling my experts, so I could understand the insulin production process. It was going to be an enormous undertaking, and the case might carry on for years.

I banished the queasy stomachache that started up at the thought. "A journey begins with the first step, and a document review begins with the first page, right?" I muttered, then clipped my hair back out of my face, pulled out a fresh legal pad, and got to work.

"Anybody home?" Mr. Ellison's voice broke into my concentration, and I looked up at the clock, blinking. It was nearly nine. Somehow two hours and most of a cup of coffee had vanished. But I'd filled half of a legal pad with notes, and my timeline was coming along, so I didn't mind the interruption.

Plus, there was the matter of the name "Percival."

He ambled into my office, hands stuffed in the pockets of green-and-pink-plaid pants, which threw me off. "Do you buy those pants on purpose to give Max fits?"

"What's wrong with my pants? These are the latest fashion!" he said, brows pulling together in the middle of his wrinkly forehead.

"In the land of dead golfers, maybe."

He ignored me. "Why shouldn't blondes get coffee breaks?"

"Oh, no. Definitely no blonde jokes. Mr. Ellison, I told you—"

"Because it takes too long to retrain them!" He slapped the doorframe with his hand, clearly overcome with his own cleverness.

I contemplated the consequences if I hit him over the head—with the ten pounds or so of my *Black's Law Dictionary*—and buried the body.

"Who wants to dig a grave in this heat?" I asked, pushing myself up out of my chair to go find more coffee.

"What? What did you ask me? What about graves?"

"Never mind, Mr. Ell— . . . *Percy.* Never mind," I said, grinning as I slipped past him to the coffeeroom.

"You . . . I . . . Hey!" he shouted. "Never, ever call me that! I hate that name. Got beat up for two years after the kids at school found out about that name."

I rolled my eyes. "Or maybe it was just your charming personality," I said under my breath, not really sure that baiting my employee was appropriate, no matter how annoying he was.

On the other hand . . . "Okay, here's the deal," I said, swinging around to face him. "You quit calling me girlie, I quit calling you Percy. If not, I may have to let it drop in front of Mrs. Zivkovich . . ." I let my voice trail off, leaving him to imagine the possible humiliation.

All the blood drained out of his face, which was even scarier than it sounds. "You wouldn't."

"I would."

"You're just . . . you're . . . evil," he whispered hoarsely.

"Duh. I'm a lawyer."

He stomped off down the hall, shouting back over his shoulder, "Fine. Deal."

I laughed and shook my head. Negotiation at its finest. Next I'd be trying the Socratic method in the grocery store.

I walked out front, wondering where Max was. She was usually the first one in the office, with her unnatural morning-person personality. As I reached reception, she walked in the front door, talking on her cell phone. "I don't care what you have to do. Put out an APB on him or something. I want to know where that furniture is, and I want to know today."

I stared at her, wondering if I'd hired *two* color-blind people. The bright lime-green dress might have been fine by itself, but the matching lime-green heeled sandals and the complementary lime-green pillbox hat put the outfit at just a teensy bit over the top.

She listened, nodding, for a few seconds, then sighed. "Well, do your best, please. Thank you. Yes, winning Miss Florida was one of my proudest moments. Thanks."

She clicked her phone shut, then caught sight of me. "I swear, some people. You'd think it was all fine and dandy that they have no idea where on God's green earth your belongings are."

"Fine and dandy?"

"Oh, hush. I go all Southern when I'm annoyed. And how are you anyway?" She stopped and gave me the once-over with her eyes, probably scanning for further injuries.

"I'm fine. Nice dress, by the way. Is there a garden party scheduled today I didn't know about? Or did you have a sudden urge to look like a citrus fruit?"

She sniffed, then carefully unpinned her hat and placed it on the side of her desk. "I don't know what you're talking about, Miss Power Suit with the elastic waist."

"Hey, it's not elastic. It has a little . . . give, that's all," I protested. "And thanks for calling again about my furniture. I assume that's what that was about?"

She made a face. "Yes, but no luck. I've tried being annoyed, demanding, friendly, and commiserating. None of them work. Still no furniture. No driver."

"We're going to have to take some kind of legal action. This is ridiculous," I said.

"What kind of legal action? Don't you think it's a little early to sue?" she asked.

I threw my hands up in the air. "I don't know. Missing

furniture is out of my area of expertise. Not that pretty much everything else isn't, too. Working at a big firm with divisions that handle everything is underrated, I think."

She shot a measuring glance my way. "Regretting starting your own practice already?"

I thought about it for a second, then touched my fingertips to the still-tender back of my head. "Nah. If I were going to have regrets, it would be over concussions, not over furniture."

Mr. Ellison walked in the room, carrying a cup of coffee. "Did you hear the one about the blonde who—"

"Mr. Ellison!" I shouted, cutting him off. "No lawyer jokes *and* no blonde jokes. Got it? Or do I have to use the 'P' word?"

He grumbled something under his breath, but he stopped. Then he looked at Max and did a double-take. "Great dress! It matches my pants."

Max moaned and started banging her head on the desk. Seemed like as good a time as any to make my escape.

Chapter 22

A few hours later, I was the one ready to bang my head on a desk. The time line wasn't making sense. The first report of any possible adverse reaction, a doctor from Orlando reporting in on the illness of one of her patients, was pretty clearly documented, as was the company's internal response, in a heavily redacted kind of way. 'Redact' means to take a couple dozen black markers (in the old days) or a couple dozen yards of white redacting tape (today) and block out anything that might possibly be helpful to the other side's case or harmful to your own.

This is not how the rules of civil procedure—the rules that courts use to run civil lawsuits—define it, but I'd seen it in action enough times to paraphrase.

Technically, you're supposed to have a good reason to redact part of a document. Like attorney-client privilege, which is a fancy way of saying that you have the right to have private communications with your lawyer. Otherwise, nobody would feel free to confide in us, and if you can't tell your own lawyer the truth, the justice system can't work.

There are exceptions, of course. My client can't tell me "I plan to murder John Smith" and expect me to keep it confidential. In fact, in that case, I'd have a duty to report my client's murderous plans.

But if my client tells me that he knows he messed up somewhere, and shipped defective insulin to consumers, that communication between us doesn't have to be disclosed to the other side. (Again, there are loopholes and exceptions even to this, but we're lawyers. We live for loopholes.)

Boring legalese explanation over, though, my problem remained, in the form of a single sheet of paper. An invoice, to be precise. I picked up the phone and called Max. "Will you and Mr. Ellison please come in for a quick huddle?"

They'd been working their way through boxes, too. Mr. Ellison, annoying sense of humor aside, had a nearly *savant* set of organizational skills, and was charting and arranging our new landslide of documents with amazing precision. When I'd mentioned it, he'd looked at me, bristling. "Forty-five years as a bus driver; damn straight I'm organized," was all he'd said, but I'd caught him grinning to himself when I left the file room.

They walked through my door, momentarily blinding with me with green and pink. I squinted my eyes. "Maybe I should wear my sunglasses for this meeting," I said, only half joking.

Max daintily arranged herself in a chair, while Mr. Ellison plopped himself down in the other one. "Very funny," he said. "Ha, ha. Now what's up? Some of us are working around here."

I ignored him and held up the invoice. "This is either a clerical error or a problem."

Max reached for it, but he got to it first, grabbing it out of my hand. "What is it? Invoice for film production, 1-800-BAD-INSULIN. I don't see . . . Wait! This can't be right."

He stabbed a finger at the date listed as DATE OF SERVICE on the invoice. "This is, what? Three weeks before that Dr. Kuebler woman reported the first reaction. I got a calendar going back in the file room."

I nodded. "Exactly right. I was going to ask if either of

you have come across any reports of earlier adverse events."

Max took the invoice from Mr. E and studied it. "No, everything I've seen has pointed directly to Dr. Kuebler's report as the first one that alerted BDC to any problem. Faith Deaver's reaction was seventeen days later."

"Yeah, plenty of time to notify people and get that product off the shelves and out of use," I said, scowling again. "Anyway, this must be a typo. How could Orange Grove Productions be filming commercials three weeks before anybody even knew there was a problem?"

I pointed at the client name and address on the bottom left corner of the invoice. "This is even more interesting: Sarah Greenberg hired this company to film these commercials. It's put as ATTENTION TO: M-somebody Ziggeran at her firm. The first name is a little hard to read."

"Damn vultures, those kinds of lawyers," Mr. Ellison muttered.

Max and I glared at him. "Don't even go there," she said. "People have a right to know about legal services that may be available to them."

I held up a hand to cut her off. "Not that I don't appreciate a spirited defense of the legal system as much as the next person, but is anybody else wondering why an invoice *from* a video production company *to* Greenberg and Smithies is in with Langley, Cowan's production of BDC discovery documents?"

Max narrowed her eyes. "That doesn't make any sense at all, does it?"

I shook my head. "No way. And there's also no way that a firm like Langley, Cowan didn't have half a dozen slave-labor associates go through this production page by page over and over. How could it get in there?"

Mr. Ellison looked back and forth between the two of us. "Will somebody explain what the heck is going on here? Don't they have to give you all the paper about the case?"

I picked up my mug, made a face at the smell of stale coffee, then put it back down. "Sorry. Yes, they do. All of the paper we *requested*. Which is why those requests the other lawyer wrote—and you made fun of—are so thorough. But we can't ask BDC to give us documents they don't have. We can't ask them for Greenberg and Smithies' communication with their film company, for example. So why would this even be in here?"

Max shrugged. "It's a mistake."

"Right. Except why would Langley, Cowan even have it in the first place? And if the date on the invoice is one mistake, then this would make two mistakes." I shook my head, getting that tingly feeling in my head that I always got when puzzle pieces didn't fit.

"It's too weird, and I don't like weird. Max, will you call Orange Grove Productions and figure out a way to ask about this date? Maybe even get a copy of the correct invoice faxed over? This is going to bug me until we figure it out."

Mr. Ellison folded his arms across his bony chest. "I betcha it's a conspiracy. The government is running bad drugs and trying to make guinea pigs out of us citizens."

Max and I both stared at him. I was the first to figure out something to say. "Um, well, how about we go with 'clerical error' for now and leave 'government conspiracy' as a future theory?"

"Sure, that's what they said about that Area 51. Then the anal probes started happening."

•   •   •

After a quick sandwich (Max had stocked our tiny kitchen with the essentials, like a giant jar of peanut butter, a jar of strawberry jam, and a loaf of honey-wheat bread), I was ready to dive back into the Deaver documents, but Max buzzed me. "December? I think you'd better come out here."

"What—"

Click.

Even my own staff hangs up on me. That is just so wrong.

I trudged out to reception, the invoice still niggling at me. Then I reached our little lobby and all thoughts of invoices vanished at the sight of a dozen or so of Aunt Celia's casserole brigade, all clutching papers and files and, in one case, a precarious pile of about four shoeboxes.

"Hi! It's so nice to see you again! Um, may I help you?"

The shoebox woman—I couldn't remember her name for anything, but I think she was one of the tuna casseroles—spoke up first. "Well, we certainly hope so! Otherwise we wasted our Monday bus ride, and Designer Shoe Warehouse is having a sale on those purple velvet heels I've been wanting."

I glanced down at her chunky white orthopedic shoes and support hose. "Um, yes. Well. I'm delighted to see you, of course, but maybe somebody could tell me—"

"Oh, for heaven's sake, shoes, shoes, shoes. That's all you think about," an elegant woman in a snazzy gold lamé tracksuit (she was definitely the apple cobbler; totally yummy!) spoke up. "We're going to start calling you Imelda, for heaven's sake."

Tracksuit woman stood up. "I'm Daribelle Dohonish, as I'm sure you remember, since you ate three pieces of my cobbler. We're here to help you get your law practice off the

ground. We all have various legal matters we've been
putting off and, well, we're not getting any younger. I'll go
first, then."

I watched, speechless, as she marched down the hallway
toward my office. The shoebox woman grumbled a little,
but the rest of them smiled at me and nodded. I looked at
Max and she shrugged, smiling.

I turned back toward my new clients. "Okay, then. Thank
you all—again—for coming. I'll find Mr. Ellison and ask
him to get coffee or cold drinks for everyone. Um, well.
Thanks."

Then I followed Mrs. Dohonish down the hall, wondering at what magic age pink-and-green pants or gold lamé
tracksuits started to look like good fashion choices.

Three hours and eight new clients later, I was tired but
happy. Straightforward legal issues, for a change. I'd be
able to help each of my new clients with a little research, all
except for one, who needed a referral to a good estate attorney. Which reminded me that I really needed to make it
to a local bar association meeting and start building up my
referral network. For now, I'd ask Aunt Celia. She knew
everybody in a three-county area.

I watched out the window as the seniors' minibus drove
off with my new clientele, only moderately embarrassed
that my Aunt Celia was sending me all of my clients. Re-
ferrals are the only way to build a business. I would work
really hard to provide the best legal representation possible
and help them with real solutions.

Tuna casserole optional.

"December? You might want to take this one in your office," Max said, holding the phone to her shoulder. "It's

Mike. Your Mike," she added, as though the expression on her face didn't give it away.

"More like Brenda's Mike," I muttered. Then I nodded and headed back to my office at a trot, wondering if he had furniture news and also wondering what I was going to say to him about dating Brenda.

"Hey Mike, how are you?"

"I'm fine, why are you out of breath?"

A wave of loneliness, homesickness, or plain old-fashioned longing washed over me at the sound of his voice. No matter how sure you are that a divorce is a good idea, there is some part of you—the part that envisioned being eighty years old together and playing with your grandchildren— that aches from the loss.

At least that's how it worked for me.

"I jogged down the hall to get the phone," I said past the lump in my throat. "How are you? Any news on my furniture?"

"What? You still don't have it? Let me know if you want me to contact an attorney and take some kind of action. This is ridiculous!"

"Mike?"

"Yes?"

"I *am* an attorney, remember?" I twirled the phone cord in my fingers, smiling. He'd always been the one to handle the little details of our lives, while I flew around the country being a hotshot trial lawyer. Looking back, I couldn't even tell you where the dry cleaners' shop was located.

He laughed. "Right. Of course. Sometimes I forget you're doing general practice now. I guess you can handle this on your own."

"Yep, no problem," I said, not mentioning that I hadn't the slightest clue when I'd ever get my furniture.

"Well, I have fabulous news, and I wanted you to be the first to know."

"You got the grant! Mike, I'm so happy for you! I know how hard you worked on that proposal, and—"

"No, no, it's not the grant. Although it looks like I might have a good shot at that. No, it's much better than that. I asked Brenda to marry me, and she said yes!"

After the phone fell out of my numb fingers, it occurred to me that I didn't have to worry about answering the "can I date your secretary" question.

Somehow, that didn't make me feel any better.

Chapter 23

Max walked in my office, shuffling some papers and a notepad. "December, that clerical error isn't one, really. In fact, the accountant at the video company was fairly annoyed that we would question her record-keeping. She sounds like a female Mr. Ellison. So I got the number of the cameraman, and . . . why are you banging your head on your desk?"

I lifted my head and stared at her. "I only banged it once, then I realized that it was stupid to hurt the front of my head when I already have stitches in the back. Not that anybody cares."

I put my head down on my folded arms on my desk and tried not to cry.

Then I tried not to think about why I wanted to cry.

Then I started crying.

Damn ex-husbands.

Max rushed over and patted my back. "Oh, honey, what's wrong?"

I sat up and dug in a desk drawer for my travel pack of tissues. After I blew my nose hugely, I took a deep breath. "Mike's marrying my secretary," I mumbled.

"*What?* That rat bastard! We hate him!"

"No, it's okay. And anyway, she's *his* secretary now," I said.

"Even worse! It's sexual harassment. We hate him!"

"No, it's not sexual harassment. He asked her to marry

him, not do him in the file room," I said, cringing at the thought.

"What kind of man gets married before the ink is even dry on your divorce papers? We hate him!" She stalked around the room, fists clenched.

My shoulders slumped, and I shook my head. "Thanks, Max, but there's no need for the best friend moral support parade. I'm the one who dumped *him,* remember? And I love Brenda like a sister. It's just . . . it's just . . . stupid."

She finally sat down and looked at me with way too much perception. Damn beauty queens. "It's just that he's not supposed to get over you so soon or so easily, right? Can we hate him for that?"

I laughed. Or at least, I think I laughed. It sounded a little hiccupy. "No hating. I'll have to call him back and congratulate him. And send them a present or something. Is there some guideline for what kind of gift you send when your ex-husband gets engaged to your ex-secretary? I bet Miss Manners doesn't have a chapter on that!"

My phone rang before I could answer. It was Mr. Ellison. "Hey, it's that cameraman from the invoice, December. He says he'll only talk to you."

"Thanks, Mr. Ellison. Please put him through. Thanks for all of your hard work today, by the way," I said.

"Fair day's work for a fair day's wage. That's how I was brought up, girlie," he said, then I heard the clicking noise that signaled a line change.

"December Vaughn here. Thanks for calling. To whom am I speaking?"

"Don't worry about that," a man said in a low voice. "Look, I can't talk about this on the phone. We have to meet."

I shot Max a puzzled glance. "I think you have the

wrong person. This is December Vaughn, and I'm only calling to ask you about the date you filmed a TV commercial
for Greenberg, Smithies."

"Yeah, I know who you are. Look, this is turning into a
big nightmare. I can't—wait," he said, then I heard muffled
talking. I waited about thirty seconds, and he finally came
back on the line. "Look, Ms. Vaughn, I can meet you tomorrow. Tomorrow at noon, at . . . at the MOSH. Do you
know it?"

"Mosh?" I asked, waving Max over to listen in. She nodded and did a thumbs-up at the word "mosh."

"Okay, noon at the mosh. Anyplace specific?"

"Uh, at the planetarium. There's a show on Mars that
starts at that time. I'll be in the back row on the left of the
door you go in, and I'll be wearing a red hat. Be on time, or
I'm outta there."

I wrote down the specifics, then looked at Max and
made a finger-twirling by my ear sign, universal symbol for
"nutcase alert." "Mars show, back row, left side, red hat. I'll
see you there, Mr. . . . ?"

"Don't be late," he warned. Then the line went dead. I
put my phone down and stared at Max. "Either I'm dreaming all of this, or I've just walked into a B movie."

"Or a bad soap opera," she offered helpfully. "The
MOSH is the Museum of Science and History, by the way.
Cool place. Are you going to meet him?"

"How can I resist, after all that buildup? Don't tell Mr.
Ellison, he'll think he was right about that government conspiracy stuff."

She shuddered. "If he ever says the words 'anal probes'
again, I'm so out of here."

I put my head back down on my desk, then popped up

again. "Hey, I need to learn something about criminal law before ten o'clock tomorrow. Any thoughts?"

If I could have found a wise, mentoring attorney through Hollywood central casting, Jim Thies would have been him. Handsome, distinguished, and with a smile that made you want to confess every crime you'd ever thought of, Jim's was the name that kept coming up in conversations about criminal law in Orange Grove. He'd worked as a prosecutor, then as a criminal defense attorney for a couple of decades, and his steel-trap mind and gregarious personality made him a favorite of the local judges and even his opposing counsel.

Naturally, I'd called Aunt Celia, but this time Uncle Nathan was the one who helped me out. "Call Jim Thies," he'd said immediately, when I'd explained my problem. "He helps me get the legal issues in my novels right, and he's a great guy."

So now I was sitting at dinner—with a man who'd forgotten more about law than I'd probably ever learn—and taking page after page of notes.

He'd just gently shot down my idea that Bear was harmless.

"Well, no theft is harmless. He took what didn't belong to him, right? A first offense is a second-degree misdemeanor. Usually he'll face a fine and a shoplifting course. If he does it again, he'll get jail time. You need to impress on Bear that this behavior has got to stop now. If you don't think he'll understand, you need to find somebody who can make him understand."

"That sounds kind of harsh. In my world, corporate executives who steal millions of dollars rarely face any jail time at all. This poor man who took a lamp home, fully intending to pay for it, is in big trouble."

He laughed. "Don't get me started on the inequities of the criminal justice system, young lady. That's why I practice on this side of the fence. My kind of criminals are much easier to understand than yours."

After another twenty minutes of helpful discussion—and he wouldn't even let me pay for dinner—I felt a lot better about Bear's hearing. I'd also decided to refer any future case that even smelled a little like criminal law to Jim's firm. "Dabbling" in law is usually called by its other name: malpractice.

I may be blond, but I'm not *that* blond.

After a couple of post-dinner hours back at the office checking in with some of my potential expert witnesses who were in West Coast time zones, my expert list was beginning to shape up. I'd disclose a few more than I planned to actually use at trial, just to be sure I had all of my bases covered. From what I'd learned from Charlie's file, his former attorney hadn't made much progress there, other than talking to a local endocrinologist about diabetes generally. I'd need way more specialized expertise against the big guns BDC would undoubtedly hire. Wouldn't a large settlement offer be wonderful all the way around?

I shut down my computer and closed my calendar, then rubbed my eyes. Probably sleep was one of those luxuries that new business owners didn't get much of for the first, oh, dozen or so years. Not that I'd slept much in my old firm, though. Maybe lawyers were doomed to chronic sleep deprivation.

The phone rang, startling me. "December Vaughn," I

said, wondering who would call me in the office at ten o'clock at night.

"Ms. Vaughn, it's Addison Langley. I'm calling to express my . . . *apologies* over the tone of our previous communications. These cases are getting to us all, I think," he said, managing to convey both warm sincerity and honest regret.

I didn't buy either for a second.

But I decided to play along. "Certainly, Mr. Langley. I agree that our clients will only benefit if we can maintain a civil and cordial tone."

"That's great," he said, and this time I believed the relief in his voice. It was too evident to be fake, unless he was Oscar-caliber. "In that regard, we'd like to offer to settle Mr. Deaver's case."

"You—*what?*" I grabbed my legal pad and started writing.

DEAVER: T/C LANGLEY
APOLOGIES—"CIVIL/CORDIAL"—SETTLEMENT??????
HOW MUCH??

"How much? I mean, what is the nature of the settlement you're proposing?" I asked, slipping on my tough negotiator shoes. The fact that I'm surprised doesn't mean my client gets a bad deal, especially since I knew exactly what he was up to. He'd lowball me, just so he could lay the paper trail of his "attempts to accommodate" and my "refusal to be reasonable." Probably something on the order of fifty grand and no admission of liability, and then—

"One million dollars."

I nearly choked.

ONE MILLION DOLLARS?!?!?!?!

"You have twenty-four hours to discuss it with your client and get back to me. Naturally, we admit no liability and would insist on a confidentiality agreement," he continued.

"Naturally," I said weakly.

"Thank you, Ms. Vaughn. I look forward to hearing from you."

After I hung up the phone, I sat and thought about the offer. One million really wasn't that much for a life, and Langley had to know that I'd refuse his offer. I'd be committing malpractice to accept an offer like that without doing more discovery on the case. What if BDC's negligence was so hideous that I'd have been able to get him tens of millions?

Why would he even make the offer, was what I didn't understand. Either way, I needed to tell my client about it.

I picked up the phone and dialed, and he answered on the first ring. "Charlie, it's December. We need to talk."

Chapter 24

Amazing how a good night's sleep doesn't do a darn thing for you when you're about to go to court on your first criminal case. I stuffed papers in my briefcase, trying to remember if we'd confirmed with Bear more than once that he'd meet me at the courthouse. I had the feeling he was a guy who needed multiple reminders.

Max, sitting across from my desk, whistled. "Pop! Here's a million dollars? Just like that, before discovery even starts?" She shook her head. "Something smells fishy about that. Do you think they've already found out that BDC screwed up somewhere in production?"

"I don't know what it is. All I know is that Charlie said no way, even before I explained why he shouldn't take it. He's afraid that they're using the confidentiality agreement to get out of taking the blame for what they did. I can't say that I disagree with him."

"So I should start sending medical records out to your experts?" Max began making notes.

"Yes, please get the copying going on that. It's going to be a massive project. Also, let's follow up with Mrs. Zivkovich and see if my cease-and-desist letter worked on her son-in-law. If not, let's go for the restraining order."

"Okay, med records copy nightmare; see if slimeball backed off. Got it. I'll also follow up on the work we're doing for our various *pro bono* clients and ask Mr. Ellison to create files for our new clients from yesterday. Is that it?"

I stopped rushing around for a moment and stood perfectly still, mentally running through my to-do list. "That's it."

She sighed and stood up. Today's outfit was a champagne-colored silk dress that looked killer on her. I looked down at my dull blue suit and sighed. "You know what we need, don't you?" she asked.

"What?" I said glumly, feeling like the ugly duckling.

"Another lawyer. If you hired an associate, you wouldn't be running in fifty directions at once."

I tried not to laugh hysterically. "Right. If I hired an associate with what money exactly? My savings is disappearing fast. I won't be able to afford *you* in another twelve weeks."

"Things always work out, D. You wait and see."

Much more waiting-and-seeing, and I'd be waiting-and-seeing in bankruptcy court. Too bad. I wouldn't be able to afford an engagement present for Mike and Brenda.

When I slipped into the back of the courtroom, one of the hottest guys I'd seen inside of a courtroom in . . . well, *ever,* was standing before the judge. He looked like an actor or a model or—well, anything but a lawyer. I wasted a few happy moments admiring the wavy blond hair and, when he turned around, the terrific cheekbones and gorgeous blue eyes.

He didn't look bad in a suit either.

Stuffing my overactive libido firmly back down where it belonged, in repression and denial-land, I opened my file on the hearing. Then I scanned the rows of people, but Bear wasn't there yet, so I read over my notes for the thirtieth time since I'd woken up with butterflies the size of law books in my stomach.

Why had I *ever* agreed to do this? Sometimes good intentions can overcome good sense, as Dad used to say.

"First offense, first offense, first offense," I muttered to myself. A shadow fell across my notes, and I looked up. The calendar model–turned–lawyer was standing there, smiling down at me, and he looked even better up close and personal.

I'm guessing it's your first offense," he said, still smiling.

"No! I mean, yes, but no. I mean, it's Mr. Anderson's first offense, not mine. I've had lots." I was babbling. I could tell, but the words just kept on coming. "Not lots of offenses, lots of clients. Just not criminal clients."

His smile had changed into a full-on grin. "Judge Bertels is taking a short recess. Would you like to get a cup of coffee and tell me all about it?"

Luckily, Bear walked in right then and saved me from fumbling around to answer. My magic "client is in the room, December morphs into competent attorney" talent kicked in to save me. "Thank you, but I see my client. Perhaps another time," I said coolly, standing up to greet Bear.

A grin quirked at the edge of pretty boy's lips, and he pulled a business card case out of his pocket and handed a card to me. "Matt Falcon. Since I have to wait for the pleasure, let's make it lunch instead. Heightened anticipation and all that," he said.

"December Vaughn," I said, holding my hand out to shake his and making a mental note to check on the status of my business cards. Suddenly, I fiercely missed the good old days when business cards magically appeared in my inbox, and toilet paper magically appeared in the office bathroom.

"If you'll excuse me, Mr. Falcon—"

"Call me Matt, since we're going to be friends." He nodded to me and walked down the aisle toward the courtroom door, passing Bear on the way. I never even peeked to see if Matt "I'm too smooth for my shoes" Falcon had a great butt or not. (He did.)

"Bear! I'm so glad you're on time. The judge is taking a break, and our case hasn't been called yet, but we should be soon. You look really nice." He'd tamed his bushy red hair, which looked damp, and trimmed his beard. Somehow, he'd even found a suit to fit his enormous girth.

I held out my hand to shake his, but he moved right past it and gave me a hug. I was so shocked, I just stood there, speechless.

Nobody ever hugged me when I did corporate work.

He let go and stepped back, biting his lip. "I'm so glad to see you, Ms. Vaughn. I told Grandma that if anybody could get me out of this mess, it was you. She can't wait to meet you," he whispered, looking around as if somebody might be waiting to handcuff him any second.

"It's okay, we're going to be fine. I talked to—" I broke off as I saw the bailiff come back in the room.

"All rise for the Honorable Judge Bernard Bertels. Court is now in session."

We all rose as the judge entered the courtroom from the narrow door which led back to his chambers. As he seated himself behind the bench, his judicial assistant handed him some papers and spoke to him in a low voice. The judge was a serious-looking man in his mid-fifties or so, maybe, with iron-gray hair and warm brown skin. His robe was so crisp and starched it seemed to crackle.

I motioned to Bear to sit down next to me on the hard wooden pew-like seat. No sooner had our bottoms hit the wood than the bailiff was calling out the next case. "Buford Anderson."

More nervous than I ever remembered being in court before, I stood up and started forward, then realized Bear hadn't moved. He was staring at the judge with terrified eyes. I walked back and grabbed his arm, then dragged him up off the bench.

Well, as much as I could drag a seven-foot-tall man. He got the point, though, and followed me up the aisle. We started to walk to one table, and the bailiff made a sort of hissing noise and pointed to the other table. I tried to pretend I'd been heading there in the first place, which fooled nobody, if the amusement on the judge's face and the disbelief on the JA's face were anything to go by.

A slender, ferret-faced man rushed up and stood behind the other table. "Your Honor," he said.

The judge nodded. "Counselor."

Then he turned to look at me again. "I don't believe I know you, Counselor. You are?"

I swallowed the lump in my throat, getting angry at myself. I wasn't some first-year baby lawyer. I'd been in hundreds of courtrooms in the past eight years. Standing a little straighter, I nodded elegantly. "I've not had the pleasure, Your Honor. December Vaughn for Mr. Anderson."

Judge Bertels narrowed his eyes. "Vaughn? The same Vaughn who was in the paper recently?"

Now would be a great time for that hole in the floor to open up.

I lifted my chin. "Yes, Your Honor. And no, Your Honor. Yes, I am that Vaughn, and no, I am not a whacked-out Yankee junkie lawyer come down to wreak havoc south of the

Mason-Dixon Line. Whatever the Mason-Dixon Line is. Your Honor."

He grinned. "You don't look much like a junkie to me, Counselor, and you'll find I make my own judgments. Welcome to the Claymore County Bar. Now if we could proceed?"

Ferret Face started to talk, but bolstered by the fervor of the persecuted, I promptly forgot everything Jim Thies had told me and cut in. Bear was special, and I needed to make the judge see it. "If I could make a brief statement, if it please the Court?"

The judge looked at the prosecutor, who twisted his face up in a grimace, but shrugged.

Judge Bertels leaned back in his chair. "Well, this is unusual, but go ahead, Ms. Vaughn."

"Thank you." I took a deep breath, and tried not to shift from foot to foot. "Your Honor, this country has a long tradition of recognizing and applauding differences in our citizens. In fact, the Founding Fathers worked on the principle that we were all unique and special and had the right to be free of oppression. If—"

"Counselor."

"—you look at—"

"Counselor!"

"Um, yes, Your Honor?"

"It's my understanding that the Founding Fathers worked on the principle that we deserved to be free from oppressive taxation by a king who wouldn't allow us representation in Parliament. Am I wrong?"

"Well, no, sir, but—"

"And the . . . what was it you said? Oh, right. 'Unique and special.' The unique and special Founding Fathers were all wealthy white men who owned land?" asked the judge, whose ancestors hadn't been among that group any more than my own poor Irish forebears had been.

"Well, yes, sir, but—" In spite of the frigid air-conditioning, I was starting to sweat. I snuck a glance at the prosecutor, and he'd dropped his papers and was staring at me, open-mouthed.

"Then would you like to tell the Court what the Founding Fathers have to do with Mr. Anderson's petty theft charges?"

"No, sir. I mean, yes, sir. It's—"

"Your Honor?" My opponent had finally found his voice, and either he'd suddenly developed a massive summer cold, or he was trying not to laugh, because he started coughing so hard he nearly choked.

"Yes, Mr. Allen? Do you have something to add that might illuminate me on the role of the Founding Fathers?" The judge smiled, but he narrowed his eyes, and I had the feeling I was in trouble.

Mr. Allen started choking again. "No, Your Honor. No illumination. Just a quick interjection to inform the Court that the state is dismissing the charges against Mr. Anderson. The complaining witness had"—he shuffled through some papers, then selected one and read from it—"a nose-piercing infection emergency, and she is thus unable to co-operate. Since it's a first offense—"

"First offense!" I added helpfully.

The judge's attention swung back to me, but he wasn't smiling anymore. "Ms. Vaughn, I'd suggest that you brush up on your criminal procedure before I see you in my court again. Mr. Anderson, in spite of your attorney, you are free to go. I would advise you to amend your behavior, as the luck of witnesses with infected piercings isn't likely to happen again."

Bear jumped up out of his chair to stand up. "Yes, sir, Your Highness."

"Honor," I whispered.

"Your Honorableness," Bear corrected himself. "I won't ever, ever take something and pay for it later, even if the clerk is very rude and calls me a bad word. I promise, cross my heart, but don't hope to die, because Grandma says that's wrong and an offense against God, just like Republicans."

The judge stared at Bear for a moment, then brought his gavel down. "I see that you two deserve each other. Case dismissed."

Bear looked at me. "Am I free? I don't have to go to jail?"

I could hardly meet his eyes as I grabbed up my files and started to hurry down the aisle toward the door, desperate to escape the laughter I heard behind me. "Yes, you're free. Please don't take anything else without paying for it, Bear. And if you get in trouble again, you have to find a criminal attorney. I have a great one for you, even. His name is Jim, and you'll really like him."

Bear followed me out the door, but stopped me in the hallway with a hand on my arm. "But I don't want anybody else! You're the best lawyer in the world! You said I was unique, and you freed me from repression!"

Chapter 25

As I drove away from the courthouse, wondering if I could move to Siberia and start all over, my cell phone rang. I flipped it open. "Hold on."

Then I pulled into a parking space on the side of the road. Emotional devastation plus supreme humiliation plus cell phone equals December smashing into the back of a truck, I always say.

I put the convertible in park, realizing I hadn't even put the top down once yet. "Okay, I'm here."

"December, it's Max. I was calling to find out if the hearing was over and give you directions to MOSH. How did it go?"

"Don't ask," I muttered.

"What? What's wrong? Did poor Bear get sent to the concrete-and-bars jungle? Did they throw away the key?"

Max gets her knowledge of criminal law from TV, too.

"No, he's free. I'm the one who went down to the concrete jungle. Or at least the humiliation jungle. I'm such an idiot. I knew better, and Jim even helped me, but I managed to make a fool out of myself in a SPECTACULAR fashion."

I moaned and dropped my head on the steering wheel. "Stupid. Stupid. Stupid."

"What happened?"

I closed my eyes. "Nothing. Except for the part where I started orating about the Founding Fathers and freedom from repression."

"What? And don't you mean *oh*-ppresion?"

"No. No. *Nooooooo*. Don't you think we need more freedom from repression? And witnesses with piercing infections? Or maybe a few more experiences that make judges rethink their conclusions that I'm not a whacked-out junkie Yankee?" I moaned again.

"What the H. E. double toothpicks are you talking about?" she yelled.

I moaned again, but held the cell phone farther away from my poor eardrum. "Forget it. I'll tell you later, if it's not on the front page of the paper. Give me the directions, please."

As I reached down in my briefcase for paper and pencil, a knock on my window scared me half to death. After I untangled my tongue, I realized I was looking through the glass at Jim Thies.

I found the car window button on the Beemer and pushed it. "Hey, Jim. Don't believe anything you hear today, okay?"

He grinned. "If you say so, but are you sure that's the way the Founding Fathers would have wanted it?"

I hate my life.

Twenty minutes later, having written down Max's directions and promised Jim I'd never, ever tell anybody that he'd helped me, I was on my way to my stupid cloak-and-dagger meeting at the MOSH. I'd decided the whole thing was an enormous waste of my time, but I was going because it was a way to hide out for a couple of hours and—hopefully—regain a little of my equilibrium, before I had to face my employees and tell them their boss was an idiot without hope of redemption.

Maybe I needed a couple of *days*.

The drive to the museum gave me time to calm down and try for some optimism. Maybe I was an idiot, but I was an idiot driving a great car (even though it wasn't mine) on a beautiful day (hot enough to melt pavement) to meet a guy who wouldn't give me his name (about an invoice that probably didn't matter a bit).

My "glass half-full" needed work.

As I drove over the bridge, then around to the road appropriately named Museum Circle, I tried to enjoy the sunshine and remember all the reasons I'd been so ready to leave Ohio.

What I wanted to do was stuff my face with donuts and spend the rest of the day in bed watching my DVD of *Pride and Prejudice*. Colin Firth never would have married Elizabeth's secretary. I slammed the steering wheel to the left, after I nearly drove right by the entrance.

I parked and got out, wondering how to put the top down for the drive back. I needed to call Jake about Gina and find out when I would get my own car back.

"He's probably already heard about the fiasco today. Something else for him to laugh at me about," I mumbled to myself, walking toward the giant building where, according to several giant banners, the DINOSAURS WERE HERE.

Maybe I'd get lucky and one would eat me.

I paid my admission fee and took the building map to figure out where the planet show would be held, wondering again why I was doing this. The guy'd sounded like a psycho. Threading my way past a hundred or so kids wearing purple Dolphin Day Camp shirts, I made it to the staircase and headed for the second floor. Gaping at the enormous robotic dinosaurs, I almost didn't see the planetarium entrance at first.

By the time I'd figured it out, a couple of teenagers dressed in MOSH shirts were getting ready to close the doors. I squeezed in behind a family of six, and tried to remember what my caller had said. I was pretty sure it was "Mars show, back row, left side, red hat."

I looked to my left, but the lights were going down fast, and I saw only the dim outline of a man wearing a hat. I couldn't tell what color the hat was. I sat down anyway. He didn't say anything, so I waited for a minute, not really wanting to humiliate myself again by asking some poor tourist about being my clandestine contact.

Two or three minutes into the show, I'd learned that Mars is red because it's rusty. The soil contains iron oxide, the planet was once wet, and now it hasn't had any rain in millions of years. A rusty planet—who knew? Speaking of rust, the planetarium stank of rust or mildew or something nasty and metallic. Maybe they were piping in a rust smell to complement the Mars show, but that was going a little overboard, if you asked me. Not to mention my horrible certainty that somebody had stashed a poopy diaper under one of the adjacent seats.

Rust and poopy diaper smell was enough to make me want to get the heck out of there. Rust and poopy diaper smell on an empty stomach was making me feel like I was going to start dry heaving any second.

I still hadn't heard a peep out of the guy next to me, but I was almost positive his hat was red. He was leaning all the way back in his seat and looked like he was asleep, but I'd had enough of Mars and its aromas.

Leaning toward him, I tried to quietly get his attention. *"Psst!"*

The smell worsened near his seat, and the acrid stink burned my eyes. Maybe he'd passed out after being asphyxiated by the fumes and would need a good lawyer. *"Psst!"*

Nothing. He didn't even move.

I tried again, louder. *"Psst!"*

Nothing.

"Oh, for Pete's sake. Hey, dude. I'm December Vaughn, and I can't take the stench. Are you the guy from Orange Grove Productions?"

He didn't move, which was kind of rude. I mean, the least he could have done was say no, if I had the wrong guy.

I hate rude people. That's my only defense for what I did next.

I leaned clear over across the two seats between us and poked him in the arm. Hard. That's when three things happened all at once: He fell forward and smashed his face into the seat in front of him, the lights came up, and I started screaming.

Because the back of his shirt was soaked with blood. His head had tilted sideways, so I had a front-row view of the four-inch gash in his neck.

Then everybody else started screaming, and there was running and yelling and a baby crying.

I sat there, unmoving, staring at the bloody man in the red hat until somebody grabbed my arm. "Did you check his pulse?" he asked. I pointed to the open wound that ringed the part of his throat where his pulse should have been—*would* have been, but I still couldn't talk. Only after he dragged me out of my seat did I realize I was shaking and tears were pouring down my face.

It was my first dead body. I couldn't stop staring at him, even as I walked away. At the body. At *it*. He didn't look like anything but what he was—dead. Not like anything I'd ever seen anywhere before. Not in movies. Not on TV.

Dead.

I fell back against the wall just outside the planetarium and stared at the people hovering near me. "I just poked the arm of a dead man," I said, then burst into tears.

"Can you tell me your name? And what you saw?" The woman frowning down at me was way too pretty to be a sheriff's deputy, but that's what her uniform said. Her hair, severely pulled back in a ponytail, said she was all business. Her name tag said her name was SMITH-SIMMERS.

Her expression said she was annoyed with me.

"Join the club, Simmers," I muttered.

"Excuse me, ma'am?" she said, leaning closer.

"I'm December Vaughn. Is that your real name?" I asked her. "I mean, Smith-Simmers, really? Is it Deputy Smith-Simmers?"

She blinked. "Yes, it's Deputy. Or you can call me Brenda. Ma'am, are you okay?"

I clamped my teeth together to keep them from chattering so hard they broke. It was suddenly so cold in the museum. Freezing. "Deputy Brenda, when did they turn the air-conditioning up so high? Was it to keep him . . . was it to keep the body fresh for evidence?"

I started to laugh. Or at least I think I was laughing. But the tears kept rolling down my face. The deputy's eyes widened, and she called out to somebody standing behind her. "Hey, Bethany! Get over here. I think she's in shock."

An EMT carrying a blanket rushed over and bent down to take my pulse. She smiled at me, all calm and peacefulness. "My name is Bethany Hilkert, can you remember that?"

"How d-d-d-d-do you d-d-d-do it?" I asked, while she wrapped a blanket around me.

"Do what?"

"How do you stay so calm when you see dead people? You must see a lot of dead people, and you're so calm, and that was my first one, and I d-d-d-don't . . . I d-don't . . ." I started crying again and scrubbed at my face. "Some tough trial lawyer, huh?"

She patted my shoulder. "We focus on the ones we can help. That's what keeps us calm. We have to stay calm to do a good job. Now, do you remember my name?"

I sniffled. "Brenda Smith. No, Simmers-Smith. No, Smith-Simmers." I gave up, frustrated. "I don't remember."

She looked over her shoulder at the deputy. "Bliss, she's a little confused. I'd like to get something warm to drink inside her before you ask your questions."

The deputy nodded grimly. "Fine, but she doesn't go anywhere. Her name is December Vaughn."

I wasn't quite following the conversation. I kept seeing the man's head falling to the side, with his neck gaping open in a way necks shouldn't gape.

Ever.

"Who's Bliss?"

The EMT smiled again. She was awfully cheerful, considering somebody just died. "I'm Bethany, remember? Deputy Smith-Simmers is a friend of mine, and her nickname is Bliss."

A fresh wave of teeth chattering hit me, and my whole body was shaking so hard it felt like I had the worst flu of my life. But the name confusion seemed like the most important thing. I had to sort it out. I had to think about something other than the neck gaping and gaping and the blood . . .

"Bliss Simmers? Are you a stripper?"

The deputy looked kind of offended. "With a name like December, you have the nerve to ask me that?"

Probably a bad idea to tick off a deputy at a murder scene, right? Oh, crap. "Am I a suspect? I watch *CSI*. I'll take a polygraph test. I'll take lots of polygraphs. You can have my fingerprints and everything. Do you need my DNA? You can scrape whatever you want out of my mouth."

I opened my mouth as wide as I could and sat there, mouth open, eyes clenched shut. Nobody scraped me, though, so I opened one eye.

Deputy Simmers stood there, hands on hips, sighing. "I hate that freaking *CSI*. Every freaking place I go people are offering me their freaking DNA. Do you know how freaking much DNA tests freaking cost?"

Bethany laughed and stood up. "I think you should carry Q-tips around and swab everybody just to make them happy."

The deputy shuddered. "Like I want all those nasty body fluids anywhere near me. Get real."

Body fluids . . . "The diaper," I said.

They both looked at me. "What?"

"The diaper. There was a poopy diaper under the seats near us. Maybe the killer was a parent who brought his or her baby along, and you can find a clue in the diaper," I said, not realizing until the words came out of my mouth how stupid they sounded.

Deputy Simmers rolled her eyes and stalked off. "I'll get some tea. You watch her for more shock or something."

Bethany shook her head. Her smile had vanished. "Ms. Vaughn," she said gently. "The body . . . releases after death, especially after a violent death like that. The smell was—"

I held one hand up in the air, and the other near my mouth in case my now-roiling stomach gave up the fight to keep from shooting acid everywhere. "Oh, *God*. I get it. I get it. Please stop. Please stop. I've had such a long day."

When my fear of hurling on, well, *near,* a crime scene had passed, I wrapped my arms around my knees and rocked back and forth, waiting for someone to tell me I could go home.

I'd never wanted to go home so badly in my entire life.

Chapter 26

By the time I'd quit shivering, the place was crawling with official-looking personnel. I'd never known how many people were part of a crime scene. Police and sheriff-type people were all over the place. Some hard-looking men in rumpled suits. A woman in a suit—I had her pegged to be an assistant state attorney. Fire and Rescue. Crime-scene investigators. People with FDLE—Florida Department of Law Enforcement—insignia.

A wave of unreality washed over me. It felt like I'd fallen through a rabbit hole into one of those TV shows with the fake corpses. I expected to see Marg Helgenberger show up any minute.

"I love her," I mumbled.

"This is December Vaughn, sir. She found the body." Deputy Blissful was back, standing stiffly at attention next to an older man who had board-straight posture.

Murder makes for good posture, I guess. I stifled the hysterical laughter that tried to bubble up through my lips.

"I'm Detective Harris. Can you stand up now, Ms. Vaughn?" he asked.

I realized I was still sitting on the floor. No wonder everyone seemed so tall.

"Yes, sorry. It's kind of . . . I never, well, I never saw a dead body before. I never smelled one either."

"How did you know the deceased?"

"I didn't. Well, I talked to him on the phone. Maybe I talked to him on the phone. I'm not really sure. Who is he?"

Harris and the deputy traded a look, as if trying to decide what to tell me. "His name is Richard Dack. Sound familiar?"

I shook my head. "No, I never knew his name. If that is the man I was here to meet."

Simmers narrowed her eyes. "What are you saying, this was some kind of midday blind date?"

"No, that's ridiculous. I was meeting him to discuss a case. Again, if it's even the same man. The man I was supposed to meet works for Orange Grove Productions. He wanted to tell me about an invoice on a case I'm working on."

Harris's eyes had sharpened when I mentioned Orange Grove Productions. "Dack worked for that company. He had business cards in his pocket. You'd better tell us about the case."

I explained the little bit I knew about the invoice with the wrong date, but I got the feeling they quit paying attention to me about the time I said "clerical error." Harris stopped to talk in a quiet voice to one of his men, then turned back toward me. "Tell me about your drug seller associates."

Oh, crap. Here we go again.

Nearly two hours later they finally let me go, with my assurances I wasn't leaving town in the near future. I almost threw up in the parking lot when I realized the last time I'd sat in the car, I hadn't known what dead bodies looked like.

Or smelled like.

My stomach calmed down enough that I managed to get in the car and head for the office. As obscene as it seemed to me to be going on with my day when poor Richard Dack was lying dead in a morgue somewhere, I didn't know what else to do.

About halfway to the office, my cell phone started ringing. I glanced at my purse, wondering if I had the strength to answer my phone. After three or four rings, I finally dug it out with one hand and answered, "Max?"

"Yep, it's me. I'm dying to hear about the mystery man, but I have three lines holding."

"Bad word choice," I muttered.

"What?"

"Nothing. I'll tell you later." I could *not* have that conversation on the phone.

"All right. I just wanted to ask you to come straight back; Mrs. Zivkovich is here and her son-in-law is worse. Also, your furniture driver was sighted in Kentucky, so he's probably finally on his way south. No ETA," she said.

"Fine. I don't care. I'll be back in the office in around twenty minutes. Will you please make some very, very strong coffee? Maybe Mr. Ellison has some rum. He seems like he might have a flask."

"What? December, are you okay? What the heck happened? Is this still about the Founding Fathers?"

I choked out a surprised laugh. "No. Life, liberty, and the pursuit of happiness. There won't be any more of any of that for Richard Dack. See you in a few, Max." I flipped my phone shut, suddenly unable to talk.

When I reached my office and pulled into my parking space, the door of the red Jeep next to me opened, and Jake climbed out. He somehow looked crisp and cool in black slacks and a white, short-sleeved shirt, in spite of the oppressive heat. I got out of the BMW and stood there for a minute, staring at him. "How many cars do you have?

Where is my Honda? And why do you always show up when bad things happen to me? Are you the death fairy?"

He walked around the front of my car and held out a hand for my briefcase. "Let me help with that, Blondie. You look like a stiff breeze would knock you down."

I laughed, the edge of hysteria still in it. "It's a good thing there are no breezes in Florida in June, isn't it?" But I let him take my briefcase and followed him to the office door, which he opened for me. I couldn't see his eyes very well through his dark glasses, but he briefly put his hand on my shoulder as I walked in, and the compassion in the gesture nearly made me start crying again.

Max looked up as we walked in, and her quick smile vanished when she saw me. Or maybe when she saw Jake. Either way, she had a good frown on by the time the door closed behind us.

"If you keep taking up so much of December's time, Brody, I'm going to start billing you."

He smiled. "Always glad to see you, too, Maxine. You might want to get your boss some hot tea or something. She's had a rough day."

Max switched her attention to me. One long look, and she came rushing out from behind her desk. "D? You look horrible!"

"Gee, thanks. I guess I forgot to freshen up my makeup after I found my witness stabbed to death at the museum." I kept walking back to my office. "Thanks, but I don't want any hot tea. I may never drink hot tea again."

The mere thought of the hot tea I'd drunk at the museum brought the sight of Dack's gaping neck back front and center in my mind. I was going to have nightmares about that sight for a long time.

"What?" Max pushed past Jake and followed me down the hall. "What are you talking about?"

Mr. Ellison appeared in the doorway of the file room. "What's all the ruckus about? I've got news for you, too, girlie," he said, then caught sight of Jake behind me. "I mean, Miz Vaughn."

I waved a hand at him. "Later, okay, Mr. Ellison? I don't think I can take any more news today."

He and Max crowded in my office behind me, and I told them what had happened. I almost threw up again when I got to the part where I'd seen his head fall sideways, which made me realize I hadn't eaten anything all day and it was nearly four.

"I may never eat again," I mumbled. The thought made me sick. How could I eat when poor Mr. Dack would never eat again?

"I think December needs a little space and something to eat," Jake said, walking in with a sandwich on a plate and a cold ginger ale.

I shuddered. "I couldn't eat."

Max stared at Jake, hands on her hips, then nodded slightly. "Okay. Mr. Ellison and I will handle things out front."

I grabbed my arms with my hands and huddled in my chair, feeling the shivering return. "The smell, Jake. I thought it was a diaper, but the body releases, and the rust like Mars, but it was coppery rust, and it was blood. So much blood."

He put the plate down and pulled me up out of my chair and hugged me. I knew I shouldn't let him, but somehow the warmth of his arms helped stopped the shivering. "What is your deal, Brody? Why *are* you always around?"

He laughed and patted my back, then stepped back.

"Hell, I don't know. Something about you has my protective instincts in overdrive. Or maybe you're a challenge. Life certainly isn't dull since you came to town."

I sank back down in my chair. "I don't need you to protect me, Jake. Or maybe I do. I don't understand any of this. I mean, there's no way this could be related to my sinus stalker, is there? Are random, unrelated bad things happening to me? What about Gina? What about Addy?"

"I talked to Gina's mom. She checked Gina into rehab right after the club incident. The rehab place said Gina has never left the facility. So she's not the one who painted your car."

"Then who is? And where is my car? I really don't want to be obligated to anybody for the loan of that Beemer anymore, Jake. I can't even pay my own rent yet. Plus, who knows when somebody will decide to paint this new car." I took a deep breath. "I hate coincidences. I don't believe in coincidences. Something is totally going on here."

He narrowed his eyes. "I'm thinking you need a security camera that covers your parking lot, especially if you're going to work late. I'll have Wrench stop by and set you up."

I shook my head. "I can't afford it. Seriously, I'll keep an eye out, but no more help or hardware, Jake."

"Okay. No more free rides. When you need investigative services, you use my firm. It's like a referral network. How's that?"

I wasn't too proud or too stupid to take advantage of the easy fix for my pride. "Okay, if you're really sure. I have to admit I'd be glad to have a little extra security. This is all getting to me in a big way."

"All right. I'm out of here. But if you need something, call me. You have my cell phone number."

I stood up to shake his hand. "Thanks, Brody. I mean it. You've been great, for whatever weird reasons you have."

He ignored my hand and reached out and tugged gently on a strand of my hair. "I'm just a weird guy, Vaughn. And you're welcome."

Then he left, leaving me standing there, staring after him, trying to think of all the reasons why getting more deeply involved with him on any level was a bad idea.

At that very moment, I couldn't think of a single one.

Chapter 27

Since I couldn't concentrate, I didn't stay long at the office. We all packed up and left together at around five. Then I went home and climbed into bed and stayed there the rest of the night, only waking up long enough to drink a glass of milk and take a couple of Tylenol.

Maybe it was the shock, or maybe it was the sheer exhaustion, but I didn't dream at all.

In the morning, I woke up before the alarm went off and stared at the clock, wondering what had happened to me. Stalkers, humiliation in court, and dead bodies. I was starting to think that leaving my boring life, boring job, and boring husband in Ohio had been the worst mistake of my life.

I showered and got ready for work in a weird funk, unable to shake the sadness and feeling of loss that swamped me. I had to work on Charlie's case today and file for a restraining order in Mrs. Zivkovich's case, and work on any number of details in my *pro bono* cases. I didn't have time to feel sorry for myself, or homesick, or whatever I was feeling.

One mental pep talk and one stale English muffin later, I was out the door, only to stop dead and stare in surprise. The BMW was gone, and my ugly Honda was back in my driveway. Except it wasn't quite as ugly.

It was . . . pink.

Hot pink.

Emily stepped outside and waved hello, then started

across her lawn toward me. I met her halfway. "Let me guess—you have my keys again?"

She laughed. "Yes, I saw that very nice Jake Brody when I went for my morning jog. Here are your keys, and he said to tell you the cameras are installed, whatever that means."

"Did he explain why my car looks like a giant bottle of Pepto-Bismol?"

We both looked at the car. "I think it looks cute," she said. "Plus, you'll never, ever have to worry about confusing it with somebody else's car at the mall. That happens to me all the time with the minivan."

I blinked. "But . . . it's pink. *Pink!* I'm a trial lawyer. I can't drive a pink car. I'll be laughed out of court."

I remembered the fiasco of the day before. "Again."

Emily laughed again. "I'm sure all the other lawyers will be jealous. Anyway, I tried to call you but your cell phone said messages over limit or something. Did you turn it off?"

"Well, kind of. It was a long day. What's up?"

"Oh, we just wanted to see if you felt like going to a picnic with us this weekend. No rush on deciding; just let me know sometime by Saturday." A sudden shriek pierced the air from her house, and she rolled her eyes. "Guess I'd better go. That was the 'Joker is ready to hit Ricky in the head with something' shriek. Have fun in your cool car."

She walked back toward her house. Only Emily would think a hot pink car was cool. Then again, she was a poker queen, so she *was* kind of trendy . . .

Shrugging, I headed for my neon car, chanting my new mantra: "Minor detail. Minor detail. Minor detail."

By the time I'd made coffee and turned on my computer, Mr. Ellison showed up and came thundering down the hall to my office, yelling my name. "December! December, are you here yet?"

"I'm in here," I said.

"I got you a present to cheer you up," he said, heaving a worn duffel bag up on my desk. Today he wore a pair of purple pants with an orange shirt in his continuing tribute to the colorblind everywhere.

I looked down at the bag. "Another toaster?"

He snorted. "Of course not. Although, doesn't toast taste better from that old toaster? There's something about it that makes toast taste special."

"Probably the rust," I muttered, then started thinking about rust and Mars and blood and had to suck in a deep breath. "So what's in the bag?" I asked, trying to distract myself from visuals of dead men.

Mr. Ellison started to talk, but then the bag moved.

And it barked.

"What the heck?" I unsnapped the top and looked inside. The tiniest ball of fur and wrinkles I'd ever seen peered up at me.

"What is it?" I asked Mr. Ellison.

He rolled his eyes. "You lawyers aren't as smart as you think you are, if you can't recognize a dog."

"I recognize a dog, but why did you put a dog in a bag? No, better yet, why did you put a dog in a bag on my desk?"

We both looked down at the dog in the bag. It was wiggling all over and squirming. Then it started to climb out of the bag, and I pulled the side of the bag up higher.

"Do something!" I said.

"She wants you to hold her," he said.

"I don't know how to hold a dog. And that's not really a dog, is it? Isn't it just a puppy? I don't know what to do with a puppy. I don't have time for a puppy!"

Meanwhile, the puppy, who evidently didn't understand Human, had figured a way out of the bag and was climbing across my desk right toward me. I put my hands out to stop it, but it climbed right over my arm and launched itself in the air toward me, knocking my empty coffee cup over with its hind leg.

"Mr. Ellison, this is very . . . um, sweet of you, but I really can't take care of a puppy. You'll have to take it back," I said, trying to hold eight or ten pounds of squirming puppy away from my face and stop my heart from melting into a big, gooshy puddle.

Max came in just then. "Hey, guys, I—*awwwww!* When did you get a pug, D? What a cutie baby lovey-dovey!" She rushed over and plucked the puppy out of my arms and held it up. "Oh, look at the precious baby girl."

"It's a girl? How can you tell?"

She laughed. "Pretty much the usual way. A lack of any boy equipment."

I felt my face heating up. "That's kind of private. I wasn't exactly staring at its—at her equipment. And I can't keep a puppy, no matter how cute she is."

Or how much I want to keep her.

Mr. Ellison shoved his hands in his pockets and grinned at me. "You need somebody. All alone, no husband, all this bad stuff happening to you. A puppy will fix you right up. Anyways, I can't take her back. The owner had to move into the nursing home, and she ain't likely to come out, with a double broken hip."

I shook my head again. "I'm sorry, but then I guess you'll have to take her. I'm at work all day. It wouldn't be fair to the dog. Or you can take her, Max."

Max gently placed the puppy back in my lap and smiled. "I think Mr. Ellison's right. You do need a puppy. Look, she likes you."

I looked down at the puppy, and watched as she turned

around on my lap three times, shedding a couple of inches of dog hair in the process, and then curled up and immediately went to sleep. Something cold and clenched deep in my stomach warmed up and let go, which was bad enough, but then I felt it.

That little twinge under my left rib cage.

I may have mentioned how much I hate that twinge. It always means I'm getting ready to do something stupid.

I sighed and thought for a moment, hardly even realizing I was petting the puppy. Then I put on my serious lawyer face and looked at each of my scheming employees in turn. "Two conditions. First, she's a company dog. She comes to work with us during the day. We'll set her up with a bed and toys in the file room with Mr. Ellison so she has company and stays out of sight when we have clients in. Second, we all agree to joint custody. We take turns taking her home at night. Otherwise, she goes to the pound."

I held my breath, knowing that there was absolutely no way I could take the little furball to the pound, but hoping they wouldn't call my bluff.

Max caved first. "Absolutely! Little Puggsley will be a sweetie. And I bet she'll even be helpful on *pro bono* days. She can play with the kids while you talk to their parents."

Mr. Ellison shrugged. "Sure. I take her for a walk, I'm gonna score bigtime. Dogs are babe magnets."

Max and I both shuddered. "Only if you promise no details," I said. "Now what's her name?"

"She's only about four months old, and doesn't really answer to any one thing. She's been called about a dozen different baby talk names," he said.

"Well, she needs a name. What about Puggsley?" said Max.

"*Euwww.* Puggsley for a pug? No, that's too ordinary.

What about Brennan, after Supreme Court Justice Brennan?" I asked. "She even kind of looks like him."

Max and Mr. Ellison both booed. "None of your fancy-pants name, December," he said. "If I'm gonna have part custody, she needs a manly kind of name."

I looked down at the tiny ball of fur in my lap. "What exactly did you have in mind?"

"I've got the perfect name," he said. "Razor Fang!"

Razor Fang picked that exact moment to stand up, yawn, and pee in my lap.

After Max and Mr. Ellison took our still-unnamed puppy off for the pet store to buy supplies, and I finished rinsing my skirt out, I sat down just as my phone rang. "December Vaughn."

"It's Sarah Greenberg. I wanted to . . . apologize for the way our first conversation went and make a kind of peace offering," she said, sounding like she was swallowing broken glass.

I'm guessing apologies don't come all that easily to her.

"That's very nice of you. I wasn't all that happy about the way we started off either. I was hoping we could cooperate on these cases," I said, willing to meet her halfway.

"Great! I have a little boat out at the Orange Grove marina. Why don't you meet me out there at seven and we'll have drinks and get to know each other a bit?" I could hear the relief in her voice, which made me wonder why it was so important to her that I'd agreed.

"I'm not that sure of my evening plans. How about lunch instead?" I didn't have any plans for the evening, but I didn't want Sarah Greenberg to see the Pink Mobile either.

"No, lunch won't work. I have a memorial service for one of our associates today. Tragic, really. He committed suicide. I guess the law was too much for him. So, drinks at seven? See you then."

"Okay, we—"

Click.

She didn't exactly sound all broken up about her colleague's death. I did a mental shrug and wrote a note on my calendar. I was curious enough about Sarah and what exactly was going on with her, Addison Langley, and the insulin cases to find a way to get out there at seven. What I needed was a way to read her devious little mind, and . . .

Emily. I needed a psychic, and one happened to live next door to me.

Before I could pick up the phone to call her, it rang again. When I answered, I felt a prickle on my neck. I'd inherited the prickle from Aunt Celia, who claimed it meant trouble was on the way. The prickle was usually right.

"This is Matt Falcon."

Hmmm.

"Hello, Matt. How are you? What can I do for you today?" I used my calm, cool, and collected voice, hoping that through some bizarre fluke of physics or universal timewarp, he hadn't heard about my idiotic performance in court yesterday.

"I'm fine. Mostly I was wondering if I could help you. I heard about yesterday."

So much for calm, cool, and collected. "So did the rest of the Orange Grove Bar, I'm assuming. Look, I don't know where that stuff on the Founding Fathers came from. I took some cold medicine, and I think it affected my brain. That's it. It was the cold medicine! I—"

"December? I'm talking about the murder at MOSH. Are you all right?"

"Oh. That. Isn't that outside of your jurisdiction?"

"Yes, more's the pity. We never get any good murders in Orange Grove," he said, voice filled with regret.

I held the phone out and stared at it, mouth open, then put it back to my ear. "You're sad that people aren't viciously murdered in Orange Grove, is that what you said to me?" My voice sounded a little shrieky, even to myself.

"No, no, that's not what I meant at all, of course. It's . . . I'm very happy that our residents aren't being murdered. It's just that working a case like that—well, you used to play in the big leagues. You must know what I mean."

Unfortunately, I did know what he meant. Working on cases where a couple of hundred dollars were at stake, like some of my *pro bono* cases, didn't have the same thrill as going into battle when millions of dollars rode on the outcome.

I didn't much like what that said about either one of us, but I did understand it. It would be like an NFL player training for years, but never allowed to play in anything but off-season games. Or what Dad had told me about why he liked going off to sea and leaving us for months at a time. "You don't train for the big leagues and want to sit on the bench, Pumpkin."

For a prosecutor, murder was the big leagues.

For me, it was something I never, ever wanted to face again.

"Are you there?" His voice cut into my mental wandering, and I sighed and hoped I'd snap out of my haze someday.

"I'm here, Matt. Big leagues, blah, blah. What's up?"

"I'm sorry to be so blunt, but if you're involved in a

criminal matter, I can help you. If you need somebody to talk to about your contacts in the drug business, I know people at the DEA. Also, we have special programs in Florida for impaired attorneys."

It took me a beat, but I got it. "WHAT?? You think I'm—you think I had something to do with that man getting killed? Hey, buddy, I'm the innocent victim here. I didn't even know him. Well, I may have talked with him on the phone, but that was for, like, thirty seconds."

"Well—"

I cut him off. "Well, *nothing.* I. Do. Not. Do. Drugs. I never have done drugs. I'm the most boring, law-abiding person you know. I have to be desperate even to take a Tylenol. I don't have drug associates or drug contacts. I don't even think I have prescription drug benefits on my health insurance!"

There was a small silence. "I have no idea what you're talking about. I'm only offering to help here. If you change your mind, call me. Oh—and would you like to have lunch with me this week?"

I stared at the phone again. "You think I'm a drug user with contacts who probably had something to do with a murder, and yet you want to take me to lunch?"

He laughed. "Live on the edge, that's my motto."

"Date sane men, that's my motto. No, thank you."

"If you change your mind . . ."

"I know. I have your number. Good-bye, Mr. Falcon." This time, I hung up first.

The bell Max had installed on the front door jingled, and I heard Max and Mr. Ellison chatting. I stood up to go investigate our new small and furry colleague's purchases, but my phone rang again. As much as I wanted to ignore it, I picked it up.

"December—"

"This is Croc," a low and gravelly voice said. "I got your letter. You'd better stay out of my business, bitch, or I'll make life real bad for you."

"You're a little late for that," I said, rolling my eyes. I grabbed a pad of paper to jot down the time and essence of the call for the restraining order and the police.

"What? Look, I'm not messing with you. Stay out of me and that old bag's business. Or else."

The word choice struck me. "Or else? Is that you? Did you buy some Claritin after all? The allergies seem to be clearing up."

"What the hell are you talking about? Are you crazy? Shut up and mind your own business, that's all I've got to say."

"Wonderful! A concise criminal. My favorite kind. Usually you're all so long-winded," I said, trying to keep him talking so I could decide whether or not it was the same voice as my sinus stalker.

He wasn't going for it, though. "This is gonna be your only warning."

Chapter 28

After a quick lunch, I spent the afternoon working on Charlie's discovery and preparing questions to ask my experts, talking to Mrs. Zivkovich and figuring out how to file a restraining order against Nervil, aka Croc, and taking half a dozen trips outside to try to convince our new puppy to pee on actual grass.

By the time I brought her in from our sixth walk around the square of grass in back of the offices, we were both worn out, but triumphant.

"There was actual pee!"

Max and Mr. Ellison broke into spontaneous applause. The puppy gave us a startled look, then plopped down on her butt and fell asleep sitting up. I caught her as she started to fall sideways and handed her to Max. "Your turn. I had to stand by while she peed all over the place. My dignity may never recover."

She put the pup in the new fake leopard-fur bed that sat on the floor next to Max's chair, where she rolled over on her side and started snoring. Loudly.

Max grinned at me. "Where'd she do it?"

I snickered. "Outside the dentist's office, of course. Mean old man."

The phone rang, and I closed my eyes. "I can't take any more phone calls, Max. Tell them I'm not here."

She answered and listened for a moment. "Yes, I under-

stand. Please hold for Ms. Vaughn. But—what—okay.
She'll be right there."

I opened one eye, afraid to ask.

Max looked worried. "That was the owner of Orange
Grove Antiques. She's holding Bear Anderson for at-
tempted theft. She says Bear gave her your name, and
if you don't go down there right now, she's calling the
police."

I groaned. "Fine. Did you get an address?"

"I know the way. I'll write down directions, but they're
kind of confusing, because it's back in a cul-de-sac-y area.
Call me on your cell if you get lost."

I found the antique store with only three wrong turns, and
steeled myself for what I was going to have to deal with inside. As I started to open the door, a wrinkly face popped
up in the window next to the door and stared at me, tongue
hanging out.

It was so unexpected I jumped a little, then looked again.
It looked exactly like a plus-size version of Razor Fang, er,
my new puppy. Then another dog just like it jumped up beside it. Their matching wrinkly, smiling faces made me
smile, in spite of the fact that my newly freed criminal
client was headed for the big house.

I wonder if they still use cigarettes for money in jail. I
wonder where I can buy him some cigarettes.

I gently pushed the door open, worried about hitting any
dog noses with the glass, then glanced to my right. Now,
three identical faces stared at me, all grinning, and I was a
goner. I tentatively reached a hand out, and when they all
started wiggling their entire bodies, I had to pet everybody.

"Aren't you the most beautiful babies? Oh, look at that sweetie."

I knelt down to pet them and they all tried to climb in my lap at the same time. "Oh, you are just like my new puppy, but even more wrinkly. Okay, okay, there's enough pets and ear scratches for everybody." I started laughing, thinking that maybe Mr. Ellison had been right about the dog thing. It was certainly hard to be anxious when you were petting one of these charmers.

A dry voice cut into my cuddlefest. "They seem to like you, but that don't mean much. They like most everybody."

I looked up and a woman old enough to be an antique herself stood by the counter, shooting eye laser beams at me. "I'm Lucinda. You say you have a pug pup?"

I stood up, attempting to brush all the hair off my skirt, then gave it up as a lost cause. "Yes, as of today. I sort of adopted a four-month-old pup, because her owner had to go into a nursing home. I don't know anything about raising a puppy, though, and it looks like you must know a lot. If you have any advice, I'd sure appreciate it. I want to take good care of her."

Lucinda smiled and seemed to warm up considerably. "Well, I'd allow as I have a good bit of advice to give about pugs. Been raising champions for near twenty years. Is yours a purebred or a mix?"

"I don't really know. I didn't think to ask. She looks exactly like yours, except smaller. Curly tail and all, although it droops kind of straight when she sleeps. Does it matter?"

"Nope, not a bit, when it comes to loving a dog. Might make a bit of difference in feeding requirements and so forth. You'll need to get her to a vet and figure it out, if the owner don't have papers on her."

A voice called my name from the back of the store. "Miss Vaughn? Is that you?"

Oh, crap. I forgot my poor client.

Lucinda's warmth iced over again. "That your client?"

"Yes, he is. What did he take?"

"He didn't take nothing. But he was fixing to, before I caught him. I confess, I don't rightly know what to do with him," she said, shaking her head. "Turns out he's kind of a savant about antiques. Knew which glaze was on the original and which was on the reproduction of a particular type of pottery that comes from—"

"Well, maybe we can work something out?" I asked, pasting a huge, hopeful smile on my face.

She narrowed her eyes thoughtfully. "Mayhap we can."

Twenty minutes later, Bear had a new job, Lucinda had a new employee, and I had a new obligation: to make good if Bear messed up.

Oh, goody.

Chapter 29

After I'd picked up my new puppy and all of her gear, we headed for home. She didn't agree with the safety concept of traveling in her new zippered travel bag and managed to work the zipper open, climb out, and crawl into my lap. I tried putting her back, but she wasn't having it. If matching stubborn personalities make for good owner-pet relations, we were in great shape already.

As I drove up to my house, Emily and the kids were in the front yard, splashing in the sprinkler. When I held up the puppy, everybody started shrieking and running toward me. I had no place to hide.

"*Awww,* she's adorable! Can I hold her? What's her name?" Joker was jumping up and down with excitement, arms stretched up for the dog. "We want a puppy, but Mommy says no until we're big enough to be asponsible for the poopy and stuff."

Ricky didn't jump on me, being a very mature six-year-old, but I could tell it was killing him. "Miss December, that is a Chinese pug. They come from China, which is a country where they speak Chinese," he said, looking exactly like a miniature professor.

I grinned at Emily, who was jumping up and down as much as her daughter, both of them dripping wet and in matching pink swimsuits. On anybody else, it would have been too cutesy. On Emily, it worked somehow.

"Oh, let me hold her, let me hold her!" she begged.

I handed the puppy, whose entire body was wiggling in a frenzy of excitement, to Emily, who promptly sat down in the grass with her and let the kids pet her. "What's her name, Miss December?" Ricky asked.

I sighed. "Maybe you can help me with that. So far the nominations are Puggsley and Razor Fang, and I don't like either one."

Emily laughed as the puppy climbed up her shirt, frantically licking any human body part that came within range. "She isn't really a Razor Fang type, if you ask me."

Glancing at my watch, I realized I had less than an hour until my meeting with Sarah at the marina. "Emily, I have a huge favor to ask . . .

Forty-five minutes later, a dry and dressed-up Emily and I were on our way to the marina, leaving my new puppy in the loving and slightly sticky hands of Ricky and Elisabeth. Rick Senior had said he'd take them all to the pet store for more supplies, if I didn't mind, and I'd thanked him about a dozen times.

Emily leaned back against the seat and sighed as we drove off. "You have the life. Nobody climbing all over you, peace and quiet all the time, no need to play in the sprinkler ever, ever again."

"I was actually thinking that very thing about you," I said. "Wonderful husband, great kids, and of course, the poker champion thing. No pressure to pay employees a salary, no humiliating yourself in court, and definitely no finding dead bodies."

"What?" She jerked her head around to stare at me. "Dead bodies? What?"

I filled her in on the previous day's events as she stared

at me, eyes wide and mouth gaping open. "Wow. Are you okay? No, that's stupid. Of course you're not okay. I'm so sorry."

"No, I'm not really okay. I keep seeing that poor man, and the way his neck . . . well. Let's just say that I hope the visual goes away really soon."

She shook her head. "I'm thinking playing in the sprinkler isn't so bad after all."

"Plus, you love it. Anybody can be around you for five minutes and know you love being a mom."

She grinned. "It's true. The little heathens drive me nuts, but I love them desperately. Sometimes I long for a free evening, though."

"That's easy enough. I'd love to babysit once in a while. Sitting alone in that house drives me nuts. Just tell me what to do. They eat real food, right? Nobody is in diapers?"

"Um, yeah. Real food, and nobody in diapers. That's a lovely offer, and after you've been around them a few more times, we might just take you up on that. Rick and I haven't been out to eat to a restaurant that doesn't offer crayons with the menus in longer than I like to remember."

"No problem," I said. "I'm a trial lawyer. How hard can babysitting a couple of kids be?"

She burst into laughter. "Oh, honey. You are so going to eat those words."

As we pulled into the marina parking lot, still chuckling, I wondered how I'd ever figure out which boat (ship?) was Sarah's. They all looked the same to me, but of course, I didn't know anything at all about boats or ships or sailing. Kind of ironic, considering my dad was in the Navy for twenty-two years, but there you have it.

They were beautiful and screamed money, money, lots of money. I hadn't even realized normal, noncelebrity types could own boats that big. I scanned them as we drove by, and realized I didn't have to worry about finding Sarah's. It was a pretty safe bet that the enormous one in the third slip was hers. The name *Tortfeasance* was my first clue.

The fact that a woman with the exact same face as Sarah's picture on the Greenberg, Smithies website stood on the dock in front of it, checking her watch, was my second.

"Okay, like we talked about," I said to Emily as I pulled the car into a parking space. "Anything at all you pick up will be helpful. Anything. But she's a trial lawyer, too, and one of the best, from what I hear. So if you don't get anything, don't worry about it."

Emily shrugged. "I'm not sure if I'll be any help at all. My expertise is in a card game, not in a courtroom." She looked at the marina. "Or on a yacht. Is that a Hatteras?"

It was my turn to shrug. "Not a clue. These boats are way out of my price range, as you can tell by the luxury automobile we're currently driving."

"Ah, yes. The luxury Pink Mobile."

We climbed out of the car and went to meet Sarah, who'd walked toward the parking lot and stood staring at my car. Probably the first time a mere Honda had graced the hallowed parking lot of the Orange Grove Marina. I threaded my way through the dozen or so European cars parked there, trying to pretend I hadn't just driven up in a car the color of esophagus.

She was a small woman, maybe five and a half feet tall, if that, and slender. She had carefully styled bottle-blond hair, worn in the dreaded "lawyer bob" that my friends and I had made fun of all through law school. Her casual clothes were effortlessly chic and obviously designer. The diamond on her wedding ring nearly blinded me. All in all, she looked more like the aging tennis-playing, country-club-going wife of some corporate type than the brilliant trial lawyer she was reputed to be.

Of course, I'd been told I looked like an airheaded bimbo. Goes to show how much looks matter.

"Sarah! Sorry we're a few minutes late. This is my friend Emily. She is a huge yacht enthusiast, and since she and I had dinner plans this evening, I thought she'd get a kick out of seeing your boat. I hope you don't mind."

Sarah's eyes narrowed noticeably behind her designer Italian sunglasses, but she was too much of a political animal to insult Emily before she knew Emily's rating on the great food chain of life. In her St. John casual wear, Emily could have been a power player—or at least the wife of one.

"Of course not. I'm Sarah Greenberg of Greenberg and Smithies. And you are?"

"Oh, I'm so sorry. Emily Kingsley, Sarah Greenberg. I'm sure we'll all be great friends and having PJ parties in no time," I said, doing my "hearty good old girl" act. "So, the *Tortfeasance*. Fun name. Should we hop aboard?"

Sarah's gaze burned into me, stopping just short of a full-out glare. The woman seemed not to like me. *Go figure.*

"Yes, right this way. I'll give you the ten-dollar tour, and we can have drinks on the deck." She motioned us to follow her across the little bridge to the boat, and I tried not to wonder about whether or not I'd get seasick while we were parked at the dock. Or anchored, or whatever the term was.

"Do you have any Dramamine?" I asked.

Sarah shot me a scornful glance. "I'm sure you'll be fine. I was planning a cruise around the harbor while we have our drinks, but if you're the type who gets sick, we'll stay here."

Ah, the familiar "mine is bigger than yours" tactic.

I smiled sweetly. "No, not at all. I'd love to go on a cruise."

Emily wandered over from where she'd been leaning on the rail. "Sure. Rick can do the kids' baths tonight."

"Oh, do you have children? What do you do, Emily?" Sarah morphed back into polite and gracious hostess before my eyes. It was kind of scary to watch.

"Yes, I have two little monsters. I stay home with them mostly," Emily replied, seemingly very relaxed. Clearly, she didn't notice the undercurrents of tension at all. I was on my own. Sarah's act was too well honed for a nonlawyer to pick up on.

"Oh, I'm sure they're lovely," Sarah cooed. "What does your husband do?"

"He's an accountant with a firm downtown."

I saw the computer behind Sarah's eyes process the information and adjust Emily's ranking on the importance-o-meter in less than half a second. "Right," she said, eyes almost visibly glazing over. "Karl? Would you be so kind as to do a quick run for us, so we can enjoy the sunset and our drinks?"

A man dressed in some kind of nautical whites stepped forward from the shadows in the doorway. I hadn't even noticed him standing there, which was rather amazing, since he was enormous. One of those tributes to steroids, he was seriously top heavy, and his bald head gleamed in the light. I had no idea how he'd found a shirt with sleeves that fit over his biceps, but I tried not to stare at him. He did a little half-bow to Sarah. "Certainly, Miss Greenberg. Any particular destination?"

"Surprise me," she said, not even looking at him. But there was something between them—some little ripple of energy—and that tingly feeling in my head zinged. I studied him as he strode off, presumably for the steering wheel. Either he didn't like his boss one teensy bit, or he was sleeping with her.

Or both.

I glanced at Emily, but she was chatting with Sarah about the teakwood on the deck, blithely oblivious to any weird vibes. I was starting to seriously doubt her claims of reading tells on the poker circuit, but maybe that was a lot different from reading ordinary people.

Twenty minutes of small talk and a nice bottle of Shiraz later, we'd come far enough that I couldn't see the marina anymore. Sarah stood up, and Karl walked through the door toward us. Sarah smiled at Emily. "Emily, December and I need to discuss some boring legal matters. I'm sure you'd rather have a nice tour of the boat than sit around and listen. Plus, of course there is that pesky little confidentiality issue. Karl would love to take you on a tour, wouldn't you, Karl?"

Karl glowered at Sarah as if he'd rather tell her to go jump, but he mumbled his assent and Emily wandered off with him, still smiling and chatting. That woman could get along with King Kong.

It was a trait I envied. A lot.

We watched them go, and then Sarah refilled my glass.

"Trying to get me drunk and take advantage of my client?" I asked, only half joking.

She put the bottle on the table between us. "As I said on the phone, in the spirit of cooperation, I'd be delighted to help with your client's case. Mr. Seaver, was it? We'll let you do many of the secondary depositions in the case and we'll be content with a seventy-five percent split."

That made more sense than her first offer. "So Mr. *Deaver* is my client, but you'll help with all the heavy lifting, and I'll take twenty-five percent of the fee?"

She shook her head. "No, no. You'll take seventy-five, since you'll be doing the deps. Seriously, December, we're not trying to steal your client. We just want to help you out."

My suspicious nature zoomed into overdrive. "Sarah, I love that everybody in this town is trying to 'help me out' so much. It warms the cockles of my heart, whatever the heck cockles are. But it also makes my naturally cynical little self wonder why."

She rubbed her temples, as if I were giving her a big headache with my questions. Gee, I hoped so.

"Here's the deal. We both know you have no idea what you're doing," she said, voice flat. "I don't want my insulin cases screwed up because some pissant little newbie sets bad precedent. I have every other reported case signed, and we're going to move to consolidate in state court. Can't you put your own stupid pride and arrogance aside long enough to see what's best for your client?"

I hate to admit it, but I was nearly speechless. "You—I—wow. You are amazing. In spite of that gracious and heartwarming speech, I think I'll keep my client. Let's go back to the marina now, please."

She leaned forward. "I heard you were even harassing my ad production company over some clerical error on an invoice. Consider this a friendly warning. Stay out of things that are none of your business."

I stood up. "I get that a lot lately. You haven't been making any threatening phone calls, have you? By the way, a man from your ad company died yesterday. He was murdered. That sounds like somebody else is doing some harassing."

She jumped out of her chair and stomped across the deck, only stopping when she was right up in my face. "Right. I heard about your drug cartel problems. Trust me, if I threaten you, you'll know it. For example, we're pretty far out here, did you notice?"

I glanced out at the water, almost involuntarily.

She lowered her voice. "If a person happened to fall overboard this far out at sea, the body would probably never be found, don't you think?"

I shoved past her and tried not to let on that she was creeping me out with her lame B-movie threats. "Very funny. Now take me back to the dock."

Before she could say anything else, Emily and the captain arrived and effectively ended the conversation. Sarah transformed again into a smiley nice person and asked Karl to take us in, then she and Emily chatted on the return trip. I spent the time staring at the water, clutching the railing so tightly that my knuckles turned white. Not that I believed for an instant that Sarah would push me overboard.

It's just that I didn't exactly know how to swim.

Chapter 30

On the drive home, I started to feel like I'd been dropped down the rabbit hole. There was no way that a successful, powerful lawyer like Sarah Greenberg had really threatened me like a cheap goon. Maybe my own paranoia was driving me nuts.

"Although who wouldn't be paranoid considering the week I've had?" I muttered.

Emily twisted in her seat and folded her arms. "You think you're imagining things?"

I tried to shake off the self-doubt. "No, I don't, really. There are things going on underneath the surface. It was unfair of me to expect you to pick up on—"

Emily cut me off. "The yacht is a Hatteras. It sleeps six in three staterooms. The master is aft with a queen-size bed and private head and shower. The master stateroom also has a built-in TV and VCR. There are two guest staterooms. One is aft with upper and lower bunks, the lower being oversize, plus it has a closet. The private head and shower is across the companionway. The second stateroom is forward with two bunks, closet, private head and shower, washer and dryer."

She stopped to suck in a breath. "As you saw, the interior also features eggshell stain-resistant Berber carpet throughout, with in-shore protection runners. The main salon has a full-size couch, two chairs, and a helm seat. It's running her six grand a month for the boat payment. Another five for Karl's salary. That doesn't include routine maintenance and upkeep, which is fairly steep, or salaries for the crew she needs whenever she goes more than an hour out from the marina. Don't even ask about how much it costs to fill that gas tank. Plus, things are not all that stable for her, financially, across the board."

"What—"

"I'm not done. She and Karl had a hot and heavy thing going, but she dumped him recently for some twenty-something boy toy. Captain Karl isn't happy about it; he was way more than casual about her." She shuddered. "Although I can't imagine why. That woman gives me the creeps. She looks like she'd stab you in the heart just as easily as she would shake your hand."

I stopped at a red light and turned to stare at her. "You got all that from a quick tour of the boat with Captain Steroid? Do you have a photographic memory or what?"

She laughed and gave me a very smug look. "Didn't think I had it in me, did you? Oh, and whatever you and she were talking about, I'd be very wary of trusting. She had massive tells for deceit, bluffing, and outright lying all over her."

"Now the question is whether she bluffed about the cases or about throwing me overboard to sing with the fishies."

"I think that's *swim* with the fishies."

"Whatever."

We dissected Sarah's actions and comments all the way back home, but other than a general WARNING, DANGER, DANGER feeling, we didn't know what she was up to. I couldn't find any motive for her wanting Charlie's case so badly that she would give up seventy-five percent of the fee. The usual motive—money—didn't work if I were getting the lion's share of it.

"That leaves me with her stated reason: self-protection. She might really be terrified that I'd screw up her cases with bad precedent. If she's sitting on millions of dollars' worth of cases, and she has money problems, that would make sense," I said. But my tingly sense was still jangling.

"What's precedent, and why is it so important?"

"Oh, sorry. I forget and slip into legal-speak sometimes. Precedent is the weight of the decisions on similar issues that have come before your case. *Stare decisis* is the first Latin term you learn on day one of law school. It means 'to stand by things decided' and is the basis for our entire justice system," I said, kind of surprised that *stare decisis* had popped out of my mouth like that. I hadn't used the term since law school.

"So, for example, if your court decided that the defendant wasn't at fault, Sarah would be out of luck?"

"Not necessarily, because each individual case will have different medical factors. But if, for example, my court ruled a certain way on key evidentiary issues, the counsel in Sarah's cases would have a strong argument that their own judge must rule the same way. If it's a bad ruling for my client, it would hurt Sarah's clients, too."

I drummed my fingers on the steering wheel. "The problem is that I can see her point. I'd be afraid some rookie would set bad precedent, too, if the tables were turned, and I were still at True, Evers. But I'd never go about it this way. This is just weird."

By the time we arrived at home and walked into Emily's house, I was tired of thinking about it. It was past nine, and we followed the sound of the TV back to the family room, where two sleeping children and a sleeping puppy were all piled on top of Rick on the couch. He held up a finger. "Shh. They only crashed about fifteen minutes ago."

Emily dropped a kiss on top of his head, and I waved hello. "How was it? Was it awful?" I whispered.

He chuckled softly. "No, no. It was huge fun. I think we might end up with a puppy sooner rather than later, if this is how it's going to be. They all kept each other occupied the whole time. I was worried about our little daredevil, but Joker was really careful with Daisy."

"Daisy?"

"Ah. Daisy is the puppy's new name, according to the kids. They were quite adamant that Razor Fang simply won't do."

I considered the puppy, who was sprawled out, upside down, half on Ricky's shoulder and half on Joker's leg. She opened one eye and blinked at me, then her tail started to wiggle. I scooped her up and looked at her tiny wrinkled face. "Are you a Daisy?"

She sneezed in my face. "*Euuww!* If that's a yes, we're going to have to work on our communication skills." I tucked her under my left arm and wiped my face with my right sleeve.

"Daisy sounds great to me, guys. Thank you so much, both of you. Talk about the bestest neighbors of all time."

Emily picked little Joker up and Rick gently shifted Ricky to the side of the couch. "Hold on, December, and I'll help you carry Daisy's loot to your house," he said.

"Loot? What loot?"

"Oh, not much. Just a couple of toys. Oh, and a bone for chewing. Puppies chew. A lot." He grabbed a large plastic bag that had been on the floor near his legs and peered into it. "A new pink collar with rhinestones—Joker picked it— a leash with attached plastic fire hydrant with little plastic poopy bags—that was Ricky's contribution—food and water bowls, a blanket, and a dog bed. Oh, and there are two 'how to raise a puppy' books, a magazine about pugs, and a crate in the kitchen."

He stopped to take a breath. "Crate training is very important, according to the books."

Emily came back from putting Elisabeth to bed and kissed Rick on the cheek. "That's my man. He's a book guy."

I blinked. "Oh, wow. I had no idea that dogs needed so much stuff. Daisy now officially owns more than I do, at least until—or if—we ever find my furniture. Please tell me how much you spent, so I can pay you back for all that stuff."

He laughed and shook his head. "Oh, no way. I figure it's the barter system. We get you some supplies, and you're forced to pay us back in babysitting and dog loan hours for a year."

"Deal! Although I think I'm getting the better end of this deal . . ." I scooped up my snoring puppy, walked toward the kitchen, and picked up the dog crate.

"It looks kind of small," I said.

"It's supposed to be only big enough for her to stand up and turn around comfortably. That way, she can't go off in a corner and go potty," Rick said from the doorway. "Trust me, it's plenty big enough for her, even when she's full grown. Pugs only grow to be fourteen to eighteen pounds when they're adults."

I grinned. "You read that entire book, didn't you?"

"It was either that or watch some movie about dancing fairy princesses for the seven thousandth time."

Shuddering, I nodded. "I can see your point."

The three of us carried Daisy and all of her new posses-

sions over to my house, and I thanked my fabulous neighbors a dozen times or so before they escaped to their snore-
free home. I put Daisy the amazingly loud pug in her crate,
on her blanket, and went to wash the day and my makeup
off my face. I'd barely taken a step before I heard a pecu-
liar, high-pitched whining sound.

I froze, scanning the room for any sign of an intruder.
The house seemed empty, but the noise escalated in volume. It was coming from behind me.

I whipped around, ready to surprise my attacker, and
pinpointed the direction of the hideous noise. The crate. Or
to be specific, the tiny furball inside the crate. Daisy was
standing at the bars, whining pitifully.

"No, the book says you have to sleep in your crate, I
think," I said firmly.

She whined again.

I shook my head. "No, Daisy. Go to sleep."

She started to howl.

I let her out.

Really, what do those book people know anyway?

The alarm clock sounded, but I ignored it. Instead, I smiled
and burrowed deeper in the covers as Jake nibbled on my
ear.

Then he sneezed on my neck.

My eyes flew open. Dream Jake evaporated, and a
small, furry face grinned at me from the top of my pillow.
"*Euww!* Definitely no dog butt on my pillow. Move over,
you annoying hound." I used my firmest voice which, since
Daisy doesn't understand Human, apparently translated
into Dog as: Climb on my neck and lick my face.

So she did.

Luckily for puppies, they're irresistibly cute. Otherwise, the incessant snoring and the butt-on-pillow thing might lead to unfortunate results. "Do you have to go outside and pee on something, Daisy? That's right, you're Daisy."

She seemed to be getting used to her name, because she wiggled and wagged even more when I said it. I put her on the floor before all that wiggling led to peeing on my bed, and then I pulled on a pair of shorts to go with the T-shirt I'd slept in and headed for the back door.

At the last minute, I remembered the leash and collar, since the backyard wasn't fenced. "Add a fence to the list of urgent things to do the second I have any money," I mumbled as I fastened the ridiculous jeweled collar around her neck. Daisy tilted her head, as if to ask why my morning breath was even worse than hers. I scratched her silky ears for a moment, then led her outside.

Ten minutes later, she was still standing two inches from my right leg and obstinately refusing to do her doggy thing. "Look, you. I know you have to pee. You're a puppy. You drank all that water, you slept all night and snored like a freight train—and thank you very much, by the way, for the bags under my eyes—and now you have to pee. So do it already."

Emily's back door swung open, and Rick ambled out, already dressed for work. "Hey, December. Hey, Daisy," he called.

Daisy, fickle creature, nearly choked herself lunging on the end of the leash to get to him. "Whoa, wait up before you hurt yourself," I told Daisy, but I started over to talk to Rick. He'd read the doggy owner manual, after all.

Rick met us halfway, and bent down to pet Daisy, who threw herself in his lap. "She's probably trying to get away from me," I said. "I make her constipated apparently."

He laughed. "You have to walk around with her to get her motor started, I think."

We both looked down. Sure enough, Daisy was squatting perilously near my left foot, finally peeing. Then she walked around me a couple of times, until I was tangled in the leash, and contorted her body into a bizarre hunching shape.

"What the heck is she doing? Is she sick? She looks like she's in pain!" I said, freaking out. If I killed the new puppy on the first day, Max would never trust me again. Plus, okay, I had to admit that she was kind of growing on me.

Except, this new thing was . . . "Oh, that's disgusting!" She was pushing a huge trail of poop out of her bottom, but it was oddly connected and wouldn't fall down. "What *is* that?" I asked Rick, trying not to gag.

He bent over and looked. "It looks like she swallowed a hair," he said calmly, then straightened back up and looked at me. "Haven't you ever had a dog, December?"

I bit my lip. "Of course. Well, only actually for one day, because my dad found out and had a fit. Then we had to give it back. I've never stood around before and watched one poop, that's for sure."

I snuck a glance down again. Everything seemed like it . . . came out . . . fine. "Now what?"

Rick was trying not to roll his eyes, I could tell. "Now you pick it up so it's not lying in the yard attracting flies or the shoes of little children."

"I PICK IT UP?"

"Use your quiet voice, December," he said, laughing. "I'm right here. Remember that fire hydrant thing? See it on the leash? You unroll a plastic bag and turn it inside out with your hand and do this." He demonstrated a "pick up the poop with your bare hand only minimally covered with a thin plastic bag" trick, and then he pulled his hand out and tied the bag shut and held it out to me.

I blinked. "Can you hire people to do this? I'm practically broke, but I'm sure I can give up eating or something to afford a designated poop-picker-upper." He shook his head, still holding the bag o' poop out to me, and I had no choice but to take it.

As I walked back to my house, leash in one hand and poop—held as far away from me as possible—in the other, I wondered which part of the snoring/eating/pooping routine made dogs man's best friend?

Oh, wait. *Man's* best friend. If dogs were *women's* best friend, they'd be more into shoe shopping.

Chapter 31

Daisy again refused into climb into the travel case. I got the feeling she was only pretending she didn't understand Human when it suited her, because she'd had no problem with the word "breakfast." The twenty minutes it took us to drive to the office left me with a half-inch of dog hair on my skirt and jacket. Between the heat and the dog hair, I felt like I'd been tarred and feathered.

That's probably how I looked, too.

Max met me at the door, looking worried.

"Oh, no. What happened? I'm not sure I can take much more of this," I said.

"What? Nothing happened. I was just worried about the puppy. Remember the fish you had in high school?" She held out her arms to take Daisy, and I tried to brush dog hair off my clothes.

"That's so unfair," I said. "You didn't tell me that fish would eat each other. How gross and cannibalistic is that?"

She was too busy making ridiculous cooing and baby talk noises at the dog to answer, so I grabbed my briefcase and followed her inside. "By the way, her name is officially Daisy. Emily's kids named her last night and, since they bought about a thousand dollars' worth of puppy supplies, I figured I owed it to them."

Max held Daisy out and studied her wrinkly face. "She looks like a Daisy. A precious wittle bittle flower."

"Okay, don't make me gag. Remember the deal: You

and Mr. Ellison have to keep her occupied during office hours. She snores really loudly, by the way, so you may want to move her bed into the file room so she doesn't scare the clients."

The phone rang, and Max answered it, listened for a moment, then handed it to me. "There's furniture news. She doesn't sound happy."

I took the phone. "Yes? You found my driver? Please tell me you found my driver."

The dispatcher's familiar nasal tones grated in my ear. "Well, not exactly."

"Then what exactly? This is ridiculous!" I grabbed a pen and Max's note pad to take notes. It was time for action.

"I know, I know. This *is* kinda ridiculous. We have some news, though. Your guy got a speeding ticket, so he's in a hurry to get your furniture there, I'm thinking," she said.

"Where?" I asked.

"Where what?"

"Where did he get a speeding ticket?"

"Oh. Um. Houston."

"HOUSTON?" I started scribbling furiously on the page. "Are you kidding me? Can we agree that Kentucky to Texas to Florida is *not* the most direct route from Ohio?"

"Oh, yeah. We agree. Look, I understand how you might be a tad upset—"

"A tad upset? Are you kidding? My furniture has been hijacked by a runaway truckdriver and you think I'm a *tad* upset?" I took a deep breath and lowered my voice. "I'm going to have to take some kind of legal action, you know. No threat, just a fact. I've got to either receive my stuff or else the money to buy new stuff, so you'd better file a claim with your insurance company."

"Well, that's another little problem," she said.

"What little problem?"

"We don't have insurance."

                       •

Reviewing the day's mail brought another shocker in the Deaver case. BDC had filed a joinder against its distributor. That meant that BDC was, in effect, suing its own distributor. I'd never seen this before in eight years of practice in drug cases. Either Addison was firing blindly, or BDC was absolutely convinced that the insulin defect did not occur in its own production process. I was still staring at the pleading when Max walked into my office.

"Okay, this is weird," I said.

"Everything you touch lately has been weird," she said. "You may want to specify."

I explained about the new development.

"That does sound odd."

"Charlie's former attorney named the distributor as a co-defendant. This is routine when you file a defective drug lawsuit—you want every possible deep pocket who may have liability in the suit."

I shook my head, tapping my pen on the desk. "But I'm really surprised by this. It's very rare that a distributor remain as a defendant. The tort laws protect those who only act as the transportation, with no opportunity to touch or tamper with the product in any way. Plus, it's extremely unusual that a manufacturer would be suing its distributor. The manufacturers usually indemnify their distributors and retailers through formal agreements early on in the case."

"Indemnify means acting as the backup or security in case of a loss, right?"

"Right. BDC must suspect tampering by somebody involved with the distributor."

"Or else BDC is trying to cover up its own negligence by suing other people," Max pointed out.

"No way. That's just not the way things work, and Langley, Cowan is no amateur to this type of lawsuit. There has to be a specific reason for this. I need for you to research the relationship between BDC and the distributor. We need to know what kind of business relationship they have. That will help us determine if BDC would risk that relationship unless it had a reason."

Max was already halfway to the door. "You got it. This case is way more interesting than those real estate deals I worked on at my old firm."

"What? You never got to meet Donald Trump?"

She laughed but kept going, leaving me to a morning of hard work following up on my other cases. Mr. Ellison came in at some point to mutter dire warnings about the fate of Mrs. Zivkovich's son-in-law Nervil, but Daisy distracted him, and the two of them went outside to commune with nature.

I made him take a plastic bag.

Detective Harris called to follow up on Richard Dack, but I didn't have anything new to add to the statement I'd given him before. Nor, much to Harris's dismay, did I want to talk about my "drug cartel," so it was a short phone call. He did tell me that Orange Grove Productions had confirmed that the date on the invoice was a clerical error—the ads had actually been filmed six weeks *after* that incorrect date—and that the company officially had no idea why the cameraman would have wanted to meet me.

"So, that's pretty much a dead end, Miss Vaughn. Although they did mention that they thought Dack had a little drug problem going on, which leads me right back to you." His voice turned cajoling. "I can't help you if you don't work with me, December. We can beat this thing together. Just let me help."

"Look, I may not be a criminal lawyer, but I'm still a trial lawyer. Don't bullshit a bullshitter, as they say. Besides, I've seen all those cop shows on TV. If I did have a drug problem—which I don't—you'd be the last person I'd tell."

He reverted to his gruff cop voice. "That's unfortunate. You'd be a natural for one of those TV specials. 'Hot Lawyers Behind Bars.' "

I shuddered. "Detective, you have no idea how much that just squicked me out. Thank you so much for sharing your perverted fantasies. I know I'll sleep better with you on the job. Now, if you don't mind—"

He barked out a laugh. "Actually, I *do* mind, but I can't see as I have much choice. You think better of this stubbornness, you know where to find me."

We hung up, and I'm sure he was thinking I was a sick and twisted human being, too. Ah, the joys of the justice system. The whole conversation depressed me so much I decided to go out for junk food.

Sometimes a girl needs french fries.

Max popped into my office around five, with Mr. Ellison trailing behind her, holding Daisy. "We made it through the entire day with no new assaults, threats, or actual crimes," she said, all perky.

"Which is how it should always be around here, considering we're a *civil* law firm," I said, not perky at all. "The Social Security disability paperwork on some of these *pro bono* cases is enough to drive a lesser attorney to drink.

Since I'm feeling a lot like a lesser attorney right about now, want to go to Mama Yang's?"

Max laughed. "I'd love to, but I can't. I'm taking Daisy to the dog park with a friend of mine who swears that dogs are guy magnets. It's my turn, right?"

Mr. Ellison tried to look disinterested, but didn't pull it off all that well, since he had a lap full of puppy. "Sure, I don't care. It's not like I ain't got nothing better to do than take care of some dog. If I'd wanted all that trouble, I would have kept her for myself."

I nodded. "Okay, then. You don't have to take a rotation on the puppy sleepovers, if you don't want to be bothered."

"Forget that! I already have a chart back in the file room with who gets what nights," he said. "That puppy is gonna have the hotties down t'the Seniors' going all gooey."

I grimaced. "Mr. Ellison, I really don't need to hear about your social life."

He snorted. "Yeah, you're jealous, on account of you don't have one."

Just because he was right didn't mean I had to admit it.

"I've called that Orange Grove Productions over and over, and they won't even talk to me anymore," he said.

Max nodded. "I haven't had any luck either. But they did just fax us a corrected invoice that puts the video shoot at a date *after* BDC reported a possible problem with the insulin and the recall." She slid the sheet of paper across my desk, and I scanned it.

"It's a new date, all right. But if this is just about a clerical error, why was Mr. Dack so hot to talk to me? Why all the cloak and dagger?"

"And who offed him?" Mr. Ellison asked.

"I don't see how the offing—I mean, the murder— could be connected to this invoice. I mean, that's got to be a coincidence, doesn't it? But the rest of it is still strange," I said.

"Cloak and dagger and offing. This is a weird job, and Miss Daisy and I are leaving you two conspiracy theorists and going to the dog park," Max said, taking Daisy from Mr. Ellison.

"Yeah, I need to go, too. Lots of stuff going on tonight. Don't work too hard, girlie," Mr. Ellison said.

I stood up to pet Daisy good-bye and walk everybody to the door, mostly to reassure myself that it was really locked, then I wandered around the office for a while. The problem was that I was getting that tingly feeling in my head.

Random coincidences don't fit into my "puzzle pieces" view of cases. When it comes to lawsuits, it has been my experience that there are very few coincidences. But— suddenly—I was surrounded by them.

The invoice.

The way Sarah and Addy had both pushed so hard for me to refer the case to Sarah.

Richard Dack.

All oddities on their own, but—combined—they made for a big ball of wrong.

I don't like big balls of wrong on my cases.

Worse, a very ugly suspicion was trying to form in the murky depths of my brain.

What if they knew?

I stopped pacing and blinked, wondering how I'd ended up in the file room, then headed for my office at a dead run. I needed to take some notes.

What if BDC knew earlier than they let on that there was a big, fat problem with the insulin? What if they spent crucial time working on getting their legal ducks in a row—

and maybe shredding documents—before they issued the recall?

What if Langley, Cowan was in on it? Or even worse, what if Langley, Cowan had advised them to do it?

I grabbed a white board I used for trial prep out of the closet and started diagramming my time line. If I assumed the invoice as originally dated was correct, then somebody was in some serious trouble. I needed to call my friend at the Food and Drug Administration and ask some "hypothetical" questions first thing in the morning.

I wrote SARAH GREENBERG??? in the middle and circled it. I couldn't figure out how she fit into the picture. She and Addy had completely opposite goals in these lawsuits; she wanted BDC to pay as much as possible, while he wanted BDC to get off scot-free.

How did that invoice wind up in the BDC production in the first place?

Was it possible that Sarah is in on it somehow? Could some terrible coverup be going on that would somehow result in favorable monetary settlements to the S&G clients? That would explain why both of them were so hot for me to transfer Charlie's case to them, but I couldn't bring myself to believe something so awful. From the defense lawyer, maybe. It has certainly happened before that a lawyer helped his client cover something up. But from the attorney on the other side of the case?

I shook my head. "I've been working with Mr. Ellison too long. Next I'll be talking about aliens and anal probes," I muttered.

Still, it was definitely time for some nonparty production requests to Orange Grove Productions. I wanted every piece of paper that had anything to do with that film shoot.

I reached for my keyboard to start drafting the document, smiling what Max would call my shark smile.

We'll just see how Sarah Greenberg responds to this.

As I opened the computer file, the buzzer on the front door sounded. I yelled for somebody to answer the door, then I realized that I was the only somebody still there. I headed for the front, my mind still on my discovery requests. As I walked out of the hallway to the lobby, I could see Charlie Deaver standing at the door. I hurried to unlock the door and let him in.

"Hey, Charlie, I'm glad to see you. How are you?"

He shook my hand, then started twisting his ball cap in his hands. "December, Greenberg and Smithies called. They said my old lawyer told them to call me."

He shuffled his feet a bit and then looked at me. "They told me you were bungling my case."

Chapter 32

"I should have shoved Sarah overboard when I had the chance," I muttered.

"What?" Charlie was chewing on the corner of his lip, and he looked moderately freaked out, so I tried to tamp down the steam boiling out of my ears.

"That's very interesting—not to mention completely unethical—in light of my current suspicions. Why don't you come back and have some coffee? I have something to show you," I said.

As he followed me back to my office, he made a few throat-clearing noises. "Look, I'm sorry, but I need to know what's going on with you. First, there was that article about the drugs, and now they say you're running around with known drug dealers who get murdered. I can't trust Faith's case to you if you're caught up in your own craziness, right?"

I stopped in the kitchen on the way and checked for coffee, but figured the sludge in the bottom of the pot wouldn't help, so I grabbed a couple of bottles of water from the fridge, and we went to sit down in my office.

"Who called you? Was it Sarah Greenberg?"

"No, it was some guy. I don't remember his name. He said that they have the home field advantage, because the judges in Claymore County love them and usually rule in their favor. So I'd be better off with them even if you weren't . . . didn't have drug issues." He mumbled the final few words, not looking at me.

I studied him for a long moment, trying to decide whether to share my suspicions at this early stage. "Oh, what the heck. The smarter thing might be to roll over, with the way they're going all full court press about this, but I have a tendency to get obstinate when people push me," I finally said. I stood up and pulled my whiteboard closer to us. "And since the people involved with this case are *really* pushing me, I want to show you something."

I used my diagram and told him of my suspicions about some kind of BDC cover-up. By the time I'd explained it all, Charlie was sitting straight up in his chair, eyes narrowed. He made the leap I didn't want to explain all by himself. "From the way things are going, it sounds like the defense lawyers might be in on it. But why is Greenberg and Smithies coming after my case so hard?"

I shrugged. "They have their stated reasons—that I'm too small to handle your case, so I'll run the risk of putting bad precedent, or bad judge's decisions, on the board. But I have a lot of experience with cases like this, so I'm a little suspicious."

I leaned the whiteboard against the desk. "Plus, none of this explains S and G taking the wholly unethical step of soliciting another lawyer's client like that. Not to mention that they could actually be sanctioned—punished—by the Bar Association for that crack about the judges here giving them the 'home field advantage.' That's casting aspersions on the integrity of the judicial process, and it's a huge no-no."

Although it did occur to me that I was getting my panties in a twist about a relatively minor ethics violation on the part of the same firm I suspected of covering up a defective drug. Naïve, much?

He shook his head. "I don't like anything about this, but I especially don't like being pushed. If S and G is practically in that BDC firm's pocket, who says they'll fight for my Faith like you would? Faith was the most honest person in the world. If they did something like this, she would want the world to know. I'm sticking with you, December, and I'm not signing any secret settlement agreements."

"That's good to hear, Charlie, because I think we should fight this one out. I don't think they'd be so worried if there weren't something big and bad to hide."

We sat there mulling that over for a few minutes, then he stood up. "I need to get going. Stay in touch, okay?"

I stood up and shook his hand. "I always do. I have a feeling BDC will want to set your deposition soon, so we're going to need to discuss that."

"Sure, just let me know," he said.

"Hold on, and I'll walk out with you. I just need to shut off a few lights." I walked through the place, flicking off lights on the way, and we left the office. He waited while I locked the door, then we both headed for our cars.

He quit walking and stared at my car as I opened the door. "Um, December, was your car pink the last time I saw you?"

I sighed. "No. It's a long story. Trust me, this is better than how it looked before."

He gave me a dubious look, but didn't ask. I waved to him as he got in his Ford Ranger and pulled out. Putting the Pink Mobile in gear, I started to follow Charlie, but then I saw a flickering light out of the corner of my eye, from the corner of the building. When I turned my head to look for it, it was gone.

"Great. Now I'm hallucinating lights. Those little green men can't be far behind," I mumbled, then pushed the lock button on my car in case aliens liked pink Hondas. As I drove off, I searched the darkness beside the building for any other flickering lights, but didn't see any. A cold tingle had taken up residence down my spine, though, and I spent more time watching my rearview mirror than the road in front of me on the way home.

By the time I pulled up in my driveway, I had a serious case of the jitters. First, a yellow sporty-looking car, like an old Camaro or something, had seemed to trail me a bit too closely. Then the Camaro turned off and a dark blue sedan took its place. The sedan followed me all the way to my street, but turned off before I'd rounded the final curve.

My hands were shaking as I fumbled for my keys at the door. Too many coincidences. Way too many coincidences. Concussions, dead bodies, and threats. I finally jammed the key in the lock, and somebody touched the back of my arm.

I screamed, dropped my purse, whirled around, and punched my attacker in the face. He jumped back, clutched his jaw with one hand, and said, "What the hell was *that* for, Vaughn?"

Oops. Well, the best offense is a good defense, right? Or something like that.

I poked Jake in the chest with my finger. "This is totally your fault. What kind of idiot sneaks up on a woman who discovered a dead body? Plus got a concussion? And a hot pink car? You scared me to death!"

He rubbed his jaw and grinned. "I scared *you* to death? You decked me! Pretty good right hook, too, Counselor. I may have to sue for assault."

I poked him again. "Get off of my sidewalk. Get out of my life."

He held up two paper bags, which I was finally noticing

smelled deliciously like Chinese takeout. "Are you sure about that? I'd hate for all this food to go to waste."

My stomach growled, and Jake laughed. "There's one vote for dinner."

Leaning down, I picked up my keys and purse, and unlocked the door. "Oh, all right. You can come in and eat, since you brought food," I said, trying to be gracious. It probably wasn't his fault that he was always around when my life blew up.

Or maybe it was.

I whipped around and held up a hand to stop him from following me inside. "Wait one minute, Brody. I want the truth right now. Are you stalking me for some nefarious purpose?"

He blinked, then grinned that slow, dangerous grin that made my brain cells go all mushy. "I've never known anybody who used the word 'nefarious' in conversation before, Vaughn. Maybe I have a fetish for women with big vocabularies."

I rolled my eyes, but moved away from the door and headed for the kitchen. "Well, we know it's not my big bazumbas," I muttered.

"What?"

"Nothing. You can put the food down here, and I'll get out my lovely fine dining china." I opened the nearest cupboard and grabbed the paper plates, trying not to notice how great he looked in jeans and a plain black T-shirt.

Trying really, really hard not to notice.

Jake looked around the house, then down at the paper plates, as he started opening the bags. "I've been meaning to ask you, where is your furniture, Vaughn? Or is that some kind of deep, dark secret?"

"No, no secret," I said, sighing. "Well, the only secret is where in the heck my furniture is these days."

He quirked an eyebrow at me, so I told him the story of my happy-go-lucky nepotist, bender-going, furniture-thief driver.

When I was done, he whistled softly. "You're a magnet, aren't you? A tall, beautiful trouble magnet."

I scooped a big pile of fried rice on my plate carefully, then glared at him. "It's not my fault . . . did you say beautiful?"

"Maybe not with your mouth hanging open like that."

I resisted the urge to stab him with his own chopsticks and carried my plate over to the card table. "I only have water and Diet Coke in the fridge, but help yourself."

He opened the other bag. "I brought beer. Want one?"

I started to say no, then stopped. "Why not? If ever a week deserved a beer, it would be this one."

He opened the bottles and brought them to the table, and we made short work of the food, not talking much. By the time we'd cracked open our fortune cookies, I was stuffed.

"Ha! 'Nothing can keep you from reaching your goals.' Yeah, right. This week, everything is keeping me from reaching my goals," I said.

"One battle isn't the war, Vaughn." Jake looked at his own fortune and smiled, but didn't read it to me.

"Hey! The rule is that all fortunes must be read out loud, Brody," I said, snatching the piece of paper. I read it and groaned.

" 'Trouble will arrive in the shape of a woman,'" he said. "Seems pretty apt to me, even if I am a nefarious stalker."

"That's not exactly what I said. Anyway, thanks for the food."

"You're welcome," he said. "Now, how about we talk?"

"About what?" My DANGER, DANGER alert shifted into high gear.

"About your client Mrs. Zivkovich, and how her son-in-law cleaned out her savings account today," he said.

I drained the rest of my beer before answering, frantically trying to remember if I'd ever mentioned Mrs. Z to him.

I hadn't.

Putting the bottle down on the table between us, but near enough so I could grab it if I needed a weapon, I still said nothing. I stared at him in silence.

He stared back.

Great. Now you think you can outstare a Navy SEAL. They probably take classes in the psychology of eye contact, you moron.

I finally had to blink. "Fine, fine. So somehow in the magic psychic world that is the wonder of Jake, you know about Mrs. Zivkovich, her son-in-law, and the fact that she's my client. Care to elaborate? Electronic listening devices? Retasked a satellite? Planted a tracking chip in my underwear?"

He laughed. "Actually, Henry told me. But let's go back to that underwear idea for a minute . . ."

My face flamed up to the color of the Orange Grove fire truck. "Forget underwear. Who's Henry?"

"Henry Ellison. Your employee," he said, giving me a weird look.

"Oh, right. Mr. Ellison. I keep forgetting he has a first name. What is he doing talking about my cases? That's a violation of client confidentiality. I'm going to have to fire him," I said, not as happy about the idea as I should have been.

"No, you don't. He didn't violate anything. He mentioned that Mrs. Zivkovich was a 'real looker,' and I extrapolated from there. Especially since I knew her car had been in your parking lot."

"He's got to quit hitting on the clients. If—*what?* What do you mean, her car had been in my parking lot?"

He stood up and started collecting dirty dishes, not quite looking at me. "Nothing."

"Are you spying on me, Brody? I can get a restraining order against you, too, you know!"

"Right. Like the one against Croc. Except all that did was piss him off, so he cleaned out her bank account, and now he's planning to leave town. Maybe do a snatch and grab on his mouse of a wife and his infant son on the way. Great job, Counselor," he said, shoving plates and bags in the trash.

I jumped up. "We have to call the police. We have to warn her. We have to—"

"We don't have to do anything, because he's sleeping off a drunk right now," he said, putting a hand on my arm. "Relax. Wrench is keeping an eye on his place and will call me the minute Nervil does so much as roll over. I think you can call your client in the morning."

"How do you know? Maybe he'll wake up in the middle of the night, and—"

"He won't, trust me."

I folded my arms across my chest. "How do you know? What aren't you telling me?"

He leaned back against the counter. "There's a lot I'm not telling you, and it's probably going to stay that way. But here's a tip. If I were a scuzzbag who'd just raided my mother-in-law's bank account, I'd have it in cash and ready to go with me. Be sure and mention that to the police when you call them."

"I—you—oh, fine. You be all Mr. Secret, and I'll just go along. That's how this is going to work, right?" I started to walk past him to the door, but he gently caught my arm in his hand.

I pretended the touch of his hand was not burning three layers of skin off my arm. That electric tingle thing never happened either, I told myself. But I couldn't help gasping a little.

Slowly, I turned to face him. "Is there something else? You've finalized all of the Social Security paperwork for the rest of my clients perhaps?"

He pulled me closer. "No, but there's always tomorrow."

"Look, Jake, this is a bad idea. I think—"

He touched my face. "You think a lot. Must get tiring, having such a huge brain, Counselor."

I felt his breath on my face and tried not to melt into a speechless blond puddle on the floor. Talk about deprived hormones going into overdrive. "Why don't you ever call me by my name?" I whispered.

"I'm going to kiss you now, December," he said. Then he touched his lips to mine, and my eyes fluttered shut, and my entire body seemed to relax into his.

The man is a great kisser.

About three seconds before my nerve endings spontaneously combusted, he stopped kissing me and stepped out from between my limp body and the kitchen counter. I stood there, blinking, wondering what the hell just happened.

He smiled at me again. "Good night, December," he said, then he walked over to the door.

"What? You can't just kiss a person and then leave!" I

shouted. "This is not some Western movie where you get to ride off into the sunset, guns blazing, after you kissed the girl."

He shook his head, but didn't say anything. As he turned the doorknob, I tried to think of a blistering put-down, but my brain cells weren't back to correct working order. So I stalked out to the foyer after him. "You, you, you—cowboy! Fine! You want to kiss and leave, fine. It wasn't all that great of a kiss anyway."

I shoved him out of the way, grabbed the doorknob, and flung the door open. That's when it exploded.

Chapter 33

"Get down!" Jake grabbed me and shoved me to the floor, landing on top of me. Something burned the top of my shoulder, but I didn't think it was lust-related this time. It hurt too much. I shoved at him. "Get off me! You weigh a ton."

My hands connected with the muscles that were hidden under his T-shirt, and I realized why he was so heavy. If I could breathe, the position might have been kind of sexy.

No air, not so much. "Get off! I can't breathe."

He shifted his body to the side and in front of me, blocking me from the doorway. Somehow, he had a gun in his hands.

"What just happened? Why is my shoulder burning? What was that noise? Was that a bomb?"

He glanced back at me and looked at my shoulder, then shifted to stare out the door again. "It was a shotgun blast, Vaughn. Somebody shot the hell out of your doorframe."

He rolled up to a crouch, then stood, still aiming the gun out into the darkness of my front yard, then he stepped out on the porch and scanned the yard. "Damn. I heard a car revving up right after I dropped you to the floor. That was probably the shooter taking off out of here."

He pulled a cell phone out of his pocket, and held his other hand out to pull me up, bumping the door shut with his shoulder. I was surprised it still closed, but there really didn't seem to be a whole lot of damage to the frame, considering how loud the explosion had been.

I snuck a peek at my shoulder, and almost fell back to the floor. "I'm bleeding!" I scrunched my eyes shut and tried to convince myself that the sight of blood didn't terrify me. Especially when it was my own.

Jake stepped closer and pulled the shoulder of my shirt to the side. "You got a splinter," he said, mouth tightening. "I could remove it, but I think you should have a doctor look at it."

My knees went a little swoozy at the words "remove it," but he caught me with an arm around my waist. "How about you sit down while I call for help?"

We walked back in the kitchen, and I collapsed onto one of the folding chairs, trying not to let the tears building up behind my eyes leak out. He touched the side of my face gently, then flipped open his phone and dialed.

"Hey, that's too many numbers to be 911. Who are you calling? I want 911," I said.

He glanced at me, then turned away and had a cryptic conversation over the phone that involved several very bad words I'd never actually heard spoken out loud before. I also caught my name and "shooter," but not much else.

When he turned back around, he closed his phone and shoved it back in his pocket. "Help is on the way. A friend of mine on the OGPD. Do you want an ambulance?"

I thought about it for a moment. "I've never ridden in an ambulance. That might be kind of cool."

He raised one eyebrow. "Yeah, except for the part where they stick a huge needle in you to start the IV. It's just a splinter, Vaughn. I can take you to the ER."

I couldn't help it; I sniffled a little. "I would have preferred somebody a touch more sympathetic for my first GSW, Brody."

"It's not a gunshot wound, it's a splinter. I'm sorry, I can be very sympathetic," he said. But then he smashed his fist into the palm of his other hand. "I'd like to be very sympathetic to whoever's doing this to you. Right after I beat the shit out of him."

"Or her," I said, feeling cheered up for some reason.

That caught his attention. "What are you talking about?"

I took a deep breath. "You have to promise me that you are not working for Addison Langley or Sarah Greenberg on the insulin cases in any way. Also that you're not spying on me for them. I want your word, Brody."

He stared at me, and for a split-second, I would have sworn he looked . . . *hurt?*

"I told you I'm not. If you don't believe me, that's your call, Counselor."

But I did. I didn't know why, since he always seemed to show up when there was trouble, but something about him registered high on the integrity meter with me. Plus, he was a SEAL. You don't grow up in a Navy household without learning about the moral fiber of those men.

I nodded. "All right. I need to hire you on the Deaver case, so I can tell you this without breaking client confidence."

He nodded. "Done."

I blew out a huge breath. "Okay. I have a story to tell you, about coincidences, dead bodies, and a possible conspiracy. Plus an implied threat that I'd be singing with the fishies."

He blinked. "Isn't that sleeping with the fishies?"

"Whatever."

In the five minutes it took for the police to arrive, I filled him in on the highlights of my suspicions about Langley, Cowan and possibly Greenberg and Smithies, including the bullying tactics and the threats. Nothing but the muscle clenching in his jaw gave away what he was thinking. He remained silent until I'd finished.

"So, it sounds crazy, but I think BDC knew about the defect and tried to cover it up before issuing the recall," I concluded.

"I think you're in some big trouble here. Shouldn't you go public with this?"

"I'm trying to figure out what to do next. For now, all I have are very far-fetched suppositions which are supported by zero admissible evidence."

"You need admissible evidence in your world, not mine," he said grimly. "All I need is proof."

The sound of sirens and then brakes squealing in my driveway stopped me from pursuing that line of conversation. As he went to open the door to the police, I called after him, "My case, my rules, Brody."

As I started to stand up, the pain in my shoulder sharpened. "For 'just a splinter,' it sure feels like a gunshot wound," I muttered as I sank back down in the chair. "And let's not forget that I have *stitches* in the back of my head still."

I tried out a few of Jake's really bad words under my breath while he let the police in the door, but it didn't really help. Jake introduced me to his good friend, Lieutenant Connors.

Connors swept his sharp gaze over me and around the room, then looked back at me. "Another drug deal gone bad?"

This totally ruined the good impression I'd been forming of him—he was tall, lean, and great-looking in a hardened "I'm the law" kind of way—but wavy brown hair and piercing, good-for-interrogating-perps blue eyes couldn't overcome his apparent stupidity.

Evidently I was getting quite the reputation. Me and my nonexistent drug cartel. Jake pulled Connors aside, and after a brief discussion that involved lots of "No shit?" and "No shit!" on the lieutenant's part, they walked back to where I still sat on the chair, getting my shoulder bandaged by the medical person from the emergency squad.

I put on my "brave and stoic" face, hoping for sympathy.

"Sorry, Miss Vaughn. Jake filled me in on the background here. You have to admit, after that newspaper article and then all the violence surrounding you these days, though, it looks bad," Connors said. "But if Jake vouches for you, you're good with me. Can you think of anybody who might want to hurt you?"

Okay, so maybe he wasn't all *that* stupid.

The medic finished and told me to see a doctor for follow-up. I thanked her, then looked up at Jake and Connors and sighed.

"Unfortunately, it's a really long list."

After I filled Connors in on what little I was willing to talk about, Jake wandered through the house with the other police officers, looking for who knows what. It's not like I had much to look at. My phone rang, and as I picked it up, somebody banged on the front door. Jake walked past me and dropped something on my lap, then headed over to answer the door. I looked down to see my favorite stuffed tiger, the one I kept on my bed.

I knew I should have been embarrassed that all the big, tough police were seeing the trial lawyer clutch a tiny stuffed animal, but I was beyond caring about that. I smiled after Jake, thinking warm thoughts about a man who would take time to bring me my tiger.

Uh-oh. Defenses going down fast.

I flipped open my phone. "Hello, Aunt Celia. I'm fine. Everything is fine. Nobody was hurt, and the police are here now."

"WHAT?" she shrieked in my ear so loudly I wondered about permanent deafness.

"Weren't you calling because you heard about me on the police scanner again?"

"No! I was calling to invite you to the community bingo and pie social at the Seniors' Center Saturday. What are you talking about? Are you okay? Do we need to come over right now? Nathan! Get your keys! December is in trouble again!"

"No! I'm fine. Look, I'll let you talk to the police," I said, and shoved my phone at Connors. "Talk to my Aunt Celia."

He shook his head and tried to escape, but I grabbed him by his shirt. "Listen here, I have been through just about ALL THAT I CAN TAKE this week. If you don't explain this to my Aunt Celia, I'm likely to lose my FREAKING MIND."

I doubt the poor man had ever been accosted by a crazed lawyer brandishing a stuffed animal before. He took the phone. "Yes? This is Lieutenant Connors. Who—"

Emily came running in the room and grabbed me in a huge hug. "December! Are you okay? We were out at a church social, and we saw all the police, and—"

Connors's voice was getting louder. "No! I did not hurt your poor baby. She is—"

"Ouch!" I pulled back out of Emily's hug, and she saw the bandage.

"Oh, no. You're wounded! Are you okay? Do you need to go to the hospital? We can take you. Do you need chicken soup? Oh, Jake, what happened to her?" Emily stood there, wringing her hands and looking terribly concerned for me.

"I am NOT an incompetent, jackbooted spawn of the devil," Connors yelled into the phone. "Your niece is fine. I'm trying to help her, if you'd let me do my job." He clicked the phone shut and shoved it at Jake, who took it, grinning.

I smiled a little, too, but for some reason, Emily's concern made me start crying. "Oh, stop being nice to me, Emily. Now see what you did." I wiped at my face and sniffled a bit, which made Emily burst into tears. She knelt down on the floor next to my chair and held my hand, and we both snuffled a bit.

Jake and Connors looked at each other with that typically male "oh, crap, not tears" expression. Perversely, that made my tears shut off completely. I scrubbed at my face again. "If you don't need anything else, Lieutenant, I'd like to get some rest now."

He nodded. "I'm sure you're tired. I have your numbers, so I'll call you if I need anything else. I'd suggest staying somewhere else tonight."

Emily held up her hand. "She's staying with me. I live next door. Emily Kingsley. That's K-I-N—"

I laughed. "You don't have to spell it, Emily. He can find us. And thanks. I don't much feel like staying here tonight, in case that lunatic comes back."

Jake finally spoke up. "I'm staying here tonight."

I shot him a look. "But what if the shotgun person shows back up?"

He smiled. "I'm hoping he does."

Connors narrowed his eyes and dragged Jake down the hall to talk. I decided to ignore them both and get my pajamas and toothbrush. After Emily helped me throw a few things in a tote bag, I put my little tiger and a bottle of pain relievers on the top.

Just the essentials.

Chapter 34

Friday morning involved trying to keep very loud small people from jumping on my wounded shoulder. Plus, there were Cocoa Puffs for breakfast. The sugar high ought to get me through till at least midnight, I figured. Plus, another twenty-minute phone call with Celia and Nathan, on top of the one I'd had with them last night after Connors'd hung up on them.

After I'd said good-bye to the kids and Emily and walked over to my house, I peered at the damage to the doorframe. Several gouges marred the surface of the wood, but it looked like most of the blast had hit the brick front of the house. Other than a few chips off the brick surface, I couldn't see much damage. Either it had been a warning shot, not meant to hurt me, or the shooter had terrible aim. Either way, I felt pretty lucky to be walking around with nothing worse than a bandage where the splinter had been.

By the time I'd showered, pulled on a simple white blouse and pinstriped slacks, and put my hair back in a French braid, my mundane morning routine had calmed my heartbeat to within range of normal. The drive to the office helped, and the thought of another day helping *pro bono* clients raised my spirits a lot.

I drove into the parking lot, smiling in anticipation of seeing another long line of clients. But the parking lot was empty. Mr. Ellison must have let them into the office already. I parked the car, making another mental note to get it painted. Anything but pink.

Then I walked into my offices, humming under my breath. No mere gunshots could dampen my spirits. I was Super Lawyer, defender of the weak and innocent. I could vanquish evildoers with a single bound. I pulled the door open and practically bounded in.

To an empty office.

Completely empty.

Super Lawyer screeched to a halt.

"But . . . but . . . where is everybody?"

Mr. Ellison stomped in from the hallway, resplendent in a sunshine-yellow shirt and pink pants. "We're out of the good cream. How come I have to do everything myself?"

I blinked. "What? Who cares about cream at a time like this? Where are my clients?"

"Oh. Well. About that," he said, shuffling his feet a little. "Nobody's coming."

"What? Why not? How do you know?"

He wouldn't look at me. "Well, one of them deadbeats, er, I mean, clients showed up earlier. But he just wanted to know if you got anything done on his case. He said nobody else from Legal Aid is coming, on account of you're involved in some murdering drug cartel."

Super Lawyer: shot down in flames.

I made it all the way back to my office and gently closed the door before I said any of my newly learned bad words.

When Max came in around nine and tried to tell me how Daisy was a guy magnet at the dog park the night before, I growled at her, picked the puppy up off the floor, and shut the door again. The less-than-friendly conversation I'd had with the folks at Legal Aid hadn't put me in a gossipy mood. Then I spent the rest of the morning working on the Deaver case with a warm puppy on my lap, only taking periodic breaks for doggy potty trips and playtime.

Max knocked around lunchtime and held a Wendy's bag inside the doorway. "Hungry?"

I wasn't much, but Daisy made trackmarks on the floor running her chubby little body over there. I sighed and stood up, contemplating the dog hair covering my pants. "Come in, Max. I need to apologize anyway."

She walked in with two bags of food and a drink carrier and put it all down on my desk. "I talked to Celia. You didn't think I'd want to know that somebody is shooting at you now?"

"I'm sorry. I was so upset about our Friday clients. Everything I've tried to do with this practice is swirling down the toilet. I'm dead in the water here, Max. I may as well just pack up the practice and go." I opened the bag, took out a sandwich, then pulled a piece off the end for Daisy, who gulped it down whole.

"You shouldn't feed her people food," Max said.

"I know. I'm a total screwup. I shouldn't be allowed to even own a dog."

Mr. Ellison walked in, carrying his own bag. "A third of a dog."

"What?"

He sucked down some soda. "Technically, you don't own a dog. You only own a third of her. And it's my turn to take her home tonight."

"Hey! I'm the one who got shot! I should get to take her home tonight," I said. Daisy ignored this debate over her sleeping schedule in favor of sticking her face and then her entire body in Mr. Ellison's lunch bag, which he'd put on the floor next to his chair.

"Um, I hope you weren't attached to that lunch," I said, pointing at the frantically wagging curly tail sticking out of the bag.

"What do you mean, shot?" he asked. Then he noticed where I was pointing. "Daisy! Get out of my lunch!" He grabbed the bag and pulled it away from her, and she stood there blinking at us for a second, three french fries sticking out of her mouth. Then she dashed away to hide under the credenza and eat them.

I couldn't help it. I had to laugh at her funny little face. "Want ketchup with those?"

I dropped into my own chair and grabbed a bag, searching for fries. Then I briefly filled them in on my evening's adventures.

Mr. Ellison clenched the arms of his chair so tightly his knuckles turned white. "This is serious, girlie. Somebody is sending you a hell of a message."

"Right. I just wish I knew what that message was," I said.

Max leaned forward. "More important, what was Jake Brody doing at your house last night?"

Mr. Ellison snorted. "If you can't figure that out on your own, you and me need to have a talk, Max. Now, back to important stuff, I have some . . . news, too."

We looked at him. "What?" I asked. "And if this is about your dating adventures, we so don't need to go there right now."

"Ha! At least somebody in this place is getting a little action," he said. "No, it's about a weird phone call I got at home last night. I figure I better tell you about it, since it was about you."

"About me?" I put my untouched hamburger down on my desk. "What about me?"

"Well, he said he was from the Claymore County Bar Association. He wanted me to report in on everything you was up to. Said you were a known drug dealer, and they needed to investigate," he said, then stopped and chewed on his lip a bit.

I couldn't believe this was happening. Now the bar was investigating me? But . . .

"That doesn't sound right. I've never been investigated before, but it seems unlikely they'd try to spy on an attorney under investigation by contacting her employees. Also, why would the county bar be investigating me? Would it even work that way?" I pulled a legal pad toward me to take notes. "Who did you say called?"

"Well, he said his name was William Rehnquist."

I dropped my pen and looked up at him. "He said his name was what?"

"William Rehnquist. I even wrote it down. It's not spelled with a K, W, but with a—"

"A Q. I know. Because William Rehnquist is the name of the late Chief Justice of the Supreme Court, Mr. Ellison!"

He tilted his head, considering. "Maybe it's a common name?"

"No! It's not a common name. Somebody is playing games with us," Max said.

"Pretty deadly games," I pointed out, touching my shoulder and then the back of my head. "First painting my car, then a rock to the back of my head, and now a shotgun? What's next, a shoulder-fired missile?"

"I know where we can get a grenade," Mr. Ellison piped up.

"No grenades!" I said, feeling my teeth clench around the words. At this rate, I was going to have to buy migraine medicine in bulk.

"What are we going to do?" Max asked, handing Daisy a piece of her chicken sandwich.

"Hey! You said no people food," I said.

Max shrugged. "It seems like the least of my worries suddenly. So what are we going to do?"

I shook off the sadness and self-pity that had swamped me all day. "We're going to figure this out," I said. "Who is doing this and why?"

Mr. Ellison jumped up. "I'll get a whiteboard. Let's make a list!"

The phone rang, and we all flinched. I laughed a little and answered it. "December Vaughn."

Jake's voice came through, staticky but clear enough. "Vaughn, Gina took off from rehab, and they can't find her. They said she kept talking about how she was going to get revenge on you."

The connection died before I could respond, and I slowly put the phone back down. Then I looked up at Max and Mr. Ellison. "We have another name for the list."

Then I smacked myself in the head, which hurt my shoulder and sent a twinge through the healing stitches in my head. Stupid. "I totally forgot about Mrs. Zivkovich. We have to call her right away. And add Croc to the list." I picked the phone back up, wondering how my life and my practice had gotten so far out of control. Maybe corporate law hadn't been all that bad, after all.

•   •   •

After an hour or so of discussion, our list of suspects looked like this:

1. Gina Schiantelli

2. Nervil/Croc

3. Addison Langley and his firm; cover-up

4. Sarah Greenberg; yacht threat?

5. Someone from BDC?

But our list of incidents didn't match up:

1. Car painting/acid

2. Rock at my head

3. Sinus stalker call

4. Murder at museum

5. Shooting last night

We could figure Gina for the shooting, but she'd been in rehab for the car painting and the rock throwing. Plus, the sinus stalker phone call had come from a man. And there was no way I believed she had anything to do with Richard Dack's murder. It didn't make sense.

"She could have talked somebody into making that call," Max said.

I shook my head. "Yeah, but it doesn't add up. She may be crazy, but this level of escalation doesn't sound right for a 'you talked to my boyfriend' issue."

"Crazy people do crazy things," she said.

"We're not getting anywhere this way," I said. "Let's see

what Jake's friend, Lieutenant Connors, turns up. He seemed pretty competent."

"Well, I gotta go," Mr. Ellison said, brushing crumbs off his lap onto the floor and standing up. "We ain't figuring out nothing like this, and I promised to help out down to the Seniors' for the big bingo party."

I looked up. "This has nothing to do with anything, but do you know my Aunt Celia?"

He stared down at me. "Know her? I woulda married her if that rotten Nathan Judson hadn't cut me out of the picture." He bent down to pick Daisy up, then stomped out of my office.

I stared at Max, my mouth hanging open. "No way. No way was Mr. Ellison almost my uncle," I said, shuddering.

Her eyes bugged out. "Talk about a narrow escape. We have *got* to get her to tell us about that."

"No way. I never, ever want to hear a conversation that has the words 'Celia,' 'dating,' and 'Henry' all in the same breath. I'm getting the creepy-crawlies just thinking about it."

She stood up. "I guess we'd better get to work. I'm assuming he's taking Daisy home tonight?"

I sighed. "Looks like it. I guess I'll get her tomorrow. You'd better give me his address so we can do the puppy handoff."

As Max walked back down the hall, my gaze strayed to our lists again. None of this made sense to me at all. What could possibly be behind all these threats and attacks?

Nobody ever shot at me when I did corporate work.

Max and I spent the rest of the afternoon deep in the Deaver case, and I barely looked up from Faith's medical records when she stopped by to tell me she was leaving. "Sure, have a great weekend," I said.

About an hour later, I couldn't ignore the loud grumblings from my stomach any longer. I gathered up a pile of work to take home with me, turned out all the lights, turned the AC down (now that I had to pay the electric bill myself, I remembered stuff like that), and left the office. As I climbed into my car, an old pickup truck with ORANGE GROVE ANTIQUES stenciled in a small sign on its side pulled in next to me.

Bear rolled down his window and gave me a huge smile. "Miss December! I'm so glad I caught you! I have a present for you!"

I smiled back at him, almost in spite of myself. He just had that kind of face. Also, that kind of *shirt*—a purple one with a giant orange giraffe on it. "Hey, Bear. How's the new job? Staying out of trouble?"

He got out of the truck and hurried around to my side, clutching a package in his hands. "Yes, I am. Most definitely. Grandma even met Miss Lucinda, and they liked each other," he said.

"That's great, Bear. I'm very happy for you," I said, meaning it. Bear may have been confused about property ownership, but at least he wasn't shooting at me or throwing rocks at my head, which made him okay in my book.

"So, what's up?"

He thrust the package at me. It was wrapped in what looked like the Sunday comics. "This is for you, to say thanks. But it's delicate, so be careful."

I took the package, feeling a lump form in my throat. It was funny how the simplest kind gesture could elicit the tears that all the assault and threat of painful, ugly death didn't. "Oh, Bear, that's so sweet. But you didn't have to do that," I said.

"I know, but I wanted to. Open it, open it!" he said, clapping his hands like a kid at Christmas.

So I opened the wrapping carefully and stared down at a truly gorgeous piece of pink Depression glass. I lifted it out of its paper nest, and caught my breath. "It's beautiful, Bear. And in perfect condition."

"It's a syrup dispenser," he said, beaming. "Pretty rare to find them in such perfect shape."

As much as I lusted after the piece, to go with my collection, I regretfully placed it back in the box. "Bear, I can't accept this. It must have cost you a fortune. You—" I stopped, suddenly worried. "You *did* pay for this, right?"

He rolled his eyes. "Miss December, I told you no more taking things without paying. I spent my savings out of my sock that I keep under my bed. You're worth it. You kept me out of jail!"

I cringed, thinking back to my hideous performance that day. "Bear, you stayed out of jail because they decided not to press charges, not because of me. Really, I can't take this from you. It's the sweetest thing anybody has done for me in a long time, but you should spend your savings on yourself."

He frowned. "I wanted to spend it on you. Don't you like it? I know you collect it, and you don't have that piece."

"It's amazing, and I love it. Please—wait a minute. How did you know I collect Depression glass?" A cold chill raced down my body, and goosebumps popped up on my arms. A neat trick, since it was about ninety degrees outside.

"Even more, how do you know what pieces I do and don't have?"

He avoided my gaze and stomped back around the front

of his truck and got in, slamming the door. "Fine. Give it away. Throw it in the trash. I don't care."

"Bear, stop! I—"

But he slammed the truck into gear, reversed, and squealed out of the parking lot, leaving me standing there with my hands full of very valuable Depression glass and my mind full of very unanswerable questions.

Chapter 35

All the way home, my gaze kept straying to the package on my passenger seat, and my mind kept straying to the conversation I'd just had. I almost needed a timeline on a whiteboard to keep up with my own life, but I was sure I'd met Bear *after* the phone call from the sinus stalker. So it didn't make any sense at all that Bear had been the caller. Plus, the voice hadn't sounded anything like Bear's.

But how had he known about my collection unless he'd been inside my house? He seemed harmless, but his mental disability might make him unstable. Had he formed an obsessive attachment to me? Was he stalking me now?

Did I have to give the syrup dispenser back?

I shook my head, and grabbed my cell phone to call . . . I don't know. Somebody. I noticed it was turned off, and flicked the on button. The "you have voice mail" music— Pachelbel's Canon, loved that piece—came on immediately. I called in to voice mail as I turned on to my street.

You have four new messages:
Jake: "I found Gina and she's in a little trouble. Will you give me a call?"

Great. With Jake's talent for understatement, that could mean anything from another bar fight to she just knocked over the local bank.

The nasal voice of the trucking company dispatcher: *"Your driver called in. He got married in Vegas, and the newly-weds are taking a little honeymoon with your furniture, but he promises he'll deliver it soon."*

Unbelievable. Just . . . unbelievable.

Uncle Nathan: *"If one of my characters kills somebody, and the victim is on death row, is it legally murder? Or could the killer argue the victim was technically already dead?"*

I laughed. Nathan always asked me the most bizarre questions for his books, and I almost never had an answer. I'd have to ask Jim Thies.

Emily: *"Pizza at our house? You may be forced to watch the new singing doll movie, sadly."*

I clicked off the phone as I pulled into my driveway. I *loved* my new neighbors.

After I'd changed into shorts and a T-shirt and called to let Emily know I'd be over shortly, I reluctantly returned Jake's call. I kinda owed him.

"Vaughn," he answered the phone.

I sighed. "I thought we were finally on a first-name basis, Brody."

"Only when we're up close and personal." I could hear the smile in his voice.

"Well, I guess we're Vaughn and Brody from here on out," I said. I didn't need that kind of complication in my life.

Silence.

I tapped my fingers on the kitchen counter, refusing to speak first. Finally he sighed. "Gina is in trouble. She bailed on rehab before her time was up. Any ideas?"

"Yes. Get her a good criminal lawyer. That is *so* not my area, and I've recently learned not to dabble."

I walked around my kitchen, realizing I was going to have to do a serious cleaning. The police had tromped dirt all over the place. Sadly, hiring somebody to clean was way out of my price range these days.

A bottle of Pine-Sol wasn't.

Suddenly I realized that Jake was still talking. "I'm sorry, Jake, my mind was wandering. The, ah, pain from that splinter is distracting me."

Another silence.

"I'm sorry, Vaughn. I shouldn't bother you with stuff like this when you have so much to deal with. Later."

Click.

The man needed to quit babbling on and on so much.

After a pleasant evening of relaxing with the Kingsleys, and three hundred or so games of Go Fish, I returned to my own house for a tense night's sleep. Emily and Rick had insisted I stay at their house again, and I'd been tempted. But the attacks seemed to concentrate on me personally, and there was no way I wanted my new friends—or their children—to be caught in the line of fire.

Line of fire. God, did that sound melodramatic or what?

I tried to work up some courage, but every sound, real or imagined, woke me, and I'd bolt upright, clutching my stuffed tiger in one hand and the rolling pin I'd borrowed from Emily in the other.

She'd thought I wanted to bake something. I almost

smiled at the idea, then settled in for a long night of staring at the alarm clock. A watched clock really does move more slowly than usual. By seven, I couldn't stand it anymore and headed for the shower, mind dull from lack of sleep.

Dragging on shorts and a sleeveless pink blouse, I shook my wet hair out, considered and passed on the idea of makeup, and headed for the office. If I couldn't sleep, I could at least work. Maybe I could figure out who was behind the attacks and threats.

I picked up donuts and coffee at the drive-through more out of habit than any real hunger. The waistband on my shorts was a little baggy, though, and my face had looked pale. I guess being threatened on a daily basis was good for the figure. I could write a book: *How to Stay Alive and Lose Weight in Thirty Days*.

At least, I hoped the "stay alive" part would hold true.

"Oh, quit being melodramatic. If anybody had wanted to kill you, they could have. This is some kind of elaborate warning scheme," I muttered to myself.

But warning about *what*?

Could this really be all about hiding the BDC cover-up of the defective insulin?

Mulling the possibilities over, I made it to the office in no time. As I pulled in, I noticed that the old Ford Escort that Mr. Ellison drove when he hadn't found a ride with one of his friends was in the parking lot. I caught myself smiling at the sight.

The guy just grew on a person.

I fumbled with my keys, then unlocked and opened the door. When I looked up as the door closed behind me, balancing my briefcase, purse, coffee, and the bag of donuts, the first thing I noticed was the alligator tail pointing at me.

The rest of the alligator was very much attached.

Chapter 36

The second thing I noticed, while I stood frozen on the spot, was Mr. Ellison standing on top of the reception desk, waving his arms and jumping up and down. "You need to get out of here while I keep its attention," he whispered.

The alligator swished its tail, and I fought to keep the scream boiling up in my chest from escaping my throat. "Why are we whispering? Did you call 911?" I whispered back, wondering—in the part of my mind that wasn't shrieking—how a ten-foot-long alligator had gotten in my office.

"Be calm, be calm, be calm," I whispered to myself. "Alligators are slow and ponderous."

The alligator whipped its head around and fixed its beady eye on me. I couldn't help it. I shrieked at the top of my lungs. Being up close and personal with an alligator had never been at the top of my wish list.

"Get out, get out, you damn fool," Mr. Ellison yelled at me.

I dropped everything but my coffee and edged toward the reception desk. My brain had shut down, but somehow it seemed wrong to leave Mr. Ellison here alone with the deadly creature. I could . . . I could throw my coffee at it.

Maybe alligators are allergic to lattes.

Maybe I'm just an idiot.

The alligator scuttled around until it faced me, and I shrieked again and threw my coffee at it. Then I hurtled up over Max's office chair and climbed on top of the three-drawer filing cabinet, banging my knee on the drawer and wrenching my injured shoulder. The alligator was right behind me and snapped at empty air as I yanked my legs up behind me. "Ow!" I shouted.

"Did it get you?" Mr. Ellison asked.

"No, I hurt my shoulder. Can you reach the phone?" The phone lay on the floor in front of the desk, so the desk itself would be between Mr. Ellison and the alligator if he could jump down and get it. Of course, he was seventy-two years old and not exactly in shape for all this jumping and climbing.

The alligator did a sort of half-jump thing and snapped at the empty air between it and me and caught a corner of Max's chair in its jaws on the way down. It made a horrible growling noise and rolled over and over with the chair in a blur of greenish-gray lumps, then finally let go.

I tried to breathe, but I couldn't seem to get my lungs to inflate. Plus, it smelled a lot like rotting fish in my office. Not exactly an air-freshener-quality aroma.

Mr. Ellison and I both stared at what was left of the chair, then looked at each other. "Use your cell phone, girlie," he gasped.

"I . . . oh, crap," I said, then pointed to my purse, lying on the floor by the door. "It's over there. Mr. Alligator might not let me climb over him to get it. And—what the heck is *that*?" I stared at the message painted on the wall next to the door.

GO HOME, YANKEY

"Great. I'm being threatened by the spelling-challenged," I mumbled.

Mr. Ellison gritted his teeth. "I can't believe you're making jokes at a time like this. Okay, it's up to me, I guess. I better get paid extra for this. Make some noise and keep its attention, willya?"

I sucked in a deep breath and started yelling, on purpose this time. "Hey, alligator! Look here! Yummy lawyer to eat. That sounds like a joke, doesn't it? Hey, alligator! I see why people turn you into purses now, you big stupid monster."

It crouched there on the floor, glaring at me with its beady eyes. Maybe it didn't like to be insulted. That purse crack had been kind of mean.

I snuck a glance at Mr. Ellison, who had made it down to the floor. He grabbed the phone and started to climb back up. The alligator must have heard a noise, because it whipped its head around and started scuttling after fresh prey. I yelled and waved my arms, but it ignored me, so I took another deep breath and did the stupidest thing I'd ever done in my life.

I jumped back off the filing cabinet.

"Here I am! Come get me! Leave the bony old man alone, he'd be tough to eat anyway. Come get me, fish-breath." I ran to the other side of the room, banging the metal filing cabinets on the way, watching the alligator as it swung its enormous head back and forth between Mr. Ellison and me. Mr. Ellison used the few moments to heave himself back on top of the reception desk, yelling at me the whole time.

"Stupid female! I thought you were okay for a lawyer, but here you go and do the damndest fool thing I've ever seen. Get back on the filing cabinet before I lose you, too," he barked.

I never took my eyes off the alligator. It advanced on me slowly, coming around the back of Max's desk. I waited until it was fully behind the desk, and then I shot around the corner and back around the front of the desk and down the hall to my office. I slammed the door and slid to the ground in front of it, flinching when a few hundred pounds of angry reptile slammed into the door.

Add whiplash to the list of OFFICIAL DECEMBER VAUGHN INJURIES.

Then I started laughing and laughing and laughing.

It was either that or cry.

By the time I'd caught my breath, the sound of sirens was louder than the sound of my heartbeat. I heard men's voices shouting in the front room. The cavalry had arrived—or at least Florida Animal Control officers.

I put my head down on the carpet and peered out through the space between the door and the carpet, half expecting to see an alligator eye peering back at me. Instead, I saw a large bulky shape moving down the hall. Knees weak, I stood up and opened my door a crack. The animal control people already had some kind of lasso things around the alligator's neck and seemed to have it under control.

Not that I was going to get close to it and test that hypothesis.

Mr. Ellison shouted down the hallway. "Girlie! I mean, Ms. Vaughn! Are you all right?"

The fact that he'd thought to call me Ms. Vaughn in front of the animal control people, at a time like that, won me over for all time. Mr. Ellison had a job with me for as long as I could meet payroll.

At this rate, that would be at least another week and a half.

"I'm here, Mr. Ellison. Are you okay?"

"I'm fine," he shouted. Then, to my utter surprise, he started sobbing. Harsh, choking sobs. I didn't know what to do, so I pretended I didn't notice, figuring I'd give him some privacy.

One of the animal handlers, a short, thick guy who looked like a fireplug with arms, yelled down the hall to me. "Miss Vaughn? Are you all right?"

"I'm fine. What about . . . that? Can you get it out of here?" I said, not stepping a foot closer, although the handlers had the beast almost completely out of the hallway by then.

The man pulled his ball cap off and shoved his hand through curly brown hair. "Yeah, we can get it out. What I'd like to know is how the hell it got in here."

Within another ten or so minutes, the handlers had dragged the thrashing alligator out the front door, leaving behind chunks of torn-up carpet and a smelly substance that I hated to think about. I ran to Mr. Ellison. "Are you all right? Do you feel okay? Did it bite you? Are you having a heart attack or something?"

He pushed me away, emotion under control by then. Blinking rapidly, as if to keep more tears at bay, he drew himself up to his full height and looked up at me. "I gotta say that was the stupidest and the bravest thing anybody's ever done for me, December. Don't think I'll ever forget it," he said hoarsely.

My lip started to quiver, and I bit it before I started crying myself. "You would have done the same for me. In fact, jumping down to grab the phone was the bravest thing *I've* ever seen, so I'd say we're even."

To my utter shock, my words seemed to drive him back over the edge. His shoulders quivered, and he pulled in a shuddering breath. "No. No, we're not. Because I got Daisy killed."

He scrubbed at his eyes. "That damn alligator done ate her."

Chapter 37

"What?" I stared at Mr. Ellison in horror. "The alligator got our puppy?"

He nodded, his whole body shaking. At that exact moment, I realized just how frail he really was.

"Here. You need to sit down. This has been a terrible morning, and you might be in shock," I said, and led him over to one of the chairs in reception, trying to ignore the huge gouge taken out of the side of my brand-new couch.

The alligator-bite-sized gouge.

Would my insurance cover alligator damage?

Do I even have insurance? I need Max.

Forget Max. I want my puppy.

I sank down on the floor next to the couch and buried my face in my hands. I could be brave for only so long, and the idea of my beautiful Daisy being a snack for that monster was the very last straw. I broke down and cried like a baby.

I don't even know how long I cried, but finally somebody touched my arm and started licking my face.

"What?" My eyes flew open. It was Daisy!

I grabbed her and rained kisses on her furry little head. "Mr. Ellison! It's her! It's her! The alligator didn't get her!"

He jumped out of his chair and squatted down next to us. "You brave little puppy! Where did you go? Hiding under the couch, I bet! Didn't I tell you that this was the smartest dog in the world?"

He rubbed her head, and I tickled her tummy, then we did a sort of snuffly group hug right there on the floor. Naturally, that's when the guy in charge of the alligator people walked back in my office.

Too emotionally drained to be embarrassed, I simply handed Daisy to Mr. Ellison and stood up, scrubbing at my face. Good thing I'd gone with no mascara, or I'd have looked like a tall, blond raccoon.

"I see you found your dog. That's great, ma'am. Can you tell me how an alligator got in your office?"

I blinked. "You're kidding, right? How the heck would I know how somebody got a ten-foot alligator in my office? That thing must have weighed a thousand pounds," I said. "Wouldn't somebody *notice* something like that?"

The man grinned. "Well, actually, she was around five feet, and maybe five hundred pounds, but still pretty damn big to sneak in under a body's hat, ma'am."

I looked at him, dazed, and said the first thing that popped into my mind (this is never a good idea). "Why in the world would you want to work at a job like this?"

He looked startled, and then he laughed. "Why, for the chance to rescue beautiful damsels in distress like you, ma'am."

"Call me December," I said. I had to admire a man who could flirt with danger—and then flirt with me—all in the space of thirty minutes.

Why is it that I only attract lunatics these days?

Speaking of lunatics, the door swung open and Jake stood in the doorway, scanning the room. "What in the hell did you do now?" he asked, shaking his head and smiling.

I rolled my eyes and turned back to the alligator guy. "Thank you so very much. If you find out anything—

anything at all—about how it got in here, will you please let me know?"

As we walked over to the door, I scooped my purse up off the floor and dug for a business card to give him. "Please give me a call if you can figure out who put this amphibian in my office."

Jake ambled over. "Reptile."

"What?"

"Alligators are reptiles," he said, putting an arm around my shoulder.

The alligator guy's eyes narrowed a little, then he grinned. "Oh, it's like that, huh? Well, I guess I'll keep that lunch invitation to myself, December. Nice to meet you."

I shook Jake's arm off my shoulders, rolling my eyes at the testosterone in the room, then peered out the front door, to where the animal handlers had already wrangled the monster up into a crate in the back of a big truck. "It's nice to meet you, too. I hope you won't be offended if I admit I hope I don't need your professional services again," I said, smiling weakly.

"Nope. I get that a lot. We'll take this big girl on down to St. Augustine to the alligator farm there. The curator will know what to do with her," he said.

"I'm glad somebody will," I said. "Thank you again."

As the alligator truck drove off, a tired-looking brown sedan drove up and pulled into the parking space next to Jake's black Mustang. Lieutenant Connors climbed out, notebook in hand. "I hear you've got a pest problem?" he said.

My shoulders slumped. "You have no idea."

• • •

I spent half an hour with the lieutenant, but other than the rather obscure connection I mentioned between the sinus stalker who asked how to spell Claritin and the fact that "Yankee" was misspelled (which neither Connors nor Jake took seriously), I hadn't a clue.

Suddenly, I looked at Jake. "The security cameras! You said you put cameras in!"

He looked grim. "I did. That's why I'm here. Wrench reported that the camera feed went down just after six this morning. Since I knew that you were home safe in bed, I didn't rush right over to check it out. So this is really my fault."

I shook my head. "No, it's not your fault. Except—hey! What do you mean you knew I was safe in bed? Are you spying on me, too?"

He ignored me and walked over to sit down next to Mr. Ellison. They started talking in low tones. I was pleased to see that Mr. Ellison looked better. He had a little pink back in his cheeks. He was still clutching poor Daisy as if her life depended on it. He nodded at something Jake said, then pulled the thin pink leash out of his pocket, snapped it on Daisy's collar, and headed outside. Daisy growled at the carpet, snuffling everywhere, all the way across the floor.

"I'm gonna take the miracle pup here outside for a potty break," he said. "Then I'd appreciate a ride. Don't much feel like driving."

Driving . . . something about the parking lot . . .

"Bear!" I said, then wished it hadn't been out loud. All three men stared at me.

"There was a bear, too? Besides the alligator?" Connors said, making one of those "you've got to be kidding me" faces.

"No, Bear Anderson, my client. He, um, he stopped by last night, and he was kind of weird. Plus, he knew about my glass collection when he's never been in my house. I was a little creeped out, and he got upset with me."

I quickly filled them in. "I just . . . you don't think he'd do something like this?" I looked at Mr. Ellison, the only one of them who knew Bear.

He pursed his lips, thinking, then nodded. "Oh, yeah. That glass thing. Don't worry about that. He called here to the office about getting you a present, and him and Max had a big long talk about glass and horses and chalkboards or something."

Now it all made sense, and I felt bad for my suspicions about poor Bear. "Chalk horses?"

"Yeah, that was it," he said, then he walked outside with Daisy.

"Okay, strike Bear off the list. He got the info about me from my office manager," I said. "December Vaughn, Queen of the Paranoiacs, I guess."

Jake shoved his hands in the pockets of his jeans. "You've got good reason to be paranoid these days," he observed.

I smiled weakly. "Yeah. People really *are* out to get me."

By the time Mr. Ellison and Daisy came back inside, mission accomplished, Connors was ready to go. "You have my number," he said. "Call me if you have any questions."

"What now?" Jake asked. "Do you want me to take you home?"

"No, we need to go eat barbecue down to the Seniors'," Mr. Ellison said.

I looked at Jake and shrugged. "I don't have any better ideas. It's not like I want to hang out here."

As we locked the door and headed for our cars, I looked at Jake. "I just have one question."

He opened the passenger door of his car for Mr. Ellison. "What is it, Vaughn?"

"Do you know anything that will get alligator pee out of a carpet?"

Chapter 38

We had to park a couple of blocks down from the newly renovated Orange Grove Senior Citizens' Center, because the parking lot and on-street parking spaces were all full. From the lively sounds of conversation and laughter we started hearing when we were still half a block away, it sounded like Aunt Celia's group was throwing a fabulous party.

I wasn't quite sure I was up for a party, not even a fabulous one.

I trudged down the street behind Jake and Mr. Ellison, who still clutched Daisy like a talisman against evil. Or at least against alligators.

It was hard to believe the puppy was alive at all. She must have some serious lucky streak to have escaped that monster. I realized Jake had dropped back to walk next to me when the air currents around me charged up with electricity. The man must cause miserable static cling in the winter.

"What?" he asked.

I looked up at him. "What, what?"

"What about static cling?"

Oh, crap. That was out loud?

"Nothing. Never mind. My brain—or what's left of it—is wandering. I mean, 'Yankee go home'? What the hell is that? Why do I feel like I'm in a bad movie?"

He shook his head. "I generally hate to play into melodrama, but I have to agree with you, Vaughn. Somebody is out to get you, and they've hired some low-rent thugs to do it."

"Some low-IQ thugs, if you ask me," I muttered.

"Quit babbling, you two," called Mr. Ellison. "We're here."

I looked at the ramp leading up to the front porch of the Center, and wasn't sure I could stand to go inside. All the shakiness I thought I'd controlled back at my office washed over me again, and I nearly stumbled. Jake caught me with an arm around my waist and pulled me in close to him.

"Henry, I'm going to take December for a walk to get some fresh air. She's a little shaken up," he said.

Mr. Ellison turned around on the ramp and studied my face. "That's a good idea, Brody. You take good care of our girl."

"I will. Tell Celia and Nathan that we'll be along in a bit," he said.

I said nothing, just stood there numbly. The fact of Daisy's near-demise had brought another near-death to my mind. Mr. Ellison could have been killed. My entire body started shaking.

Jake helped me around the corner, to where a tiny park fronted Main Street. I followed, unresisting, visions of what the alligator had done to Max's office chair playing over and over again in my mind.

"What if it got him?" I looked up at Jake as we sat down on a bench near a vibrant azalea bush. "What if it ate Mr. Ellison, and all I found when I opened the door was . . . parts?" I heard myself getting hysterical and tried to stop it, taking deep, calming, azalea-scented breaths.

"What if he died, all because somebody was trying to warn me? What if Emily's kids had been outside when that person drove by with the shotgun? What if . . . w-w-what if—"

Jake put his arms around me and pulled me into his chest, and I started crying in earnest. There's brave, and there's stubborn, and then there's stupid. Maybe if they want me gone so much, I should get myself gone.

When I calmed down enough that I was noticing how good Jake smelled, and enjoying the way he patted my back, I pulled away from him. I was still miserable, but now I was embarrassed, too. I rummaged in my purse for a tissue, and then wiped my face and blew my nose.

"I'm sorry I soaked your shirt," I said. "I'm just not used to being the potential cause of death for so many people."

That muscle in his jaw clenched again. "You're not the potential cause of anything, December. Somebody is out to warn you in a very big way. We need to find out who. I've got feelers out on BDC, Langley, and Greenberg. As soon as I hear anything, believe me, you and Connors will be the first to know."

I shook my head. "I don't care. I mean thanks, but it's not enough. What if I hurt somebody?"

I told him what I'd been thinking about Mr. Ellison and Emily's family. "These people don't care who gets hurt. What if Max had come to work first? What if . . . oh, God, what if the alligator got Max?"

I nearly started crying again, but I clenched my fingernails into my palms. "Maybe it's time to go along with their *suggestions*. Maybe it's time I moved back up North."

He folded his arms across his chest. "If you do that, they win," he said. "Are you really willing to do that? What about Celia and Nathan? Are you just going to leave them here alone? What about Charlie Deaver?"

He was getting to me, as he'd planned. Reverse psychology works for a reason. But maybe not enough of a reason. "What if Celia and Nathan wind up getting hurt in the cross fire while I try to avoid a threat I don't even understand?"

He touched my cheek where the tears had probably made horrible trackmarks. (I never was a delicate crier; another reason why I tried not to do it.) "December, I can't tell you what to do. You have to decide how far you're willing to let them push you."

I narrowed my eyes. I hated to be pushed. My dad had been the champion of pushing-December-around all my life. Now that I'd finally learned to stand up for myself, it rubbed me raw to think of buckling under to a cowardly, anonymous threat.

Stupid? Probably. But there was still time to leave. I just wanted to make a couple of phone calls first. I looked up at Jake. "I think it's time for me to push back."

We stopped in the bingo social, intending only to say hi and stay for a few minutes, but Mr. Ellison had spread the tale of the alligator escapades far and wide. Aunt Celia came running up and threw her arms around me, then burst into tears.

This made me get choked up again, and I hugged her back as fiercely as I could. Nathan walked up and cast a sideways look at Jake. "Sometimes you've got to let them get it out."

Jake nodded. "Yep."

Uncle Nathan pointed at Jake's soggy shirt. "Looks like you've been doing a spot of comforting yourself."

Jake nodded again. "Yep."

"Guess we'd better have a talk, son."

"Yes, sir," Jake said, and then he followed Uncle Nathan down the hall toward the rec room.

I pulled away from Aunt Celia, patting her on the arm, and stood staring after them. "What in the world was that about?" I asked her.

She patted her face off with a lace handkerchief she'd pulled out of a pocket. Celia, unlike me, was the epitome of a delicate crier. She got glowy. I got soggy.

"Well, of course Nathan is going to ask the boy about his intentions, dear," she said, except this time she was the one who patted my arm.

I yelped. "What? Aunt Celia, this is the twenty-first century. We don't ask men their intentions. Anyway, he works for, well, *with* me. It's not any romantic thing," I said, starting after them.

Celia gently caught my arm and stopped me. "Except he's always around when you need him, isn't he? And we've noticed the way he looks at you. Let the boys have their little chat. If your young man can't stand up to Nathan, well, then, he's not worth much, is he?"

"He's not my young man," I mumbled, but I was talking to empty air as she bustled off to make sure everything at the party worked according to her usual perfection. The air didn't stay empty for long, though, as people crowded around to hear about the alligator. I plastered the best smile I could muster on my face.

"Mr. Ellison? Oh, yes, he saved us all," I said. Then I spent the next hour and a half eating barbecue and playing bingo and telling the story of Henry Ellison the Alligator Slayer over and over and over.

By the time Jake finally rescued me (he'd won bingo twice, the turd, and worked his way through three plates of barbecue and two slices of pie), I thought my head might explode.

Exactly the right frame of mind to do some pushing of my own.

Jake followed me home, then headed off on some mysterious errands of his own. He promised to keep an eye on my house, and I wasn't stupid enough to refuse. Not after somebody had wanted to threaten me enough to deposit a live reptile in my office. Mr. Ellison had volunteered in a gruff voice to keep Daisy an extra night, since I probably had a lot of work to do. I hadn't wanted to say yes, because I was really getting attached to the little furball, but I'd seen in his eyes that he wasn't quite past his scare that she'd died. I'd thanked him and asked if he'd like to keep her till Monday, but I'd also added quickly that I'd get her for two whole days then.

He'd grinned and agreed, relief all over his apple-cheeked face, and I'd barely resisted the urge to hug him.

It had felt like the right thing to do then, but now I looked around my empty house and felt the echoes of silence resonate in the scared corners of my mind. More than likely, anybody who'd wrestled an alligator that morning had to be too tired to do much harm by afternoon, right? So a nap would be pretty safe. Just a quick power nap, then I'd get to work on Charlie's case again and try to figure out exactly what BDC might be covering up.

Or so I told myself as I fell over on my bed, clothes still on, and sank immediately into a dreamless sleep. When I woke up, it was Sunday.

Chapter 39

By Monday morning, after spending Sunday cocooned in my house, napping and working, I was back to my usual optimistic self. Or maybe, *stubborn* self. Either way, I wasn't letting some low-rent criminal with bad spelling push me out of town.

I headed straight for the courthouse, since my hearing on the nonparty production I'd served on Orange Grove Production was set for nine o'clock. I wanted all of their records about anything and everything to do with those bad insulin commercials. If I were right, and BDC was trying to cover up the fact that they'd known about the adverse reactions well before they'd reported it, somebody at BDC was in serious trouble.

It wouldn't hurt Charlie's case either.

Sarah Greenberg had filed a blistering set of objections, claiming attorney work product. Work product is the stuff lawyers prepare for actual or anticipated litigation, and it's generally exempt from discovery. That means we don't have to turn it over to the other side.

This can include reports from nonlawyer third parties. So, for example, if I hired a private investigator to research something about the case, the private investigator's findings and report would usually (remember, this is law; there are always loopholes) be considered attorney work product, and therefore exempt from discovery.

But claiming that information about the filming and

production of commercials—that not only *weren't* secret, but were actually created to be *aired on television*—could be shielded from discovery under the work-product doctrine was a *looooong* reach on Sarah's part. No judge in the country would agree with her.

Or at least, so I believed, and so I'd fired back in my responses to her objections. Now we'd find out if Greenberg and Smithies' claims of "friendly" local judges had any basis in fact. Contrary to what TV and the movies might portray, I'd never yet met a judge who didn't appear to be fair and unbiased. Call me naïve—and I'm not saying that they were all brilliant legal minds—but the bar would come down hard on any judges who played favorites.

As I drove up to the courthouse, I realized I was smiling what Max would call my shark smile. This was a courtroom I was itching to conquer, which just goes to show that I should stick to my own arena. Civil litigation was my ballpark; from now on I'd leave the criminal law to the criminal attorneys.

The shark smile reminded me to call Max. I parked and pulled out my cell phone. She answered on the first ring.

"I'm here. Getting ready to find out exactly how bad Sarah looks this early in the morning," I said.

Max laughed, but then her voice turned serious. "Watch her face when you walk in, D. If she had anything to do with the alligator, she's going to be surprised to see you, or at least expecting you to be all freaked out."

"Don't worry, I'll be watching her like a shark."

"Isn't that 'like a hawk'?"

"That, too." I flipped the phone closed, then reopened it and shut it off completely. I'd known judges who fined lawyers a thousand dollars a pop for cell phones that rang in court. I didn't exactly have that kind of cash lying around these days. I put it in the pocket of my jacket, so I'd remember to turn it back on after the hearing.

As I walked to my courtroom, I aimed my icy-lawyer-of-death glare at anybody who dared to stare at me or, worse, snicker when I walked by. It would probably take a day or seventy to live down my "Founding Fathers" snafu, but today would be a good start.

Speaking of utter humiliation, Matt Falcon rounded a corner, looking down at a file, and nearly walked into me. I stepped to the side in time to avoid a collision. As he looked up with a ready smile, I saw the recognition flicker in his eyes. "Hey, December Vaughn. How nice to almost run into you today."

I smiled. "Nice to see you, Matt. Busy saving the world from crime and hapless lawyers who cite the Founding Fathers?"

I could see he was surprised I'd brought it up (and looked so calm doing so). Lead with your weakness, as any good trial lawyer will tell you, and you leave the opponent with nothing to exploit.

It works well as a philosophy of life, too. Maybe I'd get it printed on T-shirts.

He smiled a slow smile of appreciation, both for the tactic and for the hot-pink suit with white silk chemise I wore, I was guessing. "You are a very interesting woman, December Vaughn."

"So I keep hearing. Sarah Greenberg is about to find out just how interesting," I replied. "Nice to see you again, Matt, but I have to get going."

He stepped out of my way. "Go get 'em, Counselor. But first, how about dinner?"

"I rarely have dinner at this time of the morning. I hate to litigate on a full stomach. Some other time perhaps?" I

smiled and moved on, not waiting for his response, somehow knowing that he was watching me walk off.

It seemed only fair, since I'd done the same to him. I had
the feeling Matt Falcon was the persistent type, and I'd
wind up having dinner with him before too much longer.

Might even be fun.

All thoughts of fun and dinner vanished when I swung
open the door to the courtroom and saw Sarah Greenberg
already there, standing with a small cluster of a half-dozen
men. Some looked like baby lawyers from her firm; a couple wore shirt sleeves and khaki pants, and were probably
reps from Orange Grove Productions. Those two looked
nervous and a little scared, the way their eyes kept darting
around the room.

All eyes fixed on me when I walked in, which served
only to steady my nerves even further. I thought that Sarah
paled a bit when she saw me, but that was probably my
imagination. She certainly didn't run over and say, "You
should be dead in the belly of the alligator!"—which would
have been helpful in narrowing down my suspects.

Alligators aside, I'd had the luck (although it didn't feel
like it at the time) to work for some of the worst pit bull trial
lawyers in the country at True, Evers. After being screamed
at for twenty minutes in the conference room one Thanks-
giving Day for my failure to triple-check a paralegal's work,
pretty much nothing fazed me.

Especially not Sarah "Overboard" Greenberg.

We said polite hellos, but then I crossed immediately to
my table and arranged my files on the table. The bailiff entered and announced the judge, and we "All Rise'd" for the
Honorable Judge Bernard Bertels.

I tried not to cringe. I knew that local judges heard both

civil and criminal cases, but didn't they have more than one judge in this county?

His Honor's eyes twinkled a bit when he saw me, but he merely waited for the bailiff to announce that the hearing for Deaver v. BDC, Inc., was now in session. Then Judge Bertels leaned forward. "Let's talk about these requests. Frankly, I don't see that you have a leg to stand on, Ms. Greenberg, but I take privilege and work product claims seriously, so I let you come down to make your case. Based on your filed objections alone, I'd deny them and let the plaintiff have their discovery."

Sarah stood up. "Your Honor, we clearly have valid objections based both on attorney work product and on the more stringent protections of client confidentiality."

He leaned back in his chair. "How do you see that?"

"We produced those advertisements in anticipation of litigation, as required by the work product doctrine, Your Honor. Additionally, it is possible that discussion of our targeted client base may be included in the materials on file at Orange Grove Productions, as their attorney will tell you."

One of the junior-looking lawyers popped up, eyes nearly bugging out. The judge waved an arm. "Sit down, Mr. Owens. Ms. Greenberg is claiming the privilege, we'll let her argue the motion."

"Thank you, Your Honor." The man sank bonelessly back down into his seat. Corporate lawyer types hated showing up in court. I used to make fun of them, with the usual trial lawyer arrogance. After my one and only foray into criminal law, I felt a wave of sympathy for the man.

The judge looked at me. "Counselor, your thoughts?"

I stood up. This was a lot less formal than federal court. I wasn't yet sure if I liked it or not. "Thank you, Your Honor. December Vaughn for Plaintiff Charles Deaver."

The judge did a "go ahead" twirling motion with his hand. "Yes, dementia hasn't set in yet, Ms. Vaughn. I can remember your name. Your response to Ms. Greenberg?"

"Thank you, Your Honor. As I set forth in my responses, neither Greenberg and Smithies nor their clients have absolutely any expectation of privacy related to the ad itself, or its filming. If there were any client relationship involved, it would have only been formed *after* the ad was filmed, *after* the ad aired on television, and *after* the client called the law firm in response to the ad."

I took a breath and looked the judge right in the eye, on firm ground this time. "There is not the slightest hint of work product in the filming of a television commercial, Your Honor. All those commercials do is attempt to solicit clients. Therefore, we respectfully request that you grant our nonparty production requests directed to Orange Grove Production."

Judge Bertels nodded and made a note on the papers in front of him. "Thank you, Ms. Vaughn. I've heard enough. Orange Grove Production is hereby ordered to respond in full to the nonparty production requests filed by the plaintiff in the case of Deaver v. BDC."

He looked at Sarah. "Frankly, Ms. Greenberg, I'm surprised you wasted my time with this. I've come to expect more of you."

She looked down at her table and mumbled something that may have been an apology. Then the bailiff called the next hearing, and I stuffed my files back in my briefcase and headed for the back of the courtroom. I had no desire to hear anything Sarah had to say; I'd deal directly with the production company now.

As I walked down the stairs, I could feel that the shark smile was back on my face. This time, I deserved it. I couldn't wait to call Max. I dug in my purse for my phone, then remembered putting it in my jacket pocket. I stuck my hand in my pocket, and it went straight through. A rip in the pocket lining must have opened up somewhere along the way. Since I would have heard my metal-cased phone hitting the tiled floor of the hallway, my bet was that it had happened in the carpeted courtroom.

I sighed and headed back upstairs, hoping that Sarah was gone already. I hated to ruin my triumphant exit with slinking back in search of my phone.

As I walked past the tiny counsel room outside the courtroom, where lawyers can meet privately with their clients prior to hearings, I caught sight of the back of Sarah's head through the small glass pane on the door. I stopped and snuck another look, and saw the *front* of a very unexpected head.

Addison Langley was meeting with Sarah Greenberg after my hearing. I recognized him immediately from his picture I'd seen in the newspaper. Sarah moved, and I jumped out of the way, fast, and plastered myself against the wall in the slight alcove formed between the counsel room and the courtroom door. The door opened, and they walked out, but they never even looked my way, luckily.

They stopped for a moment by the door, speaking in hushed voices. Langley had Greenberg's arm in what looked like a death grip. "Look, Sarah, this was your responsibility, and you screwed it up. This could be really bad for us."

She yanked her arm away from him. "Shut up, Addison. You haven't been much help on this. You're all about telling me to make sure the message gets across to one stupid Ohio lawyer, but you're not very helpful on the practical side."

They looked both ways down the hall, but still didn't look back toward the courtroom. Sarah spoke up again, barely above a whisper. "Too bad that loaning a judge a yacht for a weekend won't buy you justice in Claymore County like it will in some other places. Bertels turned my 'friendly offer' of the boat down flat."

Langley grabbed her arm again. "You better fix it. Now."

She said nothing, just jerked her arm away and took off down the hall, and then he hurried off in the other direction. I turned and walked back in the courtroom to retrieve my cell phone, mind reeling at what sure as heck sounded like a confession.

Alligator pee or no alligator pee, *this* stupid lawyer from Ohio was going to take some bad guys down. Now all I needed was proof.

Chapter 40

I walked into the office, still on my high from court, and screeched to a halt when I saw Gina-the-maniac sitting on our couch holding a sleeping Daisy. As the door swung shut behind me, I shot an accusing glare at Max. "What is she doing here, and why is she holding our puppy?"

Daisy heard my voice, opened one eye and peeked, then squirmed and wiggled until Gina put her down on the floor. Daisy ran to me as fast as her fat little puppy legs could carry her, which (I admit) was rather endearing.

Not that I'm a softie or anything.

Clearly, the dog has good taste, ditching psycho Gina for me. I picked her up, resigning myself to dog hair all over my suit, and petted her. She sneezed in my face, which probably means "I love you" in Dog.

Gina stood up, shoulders hunched. Her hair looked like it hadn't been washed in a few days, and strands of it hung in her face. The oversized T-shirt that hung loosely over raggedly cut-off denim shorts did nothing for her. As I studied her and wondered where the rebellious beauty from the bar had gone, leaving this defeated woman in her place, the worst possible thing happened.

That damn under-the-rib-cage twinge.

I blew out a sigh. "Okay, Gina, what's up? If this is another threat, I'm so not in the mood."

She shook her head, looking at Max almost pleadingly.

Max spoke up. "December, we need to talk. I have a favor to ask."

Oh, crap. Between my twinge and Max's "save the world" mind-set, I had the sinking feeling I was getting ready to help Gina in some way.

"What is it?"

Max bit her lip, then smiled at me. "First, the good news. Your furniture is on the way! The driver promises to have it here by the end of the week."

I rolled my eyes. "When his honeymoon is over?"

"Well, probably. And you didn't even notice! But I had the carpet cleaners in here this morning, and the place doesn't stink like alligator pee anymore."

I grinned. "Now that *is* good news."

"And your toxicologist called, too. He has some very interesting news about the insulin. He didn't want to condescend to speak to a mere assistant, so he's waiting for your call." She held up a sheet of paper. "He's already faxed us his invoice, too."

I walked over to take it, still holding Daisy and keeping my eye on Gina, in case she suddenly decided to attack us with manicure tools. I scanned the page and tried not to gasp. "Wow, guess I should have been an expert witness. It pays way better than law."

Max nodded. "Yeah, except you would have had to go to medical school, and you have that little problem with blood."

Gina sat back down on the couch, pulled her knees up to her chest, and put her arms around them. She sat there silently, her eyes fixed on me. It was a little creepy, to be honest. I jerked my head toward the hallway and asked Max to come fill me in. She followed me, first stopping to tell Gina we'd be right back. Gina nodded, but still didn't say anything.

As I walked down the hall, I realized I didn't hear Mr. Ellison clomping around or humming. "Where's our other employee, Henry the Alligator Slayer?"

"Oh, right. I forgot to tell you that. Mrs. Zivkovich called earlier, and she was really upset. Turns out her son-in-law did clean out her savings account. Mr. Ellison rushed over to her place after I took the call. She says she's afraid of Nervil. Her daughter and the baby are staying with her; they left him."

Max paused at the doorway to my office, and I glanced back at her. "December, I'm a little worried, too. She says he's after you."

I dropped my purse and briefcase on my desk. "Great. Just great. Well, look on the bright side. If he drops in, we can sic Gina on him."

"Very funny. I told her how to get in touch with the police. I don't think this is anything to joke about," Max said, giving me a disapproving look.

"I don't think so either. But what can I do? Add him to the list of people out to get me, I guess. Listen to this," I said, then filled her in on the morning's activity.

"They actually called you the 'stupid Ohio lawyer'?" Max shook her head. "That's awful! Although I have warned you about that pink suit. Especially since it kind of matches your car now."

I groaned. "Don't remind me. Did you get that appointment for car painting?"

"They quoted me five hundred dollars, and I wanted to be sure you're willing to spend that much before I set the appointment," she said.

I groaned again. "I can't afford that right now. I'm wondering how we'll keep the electricity on, to be honest. Plus, we have to pay that invoice from the toxicologist at some point."

Sinking down into my chair, I tried doing mental calculations in my head, but nothing was adding up to enough money to meet payroll. "We have to find some paying clients soon, Max."

She perched on the edge of a chair across from me. "Right. But with this junkie label hanging over you, and all the violence, which everybody hears about on the scanner, nobody wants to hire you. We're in a tough place, D. We're not even going to be able to meet payroll soon, at this rate."

I stared off into space for a long minute, then forced myself to snap out of the doom and gloom. "So tell me. What is Gina doing here?"

Max brightened. "Right. We need to hire her."

I blinked. "We have no money; we can't meet payroll; we need to hire another employee. Is this beauty queen math?"

Thirty minutes and two or three rib-cage twinges later, I surrendered. It turns out Max and Gina had chatted and found out that Gina had gone to school with some cousin of Max's, so that practically made her family to Max in that incomprehensible "Everybody is my relative" way that Southern girls have. (I'd been on the receiving end of a lot of kindness due to Max's "adopting" me when I was in high school, so I wasn't knocking it. I just didn't quite understand it.)

Anyway, Gina hated the inpatient facility. Her lawyer'd worked out some deal so she could attend outpatient rehab, as long as she could prove she'd found gainful employment.

Just call me Gainful.

Unpaid, maybe, but gainful.

"Why doesn't *he* hire her?" I muttered rebelliously, sounding a lot like Emily's daughter, Joker, when she didn't get her way.

Max glared at me. "Now you're being childish. If you're talking about *he* her attorney, he said it wouldn't fly since he represents her. If you're talking about *he* Jake, he didn't want to build into her delusions about him any further."

My ears perked up at Jake's name. "So Jake was here?" I tried to sound nonchalant, but from the look on her face, I failed miserably.

"No, he called. Look, are you going to hire her or not?"

I sighed. "Fine. As a favor to you. But you keep her out of trouble, and you supervise her. If she shows the slightest sign of going bat poop on us, she's gone."

Max jumped up and backed out of the room, probably afraid I would change my mind. "Right. No problem. I'll send her in to talk to you," she said, then practically ran off down the hall.

"Wait!" I didn't want to talk to Gina. I didn't want Gina near any sharp objects, for that matter. I grabbed my letter opener and shoved it in an open drawer. I'd already been chased around my office by one employee wielding a sharp weapon. Once was enough.

Been there, done that, almost got the stab wounds to prove it.

Gina walked into my room, still watching me with that wary expression; still saying nothing.

I gestured to a chair, and she sat down across from me. "Okay, Gina, we're going to help you out here. You can give Max all the credit for this, because it's not really my habit to go around hiring people who threaten me. But she assures me you're past all that, and that you will work hard and be responsible. No stabbing people, for example. That's definitely in the employee manual. Page thirty-seven, I think."

A little smile flickered at the edges of her lips, which gave me hope. If a person has a sense of humor, she can survive anything. Well, maybe except bullets. Or stabbings.

But she can survive *most* things.

Gina finally spoke, but her voice was so soft I could barely hear her. "Thank you. I'm sorry about calling you and yelling at you that time. My head was in a bad place. Jake and me are just friends anyway."

"What about painting my car?" I asked, playing a hunch.

She looked at me blankly. "Painting your car? What are you talking about?"

"What about having that man call me and tell me to mind my own business or else?" I leaned forward. "Why did you do that?"

She shook her head, looking at me like I was the crazy one. "I don't know what you're talking about, Miss Vaughn. I called you once about Jake, and that was it."

"Call me December," I said automatically. Unless she was a brilliant actress, she wasn't faking it. She didn't know what I was talking about. My instincts told me I could cross her off the list for the car and the sinus stalker.

Which left me back at square one. Who would have written such nasty, personal things on my car? And why?

I realized she was still sitting there, staring at me, and I stood up and held my hand out to shake hers. "Welcome aboard, Gina. We're a bit of a leaky ship right now, but we're doing our best. Please talk to Max about the paper-work you need to fill out."

She shook my hand hesitantly. "Thank you, Miss—December. I know I made a bad first impression. And a bad second impression. But I'll work hard. Thanks for helping me out."

As she left, I got the feeling that I'd just shoved the leaky ship in high gear and pointed it at an iceberg, but what could I do? It was the rib-cage twinge.

As I sat back down, my phone rang. "December, it's Addison Langley," Max said.

This ought to be interesting.

I grabbed a pen and waited till I heard the click. "Hello, Addy. What can I do for you?"

"Five million dollars to settle the Deaver case. Confidential, sealed settlement. You have twenty-four hours."

Click.

I'd been right. It was definitely interesting.

Chapter 41

Ten minutes and eight phone calls later, I looked down at my notes. Here's what I knew:

1. Jake wasn't answering either of his phones.

2. Charlie wasn't answering any of his phones.

3. Mrs. Zivkovich wasn't answering her phone.

4. My contact at the FDA was out of the office.

5. My toxicologist was in the lab, unreachable.

6. Voice mail sucked.

I slammed the phone down in its cradle, and it rang instantly. It was Charlie.

"Finally! I've been leaving messages for you everywhere," I said.

"I know. That's why I'm calling. What's up?" he asked.

"Five million dollars is what's up. Here's the deal." I filled him in on my brief call from Addy.

He whistled. "Five million dollars? It sounds like they're getting desperate to get rid of me. What did you do to them?"

"I wish I knew. There is one possible lead, but I won't know more until I receive the discovery the judge just ordered them to provide," I said. "You'll be happy to know your lawyer kicked butt in court today."

He laughed. "I'm very happy, but what do I do about this offer?"

I tossed my pen on the desk and leaned back in my chair. "That's up to you, Charlie. You told me you did not want to sign a sealed agreement under any circumstances. If that is still true, my advice has to be to decline, because there's no way BDC is going to give you five mill to go public."

"Right. But five million dollars—even after your fees and costs—would give me a huge donation to the American Cancer Society," he said slowly.

I nodded, even though he couldn't see me. "That's true. I know we didn't discuss this, but I would reduce my fee considerably if we settled at this early of a stage. And it's also true that whatever evidence I discovered, it's likely that the other plaintiffs will discover, too."

Unless Greenberg and Smithies is in on the cover-up with Langley, Cowan.

But my duty is to MY client, as much as I may wish I could effect social justice on a large scale.

"World peace," I mumbled, thinking of Max's pageant days.

"What?"

"Nothing, just thinking out loud," I said. "Look, it can't hurt to at least meet with them. Do you want to set up a meeting and find out more?"

"Yes. Can we do that? I hate making decisions in the dark," he said, sounding relieved.

"Definitely. I'll try to set up the meeting for this evening, given our twenty-four-hour time frame. I'll call you back as soon as I arrange something."

"Great. Call my cell phone," he said.

After we'd said good-bye and hung up, I asked Max to call and arrange the meeting, because I didn't want to talk to Addison again until I'd had time to think more about his offer. It's a rare trial that yields five million for the plaintiff, especially a sum that large that's not eaten away with expert witness fees, lawyer fees, and trial costs.

On the other hand, if BDC really was covering up something as heinous as early knowledge of a defect in the insulin, could I live with myself if we let it go?

Under the rules of professional responsibility—the code by which all attorneys were sworn to work—I'd have to live with it. If Charlie signed that confidentiality agreement, I could never violate attorney-client privilege to disclose a single thing about it.

Ever.

Since I believe fervently in the purpose behind the doctrine of attorney-client privilege—that a client must feel completely free to tell her attorney everything in order to assist with the preparation of her case—this wasn't even a difficult choice for me. I'd never tell.

But that didn't mean I could live *happily* with the choice either.

As I sat there, playing with all the possibilities in my mind, the phone rang again. It was my toxicologist. "What did you find out, Dr. Phillips?"

"There's no way an error in the production process caused this defect. You've got a tampering case on your hands."

I sat, stunned, at my desk for a long time after I hung up with Dr. Phillips. He'd said it was flat-out impossible that the chemical with the unpronounceable name that had infiltrated the insulin had come from any stage of the manufacturing process. I'd also learned way more than I ever thought I'd want to know about the difference between porcine and human forms of insulin, recombinant DNA, and the islets of Langerhans in the pancreas.

If it's tampering, no wonder they wanted to cover it up. If health care professionals and consumers panic because they can't trust the safety of BDC's insulin-manufacturing process, they'll all go straight to Eli Lilly or one of the other insulin manufacturers.

BDC's main source of profits is its insulin.

BDC's stock price will plummet, and the company will go bankrupt.

Holy crap.

It was time to call in the big guns. I honestly didn't know what to do with this information. But my friend at the FDA would. I needed to try to call him again.

As I picked up the phone, I heard shouting from the lobby. I shoved my chair back and ran down the hall, almost afraid to find out what was happening this time.

I skidded to a stop at the end of the hallway, mouth falling open in disbelief. A man the size and shape of a bull moose loomed over Max, yelling at the top of his lungs.

And he was clutching a baseball bat.

Normally I would have been scared stupid. But after the alligator, I was just mad. I walked out there, pasting a calm smile on my face. "Excuse me, sir, I'm December Vaughn, may I help you?"

I was careful to stand behind him and to the side, so he'd have to turn to face me, hopefully giving Max the chance to get out of there. He must have been on to me, though, because he only half turned, and he kept jerking his head from side to side to watch both of us.

I didn't know where Gina and Daisy were, but I hoped they stayed out of the way.

"You've already helped me enough, bitch," he roared. "Now my wife left me, and her crazy mother is gonna have me arrested. I needed that money. So now I'm going to make you pay."

Funny, he didn't look a thing like a Nervil. As the cold chill shot up my spine, I let out a nervous laugh. "First I'm attacked by an alligator, and now by a Croc. What is it about me and reptiles?"

He took a step closer, and raised the bat a few inches. "This Croc is gonna mess you up. Think of it as a little going-away present from me."

I tried for calm on the outside, since my inside was freaking out. *I'm going to die, I'm going to die, I'm going to die, and I haven't had sex for nearly a year. I'm going to die, and this hairy, unwashed man is going to kill me.*

"Mr. Croc, er, I mean, Nervil, you really don't want to do this," I said as soothingly as I could muster with a giant, smelly man menacing me. "You can easily work out this misunderstanding over the bank, but if you hurt me, the police will charge you with a serious crime."

He bared his teeth in a terrifying caricature of a smile. "Yeah, murder. Premeditated."

He raised the bat, and I dropped back a step. Max, who'd been frozen to her seat, jumped up and started screaming.

The door opened, and Croc whipped his head around to see who was coming in. I took the opportunity to run behind one of the chairs in the waiting area.

"Max, quit screaming and call 911!" I yelled.

Gina walked in, leading Daisy.

"Oh, crap!" I said. "Gina, get out of here—fast!"

Gina stood there, stunned, and Croc stomped over to them, shoved Gina out of the way, and slammed the door shut. Then he turned around and an evil grin spread across his entire face. "Well, well, well. Guess I got me an entire room full of pretty women. After I mess up that damn lawyer, I might have me a little fun with you two."

Daisy, who usually loved everybody, started barking and growling at him and straining at the end of her leash, as though she were going to attack Croc. Considering she weighed maybe ten pounds, I didn't think she'd do much damage.

As we watched helplessly, Croc almost casually swung out one booted foot and caught Daisy in the ribs. She yelped pitifully and flew across the floor, her tiny body smashing into the side of the couch. She fell on the floor and lay there, whimpering.

Something inside me snapped. I grabbed the nearest heavy thing I could find—which happened to be my framed, oversized law school diploma—right off the wall and went after him, screaming. "You son of a bitch. Nobody kicks my dog!"

Gina and Max snapped out of their paralysis at the same time. Gina jumped him from behind and wrapped her arms around his neck and started choking. Max grabbed her industrial-sized stapler and ran around the desk. She started smashing the stapler into his knees.

Croc roared and crashed around like the outraged moose he looked like. He threw Gina off, and she smacked her head on the side of the desk. Then he backhanded Max and knocked her down. Finally, he stood there, heaving, and stared at me. "I'm gonna kill you slowly," he snarled.

I backed up till the backs of my legs hit the couch, not allowing myself to look down at Daisy for fear I'd start crying. Then I started to lift the diploma in my hands, stopped midway, and whipped my gaze to the side to stare at the door, which was now directly behind Croc. "Thank God you're here!" I yelled.

Croc yanked his head around to stare at the closed door, and I lifted the diploma and smashed it down on his head with all my strength, glass side down. His knees crumpled, and eyes slowly glazing, he sank to the floor.

He didn't get up again.

I dropped the diploma and started sucking in sobbing breaths, then dropped to the floor to gently scoop Daisy up in my arms. Max and Gina both pulled themselves up off the floor and came over to me. Max made a wide circle around Croc's prone body, but Gina walked up to him, knelt down, and checked his pulse.

She stared up at me. "He's still alive. Do you want me to finish him?"

I looked back at her, and as much as I hate to admit it, for the tiniest split-second I was tempted. Then I shook my head. "No, of course not. Neither one of us want that on our conscience. Do we have anything to tie him up with?"

Max jumped up. "There's some rope in the kitchen, from when they delivered the refrigerator. Gina, call 911."

As Max ran down the hall, I glanced at Daisy. She looked up at me with so much love and trust in her eyes, that suddenly I was looking at her through a shimmer of tears.

Max came back with the rope just as Gina finished her brief 911 call. Then Gina tied our assaulter up with brutal efficiency. "I hope he gets rope burns," Max said and kicked him in the leg.

"Go, Max," I said. Then I stood up and very carefully handed Daisy off to Max. "We need to find an emergency vet, pronto."

The door swung open just then, and all three of us tensed

as our overhyped adrenal glands kicked our fight-or-flight responses into gear. Max and I relaxed when we saw Bear.

Gina didn't.

"Who the hell are you?" she snarled, still in a crouch.

Bear looked confused. "I'm Bear. Why are you mad at me?"

"It's okay, Gina," I said. "He's a client. Sort of."

I stepped over Croc toward Bear. "We're having a huge problem here. This man attacked us. Will you help us watch him until the police arrive?"

Bear nodded. "Sure, Miss December. I'm glad to do it. I wanted to say sorry about—"

I stopped him with a hand on his arm. "No, Bear, *I'm* sorry. I never should have jumped to conclusions, especially after you were so kind as to bring me that lovely gift. Thank you so much, and can you forgive me?"

He grinned and started to hug me.

"Ah, ah, ah! Remember the lawyer's-feet-on-ground rule?"

He let go and stood aside, still grinning. "Yep. I remember, December. Get it? I made a rhyme! Remember, December!"

I smiled weakly. "I get it, Bear. I do."

I walked to the desk to find the number of an emergency vet. "Sadly, that's about the only thing I get about all this."

By the time I talked to the vet and got instructions for transporting Daisy (move her as little as possible) and their location (behind the Harley dealership), Croc was starting to stir. His head wasn't bleeding, but that didn't mean I hadn't inflicted any internal damage. The words "subarachnoid hematoma" kept floating around in my brain, and I tried to feel some guilt about having possibly inflicted a brain swelling on the man.

Nope. Don't feel guilty at all.

Before I had time to worry about my violent tendencies, I heard sirens in the distance, and suddenly I flashed back to what Jake had told me about Croc.

Scuzzbag who'd just raided a bank account . . . I'd have it in cash.

"Gina? Will you check his pockets for keys? And then I'd like for you to go out in the parking lot—*hurry*—and find his car. Here's what you're looking for . . ."

We were all sitting on the couch and chairs (except Bear, who sat on our awakening prisoner) by the time the door burst open and the police and EMT personnel arrived. The first officer in the door swept the room with a glance and stopped at me. He groaned. "Not you again."

I stood up. "Trust me, Officer. I feel the same way."

Chapter 42

After the police had left, I wanted nothing more than to go home and bury my head under my covers. But I had a lot still to do, like prepare for the settlement conference Max had set up with Langley's office for seven o'clock. She'd made them come here to our firm, so Gina helped me drag a couple of extra chairs in my office and clean up the place a little.

As we straightened up the lobby, I looked at her and smiled. "Guess it was a great day to hire you. Thank you for all of your help."

She made a face at me. "Great for *you*, maybe. I got assaulted my first day on the job. I might have to file for worker's comp."

I groaned. "Fine, as long as I don't have to fill out the paperwork."

She stretched and glanced at her watch. "It's nearly three. I'm going to call it a day, unless you need something else. I'm not officially even working here yet."

"Sure, and thank you again."

She stopped at the door and turned back. "Be sure to call and let me know about Daisy, okay?"

"I will."

I locked the door, figuring any potential walk-ins could ring the buzzer. I'd had enough of uninvited guests for the day anyway. Then I trudged back to my office and put my head down on my arms, just for a minute.

There's nothing like looking death in the face to wear a girl out.

When the buzzer rang about half an hour later, I found Mr. Ellison and Mrs. Zivkovich at the door. I let them in, and she hugged me and burst into tears.

"The police called me and let me know we're safe," she said. "My daughter and my grandbaby don't have to worry about that awful man anymore. They said your testimony should put him away for a long time."

"Oh, don't worry," I said grimly. "I'm going to testify."

Mr. Ellison sidled up to me and gave me a very brief hug, too. "I'm glad you're okay. Heard how that rat bast— *thug*—attacked you girls. I shoulda been here to protect you," he said gruffly.

I smiled down at him. "Thank you, but it was good that you were there to protect Mrs. Zivkovich and her family. You are a very good man, Mr. Ellison. I'm lucky to know you."

He grinned and puffed out his chest. "I know. You might see a lot less of me around here, though. I'm courting Isabelle now."

She smiled and took his arm, brushing at the tears on her cheeks. "Isn't Henry just the dearest man?"

Then her smile faded. "The police said they'll do their best, but that it's unlikely that I'll ever see my money again. Most of my money is in CDs, but that was my emergency fund." She grimaced. "I only wish I'd never let him have access to my bank accounts. I'll really miss that seventeen thousand dollars."

I grinned. "That's not exactly a problem."

Striding over to my file cabinet, I opened the middle drawer and pulled out an ugly green duffel bag. Then I plopped it up on the desk and unzipped it. "Sixteen thousand, eight hundred twelve dollars. I guess he spent a couple hundred, but—hey!—it's better than nothing."

The look on her face was almost worth what I'd gone through with Croc. She promptly burst into tears again. "Oh, December, I—you—how?"

"We asked very nicely," I said, glad that Gina had remembered to wipe her fingerprints off Croc's keys before she'd returned them to his pocket. (Plus, I was a little worried about how good Gina was at stuff like fighting, tying people up, and breaking into cars, but I could worry about my new employee later.)

After many, many hugs and thank-yous and offers of homemade pie later, I finally persuaded Mr. Ellison to take Mrs. Zivkovich home. I thought about getting something to eat, but I was too worried about Daisy to be hungry. I tried to focus on preparing for my settlement meeting, but my gaze kept straying to the phone. Finally, it rang, and I snatched it up. "Max?"

"No, it's Jake. You called me?"

"Oh, it's you," I said, sighing.

"Wow. Most women don't sigh with disappointment when I call."

"I think we've already established that I'm not most women," I said. Then I briefly told him about the day.

"He attacked you with a baseball bat?" he said, his voice sharp and deadly. "Are you hurt?"

"Well, he never got a chance to hit me with it. Really, I got off the easiest. After he kicked Daisy, and knocked Max and Gina to the ground—"

"Gina?"

"Oh. Right. I hired her. So after—"

"You *what?*" The surprise in his voice made it pretty obvious he hadn't known Gina had planned to ask me for a job. For some reason, it made me feel better to know something that he didn't.

I explained. "So I'm feeling like crap here. He came after *me,* but everybody else got hurt. And poor Daisy . . . I still haven't heard . . ." I stopped talking so he wouldn't hear the tears in my voice.

"I'll swing by the emergency vet and find out what's going on with Daisy," he said. "And I'll make sure Max is okay. You stay right there and don't let anyone in the door until I come to get you."

My hackles went up at that. "Look, Brody, I appreciate everything you always seem to be doing for me, but you don't give me orders. And I have a settlement conference in about two hours. I can drive myself home perfectly well after that, but thanks."

"Damn it, Vaughn, I'm trying to keep you safe here," he said.

"I know, and I appreciate it," I said gently. "But it's not your job. I'm a big, grown-up trial lawyer here. I can take care of myself, and . . . well." I paused for a moment, seeing visions of stupid coeds in their nightgowns descending into dark basements where ax-wielding psychopaths lurked.

Suddenly, I had a change of heart. "Okay. I'm tough, but I'm not an idiot. If you really don't have anything better to do . . ."

There was a silence, and then he sighed. "Vaughn, you are making me crazy. I'll call you from the vet's."

"Thank—"

Click.

•   •   •

It was nearly seven. A fresh pot of coffee was brewing, and my offices looked as good as they could after the alligator'd gouged some of my furniture, and Croc'd bashed up a few more pieces. I'd rehung my Capital Law School diploma (way to go, Capital, for those crazy oversized diplomas!), cracked glass and all, until I found time to reframe it.

Or I might even leave it that way. Sort of a badge of honor.

The phone rang. I grabbed it, almost afraid of what I might hear. "Max?"

"Sorry, me again. I sent Max home to get some rest," Jake said.

"Is she okay? And Daisy . . . is she . . ."

"They're both fine. Daisy has a couple of cracked ribs, and they're going to keep her for observation, but she's fine. They did a lot of tests to be sure she doesn't have any internal injuries. That's why it took so long. But everybody is fine."

I sucked in a shaky breath. "I . . . thank you so much. I can't tell you how much better that makes me feel. I really appreciate it, Jake. You're—you're a good friend."

He laughed. "That's what I'm aiming for. Friend status. Take care, Vaughn."

"Wait! What about the bill? Do they need me to bring a check?"

"No, they don't charge for emergencies on Mondays, so you're covered. Max said she will come pick Daisy up in the morning on her way to work, so to expect her in a little late."

I thanked him again, and we hung up. I was nearly light-headed with relief, and had done several dancing steps across the lobby before I realized there was something wrong with what he'd just said.

The emergency vet doesn't charge for emergencies on Mondays?

Jake must have paid the bill. I groaned. One more thing I'd owe him for, even *after* I found out how much it was and reimbursed him.

The buzzer rang, and I was glad to see Charlie had arrived first. He'd dressed up his usual khakis with a button-down shirt. I let him in and we shook hands. "So, what do you think?" I asked.

He ran a hand through his hair and laughed nervously. "I haven't done much else but think about this all day, and my thoughts are all crazy running together now."

"That's understandable. Five million is a lot of money," I said, leading him back to my office.

"It's not just that, although I'd love to be able to give a big chunk of money to the Cancer Society. It's that I wouldn't have to go through this litigation process. No offense, but you must be nuts to do this job. Answering those—what did you call them? Interrogatories? Those questions the other side asked me that you sent home with me. All about Faith and our life together and what she was like. Anyway, sitting at my kitchen table, writing down my answers, brought up all the pain all over again. I'm not ashamed to tell you I broke down and cried like a baby."

I put a hand on his arm. "There's no shame in feeling pain because you lost the person you loved most in the world. And I completely understand what you mean about avoiding litigation. I spend an awful lot of time persuading people *not* to get involved in lawsuits. It's an awful, gut-wrenching process."

He looked at me, biting his lip. "What do I do? What would you do?"

I leaned back and shook my head. "I can't tell you that.

This has to be your decision. What I *can* do is talk you through the pros and cons of accepting the settlement offer."

By the time Langley and the BDC rep showed up at ten after seven (the "must show we're more important by being late" philosophy in action), we'd discussed the offer and consequences from every angle, and Charlie was leaning pretty heavily toward accepting. He'd mentioned how much research toward a cure could be funded with five million dollars, and that seemed to outweigh what he called his "petty need for vengeance."

I'd told him it wasn't petty to want justice for Faith, but that I would support him one hundred percent in either decision. I hadn't brought up my suspicions about tampering and a cover-up, because they were very serious allegations, and I didn't have any proof.

Yet.

After I brought Addison and Harold Punter, the BDC rep, back down the hall to my office, made the introductions, and poured coffee all around, Charlie seemed to be calmer. I sat down, pulled out a legal pad, and looked at Addison. "I'm surprised you don't have BDC's insurance rep here, if you're serious about this," I said.

Punter, who'd watched everything with his beady little eyes staring out of a floridly red face, started to speak, but Addison cut him off. "This is a preapproved settlement offer. Trust me, we have a check ready to go, should Mr. Deaver accept our more than generous terms," he said smoothly.

"And what exactly are those terms?" I asked.

Addison pulled out a sheaf of forms. "All the details are here. Basically, we want full confidentiality. This will be a sealed settlement, with no admission of guilt on BDC's part. Furthermore, Ms. Vaughn must turn over all copies of all discovery documents to me, and agree that she will not use her knowledge of that discovery on any further case against BDC on this matter."

Charlie shifted in his chair and looked unhappy, but resigned. I'd told him that was going to be the deal.

I took the papers from Addison, not as resigned. "Of course, I'll have to review these before we can give you an answer, you realize. Additionally, we will have to talk about the provision as it regards me."

He waved his hand, looking impatient. "We want a preliminary answer now, and the papers signed and delivered to me by noon tomorrow. There is no flexibility in any of the provisions."

I dropped the papers on my desk and glared at him. "That's more than a little unreasonable. Do you expect us to stay up all night reviewing these?"

Punter finally spoke up. "If somebody was giving me five million dollars, and I didn't even have an ex-wife to support, I'd be working hard to get the job done, little lady."

I blinked. "*What* did you—"

Charlie cut me off. "What the hell does that mean? No ex-wife to support? My wife *died* because you put bad insulin out there. We trusted you with her *life*. Thousands of people trusted you with their lives. And now you make stupid jokes at a time like this?"

He shoved his chair back and stood up. "And you want me to keep it a secret, on top of everything else? Why, so you can screw other people out of justice?"

I stood up, too. "Charlie—"

"No! Forget it! What was I thinking? I'm not accepting five million dollars to keep quiet. Hell, I wouldn't accept twenty-five million. I'm going to tell everybody about you.

You're going down!" he yelled, then he stormed out of my office.

I stood there, stunned, for a moment, then ran down the hall after him. But by the time I got to the reception area, he was slamming the door of his truck, then he squealed out of the parking lot. I closed my eyes and sent up a brief prayer for his safety. Driving while heartsick may not be illegal, but it's horribly dangerous.

When I turned around, Addison and his client were storming across my lobby. Punter got to me first. "Look here, you can't treat us like that—"

Addison cut him off again. "Mr. *Punter*, why don't you wait out in the car? I'll handle this."

Punter glared at both of us, but then shoved the door open and went outside. Addison waited until the door swung shut behind him, then grabbed my arm. "This is your last chance to be reasonable, Ms. Vaughn. Convince your client to be reasonable and accept our offer, or I will crush you and your pathetic little firm."

I yanked my arm away from him. "Are you nuts? Who do you think you are anyway? This is litigation, not . . . not *war*."

He glared at me, and whatever flickered in his eyes struck me as not a little insane. "You have no idea what war is, Ms. Vaughn. You think that little bit we leaked from your Ohio Bar app was bad? You have no idea what we can do to you. Surrender or prepare to be destroyed."

He knocked me out of the way to get to the door, and I didn't know whether to laugh or call the loony bin. *Surrender or prepare to be destroyed?*

Melodramatic much?

Two more minutes, and he would have been threatening to tie me to the railroad tracks.

I locked the door, but just stood there staring out at the parking lot as he got in his Lexus and drove off. About a minute later, Jake appeared out of nowhere in front of the door, and I let out a little screech.

I let him in. "Where did you come from?"

"I saw Langley's car, so I parked mine down at the end of the building. I figured a little discretion might be the better idea. After I saw him peel out of here, I walked over. What happened?"

Sighing, I shook my head. "I don't even know where to begin, but it ended with me nearly tied to the railroad tracks."

"What? And why was Langley here with his brother-in-law?" he asked.

"His brother-in-law works for BDC?"

Jake gave me a funny look. "What are you talking about? His brother-in-law owns a car dealership in Orlando. Are you in the market for a new car?"

"Are you saying that Harold Punter is Langley's brother-in-law?"

"Well, his name is Harold *Parker*, but yes. I've met him several times."

It finally happened. I was shocked speechless. His *brother-in-law*?

Slowly, the puzzle pieces snapped into place. Langley had played me. Big time. But why the charade?

I leaned against the door and stared at Jake. "No," I said slowly. "I'm not in the market for a new car. But I may have just been sold a lemon."

Chapter 43

Jake and I ate the pizza he'd brought with him and spent an hour trying to figure out what kind of game Langley could have been playing, to have his brother-in-law pose as a BDC rep. "Did he think I wouldn't find out? And what about the offer? Does this mean it's invalid?"

Jake shrugged, holding his hands out, palms up. "Beats me. You lawyer types are too devious for me."

I rolled my eyes. "Right. Whatever. After the three messages I left on his voice mail, you'd think he'd have called back by now."

"After that last one, where you called him the scurvy underbelly of a diseased goat, he might be waiting for you to calm down."

My cheeks got a little hot. "So I watch too many pirate movies. Sue me."

He tossed his napkin in the trashcan and leaned back in his chair, folding his arms behind his head. "So, where were we? Greenberg wanted to meet with you, but it had to be on the yacht . . ."

I nodded, tapping my pen on the paper. "Yeah, she couldn't do lunch because she had the funeral of some associate or something. Poor guy committed suicide," I said, shuddering. "Although working with her would be enough to drive anybody over the edge."

Jake had sat up straight at the word "suicide." "Who was the associate?"

It was my turn to shrug. "I don't know. Why? Is it important?"

"I don't know. I just know that I hate coincidences. Why are all these people dying? Dack at the museum, some associate of Greenberg's. I don't like it."

"I don't like it either, but it's pretty far-fetched to think the BDC cases had anything to do with a suicide."

He stood up and walked over to my side of the desk. "Humor me. Let me use your Internet for a moment."

He leaned over me while I logged back on to the computer, and I tried not to notice the tingling in the back of my neck. I rolled my chair out of the way, and he started a search. Within seconds, we were looking at an online article in the *Post-Union* about the death of Marion Ziggeran, the "much-beloved colleague" according to a quote from Sarah herself.

I rolled my head around, trying to work the knots out of my neck. "Ziggeran, Ziggeran. Why does that name sound so familiar?"

He shook his head. "I don't know it. Are you sure you don't have Zivkovich on the brain after today?"

Moving to stand behind me, he put his hands on my neck and started working the knots out with firm pressure. "Counselor, that's some tension you've got built up here. You ought to try to relax more."

Every sane thought flew out of my head at the touch of his fingers. Magic fingers.

I tried not to drool. Drooling is so unappealing.

Focus, December.

"Right. No. Not Zivkovich. Ziggeran. And *you* try to relax when you have people shooting at you, assaulting you, getting murdered next to you at the museum . . ."

The museum. What . . .

"The museum! Orange Grove Productions! Where is that invoice?" I dug around in the piles of paper on my desk, then found my URGENT CASE QUESTIONS file under an empty can of Diet Coke. I shuffled through the pages in the folder until I found the invoice.

"Ah-ha! I was right! Look at this, Brody," I said triumphantly, pointing to the invoice.

We both stared at the box marked CLIENT NAME on the bottom left corner of the invoice.

"Marion Ziggeran," Jake said softly.

I whirled around in my chair. "Marion Ziggeran. Everybody who knows about this commercial seems to wind up dead."

Jake's lips quirked in a half smile. "Not a bad fate for people in advertising, in general."

"This is no time for jokes! We've got to report this to somebody. This is too big for me to handle. I've got to reach my contact at the FDA, too. I'm going to call him right now. I have his home number," I said, reaching for the phone.

Jake walked over toward the door. "I have a friend at the FBI. I'm going to give him a call and find out where we should go with this," he said, pulling his cell phone out of his pocket as he walked.

He stopped at the doorway. "Good job, Vaughn."

I stopped, mid-dial, and looked up at him. "We make a good team, Brody."

He smiled then walked off, and I tried to shake the hormonal overdrive out of my brain. Danger. Bad guys. Imminent evil. No time for romance.

I finished dialing, and the phone rang a few times and went to voice mail. I was on my own. I left a brief name-and-number-only message and slowly hung up the phone.

Maybe Jake would have better luck with his FBI contact. As I started to stand up, the phone rang, and I grabbed it.

"Hello?"

"December, thank God I found you! Nathan never came home!" Celia was sobbing; I could hardly understand her.

"Honey, calm down. What do you mean, he never came home? From where?"

"He . . . he went to the store. Just to pick up some milk and bread. That was over an hour ago. I called the store, and he never showed up," she said, breathing hard.

It never occurred to me to doubt this. Of *course* Celia would know the people at the store, and they would know Nathan. That was so Orange Grove-y.

"I'm sure he's fine, Aunt Celia. He probably stopped off to do something else, and—"

"He's gone! Something happened to him. I have that terrible feeling in my throat, December, I just know something happened. It's almost ten o'clock at night. He never, ever drives at night," she said, practically shrieking.

Having my own personal rib-cage twinge, I didn't question Aunt Celia's bad throat feeling. It ran in the family. Plus, I knew that Nathan never drove at night. He had pretty bad astigmatism and had a hard time seeing clearly with oncoming headlights in his eyes.

Jake walked into my office, and I waved him over and held the phone so we could both hear. "Celia, did you try his cell phone?"

"He left it here. He was only going two miles away to the store. Oh, December, you have to help me!"

I quickly filled Jake in, and he leaned over and spoke into the phone. "Mrs. Judson? Celia? It's Jake Brody. I'm going to come over right now and drive the road between your house and the store, all right? I want you to remain calm and stay right there, in case he comes home."

"Jake? You're right, I should do that. I'll go right now," she said.

"No!" Jake and I shouted simultaneously.

"Aunt Celia, you're too upset, and your astigmatism isn't much better than Uncle Nathan's. We'd hate for you to get into an accident while we're out looking for him," I said.

"Celia, you stay right where you are. I will come pick you up first, and you can ride along with me. How is that?" Jake said, voice firm but gentler than I'd ever heard.

"Oh, Jake, that would be wonderful. Please hurry. I'll get ready right now."

I hung up and took a long, deep breath.

Jake put a hand on my shoulder. "Are you okay, Vaughn?"

"Honestly, I'm not sure how much more I can take. If Uncle Nathan has been in an accident, I'm going to ask them to put me in the hospital bed next to his. Maybe we can share a morphine drip." The searing pain in my chest at the thought of Uncle Nathan in a hospital bed almost knocked me down.

"Come with me," he said.

"No, there's not enough room in your car. I'll be right behind you. In fact, I'll start at the store and work my way toward the house, while you pick up Aunt Celia," I said, grabbing my purse. We were running out the door when the phone rang again.

"That might be Aunt Celia, about Nathan," I said. I ran back to pick it up. "Is he okay?"

There was a silence.

Then a raspy voice that sounded a lot like my sinus

stalker came on the line. "Tell your client that he needs to take the five million, if you want your uncle to live to write another book. We know Brody is there with you. Get him out. If you tell him anything, your uncle dies."

Jake looked at me, inquiring. It took every atom of willpower I'd ever had to keep my face calm. I held the phone away from my ear a little and forced a smile. "No, Jake. It's one of my *pro bono* clients. I have to take this; she's in trouble. I'll be on my way in five minutes."

He nodded. "Nathan will be okay, December. Don't worry." Then he strode off down the hall. After I heard the door close, I put the phone back to my ear. "He's gone. What do you want? Where is my uncle? Is he all right?"

"Shut up, bitch. I'm the one asking the questions this time."

I waited, but there was only more silence. "Well, go ahead."

"Go ahead, what?" he snarled.

"Go ahead and ask the questions," I said, trying not to scream.

"What questions?"

Oh, God. My uncle's life is in the hands of the stupidest criminal in recorded history.

"You said . . . oh, forget that. Tell me what you want me to do, and I'll do it. Please don't hurt my uncle. He's only a harmless old man. Please," I said, tears rolling down my face.

"Here's the deal. You get Deaver to accept that five million dollars. Then you bring the signed settlement papers to us at Sarah Greenberg's boat at the marina. If you call the police, we'll kill Nathan. If you call anybody else, or tell anybody else, we'll kill Nathan. If you bring anybody with you, we'll kill Nathan, and then we'll kill you."

He laughed, and ice skittered across my skull from the sound of it. "And after we kill Nathan, and you, we'll go after Nathan's wife. You got me?"

"I got you," I whispered, knees buckling. "I understand perfectly."

Chapter 44

I dropped the phone on the desk and stood there, frozen in shock. I couldn't think, I couldn't move, and I couldn't figure out what to do. My mind was babbling at me that it couldn't take one single more thing; that I had to call Jake and get help.

But he said he'll kill Nathan. I have to handle this myself.

I dug my nails into my palms, trying for clarity of thought. How did this make sense? How did it fit together? Why didn't it work?

The puzzle pieces were all wrong. The tingly feeling in my head was exploding.

If I get Charlie to sign that agreement, how will that help them? They know I'll tell the police about all of this at some point. They can't threaten me for the rest of my life.

"Yes, they can. If the rest of my life is measured in hours now, not years. They can't let Uncle Nathan go. They can't let me go. They'll have to kill us. Or make it look like we committed suicide, like Ziggeran," I muttered to myself.

I automatically grabbed my purse and headed for the door, still thinking out loud. "They can't even let Charlie live, unless he signs, no questions asked. Even then, they might consider him a loose end."

So Sarah was in on the cover-up. BDC must have one hell of a kickback scheme going on to get a top plaintiff's attorney to go along with something like that. I flew out the door and out to my car, then shoved the key in the ignition and took off.

I was heading for the marina. I'd call Charlie on the way. I couldn't put his life in jeopardy, too. I fumbled for my phone and dialed.

"Hey, hello," Charlie said.

"Charlie, it's December. Look, you have to get out of your house. I know it sounds odd, but there are some very bad people threatening us. They have . . . well, they want me to force you to settle your case. But I have a conflict now, and I can't talk to you about your case. I need—I need . . ." I fumbled, wondering what to say.

Then the perfect solution flashed into my brain.

"I need you to fire me."

"What? What are you talking about? Hey, hold on, there's somebody at the door," he said.

I'd nearly missed the turn to the marina, so I focused on screeching around the corner, but then what he'd said penetrated the fog in my brain. "No! Don't answer the door!"

I was too late. I heard shouting, then crashing noises, then a strange voice came on the line. "Vaughn? You blew it. Get down to the marina now, and you still have a chance to save the old man."

He slammed the phone down, and I choked back a cry. If they hurt Charlie . . .

I drove the rest of the way to the marina with grim determination, trying desperately to think of a way to save Nathan—trying frantically to put the pieces together. Why would such big-name hotshot lawyers go to such lengths over a single case? They could have found a way to pin the cover-up entirely on BDC, probably.

Why agree to the cover-up in the first place, for that matter? Could it really all be about money?

What about Harold Punter/Parker? He's not even with BDC. What if BDC has nothing to do with any of this?

But the suspicion forming in my mind was so monstrous, I couldn't wrap my brain around it.

Just before I pulled into the darkened parking lot, I called Jake. His cell rang straight into voice mail. "Look, I can't talk. But they've got Uncle Nathan, and I have to go to Sarah's yacht alone, to get him. It's Greenberg, definitely, and probably Langley, too. They got Charlie, Jake. I—if I don't survive this, you make sure you get them for me."

My throat closed up, and I had to force out the words. "Tell Aunt Celia I love her." Then I flipped the phone shut and shoved it down the front of my shirt and tucked it into my bra. The shirt wasn't snug, so maybe nobody would notice.

Maybe I'd be able to call somebody, when I was singing with the fishies.

I screeched to a stop and jumped out of the car, trying to send psychic "be strong" vibes to Nathan, who was almost certainly on that boat. As I ran over toward the *Tortfeasance*, three men stepped out of the shadows to flank me. They didn't follow me up the ramp to the boat, but they stood guard at the bottom.

If I hadn't already known it, that would have convinced me. I was never getting off that boat alive.

I followed the lights to the stateroom. Langley and Greenberg stood by the bar, arguing with each other. They stopped when they saw me. I walked farther into the room and saw Uncle Nathan, tied to a chair and with a bloody smear on the side of his face. I ran over to him and knelt down. "Oh, Uncle Nathan! Are you all right? I'm so sorry. I'm so sorry," I said, crying.

He tried for a smile. "I'm fine, honey. This is the most excitement I've had in years. It'll be good for a book plot, won't it?"

I saw in his eyes the knowledge that there might not be any more books, and my terror sharpened into pure fury. I leaned closer and murmured in his ear, "Watch for my sign. We're going to get out of this, I promise."

Sarah laughed. "Whispering comforting words to your uncle, December? Too bad you couldn't have listened to all of our warnings. If you'd just gotten out of this case like we told you to, your uncle would be safe at home in his bed."

Langley elbowed her. "Shut up, Sarah. We don't need to admit anything."

I stood slowly, back to them, scanning the room for something—anything—I could use as a weapon. There was nothing.

Where are the fireplace pokers when you need them?

Somebody on the deck shouted, but it cut off quickly. Then we heard a scuffling noise, and my old buddy Captain Karl shoved Charlie into the room. "Here's your other friend, Miss Greenberg."

Charlie's hands were tied behind his back, and his face was a bloody mess. I clenched my hands into fists, but tried to appear calm. I put all my contempt into my expression and sneered at Karl. "Still jumping to her bidding and even calling her Miss Greenberg, after she quit banging you?"

Sarah's eyes widened, and Karl's head whipped around to fix me with a menacing glare. "You know nothing. Shut up."

Langley, meanwhile, was staring at Sarah in disbelief. "You and Karl? That's disgusting. Sleeping with the hired help. Yet another example of your extremely bad judgment," he snarled.

She backed away from him. "How dare you talk to me about bad judgment? I had this all resolved. She was going to bring us the signed settlement papers, and we could have left Deaver alone. But you sent your thug to grab Deaver, too. Don't you think it's going to look suspicious when all of these people disappear?"

This is great. Keep fighting, you morons.

I stared at Charlie, trying to send a mental signal. We had to be ready for any chance.

Langley loomed over her. "Me? *My* bad judgment? Are you insane? You sent people to vandalize her car and shoot at her house? Plus the idiot with the allergies? You're a joke as a criminal mastermind, let me tell you."

Charlie was slowly sidling toward me when, suddenly, they both seemed to notice.

"Stop right there, Deaver," Langley said, producing a small but deadly-looking pistol and aiming it at me. "I'll happily shoot your lawyer right now." He laughed, a little hysterically. "Although maybe you wouldn't mind that. Who cares about a few dead lawyers, right?"

Sarah rolled her eyes. "You're losing it, Addison. Shut up. We'll get far enough out, and we'll dump them."

I heard the sound of the boat's engines revving and realized Karl had vanished.

"Get far enough where?" I said, looking out the window, where the dock slowly started to get farther away from the boat. Or probably, the other way around.

She laughed. "Far enough out to sea to dump your dead bodies."

Chapter 45

Sarah laughed again. "Didn't you hear? It was so sad, really. You were screwing up poor Charlie's case because of your drug use. So your grief-crazed client went berserk and shot you and then himself."

I stared at her in disbelief. "How can you be so evil? You're a lawyer!"

Charlie and Uncle Nathan both blinked. Charlie spoke up first. "I'm thinking that's kind of the point. No offense."

I realized how stupid I'd sounded, then decided to go with that. People had underestimated me before because I looked like a blond airhead. I could only pray they would this time.

"What about Uncle Nathan? How are you going to explain him?" I asked, trying to get her monologuing. She seemed like the type.

Addison sneered. "We'll dump him overboard and let the police figure it out. Karl said if you wrap enough chain around a body, it will never surface."

I noticed Uncle Nathan fiddling with his wrists, which were tied behind his back on the chair.

Go, Nathan.

Edging sideways, I asked another question to distract them as I partially blocked Nathan from their view. "Why? That's all I want to know. Why would you go to the length of murder to protect a client—especially a client who covers up something as terrible as insulin tampering? What happened to your vows as an officer of the court?"

Sarah and Addison look at each other and started laughing. "You unbelievable moron," Sarah said. "You never would have figured it out."

"Shut up, Sarah," Addison hissed.

I looked back and forth between the two of them, suddenly sure my suspicions were true. "It's you. Somehow—some way—*you* tampered with the insulin, to build more business for yourselves. BDC didn't know anything about it."

"Well, it took you long enough to figure it out. Do you think yacht payments come easy? Or house payments?" Sarah said, then she pointed at Addison. "He has five kids in private schools and colleges, plus a wife with a weakness for really big diamond jewelry."

He agitatedly stepped closer to me, still pointing the gun at my head. "There weren't any big drug cases in the past five years. The attorney fees were drying up. We had the toxicology experts and the insider contacts at the FDA. Hell, we know more about the science of pharmaceuticals than most people who work at the drug company."

Sarah slapped a hand on the bar, making me jump. Addison flinched, too, and his finger tightened on the trigger, making my heart leap into my throat. "It wasn't even difficult," she pointed out. "We planned to tamper with a batch of insulin, just a little, and make enough people sick so that the resulting round of mass tort cases would keep us all in business until the next bad drug case came along."

Addison broke in, glowering. "But your goon screwed it up, Sarah. Something went badly wrong, and over two dozen people died."

I couldn't believe what I was hearing. "You killed all those people? Plus the hundreds who went into comas?"

Charlie looked bewildered. "What are they saying, December? They ruined the insulin on purpose?" Sheer rage transformed his bloody features, and he lunged at Addison.

Addison swung the gun almost casually and smashed it into the side of Charlie's head. I screamed and started to jump on Addison, but he swung the gun back toward me as Charlie crumpled into a chair.

Sarah walked over to us. "We never meant for anyone to die. But it was way too late to back out."

I glared at her, wanting more than I'd ever wanted anything in my life to get my hands around her throat. "So poor Marion Ziggeran? And Richard Dack?"

She snorted. "More sloppiness on Addison's part."

He glared at her. "I said shut up, Sarah. It was *your* associate."

"Oh, shut up yourself, Addison. I'm tired of you telling me what to do. Yes, my associate who slipped that invoice into *your* document production. Your stupid people never double-check a discovery production?"

"It was on its way out the door," he said, looking like he wanted to shoot her, too.

"Whatever. We knew he'd found out and was trying to tell somebody. So he drove himself off that bridge. How sad," she said, smirking. "We wouldn't have had any loose ends either, if you would have just taken a hint and gotten out of town after we had those very personal messages painted on that piece of shit you call a car."

Langley was seething. "Right. No loose ends. Except you hired those damn thugs. What kind of moron tries to get somebody to drop a case by talking to her about his allergies on the phone? Or throwing rocks at her? Or shooting her doorframe? Let's not even *discuss* the damn alligator!"

He sneered at her. "A little discretion next time, Sarah, if you please."

Sarah snarled at him. "You should talk. You think having a man's throat cut in the museum in the middle of the damn day is discreet? Just because he could testify about the date of the camera shoot? We had a dozen people to testify against him and say he had it wrong, or a big, fat bribe would have been even easier."

"You're insane. You're both insane," I said, my hopes of ever making it out of this alive sinking down to my shoes. "You can't just go around killing people and keep getting away with it."

They both smiled identical smiles of triumph—so horrible I shuddered.

"But we did get away with it. And we're going to keep getting away with it," Addison said softly.

I noticed Charlie stirring, but didn't look at him, hoping Addison wouldn't shoot him.

Sarah flipped her hair back and shot an almost-flirtatious smile at me. "Too bad that hunk Jake Brody has to be next. He knows too much. We tried to send him on jobs out of town, but he turned them down to stay here and babysit you."

"No! He doesn't know anything," I said. "Leave him out of this."

"Oh, it's not just him. We may do your precious Aunt Celia just for fun," she said, and something in my mind snapped. I shouted "NOW!" as loudly as I could.

Charlie lunged forward, right on cue, and slammed his head into Addison's side, knocking him off balance. I launched myself at them, grabbing a lamp on the way and yanking the cord out of the wall socket.

Sarah screamed and rushed me, but I slammed the lamp down on Addison's gun hand before she got there. He yelled, and the gun went skittering across the floor and landed under Uncle Nathan's chair.

Sarah plowed into me and flailed her arms around, hitting me. She clocked me in the side of the head, and I saw funny lights for a second. Addison punched Charlie in the shoulder, and Charlie hit the floor. I saw my chance and swung my foot back and kicked Addison in the crotch as hard as I could. He made a weird moaning sound and sank to the floor like a stone.

Sarah jumped on my back, shrieking, and yanked clumps of my hair out. My eyes teared up, and I screamed and rammed my elbows back. One hit empty air, but the other one knocked into her chest, and it was her turn to scream.

She let go of me and dropped to the floor. "I'm going to kill you," she yelled.

"Not if I kill you first," I said, breathing hard.

Uncle Nathan's calm voice broke in. "Fortunately, I seem to have the gun."

We both whirled around to stare at him. He stood, untied, ropes on the ground, aiming the gun at Sarah.

"What? Uncle Nathan, how did you . . ." I stumbled toward him.

"I write mysteries, my dear. You think I don't know how to escape bondage?" He grinned at me, unbelievably pleased with himself.

"I'd hug you, but I think we'll turn these creeps in to the police first," I said, picking up the ropes.

Charlie pulled himself up, looking a lot worse for wear.

"I'll tie this one up," he said, nudging a howling, writhing Langley with his boot.

I tossed him the ropes and just stood there for a minute, sucking in air and enjoying the idea that we weren't going to die. Nathan stood there smiling. "Nobody expected the old man to have it in him. Ha!"

Sarah stood there, shooting death glares at us, swearing at us in a low monotone.

"Would it be bad to throw her overboard and make her swim back?" I asked, not all that rhetorically.

Then I slammed my hand on my forehead. "Karl. He must have heard all this yelling. Charlie, tie Sarah up, too."

Sarah opened her mouth to scream, but Charlie clamped his hand over it. Then he pulled a rag out of his pocket and stuffed it into her mouth, tying it behind her head. Her face turned an ugly, mottled red with rage, but she could breathe through her nose, so I didn't much care.

As Charlie tied Sarah up, I took the gun from Uncle Nathan. "I'm going after Karl to make him take us back to the dock. Oh, and here," I said, fishing my cell phone out of my bra. "Try to call for help. Police, Coast Guard, whatever. I don't know if we'll have service out here, but there must be a radio, right?"

I crossed the room, nerves on high alert. Just as I reached the door, a huge, dripping-wet man burst into the room.

He had a gun, and it was pointed right at me.

Chapter 46

I stared down the barrel of a gun for the second time that night.

Then I smiled. "Hello, Brody. Nice of you to show up."

He lowered the gun. "Hello, Counselor. I see you don't exactly need rescuing."

I lowered my own gun, which, I'd just realized, I had no idea how to fire. If some kind of safety was on, I didn't know where to find it. "I was on my way to make Captain Karl take us home."

He nodded, then crossed swiftly to me and put a hand under my chin, tilting my face up toward his. "Are you all right? Did they hurt you?"

"Did they hurt *her*? Who's bleeding around here?" Uncle Nathan asked, voice amused.

Jake let out a huge breath, then dropped a kiss on my forehead and looked at Nathan. "Are you all right, sir? Mr. Deaver?"

"We're fine," Charlie said, holding one arm at an awkward angle. "But we need to take care of that captain right away. He's in on it."

"I took care of him already," Jake said. "I've also contacted the Coast Guard. They're on their way, and the police will meet us at the marina. I had them send an ambulance, too."

Nathan nodded. "Is my wife all right?"

"Yes, sir. She's with my friend, Lieutenant Connors.

Once I got December's phone message, a lot of things started to fall into place."

Charlie half walked, half staggered over to me. "We did it, December. We did it for Faith."

He hugged me, and I started crying. Or laughing. I'm not sure what it was.

"Yes, we did, Charlie. We did it."

After Jake went back to the bridge to steer the boat to shore, I made sure Nathan and Charlie were as comfortable as I could make them. Nathan insisted on keeping the gun trained on the prisoners. "I'm the one who took that 'guns and weapons for writers' course," he said gently. "Would you even know how to shoot this thing?"

"No," I confessed. "I never needed to learn how to shoot a gun."

Then I started laughing, and laughed so hard I fell down on the floor, clutching my stomach. "Nobody . . . n-n-nobody ever tried to kill me when I did corporate work."

Four days and three press conferences later—Charlie held one, BDC held one, and the police department held one— we gathered at the office on Friday evening.

Much to my delight (and the health of my law firm), the police had told the world that Greenberg and Langley had planted the junkie lawyer story, and that I'd been instrumental in discovering their crimes. The story broke in a big way in the national news, and I'd already talked to CNN and various network news programs several times. I'd given all the credit to Charlie (Jake insisted on remaining anonymous), and the governor of Florida was going to give Charlie some kind of special recognition.

Unsurprisingly, Sarah Greenberg sang everything she

knew to put the brunt of blame on Langley and his firm, but they were all going to trial. Both of the law firms offered enormous sums to settle Charlie's case against them, mostly to try to get out of the public eye faster. Both firms claimed they had no knowledge of Greenberg's and Langley's actions.

BDC, though blameless in all of it, also offered a settlement. I figured it was mostly so the public didn't dwell on how easy it was to tamper with their product. No matter the reason, Charlie asked that they use the money to create a special fund for diabetes research.

Charlie was finally at peace. He'd found justice for his Faith, and that's all he'd ever wanted.

I was finally at peace, too.

I was also covered with dog slobber.

"Will somebody take this silly dog?" I dropped a kiss on Daisy's silky forehead, happier than I could possibly express that her injuries from Croc's violence had been so minor. She'd had one of the best dog days ever, since it was Friday, and *pro bono* day was back in full swing at the law offices of December Vaughn. Counting the ones who came mostly because of the publicity, fifty-three people had shown up, and nearly every one of them had fussed over and petted Daisy. It was seven o'clock, and we were all exhausted, but very, very happy.

Gina scooped Daisy up and sat back down on the couch with her. "Is it my night? I haven't had a turn yet," she said.

Mr. Ellison nudged her to move over and flopped down next to her on the couch. "No, it's my turn. December hogged her after the excitement on the boat," he grumped at her, winking at me.

My mind literally boggled—Mr. Ellison just *winked* at me.

Max dragged herself in from the hall and sank down in a chair. "I think my mind melted around four o'clock," she said.

I looked around at my employees—my *friends*—and beamed. "Who needs a mind? It's the weekend! I'm going to go home and sleep for two straight days," I said.

"Not so fast, Counselor." We turned to look at the open door, where Jake stood, holding an enormous cake, Aunt Celia and Uncle Nathan close behind him.

"Surprise!" As they walked into the lobby, my mouth fell open as what looked like a hundred people crowded in behind them. Everybody was there! My casserole brigade ladies, and Emily and Rick and the kids, Charlie, Mrs. Zivkovich and her family, and Bear with a sweet-faced girl who cast adoring glances at him. Even Lieutenant Connors and a few of the police I'd met in my various encounters trooped into the room.

I stared up at Jake, dazed. "What is this?"

He smiled down at me. "We figured you'd never had a proper office-warming party. So here we are."

I felt like my heart would burst from the sheer joy welling up inside. Finally, all of my dreams were coming true, and all of my new friends were here to share my happiness with me. I jumped up to hug Celia and Nathan and, pretty much, anybody else in sight. I never even heard the phone ring, but Max yelled for me over the din.

"December! It's for you!"

"Can't you take a message?" I hollered back.

"Nope. You're going to want to take this one," she said, grinning.

I made my way through the crowd to the desk and picked up the phone, putting my finger in my other ear.

"Hello? You're going to have to speak up. It's really loud here!"

"Deborah Vaygan?"

"This is December Vaughn. Can I help you?"

"I'm sitting in front of your house with your furniture. You want to hurry up and get over here, lady? I don't have all day to wait on you."

I stared at the phone, then started laughing. "I'll be right there." I hung up and turned around, waving my arms for silence. "I love you all, but I have to leave for a few minutes. Better yet, can we move this party to my house? My furniture has finally arrived, and the trucker is waiting for me."

Jake caught my eye. "I don't move furniture, Vaughn."

I just smiled. "You will for me."

NICE GIRLS FINISH FIRST

ALESIA HOLLIDAY

A HILARIOUS NOVEL ABOUT LEARNING HOW TO BE YOURSELF — EVEN IF IT KILLS YOU.

Kirby Green didn't get to be a Vice President of Marketing by being nice. But when she fires her entire staff within a few weeks, her new boss is hardly impressed. He issues a bet: If Kirby can get someone — anyone — to call her nice, she can take that long-awaited dream vacation to Italy with her best friend. If she can't, she can kiss the Coliseum and her job goodbye.

Now Kirby has thirty days to bully someone into saying she's nice — and to show her boss who's boss. If she doesn't fall hard for him first...

0-425-20405-7

Available wherever books are sold or at penguin.com